Raven Storm

Also by W. Michael Gear and Kathleen O'Neal Gear

Big Horn Legacy

Dark Inheritance

The Foundation

Fracture Event

Long Ride Home

The Mourning War

Raising Abel

Rebel Hearts Anthology

Sand in the Wind

Thin Moon and Cold Mist

Black Falcon Nation Series

Flight of the Hawk Series

The Moundville Duology

Saga of a Mountain Sage Series

The Wyoming Chronicles

The Anasazi Mysteries

The Peacemaker's Tales

Praise

"I haven't read a novel this good in a long, long time. *People of the Raven* draws you into a magnificent, sweeping world—America, circa 7,300 B.C.—that is so real you can almost breathe in the air of it. It tells a bighearted story of war and pace, love and violence, with a cast of richly drawn characters. This is a novel that will stay with you for years—I guarantee it."

— Douglas Preston, *New York Times* bestselling coauthor of *Brimstone*

"Rich in cultural detail. Both longtime fans and newcomers will be satisfied. Another fine entry in an ambitious, long-running series."

— Kirkus Reviews

Raven Storm

The Earliest Americans
Book 5

W. Michael Gear

Kathleen O'Neal Gear

WOLFPACK
PUBLISHING
— EST 2013 —

Raven Storm
Paperback Edition
Copyright © 2025 (As Revised) by W. Michael Gear and
Kathleen O'Neal Gear

Wolfpack Publishing
1707 E. Diana Street
Tampa, FL 33610

www.wolfpackpublishing.com

Illustrations by Ellisa Mitchel.

Paperback ISBN 978-1-63977-678-8
Ebook ISBN 978-1-63977-677-1

To
Howard and Belenda Willson
with fond memories of Elands and Africa,
fine meals shared, and hale and hearty drink.
All the best, dear friends

Acknowledgments

We could not have written *Raven Storm* were it not for the work of Jim Chatters, Doug Owsley, Robson Bonnichsen, Alan Schneider, James Dixon, Richard L. Jantz, Silvia Gonzalez, Jose Concepcion Jimenez Lopez, W. A. Neves, Jose Victor Moreno-Mayar, and many others who have worked to recover meaningful information on early peoples in the Western Hemisphere.

Foreword

In the fall of 1996, Dr. Jim Chatters, adjunct professor at Central Washington University and deputy coroner for Benton County, Washington, sent an urgent email to several American anthropologists saying, "Subject: Need Help ASAP."

He had in his hands an archaeological discovery that would rock the nation, and he knew it. The specimen would come to be called "Kennewick Man," and prove to be one of the most controversial archaeological finds in the history of the world.

When Kennewick Man was discovered eroding out of the banks of the Columbia River, it appeared to be a simple case. Obviously he was a Caucasoid male, forty-five to fifty-five years of age, probably a White pioneer.

Then a CAT scan revealed a "Cascade" point—a distinctive leaf-shaped prehistoric spear point—embedded in his hip. Shortly thereafter, the radiocarbon laboratory at the University of California at Riverside returned their analysis of the date:

Kennewick Man was between 9,200 and 9,500 years old.

A Caucasoid man in America 9,000 years ago? Weren't we all taught that only "Native American" people, that is, Mongoloid people, were here that long ago?

This was a stunning find that had the potential to completely rewrite our understanding of the peopling of the Americas.

Five days after the radiocarbon dates were released to the public, the Army Corps of Engineers—upon whose land Kennewick Man was found—ordered Jim Chatters to immediately halt all scientific studies and relinquish the bones. In the end, the Corps would defy orders from both Houses of Congress to leave the site alone and would cover the Kennewick Man archaeological site with six hundred tons of earth and debris. They even planted thousands of trees on top of the fill to stabilize it, very effectively concealing any undiscovered evidence that would spark additional questions about who Kennewick Man was and what he was doing in America more than 9,000 years ago.

You may think this smacks of lunacy, or at least a loathing of scientific inquiry that borders on madness, but we're dealing with a complicated story here. Let's talk about the facts.

After the radiocarbon dates became public, an alliance of five northwestern tribes—the Umatilla, Yakima, Nez Percé, Wanapum, and Colville—claimed the remains under the 1990 Native American Graves Protection and Repatriation Act, demanding that the bones be turned over to them for reburial without further study.

Why would the tribal alliance claim a White man?

Armand Minthorn, Umatilla leader, said, "Our oral history goes back 10,000 years. We know how time began and how Indian people were created. They can say whatever they want, the scientists. They are being disrespectful."

Eight scientists, in *Bonnichsen et al. v. United States of America,* sued to be able to study the remains.

The meetings of the Society for American Archaeology and the American Association of Physical Anthropologists were spiked with bitter acrimony. Since no scientists were allowed to see the remains—because they might be able to study Kennewick Man with their eyes and that was disrespectful—the vast majority of conference attendees were high on hearsay.

Next, enter the Asatru Folk Assembly.

The Asatru, based in Northern California, trace their ancestry to pre-Christian Scandinavian and Germanic peoples. In their publication, *The Runestone,* they wrote, "Native American groups have strongly contested this idea, perceiving that they have much to lose if their status as the 'First Americans' is overturned. We will not let our heritage be hidden by those who seek to obscure it." They filed suit to have Kennewick Man—whom they believed to be *their* ancestor—turned over to them.

Archaeologists around the world held their breath.

The Asatru lawsuit begged a very important question: Do some religions in America have precedence over others? Do certain racial or ethnic groups have the right to certain archaeological sites? Should Canada return the Viking archaeological sites dating to around A.D. 1000 to Canadians of Scandinavian heritage? Should the United States return all Hispanic archaeological sites to people of Hispanic heritage? Should the African American sites administered by the federal government be turned over to African Americans? If so, which people or persons? Is one-eighth blood enough? Does it have to be based on ethnicity? What about the beautiful historic Catholic missions in the California State Parks system? Should the state of California be forced to turn them back to the Catholic Church? And what happens to those sites once they're turned over? Is it all right if these groups destroy them?

The debate continued. The lead scientists analyzing Kennewick Man said he looked more like the Ainu of Japan or Polynesians.

To complicate matters even further, British scientists working in Mexico discovered two skulls, both older than 12,000 years, which appeared to be Caucasoid. Dr. Silvia Gonzalez, of John Moores University in Liverpool, said, "It looks like some of the most ancient Paleo-Americans were not of Mongoloid affinity and therefore perhaps not directly related to modern Native Americans." Working in conjunction with Jose Concepcion Jimenez Lopez, curator of Mexico City's National Museum of Anthropology, began the process of analyzing the remains, including doing DNA research.

So...now...the rest of the story:

In the past two decades since we first wrote *People of the Raven*, archaeological finds have pushed the arrival time of humans on the continent back by thousands of years, and added details to the complex story of who these groups were and where they came from. It's likely that different groups of humans arrived many times via many routes. Some survived. Others did not.

In 2020, the University of Oxford published a study saying that the "First Americans" had travelled by sea to the continent from eastern Eurasia before the last Ice Age, around 30,000 years ago—these are pre-Clovis cultures—and wrote, "It seems likely to us that the people...represent a 'failed colonization', one which may well have left no genetically detectable heritage in today's First American's populations" (https://www.ox.ac.uk/news/2020-07-22-earliest-americans-arrived-new-world-30000-years-ago).

Please, bear that in mind: "...we have no direct genetic evidence arising from populations associated with pre-Clovis sites linking them with later Native Americans. Thus, we should be careful to distinguish potential failed migrations versus the direct ancestors of Clovis and later PaleoIndians" (https://www.science.org/doi/10.1126/sciadv.aat5473).

The nuclear genomic evidence that has accumulated over the past twenty years is the most fascinating. For example, archaeologists now know that the genomes of a modern population in Brazil contains about 2 percent DNA that is closely related to ancient populations in Australasia and Southeast Asia, but has not been found in living Indigenous peoples. However, it is found in 10,000-year-old genomes from Brazil. "That's really, really puzzling," said Dr. Jose Victor Moreno-Mayar, a geogeneticist from the University of Copenhagen. "There was absolutely no way in which it was possible to make it through the Pacific," he said.

But, for the sake of argument, let's assume they did. Australasia is comprised by Australia, New Zealand,

and the Pacific Islands. We know that prehistoric populations of Polynesians, and perhaps the native peoples of Ecudor and Columbia, sailed across open ocean to get to and from Polynesia and South America by at least AD 1200, and perhaps earlier. We know that because we have a mixture of those populations' DNA in the remote South Marquesas' archipelago. (https://www.-smithsonianmag.com/science-nature/native-americans-polynesians-meet-180975269/).

But 10,000 years ago?

How did they manage to cross the Andes and the Amazon without leaving any trace to get to Brazil? A farfetched possibility is that the crossed the Atlantic ocean over 10,000 years ago. "Every new explanation we come up with is worse than the previous one," said Moreno-Mayar (https://www.the-scientist.com/new-evidence-complicates-the-story-of-the-peopling-of-the-americas-69928.

On the other hand, prehistoric peoples continue to amaze us.

Perhaps the most controversial site is found in southern California. The Cerutti Mastodon Site has truly upset the proverbial "archaeological applecart," especially since it dates to around 130,000 years ago and contains mastodon bones that appear to have been modified, worked, by human hands (https://www.nature.com/articles/nature22065). But perhaps not *modern* human hands. Archaic humans, Denisovans and Neandertals, both inhabited Siberia around 130,000 years ago (https://www.science.org/content/article/ancient-siberian-cave-hosted-neanderthals-denisovans-and-modern-humans-possibly-same).

Finally, who was Kennewick Man? After more than

twenty years of research, it's clear that while his physical features seemed to be more closely related to the Ainu or Polynesians, his genetics revealed that he was, indeed, more closely related to modern native groups in the Pacific Northwest.

In February, 2017, Kennewick Man was returned to the native peoples who claimed him as their ancestor and reburied at a secret location in the Pacific Northwest.

We hope he has found peace among the campfires of his ancestors.

—KATHLEEN O'NEAL GEAR and W. MICHAEL GEAR
September, 2024

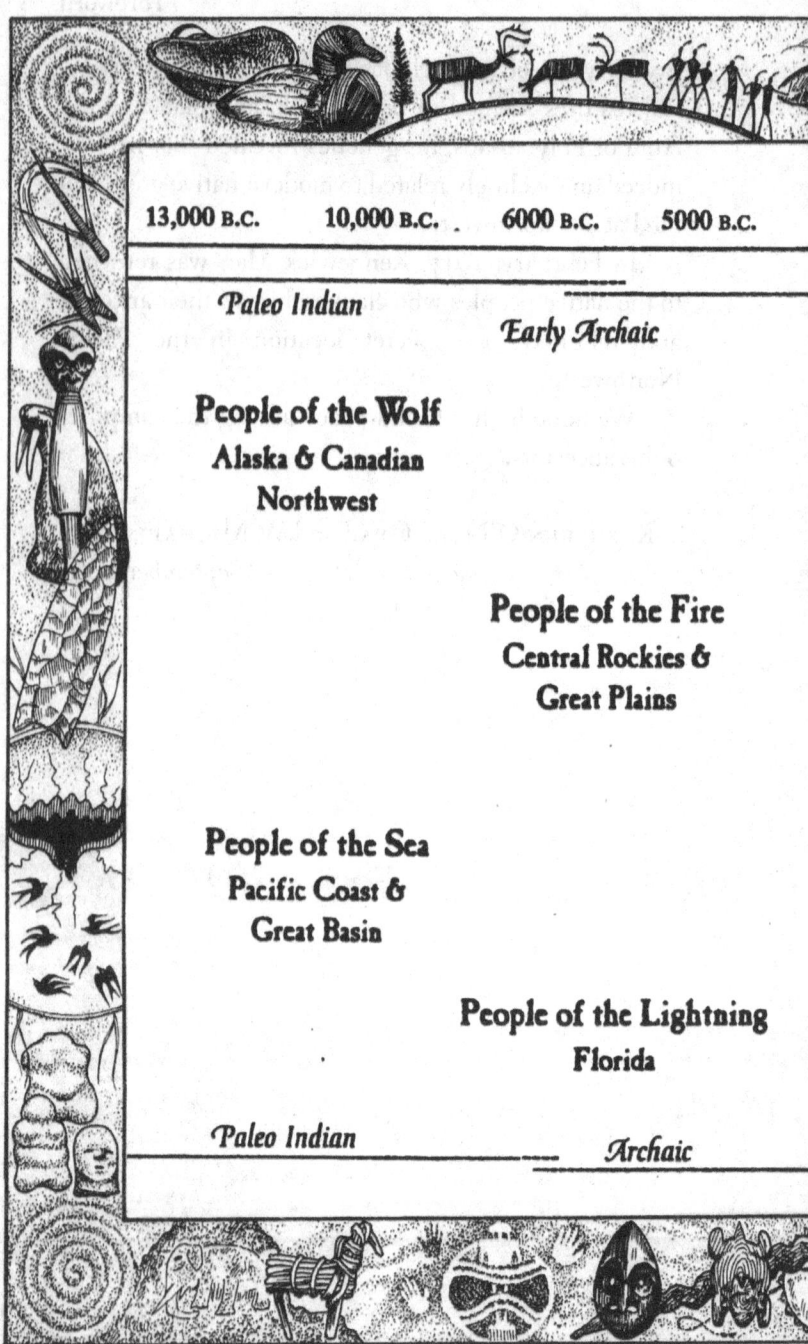

| 13,000 B.C. | 10,000 B.C. | 6000 B.C. | 5000 B.C. |

Paleo Indian

Early Archaic

People of the Wolf
Alaska & Canadian
Northwest

People of the Fire
Central Rockies &
Great Plains

People of the Sea
Pacific Coast &
Great Basin

People of the Lightning
Florida

Paleo Indian

Archaic

| B.C. | 1500 B.C. | 100 A.D. | 800 A.D. | 1000 A.D. | 1300 A.D. |

Archaic   *Woodland*   *Mississippian*

People of the Mist
Chesapeake Bay

People of the Earth
Northern Plains
& Basins

People of the River
Mississippi Valley

People of the Masks
Ontario &
Upstate New York

People of the Lakes
East Central Woodlands
& Great Lakes

People of the Silence
Southwest Anasazı

People of the Owl
Lower Mississippi
Valley

Basketmaker   *Pueblo*

People
of the
Raven

North

Deer Meadow
Village
Wake's
Nose
Cupped Finch
Village
Shell Maiden
Village
Raven
Bay
Antler
Spoons
Village
Orphan
Village
Sandy Point Village
War Gods Village
Eelgrass Village
Sea Lion
Village
Fire Mountain
Wasp
Village
Fire Village
Salmon
Village
Tortoise Shell
Village
Trailing
Raspberry
Village

NORTH

Raven Storm

Raven Storm

Chapter One

A dark blue wall of Cloud People pushed over Fire Mountain. Dzoo studied it as she shuffled up the steep trail that led around the outside of Sea Lion Village's palisade. Ecan's warriors marched in front and behind her. Everyone had their gazes fixed on the village, looking through the slats in the gaping palisade to the lodges within.

She remembered this place, had played here as a child. Then the village had contained over five tens of lodges, though only a few people had actually lived here, mostly Dreamers and caretakers. The rest of the lodges held caches of dried food, tool stone, and seashells.

The holy trails that covered their mountainous land angled off in every direction, intersecting each other, sometimes running parallel, but they all converged at Sea Lion Village. It was the spiritual crossroads to the House of Air. All lost souls began their journey here.

As they rounded the eastern end of the rickety palisade, a gray-haired acolyte dressed in a drab brown tunic hobbled out of the interior carrying a basket that brimmed with bones. He nodded as he passed. She watched him continue to a small mound of sun-bleached human bone. It gleamed in the light, cracked, flaking, and rain-washed. Thick green grass grew out of the tangle. Over the years, quite a pile of it had built up. Here and there, a battered skull stared out, the empty eyes questioning, the braincases nothing more than the perfect place for mice to build their homes. She looked back over her shoulder as the acolyte carefully placed the bones onto the pile.

The North Wind People varied in their tastes. Some wanted to be buried close to where they'd lived. Others found it worthwhile to have their bones prepared, and to send tribute to the holy people who lived here in return for having their souls prayed over, separated from the bones, and sent to the House of Air.

Dzoo tilted her head and listened to the old man's lilting voice calling the Star People to come and carry the soul to the road of light that led to the first of the Above Worlds.

"Are we traveling on to Fire Village?" she asked.

Warriors glanced at her, but no one answered. Far ahead, Ecan's white cape flashed in the sunlight as the Starwatcher led them up the trail.

"Are we going on to Fire Village?" she asked, louder.

Exhausted from days of traveling without food, Dzoo tripped over a rock, stumbled, and almost fell before she caught herself.

"Don't fall, witch!" young Hunter said from behind. "I don't want to have to pick you up."

She glanced over her shoulder, aware her vision was

swimming. Was that his soul she saw—a loose yellowish blur around his body? Must have been. He looked suddenly frightened and stopped dead in his tracks to lift his spear. In the slanting sunlight, his haunted expression turned stony. Black hair whipped around his face. Fearfully, he called, "Wind Scorpion!"

The old warrior trotted up, predatory gaze on first Hunter, and then her. "Careful, Hunter. If you're helping her up, she might snag your soul and pull it from your body."

Wind Scorpion gave her a look that sliced like freshly struck obsidian before he trotted past.

Hunter gave him an evil glance and veered wide around Dzoo, gesturing with his spear. "Walk, witch."

She walked, fixing her gaze onto Wind Scorpion's wide back. She squinted, trying to catch a glimpse of his soul. Her toe caught, and she broke contact as she flailed for balance. She turned her attention to her feet, aware she hadn't the energy for both tasks. She'd caught a glimpse, but of what?

The sensation had been of emptiness, as if the man were nothing more than a shell.

"Gods," she mumbled. "It's the hunger. I'm tired. So...tired."

Fire Mountain rose before her like a gigantic cone with a snow-covered, chopped-off top. Her hazy vision focused on the cliff just above the tree line. Was that the Fire Village palisade wall?

She shook her head. Maybe it wasn't even there. For three hands of time, she'd been seeing things. Sometimes just faces. Other times, she saw glimpses of the future. Pearl Oyster had come to speak with her. She thought he was trying to warn her about something.

She'd seen him reach out to touch her; then he'd vanished like mist on a hot day...

She stumbled again.

Hunter glared at her. "What's wrong?"

She could feel her soul growing lighter, thinning like smoke in the wind. A pink tornado formed in the air before her. Round and round it went, Dancing and bouncing.

Hunter's gaze jerked to the point on the trail where she seemed to be looking, then jerked back to her. "What's *wrong*} Do you see something."

The Noisy One, her Spirit Helper, solidified in the cold-spawned glitter, his arms moving like blades of grass underwater, sweeping up and down.

"Empty out your heart, Dzoo. Drain your soul onto the path to prepare the way."

"Prepare it for whom?" she asked, the words barely audible even to her.

"Our purpose is the boy."

"Which boy?"

"The bloody boy."

"Ecan's son?"

Hunter circled warily, his spear thrust forward. "Who are you talking to, witch?"

Dzoo couldn't feel the ground. She might have been flying, rather than walking.

The Noisy One floated just ahead of her.

"You are almost home," he whispered. *"Like a winged seed coming to ground. But beware. You are being hunted. He is close...and, oh, so Powerful. I don't know if you can beat him."*

The Noisy One raised his hands to Brother Sky,

and lightning flashed through the approaching Cloud People. Warriors spun to look. Whispers broke out.

"Witch!" Hunter shouted. "Did you do that?"

With the next brilliant flash, the Noisy One's face shattered and blew away like tumbling snowflakes.

"You had better keep walking, witch, or Til—"

Dzoo staggered, blinked, and pressed her bound hands to her forehead. The vision had been burned into her soul: a tall young man, muscular, his head back, arms raised to the blinding sun. Blood had trickled down his bronzed, sweat-slicked skin. Every muscle rippled on his naked body—a picture of male perfection. Then she saw his face. The nose was thin, aquiline, the jaw strong, slightly bearded. Wide cheeks caught the light. But where knowing and Powerful eyes should have been, dull stones filled the hollow orbits in his skull. As if he felt her presence, he turned his head, staring straight at her. The sensation was as if her soul were being sucked from her body.

Dzoo blinked and gasped, aware of the jouncing sensation. A terrible headache hammered through her skull. She forced her eyes open and saw Hunter. At first he appeared to be hanging upside down against the sky. As she fought to make sense of it, she realized that she was being carried on a sort of litter.

"Are you awake, witch?" Hunter asked.

"Yes." She sat up and put her hand to her head.

Deer Killer carried the front poles. He kept glancing uneasily over his shoulder, taking her measure.

"What happened?"

"You collapsed," Hunter sneered. "Dropped flat as a soaked cloth. Were it up to me, I'd have just cracked your skull and left you."

Deer Killer added, "The Starwatcher told us to carry you. But I'd rather you walked."

"Hurry up!" Wind Scorpion bellowed from behind. "We're almost there."

"I can walk," Dzoo said softly, the image of the stone-eyed man hovering like a bat in the back of her soul.

She felt stiff as she swung out of the makeshift litter they'd made of coats and poles. She stood on unsteady feet, but the headache began to recede.

"Make time, witch!" Hunter growled. "We're falling behind, and I, for one, don't want to be the center of Ecan's wrath again."

She filled her lungs with the cool air and forced herself into the continuing climb. As she got her bearings, she recognized the village cupped by the brow of the ridge before them like a barnacle.

The twenty-hand-tall palisade of upright poles surrounding Salmon Village had been built since the last time she'd been here. People began to trickle out the front gate to stare at her. They wore beautiful clothing —shirts made of finely tanned mink and marten hides, capes of eagle feathers. The finest dyes had been used to create geometric designs on the clothing. She had forgotten the brilliant purples, yellows, and shades of crimson manufactured by the North Wind artisans.

Ecan dropped back to walk at her side. "Just pass. Don't speak."

Dzoo smiled, turning her head to call, "Beware the blood-streaked man! He has stones for eyes."

People started, stiffening, frowning, as they puzzled over her words. Confusion and worry grew bright in their eyes.

Ecan gaped in disbelief, then raised his hand to strike her. It wavered in the air, quivering like a stressed sapling before he lowered it. "You take dangerous chances."

He stamped ahead. Perhaps he had second thoughts; for he dropped back once more to parallel her course. She cataloged the furtive glances he cast her way, wondering how long it would take.

"What blood-streaked man? What were you talking about?"

"You needn't worry. You won't live long enough to stare into his stony eyes."

"Ah, yes, my impending death again." He pointed to the path that led around the base of the palisade. "Come on. The sooner we arrive, the sooner you can sleep."

As they curved around Salmon Village and climbed higher up the mountain trail, the Fire Village palisade came into view.

"I had forgotten," she whispered in awe.

"Forgotten what?"

"The paintings."

They had been painted on hides stretched over the corduroy of the palisade wall. The bodies of the gods winked and flashed, as though encrusted with fallen stars. To create the effect, the artisans glued bits of crushed shell to the surface of the paintings of Gutginsa, Old Woman Above, Ogre, Killer Whale, Sea Cow, and Wolf.

"I'd forgotten their beauty."

For many summers after she'd arrived at the squalid lodges of the Striped Dart People, dreams of Fire Village had kept her alive. How could she have forgotten?

Her gaze moved to the gate, where two warriors leaned against the palisade. Just inside, her mother's lodge had stood to the right. Was it still there?

Ecan's eyes had an anticipatory gleam. "You are almost home."

Dzoo gazed at the towering lava cliff behind Fire Village. In the afternoon light its shadow cut upward, darkening the mountain. She could feel Power—but it was faint. Shreds crept from the lava and the high snow-patched cinder cone where once it had been a flood. What had happened here? Why had the Power fled? Dzoo concentrated on pulling the shreds around her like a protective cloak.

She asked, "Who killed it? Was it you, Star-watcher?"

"Killed what?"

"The Power. It used to run across my skin like rubbed fox fur."

His eyes tightened. "Cimmis told me the Power vanished when his daughter, Tlikit, decided to run away with Rain Bear."

It was strange to hear someone say her name. Cimmis had declared Tlikit Outcast, dead, and ordered that her name be forgotten. It was a crime to speak it.

"This is not Tlikit's work, Starwatcher." She cocked her head, raising her hands to the air. "No, I think the slow rot of human souls has led to this."

The guards stepped back, and hands still up, Dzoo walked through the gate into the village. Brown-cloaked slaves stood everywhere, watching her. In an instant, someone recognized her, and the word "Dzoo!" was whispered from person to person.

As she remembered, the bark lodges made a perfect circle around the central Council Lodge. Paintings decorated every wall. As she neared a painting of Buffalo Above, it occurred to her that the artist had mixed crushed obsidian with his paint to create the god's shimmering hair. The white eyes must contain crushed clamshells; they glittered as though alive.

Her mother's lodge still stood just inside the gate. It looked smaller than she remembered. Someone had converted it to storage.

A tall man ducked out of the last lodge near the lava cliff. She remembered it as belonging to Astcat, the matron. The tall man shielded his eyes to look in their direction. A gossamer blue cape billowed around him.

"Is that Cimmis?"

Apprehension strained Ecan's face. "That's him."

Another man, shorter and fatter, ducked through the door hanging behind the chief. "Cimmis and the leader of the Big Tail Clan, Tudab. Prepare yourself, witch. Cimmis ordered me to take no captives."

"Then perhaps I will be able to watch you die sooner than I had anticipated. I would enjoy that."

"I wasn't worried about me, Dzoo." He straightened his long white cape. "Hunter! Deer Killer! Keep an eye on the prisoner while I make my report"—he shot a final glance at Dzoo—"and see if our chief wants this worthless woman alive...or dead."

Chapter Two

After each of the chiefs had entered his lodge, Rain Bear took a moment to ensure that the guards obeyed him and stayed at least fifty hands away. They did—but no one looked happy about it. Two men stood grumbling in front of Evening Star's lodge, giving steely-eyed glances to Hornet and Wolf Spider, who returned them stare for stare.

He let the hanging fall. As it swung, bars and streaks of gold flashed over the faces of the men seated around his fire. Bluegrass, the oldest, had seen perhaps five tens of summers. A few stubborn white hairs clung to his bald head. Black Mountain, Talon's chief, was next oldest, around three tens and five summers. He had shoulder-length graying black hair, a bulbous nose, and deep wrinkles. Goldenrod, Sleeper's chief from Deer Meadow Village, was the youngest. He'd seen fewer summers than Rain Bear: two tens and six. They made a strange group.

Without waiting for them to speak, Rain Bear

asked, "Do all of you want me to kill the boy? Or just Bluegrass?"

Goldenrod shifted to sit cross-legged on the mat, and long black hair fell around his broad shoulders. He extended his hand. "Rain Bear, surely you understand the position you place us in. Most of the people gathered around your village watched Ecan destroy their homes and families."

"They want revenge. Yes, I know." Rain Bear hung his otter-hide cape on the peg, straightened his red knee-length shirt, and seated himself across from his guests. "I do not wish to fight over this. If all the chiefs agree that the boy should be executed to punish Ecan, then that is what I will do."

Relieved smiles and nods went around the circle. Black Mountain gave old Bluegrass an unpleasant look. "See? I told you Rain Bear was a reasonable man."

"Well, he wasn't earlier today." Bluegrass glared at Rain Bear. His bald head gleamed in the firelight. "What changed your heart?"

"My heart hasn't changed," Rain Bear replied. "I told you I needed to consult with the elders and other chiefs. Since we spoke, I've been trying to speak with as many as I can." That was a fanciful lie. "Not everyone agrees about the boy. Several of my own clan elders don't want him killed. They believe it's possible to use him as leverage against Ecan."

"I want him *dead!*" Bluegrass shouted. "His father tortured my wife and son to death before my eyes!"

"Bluegrass!" Goldenrod held up both hands in a *please stop this* gesture. "We can all make similar claims, but I would like to hear Rain Bear's words before I decide."

Bluegrass sucked his lips in over toothless gums and angrily flipped his arm at Rain Bear in a motion to continue.

Rain Bear said, "My elders believe that we may be able to use the boy to maneuver Ecan into a position where we can either kill him or pressure him into betraying Cimmis and the Council."

Black Mountain tilted his head skeptically. Soot smudged his bulbous nose. "How?"

"First, we need to decide where our real interests lie. Do we wish to kill Ecan?"

A mingled roar of assenting voices rose.

Rain Bear raised placating hands. "Or try to destroy Cimmis and the Council?"

Another roar.

"Then I suggest," Rain Bear said, "that we do not immediately kill the boy."

"I want him dead!" Bluegrass's elderly face contorted in rage. "I don't just want him dead; I want to slit his belly open and pull out enough of his intestines to roast in a fire while he squeals!"

Rain Bear glanced at Black Mountain and Goldenrod. They both appeared embarrassed by the vehemence. Goldenrod squinted at his moccasins. Black Mountain roughly shoved graying black hair away from his brow.

Rain Bear said, "Killing Ecan will require every skill and tool we have. Shall we destroy our best tool before we've even tried to use it?"

The chiefs started talking at once. Bluegrass shook a fist in Goldenrod's face.

Rain Bear lifted his voice. "And there is another thing I wish you to consider."

The din died down.

Bluegrass gave Rain Bear an evil look.

"By now I think all of you are aware that Ecan took Dzoo captive. If we kill Tsauz, Ecan will kill Dzoo. Is that acceptable to you?"

Bluegrass's withered mouth pinched as though he'd eaten something bitter. "I thought that was just a rumor. You're sure she was taken captive?"

Goldenrod nodded. "My war chief, Sleeper, is tracking the war party. He sent a runner back to say he'd seen Dzoo. She is definitely Ecan's prisoner."

Black Mountain looked at Bluegrass. "I believe she spent several moons at your village two summers ago. Didn't she Heal your sick son?"

Bluegrass clenched his jaw for several moments before expelling an explosive breath. "Yes. And many others in my village. She is worth ten tens of Ecan's sons."

Goldenrod looked around the circle. "If we are to save Dzoo, we cannot kill Ecan's son. At least not right away. I say that later, when Dzoo is safe, we let Bluegrass roast his guts. Who knows? By then, perhaps Ecan will be ours and he can listen along with the rest of us."

Bluegrass twisted on his mat as though ants had crawled into his cape. "For now, I agree."

Black Mountain nodded. "As do I."

Rain Bear bowed his head. "Good. There are other things I wish you to know."

Bluegrass craned his neck to look up. "Now what?"

Rain Bear gazed across the smoldering fire at Bluegrass. "When my daughter was cleaning the boy's wounds last night, she noticed...injuries."

"From rolling down the mountain when you were chasing him?" Bluegrass asked.

Rain Bear shook his head. "No, these were old bruises, yellow and purple." He let that sink in.

Bluegrass cocked his head. "You mean Ecan beats the boy?"

"That was Roe's suggestion. Either Ecan or someone else."

"I've heard this before," Black Mountain said, "from Traders."

"As have I," Goldenrod added. "Just after Ecan's wife died in that suspicious fire, I heard that he beat the boy nearly to death."

Bluegrass jerked a nod. "And that he kicked one of the boy's puppies to death. But what difference does it make?"

Rain Bear shrugged. "It's just something to think about. Ecan beats the boy, and when the battle at War Gods Village grew difficult, he abandoned his blind son and fled."

"More reasons to hate Ecan." Black Mountain drew up a knee and laced his fingers around it. "But I'm not certain it has a bearing on our decisions."

"It tells us something about the value he places on his son's life," Bluegrass said. "The boy may not be as useful a tool as we think."

"True," Rain Bear agreed in a mild voice. "It also means that killing the boy may not *hurt* Ecan as much as we imagine."

"For the sake of the gods, Rain Bear," Bluegrass exhaled the words in a rush and waved a hand. "You never wish to kill anyone. No matter how deserving! In

Raven's name, why did we vote you to lead the war party?"

Rain Bear's brows lifted. "As I recall, Bluegrass, you voted against me."

"Yes, but I was outvoted. So there we have it. At least we are all agreed that we must kill Ecan, correct?"

Everyone, including Rain Bear, nodded.

"And Cimmis, if we can, yes?"

"Of course. If we can find an opportunity."

"Anything else, Rain Bear?" Goldenrod asked expectantly.

"Not for the moment." He glanced around. "But I would like for each of you to follow out anything suspicious. We have the boy, and Cimmis knows it. If he can kill the boy before we can use him..."

Bluegrass's nose wiggled as he thought about it. "He could take any advantage away from us. That foul sea slug! If he's going to kill our captive, he's going to have to get past me first!"

Goldenrod and Black Mountain were watching him curiously.

"Very well." Bluegrass tottered as he rose to his feet. "Notify me when you wish to next meet in council."

"We will."

Bluegrass walked to the door and stepped out into the bright afternoon sunlight. People instantly began calling questions.

Goldenrod chuckled, rose to his feet, and asked, "Are we finished, Great Chief?"

"Unless you have something else to discuss," Rain Bear said.

Goldenrod shook his head, and Black Mountain said, "I have nothing more." He got up and propped his hands on his hips. "We'll be waiting to hear from you, Rain Bear."

"I will be calling on you soon."

Cimmis lifted a hand to shield his eyes against the afternoon glare of the sun and frowned at the large group of warriors who walked in through the Salmon Village gate. Several villagers ran out of the palisade gates and followed in the wake of the war party, shouting questions, hugging friends who'd been away. Ecan led the procession. Cimmis knew the Starwatcher by his long white cape. Oddly, he didn't see Ecan's boy. A woman—apparently a captive—accompanied the party.

"Ecan!" Cimmis clenched a fist. "Gutginsa strike him! Look at that! He's brought a woman! I didn't want him slowed down by captives. His need to shove his rod into her sheath might have killed them all."

"Wait, my Chief. Let's hear his story." Wind Woman tousled Tudab's thick black hair, blowing it over his face.

Cimmis said, "The Starwatcher has a bad habit of 'interpreting' my orders to his own benefit."

"Sometimes a man must make quick decisions out on the war trail."

"I spent ten and eight summers as a warrior and never had to 'explain' my actions, Clan Leader. I never disobeyed an order, never 'interpreted' an order. I just did what was expected of me."

Tudab put a hand on Cimmis's shoulder, trying to ease his mood. "We know your record, my Chief. Your complete dedication to the orders of the Council are what have placed you in such an important position. You lead by your example. You, Cimmis, are the Council's strong right arm."

Tudab, if you only knew. Where Astcat's thoughts were the strong heart-wood of our people, Old Woman North's head might be filled with punk for all the sense I get out of it.

Tudab asked, "How many did we lose?"

"If that's all of them, too many."

"Some may have been captured. Perhaps we can arrange a Trade to get them back."

"If any of our warriors were captured, they're already dead."

Tudab, a gentle little man, grimaced as though disturbed by the thought. "Is that what you would have done, my Chief?"

"Keeping captives costs too much, Tudab. You have to feed them; warriors must guard them. You never know when one will get desperate and jump for the closest guard's throat. It's safer to question them and kill them."

Cimmis could see them more clearly now. At least three had been wounded. Two limped, and one man cradled an arm to his chest. "I do not understand why White Stone sent no more messages after the battle. He should have sent one message a day telling us the status of the war party. I will have to speak with my war chief. Apparently, he does not understand his duties."

Tudab frowned. "I don't see White Stone. Perhaps he was killed in the fighting."

"Then my wrath will fall on Ecan. *He* should have sent the messages if White Stone couldn't."

Immediately after the battle, a message had been sent, signaling their victory. With White Stone dead, Ecan should have sent additional messages. Perhaps the captive had dulled his wits with her body. The thought of Ecan and his women was disturbing. Cimmis remained irritated by the mess Ecan and Kenada had made of Matron Evening Star's captivity. They were to break and humiliate her as an example to the others, not turn her into a heroine for every malcontent within a moon's journey.

Tudab interrupted his thoughts. "I just hope that our attack has dampened the Raven People's ardor for war."

"It has enflamed their hatred, Tudab, not dampened it." *That's your beloved Council at work, you dolt. Without Astcat's guidance, they're sending us down the trail of eventual disaster.*

Wind Woman flapped Tudab's cape around his pudgy body as he turned to Cimmis. "I don't understand. I thought we attacked War Gods Village to break the Raven People's will. You said we were going to teach them they cannot hide from us. If they refuse to offer tribute, we can kill them anywhere and any time."

"That's what I said, but the Four Old Women had other reasons." Cimmis studied Ecan's captive. He thought he knew her, but couldn't place her face. Red Hair? Gods, that wasn't Evening Star, was it? No, this one was older, more...what? Stately?

"What reasons?"

A cold sprinkling of rain began to patter on the lodge roofs and on the back of Cimmis's neck. He tugged up his hood. Tudab stood patiently awaiting an answer.

"Rain Bear's forces grow by the day," Cimmis said. "If we cannot force him to attack us soon with small war parties that we can eliminate, his forces will eventually move like a giant wave of locusts, destroying everything in their path. The Council is afraid the Raven People will wipe the North Wind People from the face of Our Mother Earth."

Tudab's mouth opened. Cimmis could see his coated tongue inside. Finally, he blurted, "Blessed gods, Cimmis! Have you spoken with the matron about this?"

"As you know, she's been...away," Cimmis said uncomfortably. "Besides, we will know soon enough. Rain Bear dislikes war, but when he must fight, he is swift to action."

As his leather door hanging waffled in the wind, he caught glimpses of Astcat lying inside beneath a mound of hides. Kstawl kneeled beside her.

His heart ached. She had been progressively growing worse. Every time she woke after being "away," she begged Cimmis to tell her what had been going on.

Ecan's group reached the central plaza fire, and the Starwatcher strode forward, his long white cape billowing around his tall body. How did he keep it so clean while on the trail?

The captive's gaze lingered on the painted lodges.

"What's she looking at?" Tudab asked.

"The paintings, I think."

Then her eyes turned on Cimmis. His heart leaped. He couldn't see her face—the sun was behind her and she had her hood up—but something about the way she held herself touched his memories.

People throughout the village continued to whisper with excitement and move about uneasily.

Then it struck Cimmis. He whispered, "Blessed gods. That's Dzoo."

"What?" Tudab spun around. Fear widened his eyes. "How do you know?"

"Once you've known Dzoo, you never forget."

Tudab studied the slaves huddled together in the plaza. "If that is indeed Dzoo, my Chief, we may have a problem. Many of our slaves are Raven People, and she is one of their greatest heroes."

"It's her all right—and the slaves will be the least of our problems."

"Then perhaps we should kill her immediately, before she creates dissent."

In the plaza Ecan gestured to his warriors, and they prodded Dzoo toward the dank lodge where they kept captives and disobedient slaves. Cimmis shook his head in amazement. Even after days on the trail, she moved with uncommon grace; she might have been floating across the ground.

"Tell Lion Girl I wish her to personally take care of Dzoo, and inform Ecan I want to see him immediately."

"Yes, my Chief."

Tudab bowed and waddled down the hill toward Ecan as fast as he could.

Chapter Three

Cimmis watched as Dzoo stopped in front of the opening to the captives' lodge. She stood perfectly still, her head down. The hair on the back of his arms stood on end. It was as though he could feel her soul moving about the village, touching things. Ecan pulled the door hanging back for her, but before she stepped into the lodge she turned to meet Cimmis's gaze. Long red hair fluttered around her beautiful face. She smiled at him.

It was the kind of smile an enemy warrior gave you just before he slit your throat.

A guard bravely prodded her arm with his spear, and she ducked down into the lodge.

"There's a...a traitor," Astcat weakly said.

"My wife? Are you awake?" Cimmis hurried into his lodge.

Astcat lay on her side, her jaw slack, eyes focused on nothing. Gray hair framed her wrinkled face.

"Ecan has returned," Cimmis said as he strode

across to kneel at her side, "but you do not need to concern yourself with that. Try to sleep."

Kstawl said, "I think her soul is coming back, Father. In the past hand of time, she's awakened twice."

Cimmis stroked her damp gray hair.

"What did you say?" Astcat blinked at the lodge, as if not certain where she was.

"I said Ecan is back."

"Ecan?" Astcat blinked at the painted shields. "How many warriors did we lose?"

"I don't know yet. I've sent for him."

Astcat wiped at the saliva that had run from her open mouth down her chin. "How long was I away?"

"Two days, my wife, but nothing important has happened."

Cimmis couldn't let anyone know how bad she had gotten. The Council would demand she be removed as matron of the North Wind People. They would order that another female from her lineage be installed in her place. Kstawl was the likely choice, but her three and ten summers had not prepared her for leadership.

"My Chief?" Ecan called from beyond the lodge flap.

"Enter, Starwatcher." Cimmis rose to his feet.

Ecan entered and bowed to Cimmis before striding forward. "Good news, Great Chief! We have—"

"I said *no* captives, Starwatcher. Do you take my orders so lightly?"

Ecan's handsome face tensed. Wind Woman had teased hair loose from his bun and left it hanging around his face. "No, my Chief, I do not." He untied the laces of his white cape as though they were choking him and let it fall open, revealing the beautiful red, yellow, and black shirt beneath. "This is no ordinary captive. I thought you would find her more valuable alive than dead."

"You have brought the most dangerous woman alive into my village. Are you trying to destroy us? Do you think the Raven People will just sit by and allow us to harm their precious heroine?"

"Please, my Chief, I believe that she will be a very powerful tool we can use against our enemies. If we can force Dzoo to witch—"

"Dzoo?" Astcat's eyes widened. "You captured *Dzoo?*"

Ecan bowed to Astcat. "Yes, Matron. We found her at War Gods Village."

Astcat lifted her head. "Asin's daughter?"

"Yes, Matron. Do you remember her?"

"Oh, yes." Astcat stared with such vacancy Cimmis feared her soul might have slipped loose again. But she asked, "Has she said anything, Starwatcher?"

"Mostly nonsense about the future. She collapsed on the trail this morning. We had to bear her most of the way."

Astcat's eyes cleared. "What did she say?"

Ecan made a dismissive gesture. "Something about a blood-streaked man with stones for eyes."

Astcat's frown deepened as if she didn't understand. "You must tell me if she says anything else. Anything at all."

"Yes, Matron."

Cimmis could tell that Ecan was lying. He would deal with that later, when it wouldn't upset Astcat. "What was she doing at War Gods Village?"

"I assume she came for the Moon Ceremonial."

"I always expected her to become Starwatcher." Astcat smiled in a dreamy way.

"Everyone did. She had more Power at the age of four summers"—he glanced at Ecan through heavy-lidded eyes—"than most Starwatchers do when they've seen five tens of summers."

Cimmis vividly remembered Dzoo sitting in the plaza with her clan's sacred Dolphin Bundle in her lap. She would speak, then hold it to her ear and nod, hearing the Spirit inside. Dzoo had terrified every other child in Fire Village. And many of the adults. Especially him.

Astcat whispered, "Yes, we were alike, the two of us."

"Were you?" Ecan inquired impatiently. "My Chief, I must tell you—"

Cimmis turned to Astcat. "In what way were you alike, my wife?"

Astcat's smile faded, and her eyes went vacant. Spittle trickled from the corner of her mouth.

Cimmis gently wiped it away with his sleeve. "She's probably remembering her youth. You see, at the age of nine summers, Astcat was chosen by the North Wind elders to be the Starwatcher in Fire Village."

"So I have heard," Ecan said with a nod. "Our matron was a very Powerful child." He looked at Cimmis. "But, my Chief, we must discuss—"

Astcat laughed suddenly and shouted, "Dzoo used to run with the Noisy Ones! I saw her once, spinning around, trying to fling them off her skirt."

"I remember you telling me," Cimmis said in an affectionate voice. "She spun around so fast that all the

Noisy Ones flew into the air and turned into butterflies."

"Yes." Astcat's voice wavered. "I...saw it."

Cimmis tucked the hides around Astcat and stroked her gray hair. "Sleep now. I'll tell you everything later."

He gently extricated his hand and stood up. "How many warriors did we lose?"

"Over the past two moons, we've lost two tens and three. Two were captured during the War Gods Village battle."

"Captured?"

Ecan propped his hands on his hips. "War Chief Talon ambushed us at the base of War Gods Mountain. We had to sacrifice a few to get away."

"And was my war chief one of them?"

"White Stone remained behind."

"Why?"

Ecan's perfect mouth hardened. "Rain Bear's warriors were crawling all over the mountain, and I—I lost my son. I don't know what happened. But after the battle, we were hunting down every last one of the North Wind People, to kill them, as you ordered, and my son must have..."

Astcat started weeping and whispered things that Cimmis couldn't hear, tender things.

He touched Ecan's arm. "Come, let us speak outside. I don't wish to upset her further."

He ducked beneath his door hanging, and Ecan stepped out into the cold beside him. A triumphant crowd had gathered around the returning warriors. The afternoon echoed with laughter and the rhyming work songs the slaves used to occupy themselves. In the distance, a keening arose as wives, girlfriends, and children learned of the death of their men. Dogs barked at the commotion.

"Before the battle," Ecan continued, "I hid Tsauz in a pile of rocks, but he wasn't there when we went to find him. I think he may have been captured."

"Then consider him dead, Ecan." Which saddened Cimmis; he'd genuinely liked the boy. Using him to allay Rain Bear's fears had been a stroke of brilliance. The gamble had been that Rain Bear, known for his leniency, would allow the war party to pass. Then, later, when blame had to be assigned, it would fall on Rain Bear's shoulders, further weakening his position and splintering the Raven People. Time would tell if that goal had been achieved.

Ecan's jaw muscles squirmed as he ground his teeth. Then he said, "It's possible—I'll grant that—but we searched for several hands of time looking for any sign. We found nothing. Nothing!"

Cimmis pinned him with hard eyes. "So you stayed longer than necessary. You risked, and lost, our warriors' lives searching for a little boy?"

"No longer than necessary! We searched for Tsauz while we were fulfilling your orders to hunt down the last of the North Wind People."

"Didn't it occur to you that the villagers might have found him and beaten him to death? Perhaps you just did not recognize your son."

"None of the dead wore his clothes. I think it is more likely that he was taken captive."

"If Rain Bear captured him, he's dead."

"Not necessarily," Ecan rushed to say. "Rain Bear may think he can use my son against me."

Cimmis turned. The vein in Ecan's temple

throbbed. The man's heart was beating as quickly as a trapped rabbit's, desperation in his eyes.

"Use him in what way?"

"Perhaps to convince me..." He swallowed hard.

Cimmis gazed out at the veils of windblown rain that blew across the mountain. Thunderbirds rumbled high up near the cone. "Then let us pray that a runner appears today to tell us your son is dead. That way you will not be tempted to betray me, and I will not be tempted to kill you before you have the chance."

Ecan stepped back, aghast. "I would *not* betray you, my Chief! No matter what Rain Bear offered me."

Against Cimmis's will, his gaze strayed to his swaying door flap, where he glimpsed Astcat. "Don't lie to me. I *know* what men will do to protect the people they love."

Late Afternoon

Gutginsa guards the door to the House of Air. The journey to get there is long and arduous. There are many villages in the Above Worlds, each about a moon apart, through which the soul must fly. The Spirits who live there set traps and snares to try to catch unwary souls, which they eat.

My breath rattles in my lungs. I manage to suck in enough air to say, "I know all this. Is there...a reason... you feel you must tell me...the old stories?"

"I want to make certain you understand them."

He pauses, and I manage to lift my eyelids long enough to glimpse him gazing down at the river, or perhaps at the seagulls that flutter over the deep green water. The scent is powerful this afternoon, rich and earthy.

"Now listen carefully."

I sigh and nod.

"At the end of the flight, there is one final test. Gutginsa waits at the door to the House of Air, holding a living spear with the head of a serpent. He points his *spear at each soul that arrives, because the serpent can tell good souls from evil souls. If the person has done very bad things in his life, Gutginsa's spear flies from his hand and punctures the heart of the evil soul, killing it. But if the person has been compassionate just once in his life, Gutginsa's spear hesitates."*

I can feel my lungs flutter, like a bird's wings preparing to take flight. I have to force them to settle down before I can say, "Then the soul...has a chance to explain."

"Yes, that's right. It may do no good, but it may also be your redemption."

I whisper, "I always thought...Gutginsa's spear...was too generous."

"Ah," he breathes, and I feel his cape sway as he lifts his arm in some gesture. "Then you miss the point. You see, the desire to explain is everything. It is the very heart of deliverance."

I think about that. I suppose every soul must, at some point, realize that it needs to be redeemed, or redemption is impossible.

I smile. "I want...to explain."

His gnarled old fingers touch my arm. "I know. I'm praying very hard that you have the chance."

Chapter Four

Dzoo leaned back against the damp bark wall, listening to the rain fall outside. It spattered in front of the lodge door and trickled across the plaza. The Thunderbirds grumbled unhappily as they passed over Fire Village.

As the downpour increased, the villagers moved inside the lodges, but she could still hear them. In the lodge to the right of hers, a warrior told glorious tales of the battles he'd seen in the past two moons. Wooden bowls clacked as though his wife served supper while he spoke. Occasionally, a little boy stopped him to ask a question.

Across the plaza, in the Council Lodge, women spoke. She couldn't make out the words, but their voices sounded weary and worried.

The Four Old Women. They should be worried.

Dzoo stared at the faint filament of gray that outlined the door on the other side of the lodge. Guards stood outside. Now and then, she heard them move.

She was alone.

She found it a curious sensation.

No one needed her. There were no wounded or sick to care for. The grieving didn't beg her for guidance. For the first time in moons she had only herself to think of.

She pushed back her buffalo-hide hood and examined her prison.

A smoke hole had been cut in the roof, but there was no fire hearth. Not even a ring of stones.

"Perfect," she murmured, and laughed softly.

A filth-encrusted bark container—for bodily wastes —rested near the door. Prisoners could only sit and stare at the blackness and worry about their futures.

Dzoo leaned her head back, closed her eyes, and conjured the image of the blood-streaked young man. Again she looked into his two stone eyes and felt her soul sway. She clung to that moment, feeling the few tendrils of Power slipping around her.

Feet sucked at the mud outside.

Ecan said, "Has she tried to escape?"

One of the guards responded, "I don't think she's even moved, Starwatcher."

Ecan flipped the door hanging aside and ducked into the lodge carrying a leather sack. He wore a woven bark rain hat and cape. "I thought you might be hungry."

She studied him as droplets of water sprinkled the dirt floor. "That surprises me."

"What does?"

"That the needs of another would occur to you."

Ecan roughly tossed the sack to the floor in front of her. Carved shell and bone jewelry flashed from his arms and ankles. Beneath the cape he wore a beautiful knee-length buckskin shirt dyed red, black, and white. Designs of Killer Whale, made from polished stone beads, winked in the faint light. He'd obviously bathed. His hair hung down his back in a long damp braid.

He paced before the door curtain. "You'll find a water sack and several seaweed cakes in the bag. Enjoy them or starve; I don't care."

Dzoo opened the bag. She pulled out the elk-bladder water sack first and took four swallows. Trickles ran down her chin and dripped onto her cape. After days of almost no food or water, she had to ration it or her stomach would rebel. She set the water aside and reached for the seaweed cakes. They'd been wrapped in thick layers of bark to keep them warm. She gave Ecan a wary look. Why this strange kindness?

He kept pacing.

Dzoo took a bite of the cake and chewed it slowly. It tasted salty and delicious.

Grimly, he said, "You are fortunate. Both Chief Cimmis and Matron Astcat remember you. I think if you offer to help them overcome the present crisis with the Raven People they might be inclined to spare your life."

Dzoo watched him as she chewed. She hadn't noticed before: raindrops coated his pointed face. "Why would I do that?"

"Cimmis has ways of making people do as he wishes, Dzoo. I wouldn't toy with him if I were you. Staking a person down, cutting a slit in his belly, and pulling out a length of intestines to roast in a hot fire is currently considered the most gruesome manner of—"

Dzoo laughed softly.

Ecan stalked across the room and kneeled in front

of her. He smelled fragrant, like cedar bark. Did his slaves store his clothing in a cedar box? "Your lack of humility is liable to get you killed before I can—"

"What?" she asked. "Use me for your own purposes?"

Ecan hesitated; then, as though it had just occurred to him, he touched the hem of her buffalo cape. "If I thought I could use you, Dzoo, believe me, I would." He moved his fingers tenderly over her cape. It was an intimate gesture, like stroking a lover's hand.

Dzoo leaned toward him and whispered, "Go ahead. Take me here in the dirt. A man's soul is never as vulnerable as when he is panting atop a woman. After you lay spent, I shall have more of you than just your seed."

Ecan stared at her but drew back his hand. "Will you help me or not?"

"What would you have me do? Witch your enemies? Or give your son wings so he can fly back to you?"

"Both."

Dzoo wiped the crumbs from her fingers onto her leather leggings. "Are you really surprised that Cimmis isn't already organizing a war party to run down the mountain and bring your son back?"

Ecan smiled. "Not exactly. Apparently, Cimmis fears I will betray him to get my son back."

Dzoo drew her knees up and braced her arms atop them. She finished her cake and reached for another. "Perhaps we have something in common after all."

Ecan's handsome face turned stony. "Don't even think it, Dzoo. He would kill me in less than a heartbeat if he even suspected I might do something like that."

"Then you must work very hard to keep his trust."

Ecan glanced at the door and listened for movement, afraid they'd been overheard. In the plaza, someone laughed. The guards shifted. One of them murmured something he couldn't hear.

Dzoo whispered, "You look like you just met Gutginsa's spear, Starwatcher."

His green eyes narrowed. "I believe Gutginsa's spear is pointed at us now, in this world. Not after we die. I believe it more today than I ever have."

He turned suddenly, and a thin sliver of light glinted on his water-slick rain hat. Before he exited into the pale gray gleam, he gripped the use-polished doorframe. "You understand, don't you, that I will do whatever I must to save my son?"

"You even lie to yourself, Ecan. You will do whatever you must to save yourself."

"That, too."

He pulled the curtain back, but just stood in the entry. Around his tall body, she saw the rain-soaked plaza and part of the large Council Lodge. Smoke curled from the roof.

Dzoo leaned back, waiting.

Ecan stared coldly at Dzoo as the rain began to slow.

She looked at him with those stunning midnight eyes, and he wondered if she was drinking his soul. Long red hair streamed over the front of her cape. Every move she made, every word she spoke, had a dangerous, sensual quality. She was at once frightening and frail, a combination that drew him like a wolf to a rabbit burrow. She had begun their game of dog and rabbit.

But he would finish it.

He stepped outside, where Wind Scorpion waited beside Horned Serpent. "Guard?" He motioned to Horned Serpent.

Horned Serpent trotted over and bowed. He had his brown hair tucked up beneath his rain hat. "Yes, Starwatcher?"

"Keep a close watch. Let no one pass. She is very Powerful, and she—"

"Oh, I know, Starwatcher. I have heard stories about her strange gods." The youth wiped rain from his broad cheeks.

"Stories? What stories?"

"Well..." He glanced at Ecan, then at the door hanging. "It is said that while she was a girl, the Striped Dart People taught her how to fly, and at night her soul takes the form of a bird and soars into the Underwater House to sit on the branches of a great tree hidden deep inside the Cave of First Woman. While there, she speaks with strange half-human half-buffalo men and drinks the blood of dead children."

"For the sake of..." Ecan said in exasperation. "Just let no one pass, Horned Serpent. We can't stop her from visiting the Underwater House if she wishes, but we can stop someone from trying to rescue her."

The warrior nodded vigorously. "Yes, Starwatcher. As you order. I promise to guard her with my life."

Wind Scorpion stepped forward, an eyebrow lifted. "Starwatcher, if you would prefer, I would be more than happy to stay here. The witch's wiles don't scare me."

Ecan saw the faintest flicker in the grizzled warrior's eyes, and shook his head. "No, I want you with me. I trust you like no one else."

Wind Scorpion nodded, the slightest quiver at the corners of his mouth.

Ecan stalked away from the captive's quarters. Nothing was working out as he had anticipated. By Gutginsa, why? What had he done to affect his fate this way?

The slaves still out working—pounding octopus meat on stone slabs, smoking fish on racks over the plaza fire—watched him pass in silence. Rain glistened on their hats and capes. None would dare speak to him unless spoken to first. Instead they covered their faces when he neared—especially the young women—and nodded respectfully. Only other North Wind People met his eyes, but even they did so with trepidation.

Ecan walked up the slope to his lodge, which stood just inside the palisade at the base of the lava cliff. He threw aside the leather door hanging and ducked inside. Wind Scorpion took up his position outside the door.

Home. He experienced a sudden sense of relief. Three body lengths across, the vaulted ceiling rose two body lengths over his head. Baskets filled with fragrant Healing herbs lined the walls. Skulls hung on the roof poles, four tens and four of them. They watched him from empty sockets, hollow with the memory of their death and his victory over them.

When no one could see, he leaned heavily against the wall and glared down at the flickering fire a slave had kindled in the hearth. Panic threatened to engulf him.

He clenched his fists and looked up at the skulls.

Soot blackened the curved surfaces of the braincases, brow ridges, sockets, and jaws. As the warmth of the fire rose, heat wavered around them, and their fixed grins began to deepen, as though trying to tell him something.

In the wake of the panic, a slow-burning anger stirred deep in his veins.

"Yes, my precious gods, give me rage," he whispered. "It will wipe away everything else."

The need to kill was almost overpowering. He turned, calling, "Wind Scorpion! Go and find me a girl. Someone young, untouched by another man. Someone that no one will miss. Do you understand?"

"Yes, Starwatcher."

Ecan listened as the man's steps faded, and then he turned his attention to the things he suddenly wished he could avoid.

His bedding hides lay rolled on the far right, next to his son's. Baskets stuffed with toys sat atop Tsauz's hides, and his tiny spear leaned beside Ecan's near the door.

Ecan reached for it and smoothed his fingers down the wood. He could feel Tsauz in every nick and scrape. His son's smile lived in these walls, these toys. His fault. All of it.

If he hadn't agreed to White Stone's plan... *"Enough!"* He balled a fist and slammed it into the lodgepole. *"Stop this!"*

A tripod with a tea bag hung near the flames, scenting the air with the tart fragrance of dried cranberries.

As he bent down for a wooden cup, reaction to the strain set in, and he began to shake. He stared at the blood welling on his skinned knuckles.

He got up again and started walking, shedding jewelry and garments as he went. Shell bracelets and rings slipped from his hands and bounced across the floor as if alive. When he pulled his shirt over his head and violently threw it at the wall, the garment fluttered down like a many-colored feather. Sweat glistened on his naked chest. He tried to unlace his moccasins, but his fingers could not seem to find the knots.

White Stone and Red Dog had not returned yet, and he thanked the gods for the reprieve. Every instant White Stone was still out looking for Tsauz, he could hope the boy lived. But if they returned with news that Tsauz...that his son... "Dear gods, not today. I couldn't stand it."

His dreams had been tortured. Every time he started to fall asleep, he heard Tsauz shout, *"No, Father, please! Please, don't leave me!"*

He reached for his son's bedding, crumpling it in his fingers as he pulled it to his chest, buried his face in it, and wept.

Chapter Five

White Stone pulled off his drenched cape as they entered Fire Village's palisade gate and exchanged pleasantries with the guards. He glanced at Red Dog. The old warrior looked as exhausted as White Stone felt. His graying black hair stuck to his furrowed forehead in wet locks. Mud spattered his bare legs, and his skin was threaded by red welts from branches, briars, and snags. They'd run straight up the mountain, eating and drinking as they went.

Two days before, they had rounded a bend in a patch of thick timber—and collided head-on with Sleeper's warriors, who were headed the other way. In the melee that followed, White Stone had yelled, "Run!" and he and Red Dog had burst through, beating feet as they'd never run before.

Sleeper's warriors had chased them the entire way. White Stone and Red Dog had used every trick known to them, doubling back, leaping off the trail, splashing up or down streams, then climbing out through tree branches to keep from leaving signs of their passage. Sometimes they stayed just beyond spear range. At others, it had seemed inconceivable that Sleeper's warriors could have followed the convoluted path they'd taken. Then they would magically appear several hands of time later, still dogging their trail.

White Stone made a face as he ran his hands down his trembling legs.

"Red Dog, I want you to stand guard while I speak with Ecan."

Red Dog scratched his broken nose. "Are you afraid of being overhead or afraid you might need my protection?"

Annoyed, White Stone ordered, "Just keep watch."

Red Dog grinned, flipped up his hood, and nodded as they plodded wearily toward Ecan's. Rain was falling again, the drops pattering on White Stone's head. At the moment, he couldn't have cared less. The way he felt, everything below his waist might have been made of stone.

White Stone approached Ecan's decorated lodge with a look of dread he knew he couldn't hide. His heart was beating dully as he called, "Starwatcher? War Chief White Stone wishes to speak with you."

He could hear someone scrambling about inside. The rustling of bedding and a low whimper made him look questioningly at Red Dog before he asked, "Star-watcher?"

"Maybe you'd better check," Red Dog muttered.

"Keep watch."

"Yes, War Chief." Red Dog smiled. "Just wake me when you're finished."

White Stone clapped him on the shoulder and

ducked into the interior. Larger than most domiciles, Ecan's stretched three body lengths across. His sleeping hides lay against the west wall beneath a row of weapons. A collection of finely flaked stone axes glinted in the light. From poles above stacks of bark boxes and willow baskets hung a row of skulls.

It was said that Ecan fed them powdered seaweed every day when he was home. When he was away, the slaves had instructions to keep them happy with offerings. The story was that Ecan used to abuse them until old Rides-the-Wind told him that if the souls grew unhappy they could destroy the village.

White Stone wasn't sure he believed it, but who wanted to take chances?

The bedding moved again, and White Stone squinted, making out a girl, perhaps nine or ten summers old, cowering under the hides.

"Who are you?"

She swallowed hard, eyes huge with fright, but no sound passed her lips.

"Get out of the Starwatcher's house, now!" White Stone extended a finger toward the door. "This is no place for little imps like you to be playing."

To White Stone's surprise, the little girl bolted from the covers, naked as a seal pup, and shot through the door out into the rain.

"What the...?" Red Dog cried.

"A child was hiding in here."

"You forget where you are," Red Dog replied meaningfully.

White Stone stiffened, understanding crawling through him.

"Greetings, Starwatcher!" Red Dog's coarse voice barked outside. "The war chief is waiting for you."

White Stone made a face and looked toward the door in time to see Red Dog bow as he pulled the lodge flap aside.

Ecan entered like one of the gods. His hair fell in long black waves over his broad shoulders. He hadn't even bothered to put on a rain cape. Walking directly to White Stone, he demanded, "Where is my son?"

"Rain Bear has him."

Color drained from the Starwatcher's face; a quiver pulled at his lip.

White Stone frowned and looked away. He hated weakness in another man, especially someone as brutal as Ecan. "They used the boy's dying dog to lure him out." White Stone turned back. "Did you spear the dog?"

"Of course I did!"

Fatigue made him careless. "Next time you do something that stupid, make sure you kill it."

Ecan's eyes had taken on a weird light; his voice dropped to a hiss. "If I'd let it live, Tsauz would have insisted upon taking it with him. I couldn't take the chance that the miserable little cur would give away his hiding place."

"Well, in the end, it worked out just that way."

Ecan ignored the tone in White Stone's voice. "Where did Rain Bear take my son?"

"The last we saw, they were fussing over Tsauz in the plaza during the Moon Ceremonial. We were surrounded by tens of people. We had to leave."

Ecan took a deep breath. Dark blue smudged the

flesh beneath his eyes. He looked like he hadn't slept in days.

"How did Tsauz look?"

White Stone lifted a shoulder. "He had scratches and bruises. Most of all, he looked frightened half out of his mind. He kept clutching that whimpering puppy so hard he was squeezing the guts out through the wound in its..."

A tremor, the sort icy fingers made on the spine, ran through Ecan. Then he said, "Fear can be endured. Bruises heal."

"Yes."

A frightening glitter filled Ecan's eyes. He glared at White Stone for several heartbeats, maintaining control by sheer force of will.

White Stone, fatigued past good sense, just glared back.

Ecan's dark brows lowered. "What do you think we should do next?"

White Stone shifted in confusion. "Don't you understand what I've been saying? There's nothing more *any* of us can do. If Rain Bear took him to Sandy Point Village, the boy is surrounded by tens of tens of warriors. They'd swat us like flies if we tried to rescue the boy. Unless you can talk the Council into approving a prisoner exchange, there's no hope." He could see by Ecan's eyes that that wasn't about to happen.

"Thank you, War Chief." Ecan turned away. "Please go and report to Cimmis. He's waiting for you."

White Stone stared. "I'll do that; then I must see the families of the warriors who were killed or captured. I'm sure they're—"

"One last thing." Ecan gracefully walked toward

him. "I told Cimmis that you stayed behind because of Rain Bear."

The rest remained unspoken.

White Stone picked up his rain cape. As he swung it around his shoulders, he woodenly said, "I *did* stay behind because of Rain Bear. I needed to judge the effects of our strike on War Gods Village. I needed to study his camps and count his warriors. How can we ever hope to crush him if we don't know his weaknesses?"

"I agree, War Chief."

White Stone walked by Ecan and pulled the lodge flap aside but didn't exit. "Ecan, I share the responsibility for what happened to the boy. Let me know if I—"

"Yes, War Chief," Ecan interrupted. "I will."

White Stone hesitated. "Um, you should know. I heard someone in here. There was a little girl..." He indicated the rumpled bedding.

"What?" Ecan glanced up, confused; then his eyes cleared. "Oh, yes. That. Never Mind. Cimmis is waiting in the Council Lodge for your report to him."

White Stone stepped out into the rain. Red Dog met his gaze, and White Stone tilted his head, cueing Red Dog to watch Ecan. "I'll be back soon, Red Dog."

"Yes, War Chief."

Half sick with dread, White Stone plodded wearily toward the Council Lodge.

Chapter Six

Red Dog stood in the rain beside the Starwatcher's lodge and watched White Stone slog his way through the downpour toward the Council Lodge. Had he ever been this root-sucking tired before? Fatigue, like a warm fuzziness, weighed his limbs and lay heavily in his guts. His brain felt hot inside his skull despite the cold rain pattering on his bark hat. Still, he tried to peek through the swaying flap at Ecan. The Starwatcher looked like he'd been kicked in the stomach.

After a few more moments, Ecan pulled the leather hanging aside, and Red Dog slid his gaze to the slaves still going about their duties despite the downpour.

"Is everything all right, Starwatcher?" Red Dog asked offhandedly.

Ecan stepped out into the rain. He had the kind of sculpted face that made women stare admiringly.

In a voice laced with irony, Ecan said, "Everything's fine."

Red Dog gave him a quizzical look. "Starwatcher?"

Ecan's eyes resembled shiny green beads. "I wish to hire you to undertake a special mission."

"Really?"

"I will reward you very well."

Red Dog lifted a shoulder. "I'm already wealthy, Starwatcher. When you hired me to burn down the Council Lodge where your wife's family was gathered, I made a fortune."

Ecan clamped Red Dog's wrist. "That was *necessary*, Red Dog. She was going to set my belongings outside our lodge. I would have lost my son! Her clan would have taken him away from me!"

Red Dog looked down at the Starwatcher's hand—the man had never touched him before. "I just meant I am already rich, Starwatcher."

"This is an important mission, Red Dog. Of course, it must seem as though you are strictly the chief's messenger, but we need an intermediary to work with Rain Bear. Rain Bear knows you. He once trusted you."

The cold grip of fear banished his fatigue. "That was a long time ago, Starwatcher. I guarantee he is no longer under any such illusion."

"You are still the best choice."

"I'd send someone else. Maybe Flying Fish. He's reliable." Red Dog glanced toward Cimmis's lodge. Matron Astcat was staring at him through the doorway. She gazed about warily and crooked a beckoning finger before the door hanging dropped back in place.

Ecan leaned close, his nose within a finger's width of Red Dog's. "You're going. Unless you'd like to tell me the name of the man who makes the fetishes you Trade for. I'd hire him in an instant. He's Powerful, anonymous, and living right in the middle of us."

"By Gutginsa's balls, you're right he's Powerful!" Red Dog agreed, wondering what Astcat wanted. "Powerful enough that I'm not going to cross him. Not even for you, Starwatcher."

Ecan backed away, a satiated smile on his lips. "Then perhaps you wouldn't want it whispered around that you were serving a witch, eh, Red Dog? What's his name? Coyote?"

Red Dog swallowed dryly, the fear coiling in his gut. "Look, I've never so much as seen his face. He wears a mask when we meet. He talks funny, with an accent, to hide his voice."

"A man who *says* he works for a witch, could even *be* the witch."

Red Dog shivered, but forced himself to say, "Or he could be someone like a Starwatcher, wearing a mask, hiding his voice."

Ecan laughed harshly at that. "Stop prattling. You're going, Red Dog. That's all there is to it."

Red Dog took a deep breath, knowing he had no choice. Liaison to a witch or not, Red Dog couldn't afford to cross the Starwatcher. Not yet.

Ecan said, "It means you'll have to run hard to get back by tomorrow night."

"Tomorrow! I just got home!" He had to see Astcat —and from her gesture, it was something furtive.

"It's all downhill, and you're accustomed to running for days straight. You're perfect for the task."

"Perfect for roasting over Rain Bear's coals, you mean. He will eat my liver first."

"Perhaps, but if you survive, you will be the wealthiest man in Fire Village."

Red Dog pulled his wrist away and stole a quick

glance at the lodge where he hoped Dzoo was being held. Dzoo, Astcat, Ecan...gods, this was getting complicated. "Why don't you tell me what you have in mind; then we'll discuss how much my liver is worth."

Tsauz held the dead puppy as he walked into the meadow between Evening Star and Rides-the-Wind. Scattered clouds passed above to collect in a gray, cottony mass on the volcanic mountains farther to the east. A faint breeze stirred the firs, and a ring of warriors surrounded them.

For Evening Star, the ceremony came as a relief. The dog's corpse was swollen, leaking brown liquid, and downright putrid.

How odd that a child's grief can hold an adult's common sense hostage.

It had been Rides-the-Wind who had had the courage to insist that Tsauz bury the rotting puppy. Fearing the boy might change his mind, Rain Bear had wasted no time preparing a cordon of guards to see them out of Sandy Point Village. People in the surrounding camps had watched in disbelief as the processional wound through their ragged camps. And for what? The burial of a puppy?

To Evening Star's mind, it was either the stuff of legends, or a most ridiculous comedy. She looked around the grassy meadow Rides-the-Wind had picked. Alders, pine, and a ring of birch surrounded the opening.

"How much will I owe you, Elder?" Tsauz asked as he laid the limp corpse on a rock that the Soul Keeper had led him to. "I—I don't have anything here with me, but when I get home, I give you my oath I will send you—"

"I don't wish to be paid, Tsauz. I'm just happy you asked me to help you."

Crying, Tsauz said, "I promised him, Elder. I told him I would find someone to Sing his soul to the afterlife." He wiped his cheeks on his sleeve. "Thank you, Elder."

The gratitude in the boy's voice was wrenching. "Let's get started so Runner can be on his way."

Sunlight glimmered on Rides-the-Wind's gnarled hands as he reached into his ritual pack. He pulled out a small white bag and poured powdered seaweed into his palm. It shimmered a pale green.

Rides-the-Wind touched the boy's shoulder. "Can you help me Sing him to the House of Air?"

Tsauz choked out, "Yes."

Rides-the-Wind lifted his voice in the Death Song, and after a few moments, Tsauz's voice, and then Evening Star's, joined his:

> *In a sacred manner, we send a voice.*
> *We send a voice.*
> *The path of Gutginsa is our strength.*
> *The path of Gutginsa is our hope.*
> *A praise we are making.*
> *A praise we are sending.*
> *In a sacred manner, we send a voice.*
> *Hear us, our North Wind ancestors.*
> *Come and lead this puppy's soul to the*
> *entry to the Above Worlds.*

> *In a sacred manner we are sending a
> voice.*
> *Come, Blessed Ancestors, take this
> puppy's soul to the House of Air
> where his ancestors will greet him
> and love him.*

The guards sifted through the trees around the meadow, quiet, alert, watching them. It was, perhaps, the first time any of them had heard the North Wind Death Song.

Rides-the-Wind lifted his hands. "The ancestors will find him here, Tsauz, and take his soul flying to the House of Air. Tonight he will be watching over you from high above."

Tsauz looked blankly up at the cloud-packed morning sky where ravens flapped lazily toward the sea, cawing to each other.

"Is it true, Elder, that the dead can fly down to earth and make rainbows?"

Rides-the-Wind smiled and followed Tsauz's gaze. The sky had started turning a deep shade of amber. "I think it's true. They can bring rain and call the Thunderbirds...and make rainbows. Why do you ask?"

Tsauz chewed his lip. "I'll be looking for Runner's rainbow, that's all."

Evening Star watched them, her heart heavy. How would a blind boy see a rainbow? She thought of her daughter, and all that the little girl would miss in life. Love, grief, smiles, and laughter. She would never enjoy that lift that came with a young man's smile or feel the tingle in her pelvis as she shared a man's body. No life would be conceived to grow in her womb, and the tearing pain of childbirth would never be hers. So much was lost when a child died.

Rides-the-Wind stroked Tsauz's dark hair. "You'll see Runner's rainbow. Someday soon, I imagine."

The guards shifted. Several whispered to each other and squinted at their back trail.

Evening Star could feel something happening out there. "Let's go back and eat breakfast. Soul Keeper, would you join us? Rain Bear promised to come for tea once he's finished meeting with the other chiefs."

"I would like that very much." The old man looked at her with a knowing gaze.

At that moment, a warrior loped in from the forest, breathing hard, and called, "Where's Chief Rain Bear?"

"The Council Lodge," Evening Star's guard Hornet answered. "What's happened?"

"We caught one of Ecan's assassins sneaking up on the village!"

Evening Star stiffened. "Elder, please make sure you get the boy back safely."

"What about you?" Rides-the-Wind asked.

A cold shiver went through her. "I know some of the Wolf Tails. Perhaps I can name this one."

Chapter Seven

Rain Bear shoved a low branch aside and continued up the trail behind Young Feathers. He was just a skinny boy, little more than gangly bones, but his body betrayed the terrible importance of his current position. He was guiding the great chief. No doubt his young friends were going to hear about it over and over.

The fire in the clearing ahead threw long, dancing shadows over the firs and boulders. It made the forest seem alive with translucent wings. As they drew near, Rain Bear saw Dogrib standing with three men. He was binding the middleman's hands behind his back. Two others held his arms in viselike grips.

Rain Bear called, "What have we got? Who is he?"

Dogrib called, "One of Ecan's assassins. We captured him crawling through the boulders on his belly."

"That's a lie!" the man shouted in response and struggled against Dogrib's hard hands. "I came in peace, openly!"

Rain Bear entered the halo of firelight and recognized the burly form. "Red Dog?"

"Yes. It's me. My friend, I must speak with you!" The dirt on his face had mixed with his sweat and turned to mud in the deep furrows in his forehead. "Rain Bear, get these young wolves off me! You, of all people, know I am no assassin!" He glared at the two warriors holding his muscular arms. They grinned like cougars over a freshly killed carcass.

Rain Bear halted on the opposite side of the fire. Dirty hair had come loose from Red Dog's bun and framed his round face. He appeared on the verge of panic. *Good.*

Rain Bear said, "You came in peace to do what? Try to kill one of us? Or to rescue Ecan's son?" He paused. "Sorry, old friend. Sleeper's warriors beat you back. I have just been in council with Goldenrod. He said they almost had you and White Stone more than once."

Red Dog nervously scanned the faces of the people around him. "I bring you a message from Fire Village."

"From whom?"

"Astcat, matron of the North Wind People."

Red Dog's deer-hide cape had large patches of hair missing. Not the usual garb of one of Fire Village's best warriors, but he'd probably shed everything that would tie him to Cimmis.

"Astcat has not attempted to communicate with me in six and ten cycles—not since she made her own daughter Outcast for running away with me. Why now?"

Red Dog sucked in a breath. "I can't tell you, but believe me, you truly do not wish to kill me until I've spoken with you!"

"Go ahead. I'm listening."

Red Dog glanced suspiciously at Dogrib and the rest. "My message is for you alone."

Rain Bear composed his face, deepening the lines as if in great study. "Bind him up like a trussed walrus."

He watched as a length of sturdy rope was located and Red Dog was thoroughly wrapped and secured with doubled knots. Then Rain Bear pulled his war club from his belt and motioned for Dogrib and the other men to back off. "Give us a few moments."

Unhappy with the arrangement, Dogrib said, "As you order, but we'll be close enough to see, if not hear. Should he even look like he's moving against you—"

"I expect you to kill him," Rain Bear calmly said, and thumped his club into his palm. "The fact that he knows that should make our discussions more straight-forward."

Red Dog nodded. "I assure you, it will."

Dogrib strode to the edge of the clearing with the other warriors.

Rain Bear took his time walking around the fire toward Red Dog. The grizzled warrior watched him warily.

"All right, *old friend,*" Rain Bear said in a low voice. "Tell me what's happening."

Red Dog gave him a foxy smile. "Why on earth am I doing this to myself? Look at me! I'm trussed like a pig, covered in filth! My legs feel like wooden stumps, and I'm so tired I could fall flat on my face."

"It's because you're such a scoundrel, and you know it."

Red Dog grinned like a maniac. "That's it, all right." Then his expression fell. "You have to believe me—I didn't know what was coming at War Gods Village. When you took Ecan's weapons and let him continue, I really thought we were on a peaceful errand." He made a face. "After some of the things I've seen...done...I don't want to do this anymore."

"What would you do instead?"

He jerked his head westward. "There are islands out there. I could take all of my wealth and sit on a rock, surrounded by the sea. Once a moon, I could palm off one of my trinkets to a fisherman for bringing me food."

"You'd be crazy within five days." Rain Bear crossed his arms. "I know you too well. You enjoy scheming; it's part of your soul. You find a crooked pleasure being in the presence of people who underestimate who and what you are."

"And who and what am I?"

"One of the most clever and remarkable men I've ever known."

Red Dog chuckled at that. "You know, your flattery is worth more than all the North Wind People's silly jewels." He paused. "In all of my life, only two people have seen through to my soul."

"Who's the other one?"

Red Dog shrugged. "I don't know."

"You don't have to lie to me."

"I'm not. I've never seen him in the daylight, and at night, he wears a mask."

"You're joking."

Red Dog's expression turned flat, and his voice dropped to a whisper. "About him? Never."

Rain Bear stiffened. "I don't believe it—someone actually scares you."

"Oh, yes, more than Ecan, Cimmis, or the Council.

If they found out I was your agent, they'd just torture me to death in a most grisly fashion." Red Dog's eyes glittered. "He'd steal my soul and lock it screaming and terrified into one of his little chipped fetishes."

Rain Bear cocked his head. "Coyote?"

Red Dog jerked. "You *know* him?"

"He's after Dzoo."

"After her how?"

"We think he wants to possess her."

Red Dog looked uneasily out at the darkness beyond the ring of fire. "I'm supposed to deliver Astcat's message. Then we've got to dicker over Ecan's son. After that, I've got to get back. If Coyote's after Dzoo, she's in real danger."

"Do you believe it?" Evening Star's voice held a tremor, and it angered her. Gruffly, she folded her arms and leaned against the dark trunk of a fir. This was either a dream coming true, or the beginning of a nightmare. She'd chafed and stamped when Dogrib wouldn't allow her into the meadow where Rain Bear and Red Dog were talking, and now, in the morning light, as she heard Matron Astcat's terms, she wasn't sure what to think.

Rain Bear crouched before her and studied the ragged people moving around the campfires down the slope. He had a strange look on his face. "It's possible. During her lucid moments, Astcat generally made good decisions. Do you think the Council knows about the offer?"

"I doubt it. Nevertheless, she is the matron of the North Wind People. She has the authority to make offers without their approval. I just don't understand why she would wish to."

"Perhaps it is simply an act of kindness."

She shook her head. "Offering to revoke my slave status and give me a lodge in Fire Village is more than kindness; it's very dangerous. My people would flock to me. Within days, I'd be confirmed as clan matron to succeed my mother. Potentially, if anything happened to Astcat, I would be a viable candidate for matron of the North Wind People. Surely neither she nor Cimmis wishes that."

Rain Bear rubbed his jaw. "Nevertheless she has been ill."

"Yes, but she doesn't want me to follow her. She has a daughter, Kstawl."

He propped his elbows on his knees, and she could see the red sash that belted his tan leather shirt. It accentuated the breadth of his shoulders and the narrowness of his waist. "Kstawl is very young, isn't she?"

"Three and ten summers."

Evening Star slipped her hands beneath her cape and rubbed her cold arms. The walk to the meadow had chilled her to the bone. "It is more likely that all this is a lie. Astcat wants to lure me back so that she can reward Ecan by returning his wayward slave."

Rain Bear grimaced at the ground. Tens of feet had trampled the mud; then it had frozen with the fall of night, leaving a pocked, treacherous surface. "Well, we won't let that happen."

Evening Star's throat suddenly tightened. She lifted a hand to rub it.

Rain Bear stood, and she saw the dread and hope that brimmed in his eyes. "But if there's a chance that you might be able to safely take your position as clan matron..."

He let the words hang.

"I can't."

"Answer me truly: If Astcat were dead, and the remaining North Wind People asked you to return as the North Wind matron, would you do it?"

Horrifying images flashed across her soul. She squeezed her eyes closed to avoid them, but they only intensified. People crying, lodges on fire...her daughter screaming...

"During the attack on my village," she said in a shaky voice, "I tried to plead with Ecan for the lives of the children. I had my two-summers-old daughter in my arms and five more children clinging to my cape. He was polite and understanding. He said of course he wouldn't execute children. I let his warriors take them away to a 'safe' place beyond the burning village. But it wasn't far enough. I...I...could hear..."

"You don't have to tell me this," he murmured.

"Yes, I do. You asked if I could go back to the North Wind People." Tears of anger leaked from her eyes. The memories made her feel empty and alone. "They killed Bright Cloud first. They bound her to a pole and dangled her in a fire. She kept screaming for me. I leaped upon Ecan. His guards clubbed me down." She looked at Rain Bear and found rage in his eyes. "The men who killed my daughter weren't Raven People. I *can't* go back. I *won't.*"

Rain Bear reached out and took her hand in a strong grip. "I understand, but if you..."

Evening Star stepped into his arms and buried her face in the hide over his broad shoulder. It took him a moment to realize what she'd done. Then he pulled her close.

"Would it help you if I went back?" she asked miserably. "If I went to Fire Village and secretly worked to rally the North Wind People against the Four Old Women?"

He stroked her hair. "Maybe. Think about it for a time. This isn't something you must decide today."

Wolf Spider and Hornet whispered and looked away, as though trying to give them some privacy.

Evening Star let her body melt against Rain Bear's, and a warm, tingling wave ran through her. It felt so soothing to be held by a man again.

He whispered against her hair, "Red Dog said Ecan is desperate to get his boy back. He said Cimmis wasn't concerned."

"Of course not. His assassins are already on their way. What did Ecan offer?"

"Wealth and promises of my personal safety. Mostly promises he can't keep. He will become more amenable as his desperation grows."

Rain Bear peered down into her eyes. It was like standing on a mountaintop in a lightning storm. Every nerve in her body prickled.

"Red Dog is waiting to hear your answer to Matron Astcat's request. Do you want to speak with him? You don't have to."

"Do you trust him?"

"Red Dog? He has no more scruples than a pine marten in a red squirrel's nest. For the moment he's having the time of his life playing at being everyone's spy. It delights him to no end that Ecan and White Stone think he's a dolt. Cimmis—if he ever even looked sideways at him—would think he was just another lazy unwashed warrior. A menial little better than a slave."

"Then why does he stay there?"

"They pay him. He may be the richest man in the world by now. Oh, and the other thing. He worships Dzoo. It's something I don't understand. I can't picture her ever responding to his devotion—or should I call it an obsession? May your Gutginsa have mercy on anyone who harms a hair on her body, because Red Dog, no matter the cost, will kill him."

"Where is he?"

"Dogrib has him in a secret location outside of the camps. He's under heavy guard."

Evening Star reluctantly stepped away from him, and Rain Bear folded his arms over his broad chest, as though to protect his heart. "If you went to Fire Village, it might turn ugly."

"Oh, you have no idea how ugly it might be."

Chapter Eight

Old Woman Above had left her lodge to carry the fiery ball of the sun into the sky. The dawn was so warm, a man did not even need a cape. Tiny pools of water glistened across Fire Village. Only the most sheltered ledges on the black lava cliff gleamed with frosty rimes.

White Stone had been summoned to Cimmis's quarters just after morning prayers. The chief had his square jaw clamped, as though preparing for a hand-to-hand stiletto fight. His gray hair hung loose over his shoulders.

"I don't think you should do this, my Chief," White Stone said as he strode at Cimmis's side. "It's not wise."

"If Rain Bear has shared his thoughts with anyone besides his council, it's Dzoo. If I can get anything out of her, it could make all the difference for us."

"I doubt she'll tell you anything, unless we torture her. After enough pain anyone will talk."

"We're talking about Dzoo. First, I don't think you could ever get her to talk, no matter how much pain you inflicted on her. Second, if word gets out that we're torturing her, not only will it play into Rain Bear's hands, but it might even lead to a revolt among the slaves. Do you understand? She may be the most dangerous woman in the world. Not only will I *not* hurt her, War Chief, I'm going to make her as comfortable as I can."

White Stone gave Cimmis a disbelieving look as he walked away and shook his head before following. By Gutginsa's bloody spear, didn't Cimmis understand what kind of woman he was dealing with? While on the trail, Red Dog had related some of the stories people told about Dzoo. His warriors had become so frightened, he wasn't sure they'd have had the courage to kill her under a direct order.

He glanced away, thinking. At this time of morning the palisade cast a long shadow that stretched halfway across the village. Slaves crouched around the central fire, pounding lupine root. Their haunted eyes followed Cimmis as he passed. White Stone kept his hand braced upon his belted war axe as a reminder to them. Deer Killer, on guard at Dzoo's door, straightened as they approached. His dark eyes widened. To White Stone's dismay, he always had a startled look when Cimmis came near him.

"Greetings, Deer Killer," Cimmis said. "How is our prisoner?"

"I didn't even hear her move during the night, my Chief."

Cimmis pulled the door hanging back and ducked inside.

White Stone said, "I thought Wind Scorpion was supposed to relieve you at dawn? Where—"

"You fools!" Cimmis shouted and rushed back into the daylight. *"This lodge is empty!"*

White Stone gave Deer Killer a murderous look.

"I didn't do it, *I swear!"*

White Stone ducked under the hanging. As his eyes adjusted, he saw the bark container on the far side of the circular structure...but that was all. "It's impossible! She couldn't have escaped!"

"There she is!" Deer Killer shouted. *"Look! Near Ecan's lodge!"*

White Stone scrambled out. "Where?"

Cimmis stood with a hand up to shield his eyes from the morning glare.

Dzoo stood just to the right of Ecan's lodge, facing the lava cliff. Wind Woman waffled her red dress around her long legs and played with her waist-length braid.

"War Chief!" Deer Killer blurted. "I swear to you I never left my post! Not even for an instant!" A curious expression slackened his face. "She must *have flown* out. It's the only answer! She changed herself into a bird and soared out through the smoke hole!"

White Stone made a face. Flown indeed!

"Silence!" Cimmis ordered. The slaves had started to stand up and follow their gazes.

In a clipped voice, Cimmis said, "Come with me. Both of you." Then he stalked off across the village with his long gray hair flying.

As White Stone hurried after his chief, he shot a glance over his shoulder at the horrified Deer Killer. "I'll deal with you later. Assuming Cimmis doesn't order your guts boiled first."

When they reached Dzoo, Cimmis slowed, ordering, "Deer Killer, make certain no one comes close enough to overhear my conversation. Including the Starwatcher."

"Of course, my Chief." Deer Killer trotted the two tens of paces to Ecan's lodge and stood, eyes half glazed with fear, shivers racking his body.

White Stone asked, "And me, my Chief?"

The hem of Cimmis's blue knee-length shirt fluttered in the breeze. "Keep your warrior company. Perhaps he has some last requests he might wish to make before I deal with him."

He protested, "But, my Chief, what if she attacks you? Before I could get to you, she might—"

Cimmis's dark eyes glittered. "I was a warrior for more summers than you have been alive, White Stone. I can protect myself. Go."

White Stone glanced dubiously at Cimmis's shriveled left arm and backed away to stand beside Deer Killer.

Deer Killer leaned sideways and whispered, "I've never been this terrified in my life! If she could get out of the captives' lodge, there's no place we can hold her. She can fly about as she pleases!"

White Stone glumly watched Cimmis walk toward Dzoo. Just beyond the palisade, the lava cliff rose like a rough-hewn black wall. She had her chin tipped up, as though studying the old owl nests that bristled in the clefts.

Assuming Deer Killer hadn't dozed off or left his post, how had she managed to escape? "Did you ever find the missing ropes? The ones you used to tie her up in Wasp Village?

"No, War Chief."

"Perhaps she tied them together and used them to climb out of the smoke hole. Did that occur to you?"

Relief made the young warrior's eyes widen. "Blessed gods, do you think so?"

"Maybe." He wondered if Cimmis was going to remember Deer Killer's dereliction, and if so, who would be given the disagreeable task of ending his life?

Dzoo heard him coming. Her vision of the towering black cliff quivered as his feet struck the ground. Heavy feet, pounding out authority.

He didn't speak, just took a stand behind her.

She turned and saw what he had become: tall, lanky, with a square jaw. His long gray hair hung over his broad shoulders like a mantle. His eyes were striking—the eyes of a trapped man who sees no way out.

"So," she said, "you are Chief Cimmis now. It must be difficult for you."

Cimmis's eyes narrowed. She saw him look away, trying not to let her see his fear. *I wonder if he plays this game with every person, every moment of his life.*

He exhaled. "Are you well, Dzoo? My slaves tell me that Lion Girl is ill. Is her replacement, Dance Fly, properly caring for you?"

"Your slave emptied my waste bowls before they spilled onto the floor again. If that's what you mean."

He walked over, close, as though to prove to the people below that he wasn't afraid. The hem of his blue shirt waffled around his leggings. She watched as he gathered the courage to meet her eyes. To his credit, he didn't wince when she stared past into his wounded soul.

"I did not order your capture, Dzoo. But you are here, and I cannot just release you. The other North Wind People would kill me for it. You may be a valuable tool—and these days we must use whatever we have."

"It's too late, Cimmis. The time of the North Wind People is coming to a close."

He stared at her as though uncertain. She knew him so well, could read the tracks on his soul the way a hunter read an elk's trail. She smiled as his warrior's instinct insisted that she was bluffing.

"They can't kill all of us, Dzoo, and I assure you those of us who remain will hunt down every last Raven Person who was involved—"

Her laughter came bubbling up from deep inside.

His shoulder muscles tensed.

She shot a glance at his warriors and leaned toward him to whisper, "If you were wise, Cimmis, you would start shedding every vestige of the North Wind People's way of life: their clothing, their jewelry and mannerisms. Your only hope of survival is to blend into the Raven villages and forget you ever knew anything about your own people."

His jaw hardened. In that instant she could tell that he wanted a way out, but couldn't allow himself to take it. The snare that had entangled him was called obligation.

"Dzoo, has Rain Bear managed to bind the refugees into a fighting force? Will they follow him?"

She said, "It will be difficult to disguise your wife, but it can be done. There are many battle victims who have lost their souls. My advice is to run as fast as you can to the northern Cougar People. If she ever starts talking about who she is, just tell them she is not well. Tell them the evil Chief Cimmis killed her entire family before her eyes. So many suffered the same fate. They will believe you."

His eyes might have been brown chert, hard and shiny. "I can't believe Rain Bear wishes the destruction of his daughter's relatives."

She leaned closer, their faces less than a hands-breadth apart. She watched him lose the battle to pull away, thinking it would shame him before his people. In reply he could only glare.

"Escaping your own people will be the final test. But you know that, don't you? The North Wind People will never forgive you for saving yourself and your wife. They expect both of you to die for them. To provide cover for their escape." She shrugged absently. "I will tell you truly, I have not seen that part."

"But...you have seen the rest?"

"Oh, yes."

A swallow went down his throat. "Are you telling me you have seen the end?"

"The end is only a fragment. There is much more to fear."

His teeth ground beneath the thin veneer of flesh.

"If you tell me the entire vision, Dzoo, from start to finish"—he exhaled a shaky breath—"I will set you free."

"Despite the fact that you will die for it?"

He nodded stiffly. "I give you my oath."

"Do you know what it's like to fly, Cimmis?"

"No."

"Before this is over, you will." She gestured to the beaten path that led through the middle of Fire Village. "Shall we go?"

"Go?" He squinted unsurely. "Where?"

She toyed with him like a spider tapping a trapped fly with its leg. "You had my old lodge cleaned out, didn't you? I wish to go home."

She started down the trail. He said nothing, stunned and motionless.

White Stone cried, "Stay where you are, witch!"

Cimmis hurried to catch up.

White Stone started forward, muscles flexing as he gripped his spear at the ready. "What is she doing out here, my Chief? How did she escape?"

Cimmis bluntly told him, "She is moving to her old lodge, War Chief. I want you to escort her."

"Her old lodge?" White Stone gestured in disbelief. "Why?"

Cimmis exploded. "Because I *ordered it!* I had it prepared for her. Tell the guards that she is to move about freely." He shot her a slitted stare. "But if she makes any attempt to get through the palisade, they are to kill her immediately."

White Stone lowered his spear. "I'll tell them, but they won't understand any better than I do."

Dzoo gave White Stone a teasing smile. "The chief wishes me to be comfortable. Ask yourself why."

Cimmis rolled his hands into fists, the muscles in his forearms popping and straining.

White Stone glanced at his chief. "Then you must be willing to tell us about Rain Bear's plans. I am relieved that you've come to your—"

"Rain Bear's plans?" Her laughter was crystalline. "You think Cimmis worries about Rain Bear's plans?"

Cimmis tried to hide his alarm, making his voice louder, more confident. "White Stone, take Dzoo to her old lodge. She'll tell you where it is."

"Yes, my Chief."

Cimmis walked away, slowly, acting as though he had all day to make it back to the safety of his lodge. Every eye in Fire Village watched him.

White Stone grumbled, "Deer Killer, apparently you're going to live to see sunset this day. But if I were you, I wouldn't repeat my dereliction of duty. Do you understand?"

"Yes, War Chief." His body was trembling, and Dzoo watched it with a certain glee.

When Cimmis was out of hearing range, White Stone hissed, "I don't know how you got out of the captives' lodge, witch, but I'm taking no chances with you. You'd better be very careful."

She bowed her head and smiled.

As they walked into the lower half of the village, children came racing out from behind a lodge and circled around, shrieking in joy, as barking dogs nipped at their heels. When they noticed White Stone, panic gripped them. Like a flock of spooked birds, they retreated to the edges of the plaza to let him pass, eyes like huge dark holes in the world. A strange silence descended.

"It seems, War Chief, that you have a Powerful effect on the small and frail. Would you like to know what the Dead think of you?"

"Just walk, witch."

She studied the painted lodges in awe. The lifelike

69

renderings of Eagle, Killer Whale, Grizzly Bear, and Owl were the product of a people who never had to scramble for a living. "How many North Wind People are left in Fire Village, War Chief?"

"You mean pure North Wind?"

"Yes."

His steps faltered, but he regained his composure quickly. "How many were here when you left?"

"Almost ten tens."

"There may be eight tens now."

Eight tens. "At that rate, the village is losing one a year. In another eight tens of years, there will be no purebloods left."

Water puddles dotted the ground, muddying their moccasins. She watched White Stone as he considered her words; they seemed to be eating at him like a termite in an old log.

"Did Cimmis order all of the other North Wind People killed?"

"Some of them," White Stone admitted, "but there weren't many left to begin with. Six and ten summers ago, when Tlikit fled with her lover, they started leaving. Several have died over the cycles. Astcat begged the North Wind People from the neighboring villages to come and live here. A few did."

"Does it bother you to serve a dying people?"

"I don't understand. You're one of them. A pureblood, but you favor the Raven People."

"Poor War Chief," she whispered. "How lucky you are. You need not look past your orders. I envy the simplicity, if not the quality, of your life."

White Stone's gaze shot involuntarily back up the hill. She could feel his nerves prickling, see it in the set of his shoulders. When she followed his stare, it was to see Ecan standing outside his lodge like a carved statue. His long hair hung loose around his tall body. His eyes might have been coals glowing through a darkness of hatred.

It didn't matter; she was going home. Already she could sense the ghosts of her ancestors, hear the whispers of Power coming from the aged wood and bark of the house where she was born.

As she walked up and placed a hand on the familiar doorway, she heard her mother's ghost crying.

"Yes, Mother. I know. *He* is hunting me."

Chapter Nine

Morning light fell across the ocean, reflecting from the curls of mist that twined along the beach. Rain Bear took another sip from his teacup as he stared out at the islands offshore. Despite the early hour, men were plying nets in the muddy water. Another whale had been harpooned, almost swamping the canoe as it sounded. The hunters had regaled the crowd with the story of their perfect cast—the harpoon skewering the blowhole—and their wild ride while the suffocating whale thrashed.

After the carcass had been towed ashore, people had swarmed it, using large obsidian knives to process the blubber and rich red meat. Not even darkness had slowed them. By torchlight, the whale had been rendered to bone.

Feasting had lasted until well after midnight. And while most of the village still slept, the refugees were up and moving about through the forest.

"...*today you'll speak...Thunderbird.*" Rides-the-Wind's scratchy old voice penetrated his lodge.

Rain Bear cocked his head to listen. Rides-the-Wind had been whispering to Tsauz since long before dawn, preparing him for some task. He'd caught only a few words of the conversation. Something about hunting and magical stones.

He clutched his hot cup and concentrated on the warmth that penetrated his fingers, trying to will it into the rest of his frozen body. Half of a cod was propped on sticks jammed into the charcoal-black earth and tilted so that the chevrons of meat slowly cooked over the fire's low heat. The odor was sending Rain Bear's stomach into fits.

Evening Star slipped out of her lodge, her face swollen with sleep, her eyes heavy. She glanced at him first thing, smiling as if just for him. She stood, reached for her cloak, and walked off into the forest to attend to her morning needs.

Rides-the-Wind's voice rose and fell as he regaled Tsauz with some story about Thunderbirds.

Rain Bear was pondering that when Evening Star stepped out of the dew-beaded trees, deposited a scapula comb and something else in her doorway, and walked over to accept the cup of tea he had already brewed for her.

"They're still in there?" She gave him that smile again and glanced at Rides-the-Wind's lodge.

Rain Bear yawned, watching his breath frost. "I think Tsauz has been adopted. He moved his bedding in with Rides-the-Wind. I heard last night after I returned from the island that the Soul Keeper had volunteered to train the boy."

Evening Star studied the browning cod with

hungry eyes. "I hope the boy knows just how lucky he is."

"Lucky?" Rain Bear smiled at the thought. "Half the world wants to kill him as a means of getting back at his father."

She considered. "This story about him going blind after his mother died...it seems to me the boy has already paid a terrible price for being Ecan's son."

"Do you believe he just went blind? Just like that? Without being hit in the head, or having his eyes injured?"

Her stare fixed on the distance inside her. "Oh, yes, Great Chief. I myself...I just wish I could have gone blind, and deaf, and perhaps mute as well. It's punishment, you see. The desire to atone for failing my daughter, my husband and mother...my people."

"Matron, you don't—"

She held up a hand. "Oh, yes I do. And to make sure I punish myself, I will continue to live, see, remember, and hear their screams. Taking the other route and giving up would be too easy."

He let her stew for a moment. "I never knew your husband, but I knew Naida. I wasn't aware that either she or your husband had a reputation for cruelty."

She glanced at him. "Cruelty?"

"Or that they were petty, or even mean for that matter."

"What are you talking about?"

"Just this: If you had died, and your husband had lived, I am to understand you would want him to punish himself for the rest of his life for your death?"

"Absolutely not!"

"Ah," Rain Bear added gently. "Then you would want your mother, had she lived, to blame herself for your death?"

She was giving him a suspicious look now. "If I were dead, and they alive, I would be furious with them for blaming themselves."

"Then what would you want them to do?"

"I'd want them to..." It sank in on her then, her expression getting small, her eyes seeing inward.

"To go on with their lives," Rain Bear added with assurance. "As the Naida I knew would want her daughter to do with hers. What about your husband? I've heard he was a good man, kind and thoughtful. Were he here, sitting in my spot, what would he tell you?"

She took a deep breath. "I need to think about this. I just..." She shook her head. "I don't know. I'm angry with myself. Confused."

"We're all a little confused."

Her blue eyes burned when she looked up at him. "I'm feeling doubly guilty. That's all. They're dead—their souls barely on the road to the House of Air...and all I can think about is you." She gestured. "My husband was a good man. What happened to him was wrong. I just—"

"It was an arranged marriage," Rain Bear pointed out.

She nodded. "We did our duty."

He used a stick to prod the fire where blue smoke spiraled lazily from blackened branches and puffed around the sizzling cod. "If Tlikit had done her duty, she would have pined for the rest of her life, thinking of me. She never let on, never knew that I knew, but until the day she died she believed she had failed her people."

Evening Star might have been staring into the past. "If she had stayed.."

"Would the present be different? Perhaps. She might be the North Wind matron in Astcat's place. Or she might have died in childbirth years ago, or been struck by lightning, or killed in a fall. One never knows how life would be different if one had chosen another path. And for every decision, there is a price."

She looked up, puzzled. "Was it worth the price she paid?"

"She thought so." He smiled wistfully. "We balance our lives just like children do when they play on a balancing pole in the forest. On one hand is our duty to our people, or clan, or family, and on the other is our duty to ourselves. Sometimes certain people get both. Other times they have to choose based on what they think right."

"And what should I have chosen, Great Chief?"

"You cannot change the things you've chosen, Evening Star, only the things you choose now, and in the future."

For a long time they stared at the blue smoke rising off the fire. The skin on the backside of the cod had begun to bubble. Rain Bear grinned. "While you wrestle with your choices, I suggest that you do so with a full stomach."

Her expression was thoughtful as Rain Bear removed the succulent meat from the skewers and laid it on a wooden platter.

Pitch, his arm tightly bound to his chest, picked his way through the camp. The night before, Rides-the-Wind had come and drained his wound. The process had entailed a sharpened wooden skewer that Rides-the-Wind had used to reopen the scab. Then he had carefully massaged Pitch's arm, squeezing foul-smelling contents into a small wooden bowl.

Pitch hadn't been aware that the human body could withstand a pain like that. His voice was still raw from the screams. But the fever had broken. Last night, he had been exhausted by the ordeal, relieved that the swelling was down, and overjoyed that the sour smell of the leaking punctures had dissipated. He had actually slept.

As he approached the little triangle of lodges where Rides-the-Wind, Rain Bear, and Evening Star lived, he remembered his reaction to the sight of the blood-clotted pus.

"It's all right," a solicitous Rides-the-Wind had told Roe when Pitch threw up. "He needs to be cleaned, inside and out." The old man had frowned as she carried the wooden bowl out to the roaring bonfire and tossed it into the center of the flames.

The old man had smiled as the corruption was consumed. "You'll heal now, Pitch." He had hesitated, a question in his eyes. "I wonder, would you do something for me tomorrow?"

"Yes, Elder?"

"Tsauz was awakened in the night by Thunderbirds." His eyes began to gleam.

"You want to prepare him to climb the Ladder to the Sky?"

"And I would like your help." The Soul Keeper had looked around. "This isn't the best time or place, Singer, but the boy is being called."

"He's very young. Climbing the Ladder, Elder... well, I wasn't sure I was ready when I did it last year."

The old man had only shrugged. "When you are called, Pitch, you are called."

So here he was, still light on his feet, his arm smarting in its sling, as he made his way across the damp morning camp.

The old man ducked outside. His long gray hair and beard shimmered. Tsauz came out behind him. The boy always stood so straight and tall, he reminded Pitch of an alder sapling. He wore the beautiful black-and-white cape he'd been captured in. It had been freshly washed, and the white spirals around the collar made his shoulder-length black hair seem darker.

"Good morning, Soul Keeper," Pitch called.

"How is your arm?"

"Better today. My family and I send our thanks." He glanced at Tsauz, seeing the hesitation, fright, and worry in the boy's eyes. "Have you prepared yourself, Tsauz?"

"I—I think so. Rides-the-Wind had me in a sweat lodge most of yesterday. I stayed up all last night listening for the Thunderbirds and praying."

Rides-the-Wind took Tsauz's hand. "We had best be on our way." He looked out at the gray skies and the shredded bits of misty clouds that clung to the trees. "It's a good day to go hunting."

Pitch fell into line behind them and checked the guards. A shadowy crowd silently flowed through the forest, moving as they moved. "Will the guards interfere?"

Rides-the-Wind shot him a glance. "They are an unwelcome necessity." He turned to Tsauz. "I want you to concentrate on the lightning bolts that woke you in the middle of the night, Tsauz," Rides-the-Wind instructed. "Remember every detail."

Is he ready for this? Pitch wondered as he studied the blind boy. Pitch wasn't sure but that he'd rather go through the ordeal of having his wound drained again rather than face the Ladder to the Sky.

Rides-the-Wind said, "Remembering is like shooting the bolts back at the Thunderbirds, Tsauz. If you're fortunate, you'll hit one and knock him out of the sky."

Tsauz's blind eyes searched for Rides-the-Wind's face. "But...won't that make him mad?"

"Certainly. It will make him angry enough to blast you into small pieces, and that's exactly what we want."

"I want my soul to be blasted by a lightning bolt?"

"Absolutely."

Tsauz cast a blind glance over his shoulder to where Pitch walked. The boy's expression was anything but sure.

They took the western trail that climbed steadily toward a series of low foothills. At this time of the morning, the firs whiskering the hills cast oddly shaped shadows.

Rides-the-Wind kept his pace slow and guided Tsauz around the rocks that littered the trail. The scent of damp firs was strong. They passed through a grove of white-barked alders and emerged into a grassy meadow.

Pitch took a moment to appreciate the beauty. The trail wound across the meadow and up over the top of a gray cliff that stood perhaps ten tens of hands in height. Low clouds hovered around the rim rock. In the distance, Mother Ocean's waves rose and fell.

"We'll climb to the top of the cliff and stop," Rides-the-Wind said.

As Old Woman Above carried the sun higher into the morning sky, bright yellow light flooded the cliff, and the clouds shredded into tufts of mist.

"This is high enough?" Pitch wondered as they topped the cliff and the land opened on a small meadow. His eyes fixed on the patches of cloud that blew through the jagged firs across the meadow from them.

Rides-the-Wind lowered himself to a square chunk of stone, breathing hard. The guards shuffled through the forest around them, watching with curious eyes but keeping their distance.

Pitch examined their backtrail. Several of the refugees had followed along behind. They stood with their hands propped on their hips, waiting to see what would happen next. Pitch shook his head. But then, nothing about this situation was normal. If Tsauz succeeded in his hunt—if he managed to climb the Ladder to the Sky, receive his vision, and live through it —it would be the talk of the land. People still whispered about the blessing he had received during the Moon Ceremonial, and that Rides-the-Wind himself had come for the boy. Mystery and legend were already swirling.

"I'm going to sit here for a while. Pitch, I wish you to help Tsauz with the hunt." Rides-the-Wind waved a skeletal hand.

"Of course, Elder. Has Tsauz been presented with his weapon?"

Rides-the-Wind untied his pack from his belt and pulled out a beautifully polished chert stone. It looked like it had been rolling around in the bottom of a river for tens of cycles.

"This is the most sacred of weapons. It has slain a great many Cloud People. Open your hand, Tsauz." Rides-the-Wind dropped the stone into the boy's palm.

Pitch could see a white zigzag that ran through the center of the red chert.

"Do you see the lightning bolt, Singer?" Rides-the-Wind asked.

"I do," Pitch replied. "The lightning bolt is in the shape of a zigzag, Tsauz, while the stone is the color of blood."

"A lightning bolt?" Tsauz smoothed his fingers over it. "But...how did it get in the stone, Elder?"

Rides-the-Wind rested his hands on his knees. "I found that stone in the belly of an ancient monster."

"A monster?" Tsauz whispered in awe.

"Yes, a monster from the Beginning Time who'd been turned to stone."

Roe had been telling little Stonecrop the Beginning Time stories. According to legend, when the North Wind People emerged into this world of light, they found it filled with huge lumbering monsters that wanted to eat them. The twin War Gods were given the task of killing the monsters before the North Wind People were all hunted down and devoured. But how did one kill a monster?

They had no idea. The stories of their various attempts were numerous and frightening. Time after time they barely escaped with their lives. Finally, fleeing in desperation from a pursuing monster, they climbed a rainbow to escape. Old Woman Above saw them clinging desperately to the rainbow and asked them what they were doing in such a tenuous place, since everyone knows that rainbows eventually fade. They told her of the monsters eating the North Wind People, and touched by their courage, she gave them lightning bolts to cast. Thus the twins climbed down. This time when the monsters attacked they cast the lightning bolts and turned them into stone.

Tsauz tucked the stone to his breast. "Was the lightning bolt frozen in the monster's blood when he was turned to stone?"

"Very good," Rides-the-Wind said in a perfectly normal voice. "That stone is a drop of monster blood with a fragment of lightning bolt inside."

Tsauz's blind eyes riveted on the rock. "Why did you give it to me?" he asked.

Rides-the-Wind pointed a crooked finger at Tsauz's hand. "*It's very Powerful.* Remember that. Pitch, I want you to take Tsauz out into the forest and have him kill one of those Cloud People floating in the trees."

"Kill one of the Cloud People?" Tsauz asked incredulously. "How do I do that?"

"Tsauz, you must throw that stone as hard as you can, or the Cloud Person will live and turn on you." He waggled a crooked finger. "You don't want that to happen. He might kill you...and Pitch, too."

Tsauz swallowed hard. "But, Holy Hermit, I don't want to kill one of the Cloud People."

"Do you wish to talk with Thunderbird?"

"Well...yes."

"It's the only way you can prove to Thunderbird that you are worthy of speaking with him. After all, Thunderbirds kill Cloud People for breakfast every morning. They think it's easy. You must earn their respect."

The look of terror on Tsauz's face sent a shiver through Pitch. What if the boy failed? If he didn't pass this test, he surely wouldn't survive climbing the Ladder to the Sky.

Rides-the-Wind flicked a hand.

"Now, go on, you two. Go into the forest and start hunting. You must return with a cup of Cloud People blood."

"Blood?" Tsauz wondered. "Cloud People have blood?"

Pitch took Tsauz's hand. "Are you ready to go hunting?"

The boy looked like he longed to run back to the village, but he glumly answered, "I guess I have to."

The guards moved through the trees around them as Pitch led the way forward along the path.

When they'd walked five tens of paces, Tsauz tugged on his hand and hissed, "Wait!"

Pitch stopped. "You don't want to disappoint the North Wind People's most Powerful Soul Keeper, do you?"

Tsauz wet his lips. "No, but...I'm scared."

"Well, so am I. If you miss and the Cloud Person turns on us, he'll probably eat me first. I'm bigger."

"Yes, but you can see to run. I can't!"

The boy needed reassurance more than anything. "I'll warn you. I promise."

Clouds twined among the branches like gauzy dreams. "There are a lot of Cloud People hovering around us. I don't think this is going to be too hard. Is the rock ready?"

Grudgingly, Tsauz lifted it.

"Good. Let's sneak into the trees and find a Cloud Person who's looking the other way."

Tsauz whispered, "How will we know he's looking the other way? Have you ever seen a Cloud Person's face?"

"Yes, I have." Pitch smiled. "I've killed one myself."

"You did? Was it hard?"

"It's always hard to kill." Pitch considered the filaments of mist hanging in the air. "One of the great truths is that life and death live within each other. They are like male and female: different, but necessary to each other. They lay intertwined like lovers, forever together, but separate."

Tsauz considered that. "When you killed the Cloud Person, were you afraid?"

"Oh, yes." He kneeled before the boy. "Tsauz, listen to me. If you do this thing today, you are going to face the most difficult trial of your life, but I want to ask you a question, something that I think might help."

"All right."

"When you were hiding during the attack on War Gods Village, were you afraid?"

Tsauz swallowed hard, clutching the stone as if it were the most precious possession on earth. He jerked a short nod, his expression betraying shame and reluctance. "I didn't like it," he whispered.

"I'm sure you didn't." Pitch patted his shoulder. "But you know what fear is in a way that few other boys of your age do. As unpleasant as it was, you lived through it, didn't you?"

Tsauz nodded.

"I want you to remember that in the coming days. You will be judged by your courage, and by the way you face your fear. If you can overcome it, you can speak with the Thunderbirds." He patted the boy again. "So, come on. Let's go hunting."

Pitch led Tsauz to a thick copse of leafless alders where tens of sleeping Cloud People clung to the trees like bats. "Cloud People," Pitch whispered. "They're thick in the trees ahead of us. We'll have to approach carefully. Sneak up on them."

Tsauz gripped the rock tightly as he whispered back, "All right. Show me where they are."

Pitch aimed the boy's forefinger at each Cloud Person in the trees. "See, they're everywhere."

Tsauz's eyes flitted over the branches for a long time before he suddenly stiffened and said, "I *do* see something."

"You do?"

"Yes, they look like glittering yellow serpents crawling around behind my eyes. Is that them?"

"Probably. Can you hit one?"

Tsauz lifted the stone, but he didn't cast. He started walking in a small circle, stopping, looking, then walking again.

"What are you doing?" Pitch asked in a hushed voice.

"Trying to decide which one to kill."

The dark clouds that had been hovering out over

the ocean had drifted closer. A bruised thunderhead billowed over the top of the trees to his right.

Pitch told him, "More Cloud People are coming."

"Where?"

"Behind you. There's one peeking over the fir trees we just came through."

Tsauz spun on his heel and looked straight at the thunderhead, as though he could see it. With the quickness of a weasel, he flung the stone.

Pitch watched it fly higher and higher; then it started down. It fell through a small tuft of mist and into a leafless alder, making several thunks as it clattered through the branches to the ground.

"I think you missed. But don't worry, we can..."

Thunderbird roared so loudly it knocked Tsauz off his feet. As lightning danced over their heads, the entire cliff shuddered. Pitch was just standing there, his mouth gaping, when a massive white bolt crackled from the sky and exploded in a fir to their right. Chunks of wood whipped through the air.

"Look out!"

Pitch crouched over the boy, trying to shield his hurt arm.

"Stay down, Tsauz!"

Then a strange thing happened. The tufts of mist started to rise through the rain, floating into the sky to join the other Cloud People.

All except one.

The smallest tuft of mist—the one that Tsauz's stone had fallen through—melted before his eyes. It spread out, thinned, and settled to the ground.

Pitch whispered, "Tsauz, you got one!"

Tsauz looked up in surprise. "I did?"

"Yes! Come on." He rose and grabbed the boy's hand. "Let's go see what's left."

Pitch led him through the splinters, mangled branches, and bracken to the place where the Cloud Person had fallen.

"Do you see it?" Tsauz asked breathlessly. "What does it look like?"

Pitch cocked his head. A tiny puddle of water lay cupped in a rocky hollow atop a protruding basalt boulder. "Well...like a water puddle."

"A water puddle?" Tsauz sounded disappointed.

"Yes, a water puddle, but"—he squinted at it—"it doesn't look ordinary. It has lots of colors flashing through it."

Excited, Tsauz said, "Scoop it up. We'll take it back to Rides-the-Wind. He'll know if it's a Cloud Person's blood!"

Pitch awkwardly untied the cup from his belt and dipped it into the puddle.

Tsauz looked anxiously around the forest.

"What's the matter, Tsauz? Do you see more yellow serpents behind your eyes?"

"No," Tsauz quietly answered. Deep reverence filled his young voice. "They slithered into the sky right after Thunderbird cast his lightning bolt. But...I hear something."

"What?"

"It's a—a rhythm. There's a rhythm to the shishing the drops make in the trees. Don't you hear it? It sounds like words."

"Words?"

"Yes." Tsauz nodded. "Words spoken almost too

softly to be heard. But I think if I just had the time to listen, I might be able to figure out..."

"Yes?"

"I don't know. They're so faint."

"As a Singer, I can tell you that when you're ready to hear, the words will come to you. Meanwhile, we need to get this cup of Cloud People blood back to the Soul Keeper."

Chapter Ten

Rain pattered in the trees as it fell from the brooding clouds. Pitch tucked the cup of Cloud People blood into the boy's hand when they stopped before Rides-the-Wind.

"Elder, Tsauz killed a Cloud Person." He was still trying to come to grips with what he'd seen. When he'd gone through the ritual, he'd thrown a stone through a streamer of mist, too, but it had been nothing like this. No bolt of lightning had blasted a tree. Pitch's little tuft of cloud had drifted away, unlike Tsauz's. No puddle of water had lain below the wounded mist.

Tsauz clutched the cup in both hands as he carefully felt his way forward. *"Rides-the-Wind, look."*

"Well," the old man said. "I'm surprised to see the two of you alive."

Tsauz halted in front of Rides-the-Wind, breathing hard. "Why?"

"Because I heard Thunderbird. Didn't you realize he was hunting that same cloud? You must have killed it right under his nose to make him that angry."

Huge raindrops splatted on the elder's gray hair and beaded on his hawklike nose as a sense of wonder filled Pitch. He studied the whip-thin boy again. Power was threading around them, light and pulsing, echoing from the falling rain, the winter grass, and the slumbering firs.

Gods! Just who was Tsauz, anyway? What kind of Power lay at his beck and call? Pitch was aware of Rides-the-Wind's knowing gaze.

Tsauz chirped, "But we lived! And we got it!" He held out the cup. "Look!"

The Soul Keeper took the cup and peered into it. Rain stippled the surface. "Yes, you did get him, didn't you? Did you see the thousands of tiny rainbows in the water?"

"Yes! Well, no, but Pitch told me about the colors."

"These aren't just colors. Come here, look."

Tsauz felt his way forward with his moccasins, and Rides-the-Wind put the cup in his hands again.

"Do you see them?"

Tsauz blinked. After a few moments, he said, "I see...waves. Black waves. Like looking at a lake at night."

Rides-the-Wind stared curiously at Tsauz. "Are the waves shiny, or murky?"

"Shiny."

"Do they have a voice?"

Pitch flipped up his hood and shifted uneasily. *A voice?*

Tsauz listened to the cup. "I don't hear anything, Elder."

Pitch added softly, "Elder, you should know that Tsauz heard Thunderbird's voice. Right after Thunderbird blasted the tree, he said the raindrops in the forest had a rhythm to them, like words."

Tsauz nodded. "Yes, I thought they were words, but I couldn't make them out. I guess it could have just been the rain."

"It wasn't the rain," Pitch reminded. "You *almost* heard words."

Rides-the-Wind shoved to his feet with a soft, pained grunt. "Well, let's see what Tsauz hears after he's had a sip of Cloud People blood."

Tsauz's head jerked up. "I have to drink Cloud People blood?"

"That's why we went to the trouble to kill a Cloud Person. Tonight, if you succeed in climbing the Ladder to the Sky, you will fly to the Above Worlds. Dead people do it all the time, of course, but to do it while alive, a human needs to have the blood of the Cloud People inside him." He put a hand on Tsauz's shoulder. "First, you must be properly prepared."

Tsauz stood rigid, his eyes wide.

Rides-the-Wind took Tsauz's hand, guiding him down the trail. Over his shoulder, he called, "Pitch? Would you be so kind as to see if you could find my rock?"

"I'd be honored, Elder."

Evening Star listened to the patter of rain on her roof. She had retired to her lodge after sharing Rain Bear's breakfast. He had gone off to another of his endless council sessions as he tried to hammer out an alliance with the other villages and clans.

Now she lay in the darkness, reviewing the words he had spoken. In truth, it wasn't her fault that her village had been taken and her family killed.

It's not your fault. And yes, Rain Bear was correct: Both her husband and mother would have been saddened by her behavior.

"So what are you going to do about it?" she asked herself softly. Her fire had burned down to a bed of red glowing coals; in the gloom she was left alone with herself. She heard the wood and bark of her lodge creak as if a weight had been placed upon it. Her gaze silently lifted to her sagging roof. The storm had soaked the wood. It might be rain dripping from the trees onto the lodge, or onto the ground.

She sighed, tossing onto her back to stare up at the darkness. Placing a hand to her pelvis, she realized she was cycling. With the death of her daughter and with her captivity, her milk had dried up. It was known that women missed when they were under stress of starvation, hard work, or abuse.

Having passed her moon her loins were coming alive again, and her thoughts took her straight to Rain Bear. She smiled wryly into the darkness. Life had a way of making up for death, didn't it? Here she was, safe, fed, protected, and in the presence of a man who filled her idle moments with fantasy. She watched him, and kept those moments for later so she could recall the way he moved, how he smiled. She liked little things about him: the way he held his shoulders, the lines at the corners of his eyes. That longing in his eyes touched her in particular.

Love or duty? That had been the choice Tlikit had

faced, and in the end, she had chosen this man over the needs and demands of her people.

"I have never truly been in love with a man." The simple statement shocked her. She remembered the boys she had liked and teased as a maturing girl. Then, before she could catch her breath, she had suffered through her first cramps, passed her period in the menstrual hut, and been married.

Within the year she was pregnant and slowly accepting more and more of her aging mother's responsibilities. It hadn't even crossed her mind that she might be something else besides the matron of her village.

And now? She reached down to press on the tender spot just inside the swell of her pelvic bone. Just what *did* she want for her future? The wood creaked again, as if the weight were being released. She looked up, puzzled. Then heard the soft rasping of something heavy being dragged away.

Were her guards up to something? She cocked her head, hearing stealthy steps as wet moccasins scuffed the muddy ground outside her lodge.

She crawled across the floor and picked up a piece of firewood to use as a club.

Wind Woman breathed through the lodge flap, and the coals in the firepit flared, casting a fluttering halo of red light over the walls.

A voice hissed, "I know you're alone. I just want to speak with you. Don't be afraid."

Her first impulse was to try to run, but he'd just club her as she ducked out the door, if that's what he'd come for.

Where are my guards?

An obsidian knife blade eased the flap aside, and she glimpsed a face. Then he ducked inside.

He was a thick, rough-looking man. Greasy graying black hair straggled over the front of his brown cape. *A slave's garment*. Despite his dress, he acted like anything but a slave. She thought he might even have been of the North Wind People.

He glanced down at the firewood in her hands. "You won't need that."

"Who are you?"

"A messenger."

He squinted in the dim gleam, calmly surveying the lodge. "Did you get the message? The one Red Dog was carrying?"

She swallowed hard, and jerked a quick nod, her fingers tightening on the length of firewood.

"You could be the next matron, you know. People are already starting to talk about it."

"What do you want?"

He squatted on her bedding hides. "I'm not here for your pretty head, if that's what you think. I've been sent for the boy. If you have accepted the high matron's offer, help me smuggle the boy out of here. After that, we'll meet up with a party of warriors, and I'll take the two of you back to Fire Village."

Evening Star glared at him. "Then you must be one of Cimmis's assassins."

A half-contemptuous chuckle came from his lips. "Maybe his best. Where's the boy?"

She lifted an eyebrow, thinking. "Rides-the-Wind took him. He's preparing the boy for some sort of ceremonial."

That caught the grizzled man by surprise. "The Soul Keeper has him?"

"He's training him," she said firmly.

She saw the sudden hesitation, the faint worry his eyes couldn't quite hide. *Why does that news upset him so?*

"Matron, I *need* that boy!"

Evening Star used her chin to indicate her dress— the fine one with the dentalium. It was worth a small fortune. "If you'll forget the boy and leave here, I'll give you that."

He glanced at it, eyes barely flickering as they passed over the garment. "Will you help me or not?"

Her fingers tightened around the piece of firewood. For a timeless instant, every sound and scent seemed exaggerated; the pattering of the rain on her roof, her shallow breathing, the pungent scent of the fir smoke that drifted through camp like a blue-gray snake. How had he made it this far? Rain Bear had guards everywhere.

"Tsauz is gone."

"Where to?"

"Does it matter? He's not here. Rides-the-Wind took him. You've failed. If you value your life, you'll make a run for it immediately—though I doubt you'll make it out of camp alive."

He smiled and leaned forward. She could see that a large stone gorget, or pendant, hung behind his shirt. "There are so many new arrivals here every day, all I have to do is kill you, and walk out into the crowd."

"And all I have to do is shout an alarm. Besides, I'm getting irritated by your muddy moccasins on my bedding."

He glanced down at his moccasins and smiled. "Truthfully, Matron, I don't have orders yet to kill you, only to learn your answer. If it's yes, I am to get you and the boy out of here. If it's no...well, I'll come in the middle of the night next time. When you're fast asleep and lost in your final Dreams." He propped his obsidian knife on his knee with the point aimed at her chest. "Are you going to accept Matron Astcat's offer?"

"I sent my answer with Red Dog. It was for Astcat alone. But you'll know it soon enough. I'm sure the news will run through Fire Village like a molten wave."

His face screwed up, but his eyes resembled little knives, cutting away at her, seeking to slice down to her heart. Somehow, he read the tracks of her soul. "So that's the way of it?" He chuckled softly. "I don't need to kill you, Evening Star. You'll be dead before Sister Moon rises."

He ducked out, and the hanging waffled, letting a cold gust of wind in. Evening Star sat frozen in fear, the length of wood tight in her aching hands. Not until she heard him walk away did she dare breathe.

Her heart jumped again when she heard him speak softly with another man.

Who?

Their voices dwindled as they walked away.

Evening Star got her shaking legs under her and prepared to burst from her lodge to run like a scared rabbit.

A shout split the silence; then feet pounded past her lodge, and enraged screams broke out.

Rain Bear shouted, *"No! Don't kill them! We need them alive!"*

At the sound of his voice, such relief rushed

through her that her knees buckled. She sat down hard. The entire camp must have roused. Tens of voices lifted and blended into an indecipherable din. People raced up the trail, shouting, screaming questions.

Rain Bear threw the lodge flap back, his war club in his hand. His dark eyes blazed. "Are you all right?"

"How did he get so close?"

"Evidently by working with Wolf Spider. They killed Hornet. His body is out in the trees at the end of a blood trail. Who was he? What did he want?"

"An assassin. A Wolf Tail. He wanted Ecan's son," she answered in a shaky rush. "Did you catch him?"

"Dogrib's gone after them. They took the trail that leads up toward War Gods Village. We'll get them."

As the reality of how close she'd come to doom sank in, her entire body started to quake.

Rain Bear knelt and touched her hand. "I'm sorry you had to go through that."

"I'm alive." Blood started to rush through her veins like an incoming tide.

His voice came out so soft and tender, she almost didn't recognize it. "Two guards was a mistake. I should have known better."

"Two, ten, it doesn't matter! He was dressed like a slave! He could go anywhere." She balled her fists, muscles tense against the trembling. "You've got to understand. I tried to buy him off. He didn't even look twice when I offered my dress for Tsauz's life."

Rain Bear glanced at the decorated dress. "Interesting."

"And another thing: It was eerie but I've never seen anyone so calm and self-confident. It was as if..."

"Yes?"

She glanced at him, puzzled. "He wasn't afraid in the slightest that he'd be caught." She shivered. "Something about him frightens me in a way I've never been frightened before."

"Great Chief?" Dogrib called from outside.

Still shaking, Evening Star followed Rain Bear out into the dusk. In the gray light Dogrib's white hair seemed to glow. She could see his puzzled expression. Behind him, two warriors came dragging a limp body by the armpits, the head lolling, the feet trailing in the mud.

"What's happened, War Chief?" Rain Bear asked, stepping forward.

"You're not going to believe this," Dogrib muttered uneasily. "When it became apparent that we were going to cut them off, the stranger killed Wolf Spider. Split his skull. Then he dove into a patch of bushes beneath the cliff."

Evening Star watched as Rain Bear stepped to where the body hung between the warriors' grip. He bent, caught up a handful of the blood-soaked hair, and lifted the head so that Wolf Spider's face could be seen. The wide eyes, slack features, and gaping mouth looked stunned in death.

"I take it that you surrounded him?" Rain Bear asked.

Dogrib was shifting uneasily from foot to foot, his expression a mix of anguish and disbelief. "A coyote ran out, my Chief. A single, huge coyote. It was so quick we couldn't react, wouldn't have anyway. We thrashed those bushes, sorted through them by hand."

"And?"

"Nothing!" Dogrib cried. "There was nothing there but this!" He held up a small thong from which dangled a perfectly chipped obsidian effigy in the shape of a coyote's head.

Chapter Eleven

Word of the Wolf Tail spread in ripples through the camps surrounding Sandy Point Village. Although full dark had fallen, people began to collect around the large central fire across from Pitch and Roe's lodge.

Rides-the-Wind led Tsauz down through the trees to watch. He cocked his head, curious as to how the people would respond. He could sense it: Tonight was a turning point, one way or another.

Coyote! The name was whispered from lip to lip. Rides-the-Wind studied the somber faces in the crowd. People's eyes glittered with fear, excitement, and worry. He could hear their anxious voices as they bent their heads and asked, "How did he get past the guards?"

He smiled, his hands on Tsauz's shoulders. *As if guards were any hindrance to a man of his Power.*

How curious, though, that he had come for the boy on this night, of all nights. A turning point. Yes. Rides-the-Wind leaned his head back and sniffed the cool night air. The earthy fragrance of the coming storm mixed with the odor of burning pitch torches. Power laced the air. Coyote knew it. He knew it. Did the tense boy under his grip know it as well? Those blank eyes might have been wells in the boy's soul.

"Coyote came with a message for Matron Evening Star!" Rides-the-Wind heard someone whisper. That, too, was slipping from lip to lip like an eel in the kelp.

A tense silence fell as Rain Bear and Evening Star stepped into the circle of firelight. The great chief took a moment, nodded to Talon, Goldenrod, Bluegrass, and the rest of the elders and chiefs.

It was Evening Star, however, who stepped forward, her expression serious. Every face—some reflecting hate—turned toward her. The story had circulated that she was working to betray them.

Even from where he stood, Rides-the-Wind could see her body was rigid with tension. He wondered if it was from the strain of her assault, or fear of what she was about to say.

Someone shouted, "Is it true she betrayed us to the Four Old Women of the Council?"

"Is she working with Coyote?" another demanded.

A cacophony of voices rose, shouting accusations, calling her names.

Rain Bear bellowed, "Quiet! You must hear what has occurred!"

The din subsided, and Evening Star stated, "Last night, a messenger came here from Fire Village. The rumors are correct. He *did* bring me an offer from the matron of the North Wind People. Astcat said she would revoke my slave status in exchange for cooperation."

"Go home!" a woman shouted and waved a fist. "We don't want you here!"

Mutters of assent eddied through the crowd, and expressions turned grim.

Bluegrass cried, "Cooperation? What does that mean? What does she wish you to do?"

Evening Star stood tall and still. "Astcat wants me to convince you to leave these lands. She wants you to travel in small parties, and promises that if you do, she will guarantee you safe passage through the lands of the North Wind People."

A confused babble filled the forest; then an old man stepped forward. "This is my home! My father and mother are buried here, as are two of my children! I'm not leaving!"

Another person yelled, "My ancestors died here. My clan has been here since the beginning. I won't leave!"

Yet another reached down and raised a handful of the damp soil. "Raven gave this ground to us! If Matron Astcat wants to fight Raven, let her!"

"What's Astcat trying to do?" War Chief Talon whispered. "Get rid of the Raven People so the North Wind People can have all the hunting and fishing grounds?"

Dogrib replied, "Surely she's not that foolish."

Tsauz lowered his head to peer sightlessly at the ground.

A tall burly man shoved through the crowd to glare at Evening Star. "I heard that Coyote offered you even more. Will you return to Fire Village as matron?"

"Matron?" someone whispered into the sudden silence.

Evening Star clenched her fists at her sides. "This is what I told Astcat: I would return to Fire Village if, and only if, she disbanded the Council and turned their Starwatcher over to Rain Bear."

From the darkness beyond the fire, a voice called, "Then you'd all better start running now, because Ecan is coming to kill you!"

Howls of rage broke out, the crowd surging back and forth. Fists were raised, and the cacophony of shouted threats became a roar.

"Are you all right?" Rides-the-Wind bent down to whisper into Tsauz's ear.

"They hate my father."

"We are all filled with passion, Tsauz. Each of us is the master of it, for good or ill. How will you use your passion? For hate, like this? Or to make yourself and your world better?"

Dogrib's eyes narrowed, and he motioned some of his warriors forward in a thin line between Evening Star and the crowd. A slow drizzle had begun.

Tsauz stood rigid, his blind eyes wide and still, digesting all that he heard. Then he lifted his chin. It was a royal gesture, like that of a young ruler about to make a decree. "Elder?"

"Yes?"

"I must speak with Evening Star."

"This is not a good time, Tsauz, but I'll see if I can arrange something for later. Will that be sufficient?"

Tsauz let out a shaky breath. "Yes."

Evening Star had waited out the worst of the crowd's vitriol. She raised her hands, waving until the babble died down. Her voice called loud and clear: "My people! Listen to me!"

"We're *not* your people!" an old woman shrilled.

Rain Bear threw his head back. Rides-the-Wind saw the tendons and veins standing out in his neck as he screamed the most bloodcurdling of war cries.

Silence fell over the crowd as Rain Bear's bellow died out. "Listen to her," he said into the awkward silence. "Hear her, as I did."

Evening Star pushed her way forward, passing Dogrib's line of guards as she stalked up to the old woman and shouted, "Yes! You are *my* people—as I am yours!" She whirled, pointing from face to face. "What binds us together is our hatred for the Council! For what they have done to us!" She lifted a clenched fist, her sleeve falling down to reveal a pale arm. "Cut this flesh, and my blood runs as red as yours does! My soul bled as yours did when the Council ordered my family's murder! As they have killed your relatives, sons, and daughters, *they killed mine!*"

She glared at them, pacing from person to person, her anger a burning and brilliant thing. Rides-the-Wind grinned at the authority radiating from her.

"I *killed* Kenada when I could stand no more abuse!" She raised her hands, pale fingers shining in the firelight. "With these hands I *cut his throat!*"

A low muttering of approval passed through the crowd like a lapping wave.

"Coyote," she cried, "offered me the choice of betraying you in return for little Tsauz and the promise of safety!"

Rides-the-Wind felt the boy tense.

"I refused!" Evening Star told them vehemently. "And because I did, he has sworn to kill both me and the boy!"

A muted bellow was born in the press, a rekindling of the old hatred and injustice.

Evening Star thrust her hand out, pointing at Rain Bear. She was standing among them now, one of them. "In poor murdered Hornet's name, I tell you: There is salvation for all of us! To live, we must join forces with Chief Rain Bear, *and break the Council once and for all!*"

Shouts and whistles of approbation broke out, people shaking their torches, howling their support.

Rides-the-Wind watched, fascinated. "She has won them," he noted, more for himself than for Tsauz's benefit.

But the little boy looked up, his blank eyes like pits of pain. "I'm scared, Rides-the-Wind. If I don't stop it, lots of people are going to die."

"You think you can stop this?" he asked carefully.

"I must try." The boy nodded frankly. "I've seen it in a Dream. But if I do, I may die a terrifying death."

Chapter Twelve

Tsauz heard Rides-the-Wind add more wood to the small fire the old man had built in front of his lodge. With the light drizzle, the evening had turned cold and damp. Thick mist blew through the firs, coating his face and hands. Water dripped from the brim of the bark rain hat he wore.

"I'm sure she's coming, Tsauz."

Tsauz twisted his hands in his lap. "But she's late, isn't she?"

"Her meeting with the chiefs probably took longer than she'd thought. That's all."

"What do you think they are discussing?" Tsauz straightened his black-and-white cape. He couldn't seem to keep his fingers still.

"They're probably trying to decide how to stop the assassin."

Tsauz sensed Rides-the-Wind's movement when he leaned toward the tea bag hanging on the tripod over the fire. It creaked as he dipped up a fragrant cup of fir needle tea.

"I could hear behind your voice, Rides-the-Wind. You don't think Coyote can be stopped."

"Not by guards, no." A pause. "Here." Rides-the-Wind tucked the cup into Tsauz's hand. "Drink this. It will soothe your heart."

Tsauz took the cup, smelling peppermint, but didn't drink. He stared blindly in the direction of the trail Evening Star would take when she came home.

"You heard Evening Star. Coyote will be coming to kill me next time. If the guards can't stop him..." He had to swallow the rest, unable to state what lingered in his soul like a festering barb.

"Then I will." Rides-the-Wind's voice was barely audible.

"You?"

"This isn't a battle fought by warriors, Tsauz. Coyote will either be defeated by Power, or by his unwholesome appetites. Time will tell. And you're not the only one he's hunting."

"There's Evening Star."

"Yes, that's true. Among others."

Wind Woman gusted through the forest and behind him, Rides-the-Wind's lodge puffed in and out, as though she were taking a deep breath. Tsauz shivered. Every sound affected him like a physical blow.

"Rain Bear doubled your guards, Tsauz."

"Are they still out there? Can you see them?"

Rides-the-Wind pulled Tsauz's left hand away from his cup, took hold of his first finger, and aimed it. "That man's name is Blue Frog. It wouldn't take but a half-hearted toss of a stone to make him really mad." Rides-the-Wind pointed the finger at the next guard. "That is Chases His Foot. He's leaning against a fir trunk, and over there"—he shifted the aim—"that's Elktail. He's a burly giant with shoulders like a buffalo bull. I don't know the names of the others, but this is where they're standing." Rides-the-Wind calmly aimed and pointed Tsauz's finger. When he finished he curled it around the teacup again.

The boy mouthed the words: *Elktail, Blue Frog, Chases His Foot.*

Tsauz's souls had been drifting, as though this were all a Dream: the mist, the guards, and the racket of tens of people coughing and talking at once.

He heard steps coming up the trail; his breathing went shallow. "Is it her?"

"Yes. Evening Star walks at Rain Bear's side."

"Tell me what she looks like," he asked, desperate to picture her behind his eyes.

"She looks tired. Red wisps of hair have come loose from her braid, and fringe her face. Her eyes show the day's strain, but she walks with her shoulders squared. The white concentric circles painted on her deer-hide cape blaze as she enters the fire's glow."

"And Rain Bear? Does he look angry?"

"No. Worried. His war club dangles from his hand —and his black braid hangs to the middle of his back. Two new guards walk behind Evening Star."

"Only two?"

"Only two."

Tsauz heard Rides-the-Wind pull out more cups. The odor of the peppermint tea carried on the breeze.

Evening Star said, "A pleasant evening to you, Soul Keeper, and to you, Tsauz." She sat down on the hides on the opposite side of the fire.

Tsauz heard Rain Bear take up a position behind her.

Rides-the-Wind pointed at his fire. "Would you like a hot cup of tea?"

"That sounds wonderful, thank you."

Tsauz heard Rides-the-Wind dip it full and hand it around the fire to her. Evening Star took it; her cape rustled as she leaned forward.

"Tsauz," she said gently, "I imagine you are concerned by what I said earlier."

Tsauz drew himself up and turned to face her. When he spoke, he used the North Wind People's formal dialect, usually reserved for ritual occasions. "Yes, my cousin. I thank you for coming to speak with me."

He could hear the tired smile in her voice. "What did you wish to know?"

Tsauz stammered, "I've heard the people in camp whispering all day. They think the assassin really came to kill me, not you. Is that true?"

"Not exactly, Cousin." She hesitated, and Tsauz's face slackened, sensing the worst. "He came hoping that I would side with Astcat, and that I would help him sneak you out of camp. When I told him you were with the Soul Keeper, I could tell that he was most disturbed."

"Tsauz is the center of Power," Rides-the-Wind said. "Coyote has his own goals in all this, and I can tell you now, they aren't the Council's, or Ecan's, or Cimmis's."

"Then what?" Rain Bear asked.

"Power. Pure and simple," Rides-the-Wind replied. "You delude yourself, Great Chief, if you think this is a matter of warriors, battle strategy, and defeating the forces fielded by the North Wind People. If he can't take Tsauz for his own, it will be safer to just kill him."

Tsauz swallowed hard. "Who sent him?"

Evening Star sounded unsure of herself. "I thought Coyote had been sent by the Council."

"He may be acting on his own," Rides-the-Wind said thoughtfully. "There are many people who wish you and the boy dead."

You and the boy.

"Because we are North Wind People?" she asked.

"Many wish us dead for that reason alone, yes."

Rides-the-Wind added, "Cimmis wants Tsauz dead to keep us from using Ecan against him. The Council fears him because he was witness to their attack on War Gods Village. Coyote knows that if Tsauz is not with him, he will be against him. And, of course, if we run out of enemies to worry about, there is always Bluegrass and his followers."

With all the dignity he could muster, Tsauz stared in Evening Star's direction. "My cousin, I wish to"—he tried to think of the right words—"to bargain with you."

Her cape brushed the ground. "Very well, Tsauz. Bargain about what?"

"I know some things. About the North Wind People. I would tell you, if you give me your oath that when the North Wind People turn my father over to Rain Bear, you will promise to let him live."

He had to clamp his jaw to keep it from trembling. He didn't want her to know how frightened he was. Father always said a man could never afford to appear weak before his enemies.

Evening Star sat silently, and then her clothing rustled. Was she turning toward Rain Bear?

Tsauz waited, wondering if Rain Bear had nodded yes, or shaken his head no.

He added, "My cousin, I swear to you, my father has not done the things the Raven People accuse him of doing. He is a good father to me and a good Star-watcher."

"Tsauz," she said softly, "I understand what you are trying to do. He is your father, and your defense of him earns you both honor and respect. It is because of my respect for you, Cousin, that I tell you this: Your father inflicted terrible pain on me and my family. He did things to me that will mark me for the rest of my life. I have witnessed these things, survived them. I tell you not to harm you, or to disagree with you, but so that you may understand that it will take a great deal to make it worth our while to spare your father's life."

"Because the Raven People believe he has killed many of their people?"

"That, too," she said in a low voice. "Before you speak, you must know that if you tell me this thing, I may not think it is worth saving your father. Further, the information you provide must be important enough to the Raven People that they will understand why I bargained with you."

"I understand."

"The final thing you must understand is that I have no real authority here."

Tsauz thought about that. Father had often spoken of the Raven People as an unruly mob; perhaps she truly couldn't guarantee his father's safety. If ten tens of

Raven People decided to kill him, could anyone stop them?

Tsauz saw it happen on the fabric of his souls—a sea of people with clubs and axes surrounding Father, beating him...

He listened to Evening Star's movements. She lifted her cup to drink, then turned to look at Rain Bear again.

As if a memory, he heard a voice saying, *You must choose now. And when you do, you cannot go back.*

Tsauz took a deep breath. "Cousin, as you have shown me honor in these negotiations, so I will honor you. I will tell you what I know, and in so doing, I call upon you as a kinsman and friend to do your best to protect my father." He raised his head toward where he thought Rain Bear stood. "Chief Rain Bear told me he wanted to kill Chief Cimmis. Is that still true?"

To his surprise, Rain Bear's voice came from behind. "Yes."

"Then you will wish to know that the North Wind People are going to abandon Fire Village. They have been packing in secret."

"What?" Evening Star sucked in a surprised breath.

"They have been packing in secret because they did not wish to give the Raven People time to plan an attack. They are going to move, very soon, to Wasp Village. They will be on the trail and vulnerable for several days."

A crackling sound came from Rain Bear's knees as he squatted behind Tsauz. "When?"

"Very soon, I think."

Evening Star said, "Hallowed Ancestors, it seems

inconceivable. The North Wind People have lived on Fire Mountain since the Beginning Time. The gods walk freely there, talking with the elders, guiding them. How can the North Wind People leave?"

"Old Woman North had a vision," Tsauz said. "She said that Wasp Village will be the rebirth of the North Wind People. We will grow bigger and better than we ever were on Fire Mountain."

Evening Star whispered to Rain Bear, "It's possible. She often had visions."

Rain Bear said, "What was the end of the vision, Tsauz? Did she see the North Wind People actually living in Wasp Village?"

Tsauz tried to remember what Father had told him. He shook his head. "I don't think Father told me, or if he did, I don't remember. He did tell me, though, that we must travel at night. The vision said that North Star Woman will lead us."

Rain Bear must have motioned to the guards. Several men trotted in from the forest.

"Yes, Chief?"

Rain Bear said, "Dogrib is in Algae's lodge. Tell him I know he's busy, but I need to see him. Now."

As the warrior ran away, Evening Star kept her gaze on Tsauz. The boy was shaking. Sweat beaded his face and ran down his throat.

He had the kind of spun-silk courage that only the very young could possess: frail and shining, but somehow more powerful than a thunderstorm.

She reached across the fire, taking his hand from the cup he held. "It took remarkable courage to bargain with me, and even more courage to say the things you did. You must never mention to any of the North Wind People what you've just said."

His stricken face looked ashen, his voice little more than a croak when he said, "I know, Cousin. Now I must live with the choice."

"We all live with our choices," Rides-the-Wind agreed.

She withdrew her hand and said, "I thank you, Cousin. I will do what I can to save your father. But do not expect miracles."

"I think I must talk to Rides-the-Wind. Alone please." Like a dutiful child, he rose to his feet.

Rides-the-Wind struggled up beside him. As he clasped Tsauz's hand, Rides-the-Wind said, "If you need us, we'll be awake for a time."

She watched Rides-the-Wind lead the boy into his lodge.

After the door flap fell, Evening Star heard Tsauz say, "Please, I have to fly to the Above Worlds tonight, Rides-the-Wind. I must speak with Thunderbird. I don't think I can wait any longer."

The old Soul Keeper was quiet for a moment; then he said, "Do you understand the importance of what you're asking, Tsauz? What you do tonight may change your life forever. If you are not worthy, you may even be killed."

"I understand, Elder."

"Then come over here by the fire and rest while I send for Pitch."

Wind Woman picked that moment to blast through

the village, whipping the trees and churning up old leaves and sand. Several surprised warriors grabbed for their weapons, then laughed.

Evening Star closed her eyes.

She could barely stand to think of what lay ahead.

Chapter Thirteen

Rain Bear crouched just inside Rides-the-Wind's door and chafed. He'd barely begun to give orders when Pitch had summoned him away from Dogrib's council of warriors and led him to Rides-the-Wind's. Pitch had insisted it was important. Now that he was here, he was just sitting and receiving occasional measuring glances from the old Soul Keeper.

A storm was moving in. Icy air gusted against the lodge, rattling the baskets to his right and buffeting the two red ritual capes that hung on the peg just inside the door. Until recently, this had been a storage lodge. Hide bags still hung from the ceiling poles, filled with fragrant herbs: sagewort for sore throats, ground aster root for pinkeye, bluebell for fever and heart trouble. He shivered. To his left, Tsauz lay curled on his side, staring at nothing. The fire in the center of the lodge cast a flickering gleam over his young face. Rain Bear whispered, "Are you all right, Tsauz?"

He nodded and whispered back, "What are they doing now?"

Rain Bear turned his attention to Rides-the-Wind and Pitch, who sat cross-legged in the rear of the lodge. Both wore long white shirts decorated with leather fringes. The cup of Cloud People blood sat on the hides between them. Four beautifully painted leather bags surrounded the cup. As Rides-the-Wind directed, Pitch picked up a bag and poured something into the cup; then Rides-the-Wind stirred it.

Rain Bear whispered, "They're pouring things into the Cloud Person's blood."

"What things?" Tsauz's blind eyes shimmered orange in the firelight. He had bathed a hand of time ago, and his black hair glistened.

"I can't tell. I'm not sure I'd know even if I were down there and could smell them. They're probably secret ingredients used only by very holy people."

Impressed by the gravity of his voice, Tsauz nodded. "My father won't even let me touch the bags that contain his Healing plants. He says their Spirits will fly up and kill me."

A powerful gust of wind rocked the lodge, and the walls squealed and shuddered.

"That's good, Pitch. Let's start building the spiral ladder," Rides-the-Wind said.

"What ladder?" Tsauz hissed. "The ladder to the sky?"

Rain Bear struggled to keep the impatience out of his voice. "I don't know what they're talking about."

Rides-the-Wind shot him a censoring glare, then got up and duck-walked across the lodge to reach for a coil of ropes. He handed them to Pitch and pointed to the lodge cord. "You remember how to tie them?"

Pitch smiled thoughtfully. "How could I forget?

When I climbed Grandfather Vulture's ladder, I thought I was going to fall off and die. I remember everything perfectly."

"Good." Rides-the-Wind picked up the cup of Cloud People blood. "While you're doing that, I'll prepare Tsauz."

Tsauz sat up, eyes huge. His black-and-white shirt coiled around his feet. "Is it time?"

"Almost."

Rides-the-Wind got down on one knee beside the boy and looked him straight in the eyes, as though the boy could look back. "Now listen to me, Tsauz. No matter what happens, you must be strong and brave. Thunderbird values these things. And more importantly, if you show weakness, he might kill you."

"My Spirit Helper might kill me?" Tsauz was rubbing his hands together.

"Oh, generally he doesn't do it on purpose. Thunderbird gets annoyed with you, flips over in midair, and you fall off his back and die."

Pitch was in the process of tying different lengths of rope to the ceiling pole. Since his son-in-law had only one usable hand, Rain Bear shifted far enough to help him with the knots. Once hung, the short sections of rope swung around like dead snakes.

"H-have you ever known anyone who fell and survived?" Tsauz asked.

"One. A girl...many cycles ago. She accidentally screamed when Thunderbird dove after a particularly succulent Cloud Person—she said she just couldn't help it—but it scared Thunderbird. He flew right into a mountain peak and exploded. She lived only because she jumped off at the last instant. The scars from the tree branches she hit on the way down never really healed." Rides-the-Wind put the cup in Tsauz's hand and clamped his fingers around it. "There's one more thing."

Tsauz croaked, "What?"

"You must call out to Thunderbird in his own language. Buffalo do this naturally, but it's harder for humans. Here's what the word 'come' sounds like." Rides-the-Wind formed his mouth in a circle and made a rumbling sound deep in his throat. "Try it."

Tsauz nervously smelled the contents of the cup, appeared to be thinking about it, then attempted to say "come" in Thunderbird. A high-pitched rumble-shriek vibrated his throat.

While he helped loop another knot, Rain Bear's gaze returned to Pitch. He'd started threading feathers into the ropes, pushing the quills through the twining. Vulture feathers. They bobbed and twisted.

Rides-the-Wind looked skeptical. "That was good, Tsauz, but try to make it sound deeper, more like thunder."

Tsauz swallowed hard, lifted his chin, and rumbled again, deeper this time.

It didn't sound like thunder to Rain Bear. It sounded like they both had something stuck in their throats, which perhaps explained why Tsauz looked like he wanted to throw up.

Rides-the-Wind slapped him on the back. "Excellent. Pitch, are you ready?"

Pitch softly answered, "I'm ready, Soul Keeper," and backed away from the ropes. He had a reverent, slightly frightened expression on his thin face. He wore his hair in a bun at the base of his skull, but black strands had come loose and tangled with his eyelashes.

Rain Bear noticed the beads of perspiration on Pitch's skin, the wary dart of his eyes. It wasn't the temperature in the cold lodge, nor was it any lingering fever. *Blessed Spirits, if this is bad enough to make Pitch sweat when I'm freezing half to death...*

"Follow me, Tsauz," Rides-the-Wind instructed, and started for the ropes.

Tsauz crawled after him.

"Sit right here on the hide."

Tsauz kneeled in front of the dangling ropes. Rides-the-Wind pulled the boy's left hand from the cup of Cloud People blood and let Tsauz touch the different lengths of ropes.

"What are they?" Tsauz asked.

Rides-the-Wind leaned close to Tsauz's ear and whispered, "They are feathered serpents."

Tsauz jerked his hand back. "Why do I have to touch them?"

"Because they form a spiral ladder that soars into the Above Worlds like Grandfather Vulture. In a little while, you will need to climb them."

"But I—I thought Thunderbird would come to get me, and I would climb onto his back and we'd fly away?"

"You must demonstrate your worthiness first. That means you have to climb these ropes into the Above World where he lives. Climb as high as you can. His home is beyond the Cloud People's—almost to the Star People. Thunderbird will be watching. If Thunderbird admires your courage, he'll meet you and take you flying."

"What if I can't climb high enough?"

Rides-the-Wind and Pitch exchanged a doomed look that Tsauz couldn't see, but Rain Bear did, and it shivered his very soul.

"Elder?" Tsauz asked and wet his lips. "How can I speak with Thunderbird if I only know how to say 'come' in his language?"

"If you climb high enough, Tsauz, you will be able to speak with every creature in its own language: deer, elk, Star People, even Thunderbirds. So. Are you brave enough?"

Tsauz replied, "I have to be. I have to ask Thunderbird to save my father."

Rides-the-Wind nodded. "All right, then it's time we went away."

"Went away! What do you mean? You're leaving me?" Tsauz lunged to grab a handful of Rides-the-Wind's white shirt.

Rides-the-Wind pried the boy's fingers off. "This is something you must do alone." He clamped Tsauz's fingers around the cup again. "Now, I want you to drink the Cloud People blood slowly, and when you feel you're ready to climb, grab onto the longest rope. You'll know when you're ready for the next rope, and the next. Each will lead you higher into the Above Worlds."

Rides-the-Wind motioned, and Rain Bear ducked outside into the patchy moonlight. Puffs of cloud made blots against the sky. A short while later, Rides-the-Wind and Pitch filed out. Both men unfolded beautifully painted red ritual capes and draped them around their shoulders.

Rides-the-Wind lifted a hand to Rain Bear. "You may go now. We thank you for your help."

"Outside of tying a couple of knots, I don't know what good I did."

The old eyes were knowing. "You were a witness, Chief. You have just seen the future change. One way or another."

"Will he be all right in there?"

Rides-the-Wind made a shrugging gesture. "That is up to him and the gods."

Rides-the-Wind gave him a final fierce look before he and Pitch went to take seats before the fire.

Rain Bear rubbed a hand over his face. Go back to Dogrib's? No, he had too many things to do tomorrow. If he didn't get some sleep, what kind of chief would he be?

As he passed Rides-the-Wind's lodge on the way to his, he heard Tsauz calling out to Thunderbird.

A faint smile bent his lips as he checked to see the guards lined out around Evening Star's. He watched her lodge for a long moment, thinking of her, soft and warm in her robes. If only...if only.

He sighed, ducked through his doorway, and pulled his war shirt over his head. He scratched and reached down to pull his thick buffalo robe back—only to have it move under his fingers.

"What?"

"Shhh! Be quiet or the whole camp will know."

"What are you doing?" he whispered.

Evening Star took a halting breath. "I don't want to be alone. Not tonight. Not after Coyote. I just...well, I have separate robes to sleep in if it makes you more comfortable."

He frowned into the darkness. "No. It does not."

Her skin was warm against his as he slid in beside her.

Chapter Fourteen

Tsauz wrinkled his nose. The Cloud People blood had a moldy smell. He took a tiny sip, and his mouth puckered at the bitter taste.

"I'm trying to come to you, Thunderbird," he whispered. "Please, hear me."

He rumbled the word "come" deep in his throat and listened.

Nothing happened.

Tsauz took a good drink, choked it down, and reached out to touch the ropes. They didn't feel like serpents. They weren't scaly. They felt like feathers tied to woven bark ropes.

He called again, struggling to make the deep-throated rumble Rides-the-Wind had taught him.

"Thunderbird? Are you listening? Am I saying that right?"

He was probably speaking in badly accented Thunderbird. But Spirit creatures understood things humans did not. He figured Thunderbird didn't really care about accents and hoped it was a person's heart that mattered.

"I heard them, Thunderbird," he whispered anxiously. "When Evening Star mentioned my father, the Raven People's cheers sounded like growls. If they ever get their hands on him, they'll tear him apart. I know they will."

He exhaled and ran his fingers over the cup. It felt crude. Big chips had been knocked off the wooden lip. They scratched his mouth when he drank again.

"Please help me, Thunderbird."

He tipped his face heavenward. The more Cloud People blood he drank, the more empty he felt—as though his bones were becoming as hollow as a bird's.

He tried again to make the rumble that would call Thunderbird.

Wind Woman sneaked into the lodge and batted the ropes around. They swung against each other, and he heard a strange hissing. It had to be the feathers brushing each other. Didn't it?

He rumbled again. And again.

The last four swallows of blood tasted especially awful. He set the empty cup on the hides.

The hissing came again, louder.

Rain.

It pattered the sand outside. The storm had moved in. Had Thunderbird come with it?

Closing his eyes, he concentrated on calling and calling...

The scent of wet earth filled the lodge. Tsauz reached out to touch the ropes again, and the feathers brushed his hand. They felt cool and soft. What would

Father be doing right now? Sitting before the fire in their lodge, thinking about Tsauz?

He missed Father so much it was like a fire in his chest.

A coyote yipped somewhere up on War Gods Mountain, and across the valley, an answering yip echoed. The first coyote yipped again, then howled, and up and down the shore packs of coyotes lifted their voices to join hers. The haunting melody carried on the night.

Coyote. He's going to be coming for me.

Tsauz held on to the rope and called again.

He was so tired. He'd never been this tired in his life. The lodge started to sway. Back and forth, very slowly, as though *Dancing*. He could feel it moving all around him.

Rain began to pour out of the sky. He felt sorry for Pitch and Rides-the-Wind. By now they'd be soaked. Should he call to them? Tell them to come back? They could try again tomorrow, or when it finally warmed up.

"No," he whispered through gritted teeth. "No, I have to do this! If Thunderbird is my Spirit Helper, he may be able to save Father."

Again and again, he made the deep-throated call until his throat felt like it had been sanded.

He could barely stay awake...

A hiss came from the rope, and it twisted in his fingers. Tsauz gasped and instinctively grabbed it with both hands, hanging on for dear life.

Thunderbird roared across the forest, and the lodge shook with such violence that Tsauz went rigid, ready for anything.

"I'm right here, Thunderbird," he whispered. "I'm not afraid!"

The rope coiled around his wrists, tying them together. His heart battered against his ribs with such force, he couldn't breathe.

The next roar of thunder exploded right over Tsauz's head. He cried out when the rope suddenly went stiff, like a dead snake in his hands.

"Oh, gods, what..."

"I'm coming, young Singer. Hold on very tight."

With a jerk, the rope soared upward, dragging him with it as it blasted through the roof and flew away into the rainy sky.

After a terrible night of rain, storm, and lightning, a cool morning wind blew out of the south, tousling Ecan's white cape and whirling red volcanic sand across the mountain below. He crouched on the rim of the black lava wall behind Fire Village, watching the dawn-gray trails. Red Dog would be due to return this afternoon. None of the scouts, however, had sent word that they'd seen him. Had something gone wrong in Sandy Point Village? Surely Rain Bear would not have killed a messenger from Fire Village?

Slaves walked up and down the trails carrying packs on their backs or baskets propped on their hips. In the distance, down the mountain, he could see people in the Salmon Village plaza. Their gloriously colored clothing flashed as they moved.

After Matron Gispaw's murder, her daughter, Kaska, had become the town matron. Her first order had been to build an enormous ceremonial lodge where she and a few of her most trusted allies lived—and, no doubt, where they could watch each other's backs. He didn't blame her for being frightened. The Wolf Tails were paid well enough that they could buy off almost any guard.

Dzoo emerged from her lodge, and people scattered like ripples of frightened birds across the Fire Village plaza. He watched her through slitted eyes. Every servant they sent her became seriously ill. Now, wherever she walked, people avoided her.

"Are you ever the clever witch," he mused. "No one has the courage to watch you too closely. Those who do end up vomiting their guts out for days."

She shielded her eyes and gazed out to the west.

Ecan followed her gaze. Someone ran the trail in the distance. Each time his moccasins struck the ground they left a dark dimple in the trail.

Red Dog?

He glanced back at Dzoo, and his pulse began to pound. She couldn't see the runner. The palisade blocked her view. How could she possibly know he was out there?

One of the slaves who'd been scraping hides near the central fire glanced up, noticed her, and froze. She nudged her neighbor, and within moments they had picked up their scrapers and left. Immediately thereafter, the flint knappers grabbed up their tools and scuttled inside. In the space of a dozen heartbeats the only people left outside were Ecan, Dzoo, the guards and a few of the Four Old Women's slaves. They had no choice. They'd been ordered to stay in the plaza, but hushed conversations broke out.

He rose to his feet.

Dzoo's gaze lifted to him.

It was like being struck by lightning. His fists clenched involuntarily.

Her long red hair danced in the sunlight. She wore a clean maroon dress, and her large spear point hung down between her breasts. She smiled, but her eyes remained as inhumanly luminous as polished obsidian beads.

Ecan didn't breathe until she turned away again to look in the direction of the man trotting up the trail. She tilted her head back and closed her eyes. As though she could *feel* him.

Ecan signaled to the guard who stood at the opposite end of the lava cliff.

The young man trotted toward him.

"Yes, Starwatcher?" Hunter bowed. His thin face bore a coat of dust. Dull-eyed, he must have been standing guard all day.

"Find out who that runner is. If it's Red Dog, send him to me immediately."

"Yes, Starwatcher." Hunter bowed and trotted away.

A commotion broke out when Red Dog arrived at the palisade gate. He wore a dirty brown knee-length shirt and a red headband to keep his gray-streaked black hair out of his eyes. Hunter approached him, then turned to point to where Ecan stood on the crest of the lava cliff. Red Dog dusted off his sleeves, said something, and headed around the palisade to the trail that led up over the cliff.

When he'd climbed to within three paces, Ecan called, "Greetings, Red Dog. I pray your journey was uneventful."

"Uneventful?" Red Dog walked toward him.

"Sleeper's warriors chased me half the way home. He's canny. You never know where he is or what he's up to. You just catch glimpses of him or his men running behind you."

"At least you're alive."

"Yes, well, once I've eaten and rested, I might agree with you." He mopped his sweating forehead with his brown sleeve. "I presented your offer."

"Yes, and...?"

"Rain Bear said he would not exchange your son for the witch. It seems he didn't believe you could get Dzoo out of Fire Village."

Red Dog had a strange gleam in his eyes that Ecan didn't understand, but it made him nervous. He said, "Then he refused my offer."

"I didn't say that." Red Dog braced his feet, as though he could barely keep standing. "He said he hated dealing with a spineless coward, but he had his own offer to make."

Ecan bristled at the word "coward," but said, "What offer?"

"He wishes to meet with you. Somewhere away from Fire Village. You may bring one guard, and he will bring one—"

"*What?*" he half shouted before he caught himself. "Does he think I'm a fool? Meet him with only one guard? I would never agree to something so ridiculous! Why is it important that we meet?"

"He doesn't believe he can trust your messenger." Red Dog grinned. "But then he doesn't know how much you're paying me."

Ecan would be completely vulnerable. But if Rain

Bear actually came as promised, so would he. No, no, it was too dangerous to consider.

"Did you see my son?"

"No." Red Dog shook his head, and his graying black hair fluttered over his muscular shoulders. "The instant I got close to their camp, Dogrib grabbed me and had me trussed up like a deer ready for roasting. I never got inside the village. They kept me hidden in the forest. Which probably saved my life."

Ecan felt suddenly hot. By now, Tsauz would be feeling utterly lost and alone. "Did you hear anyone speaking about my son?"

"Several of Rain Bear's warriors whispered that Tsauz was sleeping in Rides-the-Wind's lodge. They said the crazy old hermit was *teaching* your son."

"Teaching him?"

"That's what they said."

Ecan frowned. "Why would that old fool choose to teach *my* son? Tens of young Dreamers come to Rides-the-Wind every cycle begging to be taught by him."

Was it some kind of trick? Perhaps a way of turning Ecan's own son against him? "I doubt you heard correctly, Red Dog."

"Oh," Red Dog replied with arched brows, "I heard correctly, but the guards might have been lying. Perhaps they knew I was listening and said it just for my ears. Why would that be? They wished me to tell you, so that you would...what? Call down the Sea Eagles to tear the old man apart?"

Ecan couldn't think of a good answer to that. The information about Rides-the-Wind was inconsequential. It wouldn't change his actions one way or the other.

So, maybe it was true. Rides-the-Wind the Hermit was teaching his son to be a Dreamer.

Of all the would-be protectors Ecan could imagine, Rides-the-Wind was the only one with the Power to actually keep his son safe. A tiny thread of hope stitched across his chest.

"I'm tired, Starwatcher. I've told you everything important. If there's nothing else, I'd like to go."

"What about the Council's offer?"

"Refused."

Ecan narrowed his eyes, trying to think past Tsauz and his situation. "What does Rain Bear want?"

Red Dog gave him a sly glance, hesitated, and whispered, "The end of Cimmis and the Council." With an offhanded gesture, he added, "If we had different leadership, perhaps there would be peace."

Ecan's heart leaped, but he said, "Before you go, you should know that your friend Mica is dying."

"Mica?" Red Dog grimaced. "What happened? He was fine when I left."

Ecan shrugged. "I wish I knew. White Stone came to me yesterday to tell me they'd found Mica lying on his floor shaking. Every muscle in his body is twitching. I suspect he'll be dead by morning."

Red Dog's brows knit. "Isn't Mica the one who opened the witch's pack right after the battle—"

"Yes."

"But you said the bags were filled with harmless things: bat droppings and dirt!"

Down in the plaza, Dzoo stood in the same place, watching them, her full lips slightly parted as if in anticipation. He said, "Lion Girl and Dance Fly are also ill with the shaking disease."

Red Dog glanced at Dzoo and whispered, "The slaves who were tending Dzoo?"

"Yes."

"Hallowed Ancestors! And the great chief? How is he taking this?"

Ecan smiled grimly. "Cimmis wants to make her happy here. He seems to think she could be a rallying point for the Raven People if she's harmed. He's had her old lodge prepared and ordered his slaves to bring her new clothing and moccasins. He even ordered his personal jewelers to make her pendants and bracelets from the finest polished stones and shells in Fire Village. Oh, and she's free to wander about as she pleases."

Red Dog raised a pensive eyebrow. *"Free!* But that's insane! Doesn't he understand who she is? *What* she is?"

Ecan rubbed his jaw. "Yes, well, apparently we can't keep her locked up anyway. She might as well be free."

Red Dog stared at him. "Excuse me?"

"Depending on which story you believe, she walked through the wall of the captives' lodge one night. Deer Killer was standing guard. He thinks she changed herself into a bird and flew out the smoke hole. White Stone is convinced that she used the 'missing ropes' to climb out."

Red Dog's gaze fixed on Dzoo. "But if she climbed out, why didn't Deer Killer see her? He didn't fall asleep on duty, did he?"

"White Stone believes he did. That's why Deer Killer is standing double shifts."

"I'm surprised he didn't have Deer Killer skinned

alive."

"Apparently Cimmis forgot to give the order. There were four other guards posted around Fire Village that night. No one saw Deer Killer fall asleep. No one saw Dzoo escape."

Red Dog tapped his chin. "Why is she still here? If she could get out of the punishment lodge, the village palisade would be like a net bag is to a bowl of water."

Ecan gave him a thoughtful look. "That, my friend, is a good question."

"Anything else odd happen while I was gone?"

"Oh, one man said he saw ball lightning around midnight one night." Ecan lifted a hand to demonstrate. "He said it plummeted out of a starry sky, bounced around the roof of Dzoo's lodge, and vanished."

Red Dog instinctively gripped the stiletto on his belt. "Who said that?"

"Deer Killer."

Red Dog relaxed. "Why, imagine that! Deer Killer again. He probably dreamed it when he was asleep on duty."

"I think his fear has gotten in the way of his senses. He also told me he..."

Cimmis ducked out of his lodge and walked out into the plaza. He wore a plain knee-length blue war shirt belted at the waist with a braided seagrass cord. Rather than the ruler of the North Wind People, he appeared to be nothing more than an aging warrior. Astcat was sick again, which meant Cimmis rarely left his lodge.

Ecan said, "Come along. He'll wish to see you right away."

When they started down the rocks toward the palisade, Cimmis saw them and stalked for the gate.

They met him at the entry, and Ecan lifted a hand, calling, "Red Dog has returned, my Chief."

Warily, Cimmis asked, "Red Dog, when did you arrive?"

"Just now, my Chief. I was on my way to see you."

"But you stopped to report to Ecan first. Why?" Cimmis wore his gray hair in a single braid. His thin beard flipped in the wind.

Red Dog gave Ecan an uncomfortable look.

Ecan spread his arms in appeasement. "Forgive me, my Chief. I called to Red Dog and distracted him from his duties." He smiled. "If you will excuse me, you have things to discuss." He stepped through the gate, not bothering to look back.

Across the plaza, Dzoo's maroon dress waffled in the wind as she walked toward the four guards who stood near the central fire. They went rigid before shoving each other to see who could get away the quickest. Deer Killer tripped over his own feet and almost fell into the coals before he righted himself. The other guards laughed and scrambled around him.

Ecan called, *"Deer Killer?"*

The young warrior nearly twisted his neck off spinning around to look toward the palisade gate.

Ecan strode purposefully toward him. "When is your guard duty over?"

"At dusk, Starwatcher!"

"Not tonight," Ecan shouted. "I think you should be standing your post until dawn. From the clouds out to the west, we should have rain again. I wouldn't want you to miss it."

135

"Yes, Starwatcher." At Deer Killer's miserable look, the other guards chuckled.

Dzoo walked straight up to Deer Killer.

The young warrior bravely pulled his shoulders back and faced her, but his knees trembled.

She said something to him.

Deer Killer looked mesmerized, like a rabbit who's just realized he stepped into a snare.

Dzoo leaned closer and spoke again; then she smiled and walked past him. The watching guards scattered, and Deer Killer's hand twined in the fabric over his heart. He looked like he might faint.

Angry, Ecan closed the last of the distance, eyes blazing.

When he got to within ten paces, a powerful gust of wind blasted the mountain, and a tiny tornado of dirt and gravel spun into existence over Fire Village.

The whirlwind descended, gathering speed as it plunged out of the sky. It touched down, whirling coals from the fire, sucking up baskets and mats.

"Run!" someone shouted.

Ecan bellowed, "Halt! Man your posts!"

Deer Killer flinched when the first stone smacked his shoulder. Another banged across a lodge roof and sailed over the edge. Someone down below yipped.

Deer Killer spun around to greet Ecan, but before he could speak, a basket bounced off his arm with a painful crack, and Deer Killer yelled, "What the...!"

A split-cedar mat hit him in the back, then a rash of gravel and hot ash almost knocked him senseless.

Deer Killer, an arm up to fend off the wind, shrieked, *It's her! It's her!*

Ecan shouted, "Warrior! I order you to halt!"

Deer Killer bellowed, *"Make her stop! She's trying to kill me!"*

The whirlwind flipped back and forth over the plaza, dust and debris in its wake. Then it careened away down the mountain slope, kicking up dust and detritus as it went.

Dzoo seemed untouched where she stood by one of the lodges, watching with large dark eyes. Not even her dress was rippling as the blow passed.

A breathless silence settled over the village.

Ecan focused on the guards who'd fled the wind's wrath. Falling Cedar pawed at a hot coal that burned in a fold of his war shirt. The others cowered, staring wide-eyed up at the sky, and then back at Dzoo.

"If you are not back to your posts by the time I've finished calling out your names, I will assign you as the witch's personal guards, never to leave her side! Black Cod!" Men lunged to obey. "Thunder Boy!"

The warriors assembled in front of him, forming a line with their chests thrown out, their gazes focused anywhere but on Ecan. The wind had left them with eyes slitted, hair whipped around their faces. Falling Cedar's shirt still smoldered.

"I have never witnessed a more cowardly display in my life!" Ecan marched back and forth in front of them. "Deer Killer!"

The young warrior might have been on the point of tears. "Yes, Starwatcher?"

A nasty lump had already risen where the stone had bashed his temple. He seemed a little unsteady on his feet.

"What did the witch tell you before the whirlwind formed?"

Deer Killer squinted in disbelief. "She—she asked me if she knew me!"

"Knew you? Does she?"

"I've been her guard. She should know me."

Ecan's eyes narrowed. "Then she spoke to you again, didn't she?"

"Yes, but she just asked me the same question." Deer Killer's arms flapped helplessly against his sides.

Soft laughter drifted from somewhere high above him.

Ecan turned in time to see Dzoo make a sweeping gesture with her arm, a graceful winglike motion.

The remaining wind stopped. Just stopped. The air might have gone suddenly dead.

Deer Killer gasped, expression ashen. Nor was he alone. The other guards were bug-eyed, jaws locked, throats working as they swallowed dryly.

Ecan slapped Deer Killer with all the force he could manage. The young warrior staggered, stunned, and wiped at his mouth. Blood leaked onto his lips.

For a split instant, Ecan saw anger glitter in the youth's eyes. As quickly, it vanished.

"Forgive me, Starwatcher," Deer Killer whispered.

Ecan turned, glaring at Dzoo. Their eyes met across the distance. "What is she *doing* to us?"

She couldn't have heard, not from that far away; but she threw back her head, and her eerie laughter mocked them all.

Chapter Fifteen

As the whirlwind spun through the village and blasted away down the mountainside, Cimmis braced a hand against the wall. In the roar of wind, he couldn't hear his own thoughts, but he watched the twister as it played havoc with his village before rattling the palisade, whipping up red cinder, and heading down to lash the trees.

Red Dog brushed gray-streaked black hair from his dark eyes and squinted at Cimmis. "What's going on down there?"

"It has something to do with Dzoo."

Cimmis watched the ensuing drama as Ecan berated his warriors at the central fire.

"Do you think she caused the whirlwind?" Red Dog asked in a hoarse whisper.

"She'll be blamed for every unusual thing that happens in Fire Village."

People were stepping out, staring around uncertainly. Some went looking for items blown away. Here and there the village dogs came slinking back from their hiding places.

"Come," Cimmis said. "Let's talk in my lodge where we won't be overheard." He led the way to his dwelling, pulled his leather door curtain aside, and gestured for Red Dog to enter.

"Yes, my Chief." Red Dog ducked inside.

The fire in the center of the floor cast a ruddy glow over Astcat's slack face where she lay in the rear. Her soul had been gone since dawn. Cimmis had been dribbling water into her mouth to keep her body from drying up.

"You must be tired and thirsty after your run." He went to the fire and dipped a cup of gooseberry flower tea from the bag hanging on the tripod.

Red Dog eagerly took the cup and sniffed the aroma appreciatively. As he crouched opposite Cimmis, he said, "Thirsty but alive. There were moments when I doubted I'd ever see Fire Village again."

"Rain Bear treated you poorly?" Cimmis seated himself on a folded buffalo robe.

"When he realized I was your emissary, he gave me food and drink and provided a warm fire. I was surrounded by two tens of warriors, but comfortable."

As Wind Woman toyed with his door curtain, it swung and allowed the rays of sunrise to flash across his painted shields. Killer Whale and Eagle seemed to move. Red Dog turned slightly as though he saw it, too.

"All right, tell me everything." Cimmis laced his fingers over one knee. He hadn't slept well since Red Dog left. His visits to the Above Worlds had been tortured. All of his ancestors kept shouting at him, telling him he was being a fool.

"I repeated your words exactly, my Chief. I told Rain Bear that if he did not leave the Raven People and flee, your assassins would quietly kill him and his entire family." Red Dog took a long drink of tea, almost emptied his cup, and looked across at Cimmis. "He did not accept your offer."

"I see."

He'd expected as much. Now everything hinged on the second phase of his plan. His craftiest Wolf Tail would have arrived yesterday. Evening Star and Ecan's boy would be headed his way, or their bodies were being prepared for burial. The advantage fell to Cimmis with either result. If Coyote had managed to extricate them, Cimmis could quietly kill Evening Star and hand the boy to Ecan, obligating the Starwatcher forever. If it went the other way, Ecan would be rabid over the death of his son and willing to do anything to avenge himself on Rain Bear. The final advantage Cimmis accrued was the effect the murders would have on Rain Bear. His followers would know he was powerless to protect them. Perhaps, just perhaps, to save his precious family, he would choose to fade away like the morning mist. If he did, any chance for an alliance among the Raven People would go with him.

Red Dog was watching him as he thought. The old warrior wet his lips and said, "Rain Bear had an offer of his own to make. He said that in memory of Tlikit, if you would secretly send Astcat to him, he would do his best to protect her from the Raven People's wrath."

Cimmis felt a shiver run through him.

Red Dog frowned down into his cup. "He also said he regretted he could no longer do anything to protect you."

"Yes, I'm sure he regrets that very much," he said tartly. Rain Bear had shamed him before the entire village six and ten cycles ago. He could still hear Old Woman East's shouting, *You are the great chief! Your daughter has run off with a slave warrior? How could this have been going on beneath your very eyes?* Of all the things Rain Bear could have offered, this was like a slap to the face.

No, don't think about it. Not yet.

"What was your opinion of the sentiment among the Raven People? How did the attack on War Gods Village affect them?"

Red Dog chuckled. "I would say they're on the verge of scattering like a flock of quail under a hawk's shadow. Like always, each chief is ready to turn on his fellows, each carried away by his petty jealousies." He paused in consideration. "More than that, I'd say that you had them right where you wanted them."

Then perhaps Coyote has already broken their will. He would know soon enough.

Red Dog finished his tea and set the cup on the hard-packed floor.

With a flip of his hand, Cimmis dismissed him. "Go and rest. Food will be provided. I'll send for you when I require your services again."

Red Dog stood. "I'll be waiting, my Chief."

The warrior threw back the curtain to leave, then disappeared with a swishing of the hanging.

Cimmis dropped his head into his hands. His belly ached. For over a sun cycle, he'd been killing his relatives and bullying the Raven People at the Council's behest. He was too worried and tired to do otherwise.

Astcat might have been the matron, but Old Woman North wielded the true authority. And he acted in an attempt to forget his own bitterness over Astcat's illness.

He whispered, *"Blessed gods, show me a way out."*

Sunset

P owdered dust from the sage flats near the river coats my wrinkled face, and sweat trickles down my neck. The rest of my body is wrapped in hides. I actually feel a little better, more aware. More here.

"You are a good teacher," I whisper.

"There is no such thing as a good teacher. Teachers are of no consequence. They are accidental moments. Vanishing instants. Even to themselves. They must be. If a teacher pretends to offer permanence or truth, he does not give, he takes away."

"But I thought you were teaching me the ultimate truths of existence?"

"Ultimate truths?" He scoffs. "A strange pairing of words. That is the one contradiction that does not lead to enlightenment. Instead, it leads to the darkest depths of human cruelty."

"Then there are no ultimate truths?"

He pauses. "Have you ever watched water?"

If I but had the strength, I'd give him an annoyed

look. What could water possibly have to do with ultimate truth? "I've spent my entire life living on the ocean, you old fool. Of course I've watched water."

"I don't mean looked at it; I mean actively studied. For example, do you know its nature?"

"The nature of water...is to be wet." I open one eye.

He's gazing down with a stern expression, as though I'm the first real idiot he's ever seen.

"All right," I say. "What is the nature of water?"

"Water is the softest, most yielding thing in the world. It works very hard to flow over and around. It only splashes against something when it's being tormented and has no choice." His thick gray brows lower. "I suspect you've done a lot of splashing in your time."

"Yes," I answer with a smile. "But I had no choice. The jealous have always tormented me."

He chuckles and shakes his head. From the corner of my eye, I catch movement. I thought we were alone. We're not. Others wander the riverbanks.

The old Soul Keeper says, "What does water seek? Do you know?"

I remember the ocean smoothing the sand. The waves are like a heartbeat. "The earth?"

"In a way, yes; it seeks low places. Every moment is a calm, patient, sinking downward."

"I spent my life climbing upward, Soul Keeper. I always strove to soar with the Comet People. Are you telling me I wasted my life?"

"No, Chief. Nothing is ever wasted. Along with the notion of 'ultimate truth,' that is the great hoax. Every movement, every sound we make, has a purpose. But that purpose is not to soar upward."

"It is to sink downward?"

"Of course. Look at water. It settles among the smallest creatures, tiny insignificant things that dwell beneath grains of sand."

"You think the goal of life is to fraternize with small, low creatures?" I say sarcastically. I want to make up for the comment about water's nature. "That sounds particularly idiotic to me."

"Perhaps—if you're a particular idiot—it does. But it is only when you sink to the lowest place that you find the foundation of things—and others who understand it."

"I see."

"Do you? Do you understand what all this has to do with compassion?"

The old Soul Keeper rises to his feet, and his cape flaps around his tall body.

"Where are you going?" I ask.

"To get you a cup of soup. I think perhaps you're strong enough to eat. While I'm gone, think about compassion and water."

I close my eyes. Out over the lazy river, gulls flutter and squeal, as though the people are throwing them tidbits of food.

Water and compassion. Being soft and yielding. Low places and low creatures. The foundation of things, not lofty ultimate truths. Sinking downward...

I am sinking downward. I feel it every instant.

The thought terrifies me.

Chapter Sixteen

Astcat propped herself on her walking stick and stared at the darkness behind the swaying door flap. Red Dog had waited until Cimmis had left for the Council Lodge before he'd sneaked in. His meeting with her had been short, terse, and as disappointing as the rest of her life. Even though he had left, the pungent scent of his sweat lingered in his wake.

Plots within plots. She had been good at this once, back before her soul had loosened. She had no notion of how long she had been away this time.

Her knees wobbled as she slowly made her way back to the thick stack of hides beside the fire.

Most of their belongings had been packed and sent ahead to Wasp Village. The lodge felt barren. She kept looking for the baskets and bowls that had been sitting in the same spot for many summers and now were missing. The constantly lost sensation left her feeling gutted.

She combed shoulder-length gray hair away from

her wrinkled face. The coals made the very air seem awash in blood. Across from her, Killer Whale swam on his shield, his tail swaying slightly. "What do you think I should do? Hmm? Run or fight?"

The red and blue shades of Killer Whale's body had faded. At least she thought they had. Perhaps her soul sickness had affected her eyesight. She strained to think. Blessed Ancestors, she had to think...

She heard ghostly steps outside and thought it might be Red Dog returning. What had he forgotten to tell her? The steps almost weren't there, like snowflakes falling upon the ground.

Astcat stared at the door.

A tall woman lifted the flap and stood silhouetted against the starlight. She had her hood up, but long hair streamed around her familiar form.

"Ah," Astcat whispered, "I've been expecting you for a long time."

"This is a dangerous game you play, Matron, moving around the edges of your husband and the Council. Red Dog carries one secret message for Ecan, another for the Council, and a third for you. It's like playing dice with a grizzly bear."

Astcat bowed her head. How could the woman have discovered...but, then this was Dzoo. Perhaps she'd seen it in a Dream, or in the patterns of the future. Perhaps a wood rat had told her while it was carrying grass to its burrow in the rocks. "Of course it's dangerous. But what do you think would happen if I announced tomorrow that I was stepping down?"

Dzoo whispered, "The North Wind People would begin killing each other in the fight over the succession."

"Yes." Astcat nodded soberly. "And if my daughter survives, she'll struggle to find her position. As the new clan matron, the Old Women would bully her, or any other successor, into anything they wish. If I do not step down, Rain Bear will lead the Raven People against us. No matter what I choose, there will be war."

"And if Evening Star returns?"

Astcat anxiously tapped the floor with the head of her walking stick. "You think that's why I invited her back? To declare her matron? Think about this, Dzoo. Once the Raven People have amassed their warriors, how long do you think they will let her rule? How long do you think they will let her *live?*" Tears welled in Astcat's old eyes. "If I were to declare her matron tomorrow, it would be her death sentence."

Wind Woman teased the hood masking Dzoo's face. "She will not accept no matter what you offer."

"She must. She has to. She cares too much. She knows how young my daughter is. I'm sure Evening Star has regretted that her mother ever opposed us. Were it not for Naida's obstinacy, Evening Star would be a village matron now, and on her way to being matron of the North Wind People."

Dzoo placed a hand on one of the lodgepoles and leaned in the entry to whisper, "There is *another* way."

Her face reflected the red gleam of the lodge like a pool of water. "What other way? Give up? Throw myself upon Rain Bear's mercy?"

"I am not the Dreamer you must listen to." Lightning flashed, silhouetting her tall body in the doorway. Dzoo cocked her head. "He has found his wings."

"Who?"

"You will know."

The night sky seemed to darken behind Dzoo as thunder rumbled across the rugged land.

Astcat wiped at the tears that ran down her cheeks. "Why don't you come and sit with me? I haven't had a woman to talk with for a long time—except the old hags in the Council, and they're not much company."

As Dzoo stepped into the lodge, her buffalo cape billowed, blocking the light.

For an instant, Astcat's lodge went as black as the tunnel to the Underwater House.

Pitch yawned and shivered in his wet cape. Thunder rumbled over the mountains. Rain had begun to fall with the morning and softened the lines of the sea and shore. In the murky blue radiance before dawn, the bark lodges resembled a slumbering herd of wet animals. The only people awake—other than he and Rides-the-Wind—were guards. Occasionally, he glimpsed them fighting fatigue as they stalked the forest.

Pitch adjusted his arm. The pain wasn't quite so bad, but the sling had started to cut into his shoulder. Best of all the swelling was down, and he could move his fingers.

Rides-the-Wind lay wrapped in hides to Pitch's right, his gray head propped on his arm. He'd been silently staring at the fire for over a hand of time. A hide bag full of seal meat and onions simmered where it hung from a tripod beside the fire.

"Why don't you try to sleep, Pitch. I'll stay awake."

He shook his head. Wet black hair stuck to his cheeks, making his beaked nose look long and sharp. He'd barely slept in the past day and a half. "I'm all right, Elder. Just worried. Does it always take this long before a Dreamer wakes?"

"It depends on how far he's gone." A pause. "And if he's coming back."

Pitch turned to look at Rides-the-Wind's lodge where Tsauz still dreamed. Raindrops beaded the roof like tiny glistening shells. The last time he'd checked, the boy lay on his back staring blindly at the ropes swaying above him.

Lightning flashed, strobing the peaks, and thunder rolled through the village.

"How many times have you done this?" Pitch asked. "Helped a young Dreamer to climb Grandfather Vulture's ladder to the Above Worlds?"

A soft shishing could be heard as the rain increased.

"Many times. Two tens, maybe three tens."

"Tsauz is so young. I was surprised you permitted him to try."

"I generally know people's souls, what they're capable of."

"Have you ever been wrong?"

"Yes," he answered softly. "If he survives this, Pitch, he'll become a very powerful holy man."

Pitch twisted to look at Rides-the-Wind's lodge again. Off to the right, a faint coil of gray rose through the smoke hole of Rain Bear's lodge. He had seen the furtive shape slip from the doorway just before dawn and watched Evening Star scuttle to her own lodge. Neither he nor anyone else had missed the way she and Rain Bear had started to look at each other. People had begun to say unkind things. And even Roe was unsure if she approved of where this relationship might be going.

Rides-the-Wind indicated his lodge. "Make sure he's all right."

"Yes, Elder."

He quietly walked to the lodge and pulled the flap back. He stared in for a long time, before calling, "Elder? I think you'd better come."

"What's wrong?" Rides-the-Wind sat up in his hides, and long gray hair fell around his shoulders.

"Tsauz is having trouble breathing. It—it sounds like he's suffocating."

Rides-the-Wind walked stiffly across the wet fir needles and kneeled before the flap.

Tsauz lay on his back with his knees crooked and his arms spread. The position had drawn his black-and-white cape out like wings. Wet black hair haloed his head. He *was* having trouble breathing. He wheezed and sucked at the air as though he couldn't get enough.

"He's flying very high now," Rides-the-Wind murmured. "The air is thin up there. Leave him alone and let him concentrate. This is the most dangerous part of the journey."

In a hushed voice, Pitch asked, "Is he riding Thunderbird yet?"

"Oh, yes."

"Why is his hair wet? The hides are dry. Almost no rain blew in."

"Thunderbird may be soaring through rain showers. We won't know until Tsauz comes back to us. Now come, let's go back to our fire."

As Pitch turned to follow, lightning cut a brilliant

gash across the sky. It took Thunderbird's voice a few instants to reach them, but when it did, they both jumped and looked up into the rainy sky. Lightning flashed in all directions, creating an eerie luminescent web over the trees.

Pitch walked back and sat on the log, his gaze lost in the faint flickers of fire. Rides-the-Wind returned to his hides.

"Elder?" Pitch asked. "What's it like to ride on Thunderbird's back?"

"Where did you go when you climbed Grandfather Vulture's ladder?"

"For me, the ladder led to the Underwater House. I talked with my dead mother. That was just after I discovered Roe was pregnant with Stonecrop. Mother helped me to understand what made a good father. I have heard the ladder leads each person to a different place."

"Usually, yes."

Pitch caught the tantalizing odor of boiling seal meat as steam drifted his way. Off and on throughout the night, they'd eaten small amounts to keep up their strength.

A massive white bolt of lightning crackled right over their heads. Pitch let out a cry—drowned out by the deafening booming that shook Sandy Point Village. After images burned his eyes.

When the sound trailed away, Pitch saw Rides-the-Wind staring pensively at his lodge.

A low whimper came from inside.

Pitch leaped for the lodge. When he threw back the flap, he found Tsauz standing, hunched over, hands on his knees, shaking like a leaf in a spring gale. Bloody scratches covered his face and hands.

Pitch ducked into the lodge. "Are you all right?"

Tsauz staggered, about to topple face-first to the floor. Pitch steadied him and felt the boy's flesh, like ice. He wrapped him in a section of elk hide and dragged him out to the fire. Tsauz collapsed on the ground like a child who'd been spinning around with his arms out.

"Tsauz? It's Pitch. Can you answer me? Are you all right?"

Rides-the-Wind stepped to the wet pile of wood and tossed more branches onto the fire. Then he bent over the boy, peering intently into his eyes.

Tsauz sucked desperately at the air, filling his lungs, letting it out and filling them again. "We dove through the top of the forest to get here."

"Thunderbird was in a hurry?" Rides-the-Wind asked.

He nodded. "I had to close my eyes. The light was too bright."

Pitch waved a hand in front of the boy's eyes. Nothing. He'd been hoping...but it didn't matter. He stroked the boy's hair. "You did well, Tsauz. We're so proud of you."

Rides-the-Wind stopped and surveyed Tsauz with expert old eyes. "Are you hungry?"

The boy wiped his runny nose on his sleeve. "Yes. But I must see Rain Bear first."

"Pitch, these scratches need tending to. Please, fetch my Healer's bag."

Pitch scrambled into Rides-the-Wind's lodge while Rides-the-Wind draped the hide closer around Tsauz's shoulders.

When Pitch returned with the bag, Rides-the-Wind said, "Tsauz, we need you to relax for the moment. When you're warm and we've tended your injuries, we'll send for—"

"I must see Rain Bear now!" His blind eyes widened in terror. "I saw...saw all of you...and you were *dead*."

Chapter Seventeen

Rain Bear sat across the fire with his teacup braced on his knee. Morning was breaking, sending a shallow light through the camp. It illuminated the low blue wreaths of smoke that hung in flat layers. Every muscle in his body cried out for more sleep, but he forced himself to sip his tea and struggled to come awake.

Little Tsauz sat across the fire, Rides-the-Wind and Pitch flanking him on either side. The boy's dark eyes looked strangely luminous, as though some of Thunderbird's light had suffused his young body. Rides-the-Wind had cleaned and treated his facial wounds, but a few of the deepest cuts across his forehead still oozed blood.

Rain Bear's sleep-hazy mind wasn't capable of rational thought this morning. Instead it kept clinging to memories of Evening Star's body against his. He had never made love with a woman who fit so perfectly against him.

He glanced surreptitiously at her lodge, wondering

when she had slipped away last night. Waking without her this morning had left him with a sense of desolation and loss.

He sniffed at the cold, sipped his tea, and forced himself to concentrate on the here and now.

"What happened?" Rain Bear gestured to the boy's wounds.

"He flew through the treetops on Thunderbird's back," Rides-the-Wind answered matter-of-factly. "The branches scratched him."

The branches scratched him? Rain Bear put more faith in good clubs and spears than he did in gods, but he didn't exactly disbelieve.

Pitch handed Rain Bear a bowl of seal meat stew, and he nodded his thanks while he tried to sort this all out. As he stirred the stew, the mingled scents of seaweed and seal encircled his face. He took a bite. Tender and succulent, the seal melted in his mouth. Swallowing, he gestured questioningly. "I'm glad the boy had a vision, but why am I here?"

Tsauz clasped the bowl Pitch inserted into his hands and slowly let out a deep breath. "Chief Rain Bear, I spoke with Thunderbird."

Rides-the-Wind gave the boy an intense look. "Did he meet you at the top of the ladder?"

"No. He grabbed the rope and dragged it away, but he made me climb to the middle while it swung through the air"—his lips parted, as though seeing it all again on the fabric of his soul—"and then we soared away."

Rides-the-Wind leaned forward. A clean dry deer hide rested over his shoulders, but he still shivered periodically, as though the cold night had settled in his bones. "Where did you go?"

"We flew to Fire Village." Steam curled around Tsauz's face as he ate a bite of stew. He chewed it thoughtfully and swallowed. "I saw my father."

That got Rain Bear's attention. He perked up, studying the boy.

Rides-the-Wind asked, "Did you speak with him?"

"Thunderbird wouldn't let me." Grief strained his voice, but his eyes remained clear.

"Then Thunderbird had good reasons. Did you ask him to save your father?"

"Yes."

"What did he say?"

Tsauz lowered his bowl to his lap and fumbled with it. The words were almost too soft to hear. "He told me that I could either save my father or save all of our peoples. One or the other."

"Did he say why?"

"No."

Rides-the-Wind's gray brows slanted down. "How are you supposed to do that?"

"He wouldn't tell me. He said he'll come back and tell me more later. Right now, he just wanted me to get word to Matron Astcat."

"Word about what?"

Tsauz ran his thumb around the rim of his bowl. "He told me how to stop the war."

Rain Bear's spoon stopped halfway to his mouth. He put it back in his bowl with a clunk. "How?"

Tsauz's blind eyes drifted in his direction. "It's not something for you. Great Chief. Only Matron Astcat and I can stop it."

The hair at the nape of Rain Bear's neck prickled. "Tsauz, I must insist—"

"No, you must not." Rides-the-Wind gave a shake of his finger. "If Tsauz were to betray the trust of his Spirit Helper by revealing the Dream to you, it might anger Thunderbird. We would be worse off than we are now. At least we know there *is* a way to stop the war."

Rain Bear set his half-eaten bowl on a warm hearth-stone. "You mean that I'm supposed to trust Tsauz when tens of tens of lives are at stake?"

"Apparently. So let's spend our time thinking about a runner. Who should we send with Tsauz's message?"

"Just a moment!" Rain Bear glared back and forth. "You're asking me to bet the future of my people, clan, family, and warriors on the vision of a ten-winters-old boy?"

Rides-the-Wind gave him a thoughtful appraisal. "Do you remember when we talked about why I came here? I told you that Power brought me here. Just as it brought you, Tsauz, and Evening Star to this place. I told you that you would have to make a choice. Do you trust Tsauz's vision? Or prosecute your war in an attempt to exterminate the North Wind People?"

"I have no wish to exterminate the North Wind People." He scowled at the old man.

In a gentler voice, Rides-the-Wind asked, "What will be the ultimate price of your alliance, Great Chief? What will Bluegrass, Goldenrod, and Talon demand in return for their service?"

Rain Bear started to shake his head, and then a cold realization sank in. Yes, that would be it, wouldn't it? He might start out with the assurance that his forces were only going to break the Council's authority, but once the warfare began, who would keep the pent rage from feeding on a desire for revenge?

"Ah, yes." Rides-the-Wind read his expression. "Where will it end?" He turned back to Pitch. "Let's see. We were talking about a way to get Tsauz's message to Matron Astcat."

Rain Bear was painfully aware of Tsauz. The boy was staring at him with such intensity Rain Bear would have sworn the boy could see him. It went against every fiber in his body, but he said, "Whatever we do must be done immediately. The next time Coyote prowls Sandy Point Village, he'll kill Tsauz."

Pitch's beaked nose caught the gleam of firelight as he glanced uncertainly at his father-in-law. "It has to be someone special, doesn't it? Carrying the message will be dangerous."

"It has to be someone they wouldn't kill right off," Rides-the-Wind said. "Someone important enough that they would listen to him."

"Someone like me."

Rain Bear and Rides-the-Wind turned to Pitch, asking in unison, "You?"

"I'm perfect for it."

Rain Bear placed a hand on Pitch's shoulder. "What about your wound?"

"It's healed enough. The swelling has gone down. I can do this. And, given my wound, I'm surely not intimidating to them."

Rain Bear mused, "Roe isn't going to like this, but if I'm stuck with this lunacy, you're the best choice. Not only that, you're my son-in-law—married to Astcat's granddaughter, for what that's worth."

Rides-the-Wind smoothed his hand over his gray beard. "By sending you, they will know the value we place on Tsauz's vision."

Pitch muttered, "Tell that to the assassins who speared me on the trail home from Antler Spoon's village."

"Yes," Rides-the-Wind said softly. "I've been thinking about that."

Pitch frowned and looked back and forth between them. "But I thought we'd decided Coyote hired them, and Coyote was Ecan."

Rides-the-Wind's eyes glimmered. "If Coyote were Ecan, Evening Star would have recognized him the other night. No, this is someone who can play many roles. Someone smart enough to let other people believe him harmless."

"If Dzoo was right, and he's obsessed with her, why isn't he trying to get her out of Fire Village?"

The old Soul Keeper's smile was anything but friendly. "Oh, he hasn't forgotten her. You see, when I say he's clever, I mean it. How patient he must be, seeing her every day, waiting, knowing that the entire world is about to explode in warfare."

"And in the chaos..."

"Exactly."

Rain Bear pinched the bridge of his nose. "We must warn her."

Rides-the-Wind was watching him from the corner of his eye. "Do not worry about Dzoo, Great Chief. She and Coyote are already Dancing and darting. They have locked themselves in a duel. What happens between them is out of your control."

Rain Bear shot him a mistrustful look.

Rides-the-Wind replied, "Why do you think she let Ecan take her to Fire Village in the first place?"

Pitch rose. His red ritual cape swung around his

long legs. "Let me get my pack. I'll be ready in moments."

Rides-the-Wind gripped Pitch's free hand as the Singer walked past, and whispered, "Take the obsidian amulets to Dzoo. She may need them."

"Yes, I will." He sprinted away.

Rain Bear studied Tsauz. The boy had his chin up, bravely facing them, but his fingers had twined in his cape and hardened to fists.

What had Tsauz really experienced last night? Had he truly flown with the god, or was he just a very imaginative child? One touched by Power, to be sure, but the boy had been desperate to get a message to his father. *And now I have given him a way to do just that.*

Would the message actually stop the war?

Or start it?

His gaze returned to Rides-the-Wind, and he found the elder staring at him with dark penetrating eyes.

"Quite the unsettling decision, isn't it?" the Soul Keeper asked.

"I was just wishing I was the only one I had to trust."

A grim smile curled the old man's lips. "Then you'd be in real trouble."

Chapter Eighteen

Ecan ducked out of his lodge, his prayer bag in hand, and looked across the mountain. The gleam of dawn painted the belly of Brother Sky, turning it into an iridescent lavender bowl. At least twenty people already stood on the high points around Fire Village, facing east, toward the mountain peak.

He nodded to the young woman who kneeled on a woven seagrass mat ten paces away and proceeded up the trail toward the eastern palisade gate. Wind Woman blew his long black hair and stirred the wolf tails on his knee-high moccasins. They made a pleasant swishing sound.

North Wind People rarely appeared to offer morning prayers, which he thought foolish. Of course it meant associating with the unwashed rabble, but it was also a powerful symbol. If Matron Astcat were any sort of leader, she would order everyone except North Wind People to stay in at dawn, so that the sun shed its newborn light on North Wind People alone.

As he passed a lodge, he glimpsed the knot of slaves

bent over a still form. Wind Scorpion stood there, his grizzled face stern, arms crossed resolutely. Ecan had never really liked the man. He was taciturn, quiet, and watched the world through predatory eyes. Cimmis placed a great deal of credence in his skills, sending him constantly on scouting chores.

Ecan stepped over, stopping at his side to see what the commotion was.

"Good morning to you, Starwatcher." Wind Scorpion didn't raise his eyes to Ecan's, but continued to stare suspiciously at the proceedings.

"Warrior." The slaves were busy rubbing Lion Girl's body with mint leaves and crushed fir needles. "So she died, did she?"

Wind Scorpion's lip lifted in a sneer. "I asked Cimmis to let me take the witch out into the forest." He lifted a war club in his bony right hand. "One smack. Right in the back of the head. And she'd never kill another of our people with her potions."

Ecan glanced at the corpse. "It does seem that everyone around her becomes ill, doesn't it?"

"Deer Killer is complaining of a stomachache this morning." Wind Scorpion shook his head. "Ask our chief, will you? See if you can get him to be rid of the witch before we're all as dead as that girl."

"And Dance Fly?"

Slaves usually cared for their own. They dared to call upon Ecan's skills only in the direst of circumstances.

As they had yesterday for Lion Girl and Dance Fly.

When he'd entered the slave lodge, he'd been horrified by the raised wartlike lesions that covered their faces, hands, and legs. They'd been trembling spastically. He'd left willow bark tea and larkspur ointments —both very valuable because they, too, came as tribute —to relieve their pain. Now, seeing how Lion Girl had turned out, he wished he'd saved his precious ointments.

"If Dance Fly isn't dead by midday, it'll be a miracle. She's lost her soul; her breathing is so fast you'd think she'd run for miles." Anger welled in Wind Scorpion's voice. But then, it was known that he consorted with most of the slave women.

"If she dies, the rumors about Dzoo will be flying like bats."

"She's doing this to scare us." Wind Scorpion's war club bounced in his hand. "Just mention it to the great chief, will you, Starwatcher? I'll drag her out of here on the end of a rope. I'm not afraid."

Ecan remembered how Wind Scorpion had been with Hunter on the trail back from War Gods Village. No, he wasn't afraid. Not in the light of day like now. But come nightfall and Dzoo's proximity, and well, it would be another thing.

"I'll mention it," Ecan agreed as he turned back to his duties.

The guard standing at the far northern end of the cliff lifted a hand to him. Ecan couldn't tell if it was Hunter, or that bellyaching fool, Deer Killer. He lifted a hand in return and continued on his way through the palisade.

The cliff rose like a giant midnight wall. Another guard stood two hundred hands above. No, not a guard. Ecan knew White Stone's stance. The war chief always stood with his back straight and legs spread.

White Stone had been acting strangely since Red

Dog's return. Sensing that Red Dog carried important messages, he would rightly assume that plans were being laid in secret.

Ecan shrugged it off. He hadn't slept well. Tsauz had wakened him several times in the night, calling out as though he was hurt and needed Ecan. The visions had left him drained and anxious.

He reached the trail that led to the top of the lava cliff and climbed. Footprints disturbed the frost. Anger warmed his veins. He'd given strict orders that no one should ever disturb his morning prayers...

Dzoo leaned over the edge of the cliff above him.

Ecan froze. How had she managed to pass the guard at the palisade gate? Cimmis had ordered her death if she even tried to pass. Now she turned to study him. Inside the frame of her hood, her beautiful face looked pale, like polished chalcedony. Her black eyes shone.

The town had gone quiet. He turned to see people staring, waiting to see what he'd do.

As he stepped off onto the rimrock, her gaze followed him. Just her gaze. She stood three paces away, tall and willowy, silhouetted against the pink sunrise like a dark Earth Spirit.

"A pleasant morning to you, Dzoo," he greeted, and went to stand at the southern point of the rim, where he always offered his prayers. "They were supposed to kill you if you tried to leave the palisade."

"My guard said he was sick this morning."

"Yes. Lion Girl died last night."

"He's good, isn't he?"

Ecan turned his head. "He? Who?"

"The man who killed them."

"People think you killed them."

"Yes. They are supposed to."

He ignored it as another of her ploys. As he loosened the laces of his prayer bag, she moved up behind him, her steps silken.

Ecan's back muscles crawled. He said, "I'm glad you're here. It will give us a chance to speak."

He pulled four small leather pouches—each a different color—from his prayer bag.

As he opened the yellow pouch; he said, "It is considered ordinary courtesy to talk back when—"

"You have no interest in my courtesy."

Her deep voice had a curiously penetrating quality. It seemed to echo inside him. "I saw you enter Matron Astcat's lodge last night. You were there for a long time. It would be worth a great deal to know what you discussed."

He hadn't heard her approach. Barely more than a handsbreadth from his ear, she whispered, *"Your death."*

Annoyed that he'd jumped, Ecan dumped powdered red cedar bark into his hand and as he sprinkled it to the east, Sang, *"Come Old Woman Above, rise and carry the sun across the sky."*

He stuffed the yellow bag back into his pack and jerked open the laces of the red bag. As he poured powdered clamshell to the south, he said, "Is that something you will accomplish, Dzoo?"

She turned to stare up at the mountainside where White Stone was perched. "What will you do now that Rain Bear has rejected your offer?"

Ecan's hand stopped. Shell blew from his fingers in a haze. How could she know?

"You must find another way to recover your son—

and soon."

"Or what?"

She paused. "Or he'll kill you."

"Who will?"

She just smiled.

Ecan finished his prayers, sprinkling bitter cherry bark to the west and ground oyster shell to the north. Then he offered his shell-covered hands to Brother Sky, and bent to touch Our Mother Earth, chanting, *"Come Old Woman Above, be on your way to the Dark Place."*

Wind Woman swept the lines of bark and shell together, blending them into a rainbow haze before carrying them away down the mountain. They fell over Fire Village like a glistening mist, blessing it.

"Cimmis's assassin failed. That must make you happy."

Ecan's head jerked around. "What assassin?"

"You didn't know?"

"What assassin?"

Her gaze had fixed on the cliff where White Stone stood, as though waiting for something. Waist-length red hair streamed around her hood like long dancing legs. From his angle, he could see the lavender light shining on her turned-up nose and full lips. The rest of her face remained hidden by her hair.

"You really don't know, do you?"

"Is this some trick? A lie designed to make me..."

She turned, and Ecan went still. His loins stirred, though he couldn't say why. Something...lethal...gazed at him from those ebony depths. Something not quite human.

"Your chief sent an assassin to kill your son. He

failed. Barely made his escape. A worrisome thing for a man of his skill."

Ecan's heart thundered. "You're lying!"

She didn't even blink.

His hand quaked as he stuffed his blue pouch back into his prayer bag and tied it to his belt. It wasn't that he doubted Cimmis would do something so heinous; he just couldn't fathom why his own spies hadn't informed him. Cimmis would certainly make another attempt.

"When did this happen, Dzoo?"

"Two days ago."

"Did Astcat tell you?"

"Are you ready?" She smiled, and he felt it like the final plunge of an assassin's knife.

"Ready for what? Stop playing games with me."

"It's almost over now." She extended her palm and breathed across it, as though blowing dust to the wind.

"What is?"

"Your life, Starwatcher."

Chapter Nineteen

T he news had traveled like a racing wolf. Within a single hand of time, everyone around Sandy Point Village knew that Pitch had left to carry a message to the matron of the North Wind People—a message Thunderbird had given Tsauz in a Dream. Many people, tired from running and heartsick over their losses, rejoiced that Thunderbird had told Tsauz how to stop the war. But there were others— Raven People who'd been looking forward to killing North Wind People—who grumbled around their fires while they crafted enough spears to serve their needs five times over.

Rain Bear's elk-hide cape billowed as he and Evening Star slowly continued up the trail toward the hastily arranged meeting place. He had picked an old hunter's storage lodge some distance from the camps. Dogrib's warriors had kicked out the squatters who occupied it and had seen to the refurbishment of the place. Rain Bear hoped they would be away from prying eyes and interference. Guards stood every ten paces, ringing the lodge like hard-eyed statues.

"My Chief, let me examine this place before you enter." Dogrib trotted toward the moss-covered lodge in the trees ahead. Warriors, thicker than the trees themselves, stood around talking, laughing, casting curious glances at each other.

"At least no one has thrown anything pointed in our direction," Evening Star mused wryly.

He shot her a glance from the corner of his eye. "We just got here. There'll be plenty of time for that after the council."

"I love optimists."

He was puzzled by her, and still more than a little off balance by what had occurred that night in his lodge. He hadn't been prepared for the passion of their lovemaking—either for his reaction, or for how she had clung to him as her body tensed and undulated under his.

Nor was that all. Since their coupling she had changed. He'd been surprised by the emergence of a cutting wit and subtle but dry sense of humor. He had heard her laugh, and periodically, a sparkle lit her blue eyes.

A terrible longing grew within him. More than anything, he just wanted time to learn her moods, see her laugh. From somewhere came the memory of Cimmis's offer: He could leave. Take this marvelous woman, load his canoe, and paddle off into the north with his family. They could build a lodge on one of the small islands, fish, pick berries, and live out their lives.

If only...if only...

Dogrib reemerged from the lodge; his long white hair blazed in the morning's yellow gleam. He waved Rain Bear forward. At that moment the other chiefs emerged from the trees, maintaining the fiction that they had all arrived together.

Rain Bear nodded to this one and that, wondering if the old lodge would hold them all. Before he could enter, Dogrib grasped his arm and whispered, "There is a new war chief here: Brush Wasp. Says he's Gray Owl Clan from Trailing Raspberry Village. I don't believe it."

"Why not?" Rain Bear whispered and glanced at the two guards.

Dogrib's eyes bored into Rain Bear's. "Look at his earrings."

Rain Bear followed the others under the flap into the council.

Nearly two tens of chiefs packed themselves in two concentric circles around the fire. The chiefs formed the inner ring while their war chiefs knelt behind them. Rain Bear knew Brush Wasp instantly. The rough-looking young man sat cross-legged to his right, alone. He had seen perhaps twenty summers, but the battles he'd fought showed on his face. A long scar cut across his forehead, as though someone had almost succeeded in scalping him. He obviously had no chief here. His appearance would have meant little were it not for his earrings. They had been beaten from copper nuggets.

Copper was the property of the North Wind People. The rare nuggets were jealously guarded and only given to Raven servants for the most meritorious of service.

Had Brush Wasp simply forgotten he was wearing them?

The grizzled old Talon nodded as Rain Bear walked around the circle. He and Evening Star took seats beside Goldenrod, Dogrib settling close behind them. They made a stark contrast. Goldenrod was twenty-six and wore his black hair coiled in a stern bun over his right ear. Evening Star, on the other hand, had left her long hair loose. It fell over the shoulders of her elk suede dress in glossy red waves. It seemed that all eyes were upon her.

Goldenrod whispered, "The warriors outside are growing restless."

Rain Bear raised his hands to the assembly. "I pray that the Ancestors will watch over us today and grant us wisdom. We have many decisions to make."

Chief Black Mountain leaned forward. His bulbous nose and shoulder-length graying black hair shone, as though freshly washed. "Let's begin with the boy's 'vision.' We have all heard the stories. It is said that Ecan's son flew on the back of Thunderbird. That Thunderbird told him how to stop the war. Do you believe it?"

Whispers eddied through the lodge. Several chiefs shook their heads in doubt.

Rain Bear looked around the room, meeting each pair of eyes. "Rides-the-Wind believes it; so, too, does Singer Pitch. As to whether I believe it? Honestly, I don't know. I've always placed more faith in the actions of men and women. But I was there for part of it. Something happened to the boy. I watched him prepare, and I saw him after he came out of the lodge. Much of what happened to him cannot be explained. How did a boy inside a lodge get soaked while the rest of the lodge remained dry? How did he get the scratches that he said were from branches?"

"I saw him at the Moon Ceremonial," Talon said reverently. "A shaft of white light fell only on him. He seemed to glow in the night."

"His little dog took a message to the gods," old White Flicker added. "The Soul Keeper himself saw the dog rise like smoke."

Several grunts of assent followed this. Rain Bear said nothing but wondered at the awe in so many of the chiefs' eyes. They *wanted* to believe.

Black Mountain was among the skeptics. "What was in this vision, Great Chief? What did the boy say? That he can do what? Turn himself into a shaft of white light and burn the Council away, or send his Spirit Dog to rip Ecan's throat out? Or will he simply walk up to Fire Village and order Cimmis to leave us alone?"

Mutters of both assent and dissent rose in response.

Rain Bear spread his hands in a gesture for silence. "I do not know the whole vision. He would not say. I do know, however, that Thunderbird told Tsauz that only the matron of the North Wind People could stop the war. His message was for her alone."

Talon straightened where he sat behind Black Mountain, and his white hair glinted in the firelight. "Then, you do not know what message Pitch carries to Matron Astcat?"

"Tsauz told no one except Pitch."

Disagreeable grumbling broke out.

He shouted above the din, "But Tsauz told us other things you must know! They are the reason I called this council." He lifted his arms again and waited for the din to hush. "Tsauz told us that the North Wind People will be leaving Fire Mountain, abandoning Fire Village, and moving to Wasp Village. They will be on the trail and vulnerable for several days."

"Then this may be our chance!" old Bluegrass shouted. "When?"

Black Mountain twisted around to speak to Talon, then turned back and called, "None of us wish to fight, unless we have to. Have you received an answer from Cimmis? Will he and his wife step down and turn over their Starwatcher to us?"

"We have received no answer. But it no longer matters. If we are to end the North Wind People's attacks, *we must strike in the next few days.*"

Every chief turned to whisper to his war chief, and a rumble of voices filled the lodge.

Goldenrod loudly called, "As you know, my war chief is not here. He and several of our warriors are still out keeping vigil along the trails, so I am hindered by not having his counsel today—but I have serious doubts about all this." He turned to Rain Bear. "You lived in Fire Village for many summers. Chief Cimmis is not a fool, is he?"

"He is not a fool," Rain Bear agreed.

"Then isn't it possible that the boy was left behind at War Gods Village just to give us these words? Perhaps if we attack the North Wind People on the trail to Wasp Village, we will be leading our warriors into an ambush. Perhaps they are not moving at all."

Heads nodded and conversations hushed.

Rain Bear gave them a serious nod. "It's possible. Cimmis would love to crush our forces in a single blow.

But I think the boy was telling the truth. Regardless, I believe it is prudent to attack the North Wind People if they leave Fire Mountain."

Brush Wasp clamped his jaw.

Rain Bear noted it and let his gaze drift around the circle. Many of the chiefs here were new to him. They'd come in for the Moon Ceremonial and had remained to hear this new talk of an alliance.

Bluegrass rose to his knees and propped his hands on his narrow hips. "Would someone please tell me why the boy would reveal this? He has no reason to. We are his enemies. Telling us about the North Wind People's move will endanger the lives of his relatives." He waved a hand in self-deprecation. "This makes no sense to me, but perhaps I am just not seeing as clearly as others in this lodge."

Black Mountain glared across the fire at Rain Bear. "Bluegrass is right. Why would the boy tell us this?"

Evening Star said, "He was bargaining with me."

"Bargaining? To what end?" Black Mountain asked.

She answered, "He asked me to help save his father's life."

"*Save Ecan!*" Bluegrass cracked his walking stick across a hearthstone, and his toothless mouth twisted in rage. "Over the dead bodies of every member of my clan!"

"Hear me out!" Evening Star shouted as the lodge exploded with questions. "If you can attack and win against Cimmis's warriors, you can break the North Wind People once and for all! Isn't that worth sparing the life of one man?"

"No!" Bluegrass struggled to his feet. He had to brace both hands on his walking stick to remain standing while he glowered at the other chiefs in the circle. "How many of you watched your families murdered before your eyes while Ecan stood on a hilltop out of spear range giving orders?"

"I did." A young man to Rain Bear's left rose. His fists clenched at his sides. "My mother was tortured to death while Ecan roasted my father's intestines five paces away! If I have the chance, I'll kill him myself! No matter what agreements you've made, Evening Star! Who are you to say what happens to Ecan?"

Just above a whisper, she answered, "No one."

Bluegrass pounded his walking stick on the floor. "Have you agreed to this, Rain Bear?"

He glanced at Evening Star. She had her head down. Red hair spilled down the front of her cape, glinting in the firelight.

"No," he answered. "I have *not* agreed to it."

A clamor of shouted questions rose. Many people waved their hands, trying to get his attention. He pointed to Bluegrass. "Yes, Elder?"

"I want to know why she's here. Has it occurred to you that she might be playing us like a spider luring bugs into its web? That she and the boy are working together to get us all killed?"

Roars went up from every part of the lodge.

Rain Bear lifted his voice above the din. "I asked her here because I thought she might be able to help us understand the North Wind—"

"*Why do you trust her?*" Bluegrass spat the words. He wobbled on his walking stick. "She is one of *them!*"

He didn't see who muttered, "He's just thinking with his penis."

People began to stand up, as if preparing to walk out on the meeting.

"Fools!" Evening Star shouted as she stood. Before Rain Bear could react, she had whipped a hafted obsidian knife from her belt pouch and raised her other arm. Her sleeve fell back, revealing her pale forearm.

As the stunned chiefs watched, she slashed the underside of her arm. A thin line of red widened as blood began to leak down her arm.

"I give you my oath!" Her blue eyes were flashing, daring each of them. "The Council, Great Chief Cimmis, and that foul maggot Ecan are my enemies!"

Dropping her knife into her pouch, she wiped at the welling blood until it dripped from her fingers. Then, with a dramatic gesture, she flicked blood into the fire, where it sizzled and hissed.

"With the blood of my body, I seal that oath!" One by one, she glared at them. "I am here because I am *tired* of tribute and raiding. The old ways serve none of us anymore—neither the Raven People nor the North Wind People. The Council is led by the insane. Wolf Tails stalk the North Wind families while North Wind war parties sack Raven villages. And all the while the world grows warmer and the sea levels rise. Mud chokes the beaches and kills the fish." She might have been a trapped cougar the way she looked at them. "Our world is changing. I, for one, am ready to change it more."

"Then why do you plead for Ecan?" Bluegrass demanded. "That's just like the North Wind, forever protecting their own!"

Shouts rose in support.

Evening Star, heedless of the blood dripping down her arm, walked and stood face-to-face with Bluegrass.

"Chief, I have as much claim on Ecan as anyone in this room. I'm not the only one here who witnessed the Starwatcher burn my village, kill my mother, boil my husband's intestines while he screamed, and had to hear my daughter killed. I *know* what he does to women, because he kept me for almost two moons!"

She was nose to nose now as her voice dropped. "Unfortunately, I have to be more than just a woman crying for revenge. I have to consider more than just my grief and rage. I have to be a *leader*. Do you understand?"

"Of course." Bluegrass didn't sound so sure of himself.

"Then you know that to *lead*, you have to think beyond yourself. Beyond this moment when we all cry for revenge! Sometimes you have to make bargains you don't like in order to serve the better interests of your people. Isn't that right, Bluegrass?"

He swallowed hard. "Yes."

"Then you can understand why I gave Tsauz my oath that I would try to save his father in return for his help in destroying the North Wind Council."

The only sound in the lodge was the crackle and hiss of the fire as Evening Star met each chief's eyes. "We have the chance to break the Council and change the way we live. We can only do this if we act together. Sometimes you have to give up a little to receive a lot." She returned to Rain Bear's side.

"Hear, hear!" Black Mountain cried.

Rain Bear rose to his feet. "We must attack together, all of us pooling our warriors and resources, or we will fail."

Goldenrod got up and stood shoulder to shoulder

with Rain Bear. "I agree! My warriors will join Rain Bear! Who will fight with us?"

Over a dozen chiefs rose to their feet calling in assent.

Bluegrass slapped his war chief on the shoulder, turned his back to Rain Bear, and headed for the lodge flap. Four others followed him out into the cold morning wind.

Evening Star folded her arms and waited until they'd gone. "Forgive me," she murmured miserably. "I shouldn't have said anything."

Black Mountain gave her a narrow-eyed stare. "Bah! Without you, Bluegrass would have taken half of them out with him." He shot her a grin before he stood to speak with two other chiefs.

Rain Bear glanced at Brush Wasp. He had the unhappiest face Rain Bear had ever seen: a face from which all hope of peace had fled. Etched in every line, resolution battled with despair. He remained seated as the others slowly filtered out into the morning.

Rain Bear called, "I thank you all for coming. Please, go home now and discuss this. The next time we meet, it will be a war council."

As people began to file out, Goldenrod said, "Evening Star is right. Sometimes you give up a little to get a lot more." The tone in his voice wasn't pleasant.

"What do you mean? Only five refused to join us. That's better than I'd hoped for."

"They didn't refuse to join us, Rain Bear. They set themselves up against us. We're going to have to dispatch half our forces to guard our backs while the other half attacks the North Wind People. I'm not sure where the greater threat will lie. In front of us...or behind us."

"They need some time to think. They may yet join us once they understand the stakes."

Goldenrod wasn't convinced. "I pray you're right."

Black Mountain gestured to Goldenrod, who touched Rain Bear's shoulder in a show of support and followed Black Mountain outside.

Brush Wasp waited until the lodge was almost empty before rising and crossing the floor. He bowed to Rain Bear, then kneeled in front of Evening Star. "Matron, I must speak with you."

Evening Star frowned. "Yes?"

"I carry important news, Great Matron."

"I am not a great matron."

"Not yet. But you will be."

She cautiously asked, "Who are you?"

Brush Wasp glanced around warily, then whispered, "I am Sand Wasp, war chief to Kaska, matron of Salmon Village."

Rain Bear heard Evening Star gasp.

Sand Wasp continued, "She wishes you to know that the North Wind People will be leaving Fire Village by the dark of the moon in seven days."

Evening Star studied him, as though searching for treachery. "Why would she tell me this?"

"Because her mother was murdered by Chief Cimmis's assassins. She wants him dead. She believes you are her friend." His gaze searched her face. "That's true, isn't it?"

"Tell my cousin that I love her as much today as ever."

"I was sent to determine if you really were working

with these people to attack Cimmis. After the things that were said here, I'm sure." He glanced uneasily at Rain Bear. "Can you trust him?"

"I can."

Sand Wasp held her gaze for several moments before he whispered, "Very well. Know this: If you can arrange for an attack on Cimmis, Matron Kaska promises her forces will be at your command."

Evening Star's shoulders tensed. Rain Bear waited anxiously for her response. Another fifty trained warriors...

Evening Star said, "What does Kaska think she may gain from this?"

"Cimmis's death."

"Others may be killed, as well. Perhaps Matron Astcat and the Four Old Women. Does she hope to become the next great matron of the North Wind People?"

Sand Wasp was taken off guard by the accusation. "No. I mean, she does not! In fact, she suggested that perhaps *you* might ascend to that position."

"I cannot accept her offer."

Sand Wasp blinked in surprise. "Why? After seeing you face down that chief, I'm convinced you are more worthy than ever."

"You heard what was said here today. Take it to her. Tell her Rain Bear's intention is to break the North Wind People—not just Cimmis. If she agrees—"

"Wait." Dogrib held out a hand to Rain Bear. "Great Chief, we can't allow him to return to Fire Village. He may be an emissary from Matron Kaska, but he could just as easily be a spy for Cimmis."

Sand Wasp's mouth tightened. He carefully drew

back his cape, allowing them to see his hands, then reached into his belt pouch. He pulled out a magnificent spear point pendant. "Matron Kaska sends you her mother's pendant as a token of her loyalty."

He handed it to Evening Star.

Evening Star's fist closed around the precious gift. "Gispaw was a good friend," she whispered, "and a great leader of our people."

Dogrib stepped closer. "Cimmis may have ripped it from her corpse and sent it to you himself. We have no way of knowing if Kaska actually sent it."

Sand Wasp gave Dogrib an evil look.

Rain Bear considered as he tried to read past Sand Wasp's building anger. "I say we fill Sand Wasp's pack with food and let him go."

"What?" Dogrib asked. "Why?"

Rain Bear's gaze remained locked with Sand Wasp's, judging the set of the man's jaw, the fire in his eyes. "Because even if Sand Wasp repeated every word he heard today, it wouldn't change our plans. Nor would it change the Council's. Cimmis already expects us to attack him on the trail to Wasp Village."

Sand Wasp granted him a wary smile of respect. "You are right, Great Chief. He sent White Stone to us several days ago and laid out our defensive strategy." He kneeled on the floor, and his cape folded around his moccasins. "I will show you how he plans to defend against your attack."

Dogrib exchanged a look with Rain Bear before he knelt beside Sand Wasp.

"These are the places Cimmis thinks the North Wind People will be vulnerable." Sand Wasp made a dot in the dirt with his finger.

"Fire Mountain." He drew the main trail down the mountain between Fire Village and Wasp Village. "Tomorrow, he will send war parties to begin securing narrow, confined, and dangerous sections along the trail. Scouts will sweep the country for hidden enemy warriors in an attempt to deny you the element of surprise."

He tapped the dirt. "But he still expects you to reach the trail with enough warriors to pose a threat. His best spear throwers will encircle the North Wind People like a great wall as they travel."

Dogrib smoothed a hand over his jaw. "How many warriors does he have at his disposal?"

"He has ten tens of his own and another ten tens from nearby North Wind villages, but five tens of those belong to Matron Kaska."

Dogrib's eyes narrowed as he looked at Rain Bear. "We may be able to glean ten tens of warriors from the camps here, but I suspect it will be more like eight tens, and many of those will be inexperienced youths. We will be badly outnumbered."

"Yes," Rain Bear said quietly, "but there will be a few hands of time where Cimmis's forces are split three ways. That is when we must attack—before they can reunite around the North Wind People."

"That will be tricky." Dogrib tapped the map on the ground. "If we're not *very* careful, we will end up with enemy warriors in front of us—and behind us."

Sand Wasp rose to his feet. "Matron Evening Star, if you have no further need of me, I will leave you to your plans. It will take me two days to get home. Matron Kaska will send a messenger with her answer."

"Go, Sand Wasp. I pray the Star People watch over you."

He bowed to her and left.

"Seven days," she said and gave Rain Bear a heartrending look.

"We don't have much time." He smiled encouragement to her. "But first, let's attend to that arm. We can't have the next great matron bleed to death from an oath."

Chapter Twenty

Word had arrived long before Pitch's party could make its way up the trails. Ecan watched his son's messenger as he was borne on a litter up the trail from Salmon Village.

Sunset's soft amber gleam flooded Fire Mountain, turning the men who carried Pitch's litter into wavering shadows. People crowded the trail, calling greetings, shouting questions.

Ecan smoothed his hair. In preparation, he had pulled it away from his face and twisted it into a bun at the rear of his head. The style gave his chiseled features a stark look that he liked.

He shielded his eyes. No less than six warriors bore the litter. Pitch had one arm in a sling, and it left him off balance. Though he gripped the side poles with his good hand, he bounced every time the warriors' feet struck the ground. The party had been traveling for two days to reach Fire Village.

Ecan straightened his long white cape and headed for the gate. As he marched down the trail, Cimmis stepped out of a group of warriors. His blue cape flapped around his tall body.

When Cimmis caught Ecan's eye, he broke away from the warriors and strode toward him. Two guards, Hunter and Deer Killer, followed. Cimmis had his square jaw clamped, and his windblown hair and beard made a snarled gray halo around his face.

"The matron and I will meet with the messenger in the Council Lodge, Starwatcher. We will send for you when we are finished."

"But, my Chief," Ecan said in surprise, "my son sent the messenger. He may—"

"I am aware of who sent the messenger. If Singer Pitch does carry a message for you from your son, I will make certain you have the opportunity to speak with him *after* the matron and I do."

"But that's foolish! I may be able to understand things that no one else can."

Hearing the unbridled anger, Cimmis gave him a narrow-eyed glare, then swept past him and headed toward the Council Lodge. Hunter and Deer Killer stood uneasily to either side. Wind Scorpion leaned on a nearby lodge, his dark eyes missing nothing.

Sharply, Ecan asked, "What are your duties, warriors?" "The chief ordered us to bring the messenger to him, Starwatcher," Hunter said, squaring his shoulders. "Then he wishes us to stand guard at the entry to make certain they are not disturbed."

"I see."

Deer Killer gave Ecan a half-panicked glance, then fixed his gaze on the gate. He'd coiled his black braids over his ears and secured them with rabbit-bone pins. It made him look like a big-eared bat.

"How's your stomach these days?" Ecan asked slyly.

Deer Killer swallowed hard, placing a hand to it as if it were tender. The guards standing on either side of the entry shouted the arrival of the messenger.

Ecan said, "I want you to bring the messenger to me immediately after Matron Astcat is finished with him. Do you understand?"

"Of course, Starwatcher." They fled with unaccustomed swiftness.

As the litter was lowered to the ground, Pitch jumped off and clutched his slung arm, as though in pain. He looked like a skinny boy. Nothing more. His thin face and hooked nose glistened with sweat. He wore a tattered elk-hide cape. Ecan's eyes narrowed. So this was Pitch? Rain Bear's son-in-law?

Pitch spoke quietly to the guards. Hunter and Deer Killer escorted him up the trail to the Council Lodge, where he ducked beneath the door flap and disappeared. Hunter and Deer Killer took up positions outside.

Ecan gruffly folded his arms. Odd, he didn't even remember Pitch, though he must have seen him in Rain Bear's camp, which proved how much of an impression the youth had made. He stared at the Council Lodge for a time, then turned.

Dzoo stood behind him—perfectly still, as though not quite real.

"Greetings, witch." He instinctively clenched his fists. Wind Scorpion had a slight smile on his lips, as if expecting something.

Her deep voice had a velvet quality. "Where is the matron?"

Ecan looked up the trail to her lodge. No guards waited to take her to the meeting. "She must already be in the Council Lodge."

Which meant Cimmis had received advance warning from a scout. He had had time to both rouse his wife and escort her to the Council Lodge long before he'd sent runners to notify Ecan.

"What are you doing out here?" he asked.

"Waiting," she whispered, and tipped her chin toward the Council Lodge. "For that."

Cimmis ducked under the door hanging and walked out into the plaza. He looked angry as he paced back and forth with his arms folded tightly across his broad chest. Finally, he stopped short, glancing this way and that until he picked out Wind Scorpion. He summoned the grizzled warrior with an angry gesture.

Ecan would have sworn that Wind Scorpion smiled ironically as he trotted toward the great chief. Smiled? When Cimmis looked as if all the fury on earth was building in that old battered body?

Ecan said, "Now, there's a curious development."

Dzoo's voice was as musical as the wind. "The message Pitch carries is for Astcat alone, but I wasn't sure if she would have the courage to dismiss her husband."

He stared at her. "How do you know this?"

"Do you know what they're discussing in there, Ecan?" Dzoo whispered, as though she didn't wish anyone to overhear them. Her eyes seemed to have no pupils.

"No. Do you?"

She leaned forward to hiss, "They're selling you.

It's like the summer solstice market. They'll haggle over price for a short time, and then—"

He cut her off with a gesture and untied his cape laces, opening the front to the wind. He was sweating. "Do you really think I believe your threats?"

Her gaze drifted over Fire Village before she asked, "How is Mica?"

The change of subject left him floundering for an instant. "Dead. But he lasted a lot longer than I thought he would."

Ecan boldly stepped to within a hand's breadth of her, close enough to smell the earthy scent that clung to her hair. "What did you do to them, Dzoo? Some sort of poison? Some strange plant you brought from those buffalo hunters out on the plains?"

She softly laughed, "He's taking them one by one— everyone who was near me. Hunter and Deer Killer will have to be next. Eventually he will have to eliminate White Stone and then…you."

Matron Astcat was seated on a log before the fire, her long seashell-covered leather cape spreading around her feet in firelit folds. A walking stick leaned against the log beside her. She wore her gray hair twisted into a bun on top of her head, which accentuated the gaunt lines of her wrinkled face.

"Matron Astcat, I bring a message from Tsauz, son of Starwatcher Ecan," Pitch called formally as he knelt before her.

"Before you deliver the message"—she put a bony hand on his shoulder—"I want you to verify a rumor."

"If I can, Great Matron."

"Two hands of time ago, a Trader passed through here. He said there was a great uproar in your village because Ecan's son had had a Spirit Dream. Is it true?"

"Yes, Great Matron." Pitch nodded, eyes still downcast. "There is indeed an uproar. Our people—"

"I mean about the Spirit Dream. He really did fly on Thunderbird's back?"

Pitch nodded again. "Yes, Great Matron. Rides-the-Wind and I were both witnesses. As a Singer, I have no doubt. The Soul Keeper thinks Tsauz will be a very great Dreamer someday."

She let her hand fall.

Pitch looked up.

She had kind, vulnerable blue eyes. "Then perhaps he is the Dreamer I am supposed to listen to."

Pitch frowned, not sure what she meant.

She smoothed her hands over the cape that covered her knees. "What is the message?"

"Tsauz was told that our peoples are like Eagle and Raven with their taloned feet locked together in a death grip. So long as we fight this way, neither can fly."

"An apt analogy," she whispered absently, her blue eyes distant.

Pitch nerved himself. "Thunderbird told Tsauz that all we can do is spiral ever downward, no matter how hard we beat our wings. He said that even if one of us manages to kill the other, we shall still be locked in the death grip." He winced. "And, in the end, we shall spiral, exhausted, into the waves."

"Neither an eagle nor a raven can swim," she noted.

"No, Matron. In Tsauz's vision, we are swallowed

up by the sea. But it does not have to end that way. Tsauz was told a way to stop it."

Her gray brows slanted down. "How?"

"You must make the most painful decision of your life."

"What? Must I forgive my enemies? Surrender my position as matron? Deny my daughter her rightful succession?"

"You must take another husband."

"Another husband?" Matron Astcat's wrinkled mouth hung open in surprise. "Why?"

"Tsauz did not tell me why, Great Matron. Just who."

Astcat straightened. Behind her, firelight fluttered over the bark walls in golden waves. "Who is this man I am supposed to marry?"

"Tsauz, Great Matron. You must marry Tsauz to end the war."

A mixture of anger and disbelief creased her face. "Is this some joke? One of Ecan's charades? I will not marry a ten-summers-old boy!"

Pitch bowed his head and stared at the floor. Tiny flakes of obsidian, the debris from stone toolmaking, had been pressed into the dirt and glittered around her moccasins. "Tsauz said that you do not have to divorce Cimmis; he will be content as a second husband, but Cimmis must step down as chief."

"That's *preposterous!*" she exploded, then consciously lowered her voice. "Force Cimmis to step down and install a boy in his place! Never!"

Pitch continued staring at the floor. "Tsauz also said to tell you that you must marry and announce him as chief quickly...or within days you will be crying over

Cimmis's dead body, and nothing will stop our peoples from destroying themselves."

She picked up her walking stick and propped her hands on the polished knob. For a long time, she stabbed the stick at anything nearby: the hearthstones, the woodpile, the tripod holding the tea basket.

Finally, she gruffly asked, "You say the Soul Keeper, Rides-the-Wind, believes this Dream?"

Pitch nodded solemnly. "He does."

Matron Astcat made an irritated sound. "Did he send a message to go along with the boy's?"

"No, Great Matron."

"No explanation at all?"

"No."

"The old fool. I suppose he just expects me to do it."

Pitch lifted his eyes. Wan evening light from the smoke hole slanted across her face and shimmered in the last red hairs that threaded her bun. They were the same color as Roe's hair. This was his wife's grandmother, yet they'd never met. He felt oddly as though it were his fault. Perhaps he should have made some attempt to run up the mountain to speak with her before his marriage to Roe. Roe would have hated the idea, but...

"Go now." Matron Astcat took a deep breath and let it out slowly before adding, "Send my husband to me."

Ecan spun around when voices rose. A chastened-looking Pitch walked out of the Council Lodge to speak briefly with Cimmis, who immediately ducked back inside.

Hunter used his war club to gesture to Ecan. Pitch marched toward him with Hunter and Deer Killer on his heels.

When Pitch approached, Dzoo's expression softened, as though she was glad to see him.

Ecan stepped deliberately in front of her. "He's coming to speak with me. Back away."

Dzoo only gave him a cold smile.

Pitch strode up and bowed respectfully to Ecan. "Greetings, Starwatcher. I bring a message from your son."

"Yes, what is it?"

"He said to tell you he loves you and is trying very hard to save you."

"Save me? *Me?*" Ecan asked in confusion. "From what?"

Pitch walked around him and embraced Dzoo. She rested her chin on his shoulder and stroked his back, as though comforting him. In a soft voice, she asked, "You told her?"

"I did." Pitch pushed away to meet her gaze. They just looked at each other. Each appeared relieved and happy to see the other.

Ecan frowned. How could she know what message he'd brought?

How can she know any of the things she seems to? Does she truly see the future? Or is there a spy in Fire Village? Someone carrying messages between her and...

He suddenly felt weak.

It was the only answer.

Dzoo said to Pitch, "Have they assigned you a lodge?"

"Chief Cimmis told me that after I spoke with you and the Starwatcher, I would be confined to—"

"No. You will stay with me." She glanced at his arm. "I need to see to your wound. Your journey may have harmed it."

He wet his lips nervously and looked around Fire Village. "Will they allow it?"

"Let us hope they do not interfere." She gave Ecan a lethal glance, put her arm through Pitch's, and started leading him toward her lodge. Just loud enough for Ecan to hear, she said, "What of the fetishes? Did you bring them with you?"

"Yes." Pitch touched his belt pouch.

"What fetishes?" Ecan called.

Pitch looked like a boy with his hand caught in the berry basket. "I—I brought something for Dzoo. It's actually hers to begin—"

"Hunter! Remove his belt pouch and bring it to me."

The young warrior trotted forward, untied the hide pouch from Pitch's belt, and handed it to Ecan. He jerked the laces open and pulled out a small leather bag painted with red coyote prints.

In less than three heartbeats, his hand stung, as though being bitten by a thousand tiny ants. Fearfully, he whispered, "Where did you get these?"

"You don't know?" Dzoo asked.

"No!" Ecan hastily tied the bag to his belt and tossed the empty pouch back to Hunter. "Return this."

Pitch stared in shock. "Starwatcher, you can't take that! I'm a messenger! Under the protection of—"

"They do not belong to you, young Healer," he said.

Dzoo whispered, "Lift the sack to your ear, Ecan. Tell me what you hear?"

Ecan hesitated, searching her half-lidded expression for some sign of a trick. Pitch had a wide-eyed look, part wary, part fearful. Ecan lifted the sack, and never taking his eyes off Dzoo, listened.

Only the faintest of voices seemed to come from the bag, but voices nonetheless. The rim of his ear began to burn, prickling like his hand. A cold shiver, as if driven by a winter blackness, ran down his spine.

"I heard nothing," he lied.

Dzoo's lips parted, her eyes like the swells on a midnight ocean. "Did you hear your own voice, Starwatcher?"

"My voice? Don't be ridiculous."

She tilted her head, red hair spilling. "Then perhaps he'll just let you die in peace. I thought he would want you, too."

"What are you talking about? He? He who? And why would he want me?"

"I want my bag back," Pitch said stiffly, and extended his hand.

Dzoo's long hair fluttered around her shoulders as she released Pitch's arm and walked toward Ecan. "Do they belong to *you*, Ecan?"

He opened his mouth to respond, but Hunter said, "Starwatcher? The chief is motioning you to the Council Lodge."

Ecan shot a quick glance to confirm that Cimmis was waving. He started up the trail, but his steps faltered when a sudden dark sensation swelled from the bag and filtered through his chest. He looked down.

Whispers. I hear whispers. They're calling my name.

In a series of flashes, he saw dozens of faces: some old, some very young. All had their mouths open: screaming or crying, he couldn't tell. They reached out to him.

"Yes," Dzoo said softly, her voice penetrating past the whispers. "They think you can save them, Ecan. They don't know you, do they? And more important, *you* don't know them."

It required great effort for Ecan to walk all the way to the Council Lodge.

Chapter Twenty-One

Cimmis crouched before the fire that Kstawl had built in their lodge. Worried in a way he hadn't been in years, he laced his hands over one knee and watched Astcat pace near the door. On the way back from the Council Lodge, wind had torn locks of hair loose from her bun; it hung around her face in glistening silver threads. She kept propping her walking stick, staring at the floor, then taking a step, turning, and walking back in the other direction.

"Mother?" Kstawl called from outside, then thrust her head past the hanging. She looked as if some terrible thing were about to befall her. "Old Woman North has convened the Council and demands your presence. She's sending warriors to—"

Astcat turned. "Who is great matron? Me or that vision-racked old hag?"

Kstawl's mouth worked like a beached salmon's.

From outside, White Stone's voice called, "You are, Great Matron. I will take your regrets to the Council and inform them that you will call them at your convenience."

Kstawl, looking slightly sick to her stomach, withdrew. Cimmis sat stunned, hearing footsteps beating a hasty path away from their lodge.

"As if I didn't have enough to fret about!" Astcat snapped irritably.

"Please, don't drive your soul away."

"Drive my soul away?" She raised her thin arms. "As if that was my only worry!"

"My wife, please, your hold on your soul—"

"My soul will stay where it is for the moment." She closed her eyes, looking pained.

"Why won't you tell me the message? Is it so terrible that you—"

"I need to think about it." She heaved a tired breath and looked at him. Love sparkled in those blue depths. "I wouldn't hurt you for anything in the world. Do you know that?"

"Yes, of course," he said shortly. "What does that have to do with the message from Ecan's son? By Gutginsa, he's just a silly little boy."

As she walked toward him, the seashells on her cape winked in the firelight. "Apparently, that silly little boy has become a Dreamer."

Cimmis shrugged, but dread knotted in his belly. The news must be bad or she wouldn't be using this roundabout way of telling him. "Did he Dream our deaths?"

She stopped in front of him and lowered a hand to stroke his hair. In a tender voice, she said, "Not our deaths...yours."

Dzoo slowed as she approached her lodge, turning so the sunlight filled her face. It burned in her red hair and turned her eyes into black pits. She fixed her attention on Hunter and Deer Killer, who walked behind them.

"Of the two of you, only Hunter has a child. A boy." She smiled with deadly earnest. "And you, Deer Killer, you are thinking of marrying New Fawn."

Pitch watched as both warriors swallowed hard and backpedaled. They wore expressions that were a mixture of loathing and horror.

"If you desire to sire children in the future ..." Her voice dropped. "No, let's say if you would ever even *enjoy* lying with a woman again, you will stay as far from this lodge as you can tonight."

To Pitch's astonishment, the guards almost shook their heads off their shoulders, nodding in agreement.

"Good," Dzoo said simply. "The Singer and I are going to be mixing potions. Try not to breathe the fumes. Some...well, never mind."

Pitch followed her into the lodge, where a fire had burned down to coals. Dzoo indicated a place by the hearth, where a roll of buffalo hide made a cushion. "Let me check your wound."

Pitch stopped long enough to glance out the thin slit at the door's side. Both guards were well out of earshot.

"Hungry?" She raised an eyebrow and pointed to a carved wooden bowl beside the hides.

Pitch sat and exhaled in relief. As she dipped stew out and handed it to him, he took inventory of the lodge and related all the events leading up to his departure.

"He's going to be great," Dzoo said thoughtfully after Pitch told her of Tsauz's flight with Thunderbird. "If this coming trial doesn't kill him."

Pitch ate a spoonful of sea lion stew, relishing the rich flavor. In addition to the meat, the stew contained red laver and dried skunk cabbage. It had been a long time since he'd eaten such a meal. But no matter how much he ate, his stomach squealed for more. "Forgive me," he said and awkwardly repositioned his injured arm. The sling had started to saw into his shoulder. "I know I'm not very pleasant company. The only thing I've had to eat in two days is dried packrat jerky. I'm starving."

"Eat as much as you can hold, Pitch. Meanwhile, let me see that wound."

"No, there are many things I must tell you."

While Dzoo undid the sling, Pitch examined the beautiful painted leather dress she wore—the scarlet color was stunning. Her long red hair tangled with the tiny shell beads that covered the bodice.

Pitch gestured with his horn spoon. "We heard you were locked in the captives' lodge."

"I was."

"Who gave the order to release you?"

"Cimmis, when it became apparent that I wasn't interested in leaving."

"How did they capture you?"

"They didn't. I surrendered to them at War Gods Village." She stared thoughtfully at his wound. "Sometimes, the choices we make condemn us either way."

"Why didn't you warn the people at War Gods Village?"

She stared at him, a terrible pain in her eyes. "I had

to choose between Coyote and all those people. To defeat Coyote, I had to be captured, had to be brought here under constant guard."

"He's that dangerous?"

"Stopping him may be more important than defeating the North Wind Council."

Pitch nodded, chewing thoughtfully. "What of Astcat? She wasn't what I expected."

"Astcat is not well."

He swallowed a bite of sea lion and said, "I know she's supposed to have blank spells where her soul flies away, but she seemed fine when I spoke with her. Alert, intent on hearing my words."

"Then she's having a good day. That is not always the case. How did she react?"

"With shock and dismay. But not with the vehemence I was expecting. In my dread, I thought she'd scream and have me thrown out, maybe even order my death."

She studied him thoughtfully. "But you came anyway?"

"It is a matter of Power. How could I have refused?"

On the eastern wall, two sacred bundles hung from the lodgepole. He scooped up his last succulent bite of meat and studied them while he ate. The bundle on the left was decorated with red and yellow circles, imitating the pattern of the Star People in the Wolf Pup constellation. An eye glared from the center of the bundle, black and glistening as though alive. Beside it, Dzoo's Noisy One bundle hung. The miniature face of her Spirit Helper covered the leather. The Noisy One had empty white eyes, a black circle for a mouth, and a squat, hair-covered body. The longer Pitch looked at Dzoo's sacred Power bundles, the more he felt their souls creeping around inside him, testing him to see if he was worthy to touch them, whispering just below his ability to hear.

She followed his gaze. "Ecan had them returned to me. I think he was having bad dreams while they were in his possession."

Pitch set down his empty bowl and wiped his mouth on his sleeve. "Hallowed gods, that was good. Do you eat this way every night?"

"Living here is very much as I recall from my childhood. At dawn and dusk, slaves bring bowls of food, carry away waste bowls, deliver clean clothing, sweep and straighten the lodge. The only thing that's really changed is they know the tribute is running out. They've been stockpiling it for many cycles, but it will be gone soon. Long ago, they wiped out the sparse resources on the mountain. Without tribute, they can't survive here...and the ghosts have changed."

He reached for a seaweed cake. As he ate it, green crumbs trickled down the front of his white shirt. "How so?"

Her gaze fixed on the doorway. The curtain swung gently in the draught that constantly breathed up the mountain slope. "They used to be happy ghosts, going about their days laughing and talking. Now they're frightened. They roam the village at night, crying, screaming the names of people I suspect are long gone." Dzoo turned to look at him. "You'll hear them. Just wait. They wake me every night."

"You often hear things I don't." He finished his cake

and wiped his hands on his red leggings. "What about Astcat? If she agrees to this marriage, it will drastically change the balance of Power. Imagine what the other North Wind People will do if she goes through with it."

"I suspect they'll assassinate her."

Pitch ate another cake and studied the doorway. Past the door curtain, he could see one of the guards keeping his distance in the gathering dusk. The man kept shooting owlish glances at Dzoo's lodge, as if he expected grizzly bears to bolt from the door at any instant.

Pitch whispered, "Why do you think Thunderbird told Tsauz this was the only way?"

"It probably is."

"If she marries him, will the Raven People be content? Or do you think they will still demand the deaths of the North Wind People?" His wife and son were North Wind People. Pitch had already begun to plan his family's escape. They would flee southward, perhaps run all the way to the Elderberry People...

Dzoo said, "I can't say."

He brushed at the green crumbs on his shirt. "You know that Evening Star is trying to save Ecan, don't you?"

Dzoo nodded. "Tell me about Evening Star and Rain Bear, Pitch. Are they...together?"

He lifted a hand. "I think so."

Dzoo closed her eyes for a moment, as though thanking the gods. "And the fetishes. Why did you bring them?"

Pitch let out a breath. The lodge smelled fragrant, a mixture of roasted sea lion and black seaweed. "Rides-the-Wind wanted me to ask you about one of the fetishes."

"Which one?"

He held up his thumb and forefinger to show her the large size. "It's obsidian—in the shape of a coyote. It took me a long time to determine the one that—"

"Contained the man's voice?"

Pitch went numb. The hair on his arms prickled. "How did you know?"

Dzoo smiled. "I heard his voice the first time I touched the bag."

Filled with dread, Pitch asked, "Why didn't you tell me?"

"Because he was calling to you. You had to hear it for yourself, or it meant nothing."

"Hallowed Ancestors, Dzoo," he said loudly without thinking, then made an effort to lower his voice again. "What does it mean? Who is he? And how did his voice get into the Coyote fetish?"

She shoved long red hair over her shoulder, and the tiny lines around her eyes deepened. "Now you know why I have to hunt down Coyote. He has enough Power to capture souls and imprison them inside those fetishes. I just don't know if it was in the past or in the future."

Pitch sank back against the wall and rubbed his forehead. The orange gleam of the fire fluttered over his hand. "If we knew whose voice that was, maybe we could stop it from happening."

A strange haunted smile touched her lips. "What if he deserves this fate?"

He just stared at her.

She smoothed her fingers over the soft buffalo hide

she sat upon. "Those fetishes are more than just magical stones. You know that, don't you?"

It felt like an earthquake building in his heart, ready to shake his world apart. "Yes. And?"

Her black eyes flared. "That bag is an army of ghosts for the man who knows how to use it."

Pitch had trouble swallowing. The fire's gleam seemed to close in around him. "Rides-the-Wind thinks he's the most Powerful witch to exist in a long time."

"Very possibly." She ran a hand through her long hair. "I haven't had the chance to ask him."

Fear swelled like a black bubble in Pitch's chest. "Are you saying he's here? In Fire Village?"

Dzoo tilted her head, as though considering. "He is often here. He comes and goes. But he's never far from me for long."

Pitch reached out to touch her hand. "Do you know who he is?"

"Not yet. But I will. When he wears the mask, I can smell damp moss. At other times..."

Her voice faded as footsteps crunched the sand outside.

A man gruffly asked, "What are you two fools doing? And why do you both have your hands cupped over your balls? War Chief White Stone wishes to see both of you. I'll stand guard while you're gone."

Dzoo sat up straighter, one elegant eyebrow cocked.

"But, Red Dog," Deer Killer objected, "Ecan told us to stay here until dawn. I'm in enough trouble, I don't wish to—"

"Yes, yes," Red Dog said irritably. "That was before the great chief changed his mind. White Stone has convened a war council around the central fire. That

206

lazy Wind Scorpion is missing, so you are each going to be leading war parties tomorrow."

Whispers broke out, both men asking questions at the same time.

"Don't ask me," Red Dog said. "Go and get your orders straight from the war chief. I wouldn't keep him waiting too long. He's in a foul mood."

The guards grumbled, then pounded away into the dusk.

Dzoo rose to her feet with the silence of Wolf and stared at the doorway.

A few instants passed.

Red Dog ducked his head through the curtain. He gave Pitch a gap-toothed grin that was anything but reassuring. His gray-streaked black hair was pinned back in a bun, which made his broken nose stand out even more. A tattered deer-hide cape draped his burly shoulders.

"Tell me quickly," he whispered. "I'm leaving tonight."

Dzoo hissed, "The slaves say that Astcat and the other matrons will lead the group, encircled by the best spear throwers. Cimmis will bring up the rear. He'll be dressed as an ordinary warrior. It won't be easy to spot him. He—"

Someone walked up the trail outside, his steps as soft as spider silk. He carried a torch; its orange gleam edged the door like liquid flame. Red Dog's eyes went wide a second before he ducked back outside, taking up his proper guard position.

The torch's gleam strengthened as the man came closer.

Pitch held his breath, listening.

Ecan's deathly quiet voice called, "Well, well, Red Dog, imagine finding you here."

Pitch rose to his feet, but Dzoo stopped him short when she asked casually, "Tsauz said Ecan would die?"

He frowned. It took him a moment to understand; then he replied, "Poor little boy, he's frightened half to death for his father."

"Why didn't Tsauz ask you to tell Ecan?"

"I—I think he was afraid." Pitch shrugged in mimic. "How does a boy like that tell his father he's going to die?"

"But if Ecan is going to die before he gets to Wasp Village, something must happen on the trail. Is he killed in the fighting?"

Pitch tried to decide what to say next. Outside, an unearthly silence had descended. Ecan's ears must be trained on their voices. "Tsauz didn't tell me, Dzoo."

She lowered her voice and said, "Death has already wrapped its tendrils around Ecan. That cannot be changed. What of Tsauz? Does he survive?"

They continued talking for what seemed a long time, making up this and that.

"You've heard enough," Ecan growled outside. "Get out of here, Red Dog. And don't go spreading their poison, or I'll slice your liver out of your body."

Steps sounded as Red Dog left, followed shortly by the wavering of Ecan's departing torch.

When the same two guards returned to their door, Pitch slumped to the floor, breathing hard. He whispered, "I don't understand. What is—"

Dzoo clenched a fist to order silence. "You must be exhausted, Pitch. Why don't you try to sleep?"

So. Even at a whisper, it was not safe to discuss Red Dog. Pitch's thoughts twined around that fact.

Dzoo paced back and forth in front of the fire, clearly distressed. Firelight sparkled across her beaded dress.

Pitch curled up on the buffalo hide, but his heart pounded like a drum at a ceremonial.

"So much at risk," Dzoo whispered to herself.

Chapter Twenty-Two

"Those were her exact words?" Kaska asked.

"Yes."

She stood beside Sand Wasp outside her lodge in Salmon Village and gazed up at the glittering Star People who arced like a giant wheel around the cone of the mountain.

When she'd been notified that Sand Wasp had returned, she'd risen straight from her husband's arms. She must look it. She was barefoot, and long red hair streamed over her cape. "Do you think Rain Bear can do this?"

Sand Wasp braced his hands on his hips. "With enough warriors, he and Evening Star can do anything, Matron."

The soft hum of conversations radiated around Salmon Village. She could hear children crying and dogs barking. Old Woman Shuffling Feet snored loudly, as she had for as long as Kaska could remember.

It was so hard to imagine anything but this. Where would she go? What would she do? She had taken for granted that her two-summers-old daughter would grow up as she had: beloved and respected, with everyone knowing she would eventually be the matron of Salmon Village. She loathed the idea of telling little Sotic that instead of being one of the most powerful women in their world, she was going to spend the rest of her life in hiding, trying to scratch out a living with her bare hands. Assuming, that is, that a band of blood-thirsty Raven People didn't smack the brains out of her little skull first.

"How many warriors does Rain Bear have?" Kaska asked.

"Ten tens at most. Those are his trained warriors. In addition he has plenty of hunters, fishermen, old men, and boys. They're mad enough to fight, but probably won't stand when they see their best friend speared through the guts." The long scar that slashed Sand Wasp's forehead gleamed whitely when he turned to her. "If we add our warriors to his, however, we'll even the odds. If not, he will be badly outnumbered."

Wind Woman rushed up the slope, and the hem of Kaska's cape flapped around her legs. Her toes were quickly turning to ice. "What is your advice, War Chief?"

"I cannot advise you, Matron, beyond telling you that joining an alliance of Raven People to make war on North Wind People makes me most uncomfortable."

"A bit like sleeping with a rattlesnake, isn't it?"

"Very much so, Matron."

Kaska smiled wanly. On the night of Gispaw's murder, her mother had told her, *The North Wind People are doomed, my daughter. Leave now. Take your family and run.* Kaska had, of course, vehemently disagreed.

That was two moons ago.

After her mother's murder—and so many others— she had begun to fear that Mother may have been right. If the Raven People didn't kill them, her people would murder each other just for spite.

But Evening Star has joined them. Could Naida's daughter be making such a terrible mistake?

"Tell me how the Raven People reacted to Evening Star speaking in their council."

"She won most of the doubters over, Matron." He smiled in the darkness. "She might have had the support of a couple of the chiefs going in, but when it was over she had even won the respect, if not the hearts, of the dissidents."

"How did she look, act?"

He gave her a piercing glance. "Like a great matron should." A pause. "And I mean no disrespect, but if I were Astcat, let alone Old Woman North, I'd be sending every Wolf Tail I could find to cut her head off."

"That persuasive, was she?"

"Yes, Matron. Even while arguing for Ecan's life."

Kaska took a deep breath. The future was looming before her. In a stroke, she could be destroying her whole family. A loyal Kaska would be worth a great deal to the Council. Her heart ached for Astcat. Then she imagined Evening Star, haunted, hunted, fleeing desperately through the forest...

"How would I go about putting our warriors under Rain Bear's command?"

"It won't be easy. They think they're supposed to

fight Raven People, not help them." Sand Wasp gave her a somber look. "If we do this, we will have to get word to Rain Bear soon. He must have time to plan how to use our warriors, and we must get our people into position without arousing the suspicions of the great chief, his Starwatcher, or White Stone."

Kaska curled her toes to keep them warm. "I need you here to help me. Can you find someone else to deliver the message to Rain Bear?"

"I can, but it will cost a great deal, Matron. To assure secrecy, we must *buy* a messenger."

"I will pay whatever is necessary. But choose well, Sand Wasp. What little tribute we have left is rapidly disappearing. Make him aware of the consequences if he betrays us."

Sand Wasp stood quietly for a time, then whispered, "What will happen to us if Rain Bear wins, Matron?"

Kaska studied the wealth of sparkling Star People, wondering how her ancestors would answer that. They were probably all glaring down at her this instant, asking how one of Gispaw's children could betray her own people. She prayed with all her heart that her mother could explain it to them.

"The North Wind People will be reborn as something else, Sand Wasp. But for good or ill, I cannot say."

"Where will we go?"

"I suppose we will live at Wasp Village for a time. After that...who can say?"

Sand Wasp took a deep breath and whispered, "Know this, Matron. No matter what happens, I am your servant."

Tears sprang to her eyes. She lightly touched his

shoulder. "Thank you, my friend. Now, leave me. Find a messenger."

Sand Wasp bowed and left.

Kaska's gaze followed the steep mountain slope up to Fire Village. Even at night, the images of the gods painted on the palisade wall shimmered as though alive.

She walked back to her doorway. Just before she ducked through into her firelit lodge, she murmured, *"Forgive me, my daughter."*

Chapter Twenty-Three

The air cooled with the coming of night, and the savory tang of the fires and burning alder filled the forest. Rides-the-Wind drew it into his lungs as fingers of breeze stirred.

Rain Bear and four people—Tsauz, Dogrib, Talon, and Evening Star—sat around the great chief's fire.

"If I can pull Matron Kaska's forces into mine on the south"—Talon leaned over the map they had sketched into the charcoal-stained soil near the hearth-stones—"it will create an opening to Cimmis's inner circle. Assuming, that is, that Kaska's warriors obey my commands."

Dogrib pointed. "If you can create that opening, I'll rush my forces into the center as quickly as I can." He kept his voice low. "But by the time we get there, his strength will be closing around the North Wind People. No matter how well this goes, it's going to be precarious. One wrong move, one delay, and the battle will fall into chaos, every warrior fighting for himself."

Rain Bear said, "We can't let that happen."

Rides-the-Wind looked out at the ring of guards that encircled them. The warriors stood fifty paces away in the forest, or perched on boulders overlooking the ocean, but their ears were trained on the conversation going on around the fire.

"We must take the boy." Talon shoved age-silvered hair away from his sharp eyes. "We may need him."

"Too dangerous." Evening Star straightened. "The boy should stay here. Tsauz is only valuable to us if he's alive."

"It's no more dangerous for him than it will be for the rest of us, Matron," Talon replied.

Dogrib braced his elbows on his knees. "Talon is right. If our situation grows desperate, we may need to hand Tsauz over to save people we care about."

Tsauz's blank eyes seemed to quiver in their sockets.

Rain Bear leaned sideways to whisper, "It's all right. We're just talking. We haven't made any decisions."

"He must go along," Dogrib said. "What if we cannot free Pitch and Dzoo? Cimmis will certainly use them against us. Tsauz gives us a bargaining piece."

"Cimmis will not bargain for the boy," Evening Star said. "Tsauz will only be useful if we are bargaining with Ecan. Or have you forgotten Coyote's visit not so long ago?"

Rain Bear nodded. "Tsauz is only valuable if we can wring concessions from Ecan. And who is to say he's safer here? At least if he goes with us, he'll be surrounded by friends. Here he's easy prey for the next Wolf Tail who prowls through."

Rides-the-Wind's gaze turned to the pebble-strewn beach where the canoes were drawn up. There, on the landing, refugees walked the shore looking for crabs or anything else that was edible. Beyond the soft whisper of the surf, an odd stillness cloaked the camps.

He propped his walking stick and said, "Perhaps it would be helpful if you asked Tsauz what he thinks."

Tsauz blinked.

Rain Bear's brows lowered, but he said, "Tsauz, should we take you with us?"

Tsauz licked his lips. "If you leave me here, you will have to leave fifty warriors to guard me, won't you?"

"Probably."

He lowered his gaze to assure Rain Bear he meant no disrespect. "You *will* need those warriors in the battle."

"I would rather not risk having you hurt, Tsauz. I promised I would make sure you got home, and I must try to do that."

"I—I would rather go with you."

Evening Star tilted her head. "Why is that?"

"Two reasons: If you do not take me, Cousin, my father will assume I am dead. Second, Coyote will find it harder to kill me when I'm with you."

Dogrib nodded, and his pale hair glinted in the fire-light. "Smart boy."

Wind Woman gusted through the forest. Rides-the-Wind shivered and tugged at the deer hide over his shoulders.

Rain Bear exhaled hard. "There is one last thing we must plan for."

"Yes?" Talon asked.

"Kaska may be working with Cimmis."

Evening Star said, "No, she wouldn't. She's not—"

Rain Bear held up a hand to halt her words. "If she

is, at a critical point in the battle, her warriors will turn on us."

Dogrib nodded. "It would make a perfect trap."

"I know Kaska. We almost grew up together. She wouldn't do such a thing," Evening Star insisted stubbornly.

"Wouldn't she?" Dogrib asked, "Forgive me, Matron, but you have no idea what pressure the Council might have put upon her. What if Coyote drops in on her every so often to remind her how simple it would be to kill her family? Her warriors are another matter. Will they obey her when she orders them to fight against their chief?"

Evening Star stared at him for a moment, took a deep breath, and nodded. "Yes, you're right, War Chief. We must plan for that eventuality."

Everyone started talking at once, and Tsauz's blind eyes turned to Rides-the-Wind.

He walked over and lowered himself to the mat beside the boy. "What is it, Tsauz?"

Tsauz felt for Rides-the-Wind's ear and pulled it down to his mouth. He whispered, "Thunderbird told me something."

When the boy didn't continue, he asked, "What did he tell you?"

"That Rain Bear doesn't know how to win."

Rides-the-Wind pulled away and looked down at the boy. "Did Thunderbird say how?"

Tsauz swallowed anxiously. "No. I just have to be there. But you can't tell Rain Bear I said so."

"No, of course not," Rides-the-Wind said.

In the distance, over Fire Mountain, thunder rumbled.

Tsauz spun around to look. "Did you hear that?"

The old Soul Keeper said, "I heard. What did Thunderbird say?"

"It's beginning," Tsauz whispered.

Sister Moon had risen into the sky; her gleam flooded the forest, shimmering in the trees and outlining every dark boulder. Shadows fell across the forest floor like a tracery of black lace.

Rain Bear hunkered on a fallen log across from Red Dog and studied his old friend. The silver glow reflected from the thick coating of grime on the battered warrior's face. He smelled dankly of sweat, and his gray-streaked black hair straggled around his face as though he hadn't combed it in days.

Red Dog had pledged his loyalty to Rain Bear over a cycle ago. He'd been badly wounded in a fight with Talon. Dzoo had worked day and night to save his life. Since then Red Dog had periodically passed information about the happenings in Fire Village. Of course, Rain Bear wasn't gullible enough to believe all of it. He knew for a fact that Red Dog played his own game for his own reasons, many of them no doubt unsavory, but he seemed to worship Dzoo. How many times had Rain Bear seen that look of longing in Red Dog's eyes as he watched her from afar?

"Thank Raven it's all downhill from Fire Village. I've never felt so tired." Red Dog sighed. "Kaska needs instructions. What do you want her to do with her warriors?"

Rain Bear outlined the proposed plan of attack. When he finished, he asked, "Do you understand?"

"Yes. You want her people to fall on the rear of the North Wind warriors that are fighting Dogrib."

A weight seemed to lift from Rain Bear's shoulders.

"What have you got for warriors?"

Rain Bear chuckled. "I have a core of eight tens of capable men and a couple of women. The rest are an angry rabble. They're the ones who are unpredictable."

Red Dog said, "Tell me truly, old friend. Are you ready for this?"

Wind Woman swept the forest, and the firs creaked in the wind.

"I'd better be. We set out at dawn. Did you speak with Dzoo?"

"Yes." Red Dog licked his chapped lips and winced as though they hurt. "Dzoo heard the slaves whispering. Cimmis will be dressed as an ordinary warrior—blue war shirt, hide cape. Spotting him is not going to be easy."

"Will he walk with the Four Old Women?"

"No." Red Dog looked bone weary. "He will march in the rear."

Rain Bear frowned. "Why?"

"If you ask me, it's so he can run away if it all goes wrong."

"What does White Stone think of this?"

"He's not happy. He growled to me that since the chief insists upon exposing himself, he can defend himself."

Rain Bear plucked a twig from the ground and twirled it in his calloused fingers. If White Stone had gone so far as to tell his warriors the chief could defend himself...he was a very discontented war chief. Could Rain Bear use that?

Red Dog shot a curious look at Rain Bear. "He also told us to expect an attack around Gull Inlet. Anything to that?"

Rain Bear rubbed his jaw with the back of his hand. He hadn't given Gull Inlet more than a passing thought.

"What's at Gull Inlet?"

Red Dog drew the U-shaped inlet in the frost. "The trail turns along the sea cliff like this—and branches here. A wise war chief could use the cliffs to his advantage to box his enemies in and slaughter them like scurrying mice."

"I'll keep that in mind. How soon can you go back?"

Red Dog smoothed a hand over his dirty face. "Ecan knows I'm up to something. If he hasn't already hired someone to kill me, it's just a matter of time."

Rain Bear steeled himself. "I must ask that you go back, my friend."

Red Dog stared at the frosty ground. "Isn't there someone else?"

"My message to Kaska must be delivered by someone she trusts. That leaves you or Sand Wasp."

Red Dog's burly shoulders sagged. He closed his eyes for a few moments. "I can't guarantee I'll make it. The first war parties headed down the mountain trail two days ago. If they catch me coming up from the coast, don't assume I'll be able to talk my way out of it. Do *not* count on Kaska receiving the message I'm carrying."

Rain Bear gave Red Dog a sober look. "Do you have friends among the warriors who guard Kaska?"

"I did when I left. But if Ecan has gotten to them, told them I'm a traitor..."

An owl sailed over their heads, and its dark shadow flitted among the branches.

"One way or another, this is almost over. If you and I both live through this, I'll find some way to reward you for the risks. I don't know what or how I—"

"Forget it." Red Dog grinned wearily. "I'm doing this for Dzoo. I wouldn't be here but for her." He shrugged self-consciously. "And, who knows, perhaps someday she will be ready to marry again."

Rain Bear nodded in sudden understanding. Then he tugged open the laces of his belt pouch and drew out a bag of seaweed cakes. "Here. Roe made these. She flavored them with smoked salmon and hazelnuts."

"Thank you." Red Dog stuffed them in his belt pouch and playfully punched Rain Bear's shoulder.

"You know that if there were anyone else..."

"You don't have to say it."

Chapter Twenty-Four

T he village cooking fires blushed color into the towering lava cliff and gave the cold evening air a pungent smoky fragrance.

Ecan hurried along the base of an old lava flow that stuck out of the side of Fire Mountain like a low shoulder. He was just east of Salmon Village, where the trees gave way to a basalt cliff.

He kept glancing over his shoulder as he hurried along the dark trail. Cycles ago chunks of stone had cracked loose from the sheer cliff and tumbled down to create a wind-smoothed garden of boulders. These in turn provided a home for brambles of raspberries, currants, and, where the water seeped, cranberries. As night deepened, the place turned black and foreboding. Angular sections of basalt overhung the trail like monsters bent on hearing his passage.

Paintings covered the rocks. At the tops of the tallest boulders, white spirals glowed in the pale winter moonlight. Lightning bolts zigzagged out from the spirals and punctured the red hearts of wolves and bats.

When the path entered a stand of firs, it became pitch black. He could barely see two paces ahead, and slowed, letting his fingers glide along the porous rocks.

The sweet smell of moss seeped from the cave hidden in the boulders ahead. He placed his feet with care. In summer, the cave provided a cool haven, but in winter, the moisture turned to ice.

Ecan stepped around the last turn. The old lava tube resembled a dark womb cut into the cliff.

He stopped at the mouth of the cave. "Are you here?"

His voice echoed, coming back to him sounding tense and edgy.

No one answered.

"Wind Scorpion sent me."

Nothing.

He ducked inside and blinked at the utter darkness. Though he couldn't see it, he knew the cave stretched three tens of hands across and two tens high. A steady stream of water dripped from the ceiling and splashed into a small pool in the rear.

The scent of moss bathed his face.

Ecan braced his back against the entry. The stone fetishes in the bag tied to his belt clicked with his movements. He could feel them, hear them, whispering with excitement.

Since Dzoo had told him about the assassins Cimmis had sent to kill his boy, he'd been able to think of nothing else. His son's face and laughter filled Ecan's every waking moment. He *had* to do something. No matter how much it cost, or—

Someone breathed in the rear of the cave, near the pool.

Fear tickled the base of Ecan's throat. His hand dropped to the stiletto on his belt. "Show yourself."

A form moved in the darkness, no more than a stirring of shadows.

"Wind Scorpion sent you?" The voice was little more than a hoarse whisper.

"I am—"

"I know who you are, Starwatcher."

A tall body moved forward, gradually changing from a black silhouette to a gray apparition. He wore an obsidian-black cape decorated with red coyote tracks. The head remained deeper in shadow, and at first all Ecan could see were the eyes, gleaming with an unnatural light. As the apparition took another step, Ecan's breath caught in his throat.

It had to be a mask, but in the darkness, he would have sworn he saw a huge coyote's head perched atop a human body.

"Why would Wind Scorpion send you here?" the breathy voice asked.

"I asked if he knew who Cimmis might send to murder my son. He told me that if I came here, I might find someone who would be of service."

A long silence passed. Then the breathy voice took on an eerie sibilance. "I shall have to have a *talk* with this Wind Scorpion."

The shiver of fear ate through Ecan. He was used to inspiring terror, not experiencing it.

The masked figure stopped opposite Ecan and gazed outside at the starlit boulders. "You must be desperate to have called upon me, Starwatcher."

"I *am* desperate."

"What do you want?" The coyote mask with its

white teeth, pointed ears, and furred brows shone when he turned.

"I have a job for you."

"Indeed? How will you pay me? My fees are exorbitant."

Ecan took the bag from his belt and held it out to the dark figure.

The eyes behind the mask fixed on the bag. "What is it?"

"Open it and look."

The second Coyote's hand touched the bag, he stopped, as if frozen. "Where did you get these?"

"It doesn't matter, but I assure you, they are fetishes of great Power. With them—"

"I *know* what they are!" The voice boomed now, undertones laced with anger. *"Where did you get them!"*

"The Singer, Pitch, had them." Ecan tried to swallow his fear and failed.

"Fascinating."

Ecan waited, locking his knees to kill the weakness in his legs. Coyote remained as he was, still holding the leather sack, his head cocked as if listening to the voices.

"My son—" Ecan began.

"Yes.." The voice seemed to come from far away.

"Will you save his life?"

A pause. "You take great chances, crossing Cimmis this way."

Ecan said nothing.

"I see into your soul, Starwatcher. What else do you want?"

"A small favor."

"Really?" the voice mocked.

"Our people are moving to Wasp Village. Supposedly as a rebirth of our Power."

"But you and I know that is a lie," Coyote added.

"Yes, to survive we need to be closer to the resources in Raven Bay. From there we can exterminate the Raven villages closest to us before raiding villages offshore. But that isn't what concerns me now."

"You want me to kill Cimmis and Astcat."

Ecan shifted. Gods, how did he know?

Coyote continued. "Then, with you as the new chief, and the Council aging and dying, you will be the leader of the North Wind People. Who will be your great matron?"

"Astcat's daughter, Kstawl."

"Who is a child, easily intimidated to do your bidding." Coyote laughed. "How soon do you want them dead?"

"Within days of our arrival at Wasp Village. Not before. It wouldn't be wise to create a hole in our leadership before the village moves."

"You are smart, Starwatcher. But what if the Raven People succeed in defeating Cimmis's forces before you get there?"

"I must take that chance."

"What if I could assure you that Rain Bear's alliance was nothing more than a nuisance? Would that be worth something to you?"

A premonition ran up Ecan's spine. "It would be worth a lot."

"How much?"

"A great deal."

"Ah," the hollow voice breathed out. "When this is

all over, I want Rides-the-Wind, Evening Star, Singer Pitch, Rain Bear, and most of all...*Dzoo*."

"Consider them yours."

Coyote chuckled. It sounded like brittle bones rattling in the wind. His black cape seemed to breathe, filling with air and letting it out.

Chapter Twenty-Five

Astcat stepped out of her lodge and set two packs beside the door. Throughout the day slaves would be collecting the North Wind People's last belongings and carrying them down to the plaza to bundle them up for tomorrow's journey.

On the lava cliff high above, she heard Ecan chanting, *"Come Old Woman Above, be on your way to the Dark Place."*

A veil of ground shell swirled through the cold air and swept down across the village plaza where the slaves cooked breakfast. The sweet aromas of roasted lupine root and boiling oysters rose.

Just as they did every morning, people in brightly colored capes bowed to the east before they slowly returned to the warmth of their lodges. A few stopped to speak to their neighbors.

Watching this familiar ritual made her soul ache. Long moments passed as she tried to remember, to place the sights and sounds deep in her souls. She would never see it again. The North Wind People would be on the trail before dawn tomorrow. This was the last day she would be able to placidly stand and look out over the shining majesty of Fire Village at sunrise.

"A pleasant morning to you, Great Matron," Ecan said as he entered through the gate on his return from the cliff. He had plaited his obsidian-black hair into a single long braid. Shell, polished copper nuggets, bone, and stone jewels flashed on his wrists and around his throat.

"Good morning, Starwatcher. You delivered a beautiful prayer this morning." She looked into his eyes, seeing the cunning gleam of what? Triumph? She had never liked him.

"I see you're ready." He gestured to the packs.

"I'm ready for the trip, Starwatcher. Not for what leaving here will entail."

"Well, if our plan works, it will be the last battle. The Raven People will be broken for good."

Wind Woman whipped her cape about her frail legs. "For good? Do you really think we can deal them such a devastating blow?"

He smiled. "Well, let us say they will be no more trouble during our lifetimes. Everything is being handled. The great chief has left nothing to chance. A signal fire last night informed him that Rain Bear's pathetic alliance is on the move."

Cimmis had been planning this for moons, working out every possible permutation, every last detail of the timing—who was friend, who was foe, who *might* be a foe. But there were so many factors he could not anticipate. Exactly *when* would Rain Bear attack and *where*.

She blinked. *Already on the move?* Why hadn't her

husband said something? Or had he, and her soul had been loose, flitting about like a bat when it should have been paying attention?

"Thank you, Starwatcher." She turned to peer about.

"Er, you are more than welcome, Great Matron." He seemed confused over what she would thank him for.

"My husband was sending four warriors to carry some things. Where could they be?"

Ecan glanced at the packs. "Four warriors, for these?"

As she started to speak, she caught herself. By the Spirits of the night, was she that doddering? She took a breath. "Oh, I need not bore you, Starwatcher. I'm sure you have important things to do." She made a shooing gesture with her hands.

Her litter was behind the door. But even if he'd seen it, he wouldn't suspect. No one would. Not even her husband, who thought he had planned for everything.

The first sliver of sun glimmered on the eastern horizon. As Old Woman Above carried the glowing orb through the thin layer of clouds, yellow light lanced across the mountain slopes, falling in golden ribbons on the tree-tops. Pitch had been rudely pulled from Dzoo's lodge before he even had the chance to relieve himself. He was prodded past the Council Lodge, and up the path that led to Cimmis's lodge. Slaves watched them pass with wide eyes.

"Where are we going?" Pitch asked the guards as they shoved him from behind.

The younger man prodded him with his spear. "Just keep moving."

Pitch had a sick feeling in the pit of his stomach. From the instant he'd left Sandy Point Village, he'd feared being interrogated by Cimmis, or Ecan, or both. He wondered what it felt like to have someone cut a slit through his abdomen, reach inside his living body, and pull out a length of intestine. He knew that people screamed for hours as loops of their guts were slowly roasted. The sizzling sound was said to drive one mad long before pain and thirst could kill.

They halted before Cimmis's lodge, and the guard announced, "He is here, my Chief."

"Bring him."

One of the guards pulled the door flap aside and gestured for Pitch to duck under. He stood blinking to allow his eyes to adjust to the dim reddish glow cast by the fire. A hissing sound came from the middle of the room. He tried to focus on it and saw a black form shift.

Cimmis kneeled beside the fire with a large basket, a plain wooden bowl, and two dozen spears resting on the floor beside him. He wore a knee-length buckskin shirt, and his gray hair hung loosely about his shoulders.

Cimmis said, "Come over here."

As Pitch walked across the floor, Cimmis removed the lid from the basket, and the hissing grew louder. He reached inside, grabbed at something, and drew out a writhing snake.

Pitch jumped back.

Cimmis held the rattlesnake behind the triangular

head, but its long body twisted as it wrapped around Cimmis's arm. The tail made a constant angry shishing.

"Sit down. We must talk."

Pitch forced a swallow down his tight throat and squatted. His hide cape spread across the hard-packed floor.

Cimmis deftly hooked the snake's fangs over the lip of the bowl and worked its jaws to drain the venom. As the fluid trickled out, he said, "Who is the traitor?"

Pitch stared at him. "What traitor?"

"The man who carries messages between Dzoo and Rain Bear. He's very clever. I almost had him twice, but he slipped away."

Cimmis stood and dropped the snake back into the basket. Wild hisses and furious rattling rose. The basket rocked. How many snakes were in there?

"Ecan thinks it's Red Dog."

"I don't know Red Dog."

"No?" Cimmis smiled. "Well, perhaps he goes by another name when he is in your village. He's an old warrior, gray-streaked black hair, bent nose. About this tall." Cimmis held up a hand. "Have you seen him?"

"There are ten tens of refugees there. I can't know them all."

"Yes, I've heard the camps around Sandy Point Village are very large, and more people arrive every day, don't they?"

"They do."

He had the terrible feeling this was all staged, like the spring Kelp Dances. Cimmis knew the answer to every question he asked.

The old chief lifted one of the spears from the floor

and dipped the obsidian tip into the poison. "I'm debating which of you to kill."

Confused, Pitch asked, "Who? Me or this mysterious Red Dog?"

"I've already given orders to have Red Dog killed the moment he sets foot inside the palisade. I mean you or Dzoo."

"Why should you kill either of us?"

Cimmis smiled, laid his spear aside to dry, and picked up another. "Because I don't like being betrayed. Killing you sends a message to Rain Bear. Killing Dzoo sends a message to the Raven People."

He dipped the spear and rolled it in the venom.

"Personally, I think it would be far wiser to keep both of us alive. It's a bad decision to kill the messengers —one that, like that snake there, might turn around and bite you unexpectedly. It not only makes people reluctant to talk to you, but it invites retaliation. And someday, Great Chief, you really might want to send an important message."

Cimmis pulled the spear from the bowl and blew on it to dry it faster. The wet tip glittered. All he had to do was plunge that into Pitch's flesh.

Pitch tried to keep his voice reasonable as he continued, "Nor would I kill Dzoo. She is beloved by a great many people, both North Wind and Raven. Harming her might ruin your last chance for peace."

Cimmis nodded. "From the viewpoint of the Raven People, Dzoo is probably a more valuable hostage, but you are Rain Bear's son-in-law. Will he make more concessions to get you back, or Dzoo?"

"Rain Bear? Make concessions?" Pitch laughed.

Cimmis propped his spear on his drawn-up knee,

studied the basket, and grabbed out another snake. More hissing could be heard. "I've seen Rain Bear risk an entire war party to rescue one warrior. One friend. He will bargain."

"Then you are wiser to bargain for two rather than one. Any Trader can tell you that."

He gave Pitch a measuring glance. "Here is the choice I must make: As much as I would enjoy killing Dzoo, I know how important you must be to Rain Bear. Even if he doesn't die fighting the next few days, I want to punish him for making this alliance. Your death would do that. He would blame himself."

Yes, he would. Pitch felt his guts sink. With all the courage he could muster, he said, "If you decide to kill one of us, kill me."

Cimmis held the rattlesnake up level with his head. Pitch couldn't help but note the same flat stare in their eyes. "Since you are noble enough to offer yourself in Dzoo's place, I shall kill her. Now for the rest of your life, you can blame yourself for not saving her."

Pitch balled his fists, a sensation of panic rising within him as he blurted, "Kill her, and you'll die for it!"

Cimmis gave him a sidelong look as he ran a finger across the writhing snake's head. "Oh, why?"

"Because...because she is under the protection of the witch Coyote!"

Pitch saw the color drain from Cimmis's face. In that moment, the man was truly afraid. He almost dropped the rattlesnake as he replaced it in the basket.

"Go," Cimmis ordered hoarsely.

As Pitch scrambled to his feet and ducked out the door, his legs were charged. The guards stepped in behind him as he blinked in the bright sunlight. A numb sensation began in his head and spread through his limbs. The shaking didn't start until Pitch was halfway down the trail.

Then it struck him like a palsy.

Blessed gods, what have I done?

Chapter Twenty-Six

Red Dog kneeled in the rocks east of Salmon Village, watching people walk back and forth before the firelit palisade. Matron Kaska's lodge stood to the south of the palisade in a nest of interconnected lodges. If he sneaked in they'd certainly assume the worst and kill him as a spy.

He climbed to the top of the lava outcrop. Cold wind stung his face. From this vantage he could see the village clearly. Rather than being circular, like Fire Village, the lodges were arranged in a large square around a central plaza. Several interconnected lodges nestled together on the south. Those were Kaska's.

He scanned the uneven ground between his perch and the palisade and counted seven guards—three along the trail and another four scattered on high points. Which meant there were probably another twenty he couldn't see. There would be many more inside, stationed along the path that led to the matron's.

He stepped down into the dark shadows cast by the boulders. Fifty body lengths away, he spotted a guard on the talus slope. Short and pudgy, the man was turned away, gazing toward Salmon Village.

Voices carried on the cold night air: infants laughing, different strains of conversation, dogs growling. Deep in the belly of the village, someone played a drum. The beautiful rhythm drifted down the mountain like butterfly wings.

"Hallowed Ancestors," he hissed to himself, "this is something only a foaming-mouth dog would do."

He hung his atlatl on his belt and trotted up the trail toward the guard.

The warrior saw him almost immediately and yelled, "Halt! Who are you?"

"A messenger!" Red Dog spread his arms wide. "I carry important information for Matron Kaska!"

"What is your name?"

"Red Dog. From Fire Village." He continued up the low rise to where the guard stood. The man had shoulder-length black hair. He'd seen perhaps eight and ten cycles, but had the wary look of a seasoned warrior. He gestured with his stone-headed war club. "I know you. Walk toward the village. I'll take you to the war chief."

The trail curved to the south of the palisade. Red Dog had to bend his head far back to see the guards who stood looking over the lip of the twenty-hand-tall wall. They watched him pass in silence, their eyes occasionally glinting in the light of the Star People.

The guard took him not to the main gate, but to a smaller side gate he'd never been through before. It opened behind the interconnected lodges where Matron Kaska had her quarters and held her village council sessions.

"Walk to the middle lodge, and remember, since

you're not expected, you'll be watched by two tens of guards."

"I understand." Kaska wasn't taking any chances since Gispaw's death.

Red Dog passed through the gate and ducked beneath the door hanging the man indicated. The sight that met his eyes stunned him. He had seen Salmon Village many times from outside, but he'd never been allowed into the matron's lodge. Magnificent painted shields lined the walls. He saw Cougar and Mink, Wolf and Grizzly Bear, and many other sacred animals.

"Walk," the guard ordered.

"Forgive me, it's just that...these are the most beautiful shields I have ever seen."

"Yes, they are. The matron painted them herself."

Red Dog glanced over his shoulder at the man and continued walking.

"Go through the rear door."

When he ducked through, he entered another lodge, and a rich fruity scent filled the air. It took him a few moments to identify it: blue paint made from dried blueberries. The painter crushed the berries and mixed them with fat; the sweet fragrance smelled intense.

"Don't move," the guard ordered.

Red Dog heard soft calculated steps and turned to see Sand Wasp coming up behind him. The long scar across his forehead looked oddly pale in the light. He had a dangerous look about him, as though it wouldn't take much to push him to kill.

"Hello, Red Dog. I didn't expect to see you back so soon."

"I've covered so much ground my legs feel like they are made of wood."

Sand Wasp examined Red Dog carefully, noting the atlatl and bone stiletto on his belt.

"Take his weapons."

"Yes, War Chief."

The guard relieved Red Dog of his atlatl and stiletto, then untied his belt pouch and removed it. Finally, he patted Red Dog down. In the process he found the other two stilettos Red Dog kept tucked in his black leggings. He laid them all in a pile beside Sand Wasp's feet.

"Can't you find a pretty young girl to do that?" Red Dog groused. "That way I could enjoy it, too."

"He is ready, War Chief," the guard said as he rose.

Sand Wasp's eyes narrowed. "Thank you, Banded Eagle. You may return to your post. I will conduct the messenger to the matron."

"Yes, War Chief." The guard bowed and marched down the corridor.

Sand Wasp waited until he could no longer hear the man's steps. "Who sent you back so quickly?"

Red Dog whispered, "Rain Bear."

Sand Wasp's gaze bored into Red Dog's as though searching for any hint of treachery.

"Hey, what's wrong with you?" He narrowed an eye. "You hired me!"

Sand Wasp swallowed as if something were stuck in his throat. Then he smiled weakly. "Lies within lies, old friend. Treachery, double-dealing, no wonder I'm not sleeping."

"It will be over soon."

Sand Wasp's eyes were full of promise. "Yes," he said simply as he led Red Dog into the matron's lodge, "it will."

A woman called, "What is it, War Chief?"

"I bring a messenger, Matron."

"You may enter."

Sand Wasp walked up and pulled the door hanging aside.

Red Dog stepped into the lodge, Sand Wasp close behind, and looked around in genuine awe. More painted shields covered the walls, but these were even more extraordinary: glorious half-animal and half-human gods danced around the walls as though alive. He could almost hear eerie voices coming from their open beaks and muzzles.

"I see you have had a safe, if fast, trip, Red Dog," Kaska greeted.

Their last meeting had been at night beside a spring not far outside the gates. Red Dog had never really seen her up close in the light. A tiny, slender woman with a delicately beautiful face, she looked to have seen perhaps two tens of summers.

"I carry word from Rain Bear, Matron."

"Yes?" She stepped forward, concern in her soft dark eyes. "You saw him? Gave him my message?"

"He wants you to bring up the rear of the procession. Be ready to pull your warriors off near the signal point at Whispering Waters Spring."

Impulsively she reached beneath her cape and smoothed her fingers over her belted stiletto. After what had happened to her mother, he didn't blame her for going armed.

"Is that all?" Kaska asked.

Red Dog carefully laid out Rain Bear's battle plan, squatting to re-create the map Rain Bear had drawn for him. "So, there it is, Matron."

Her red-and-black cape hissed as she walked across the floor. "I thank you for your service, Red Dog. Are you heading back to Rain Bear tonight?"

"No, Matron." He winced as he stood on his aching legs. "I am making one last desperate attempt to rescue Dzoo and the young Singer Pitch."

Her dark eyes fixed on his. "That may be very dangerous. Given that Fire Village is packing for the move, your absence has surely been noted, and commented on."

He gave her a crooked grin. "I have lived for a whole turning of seasons because of *Dzoo-noo-qua*. Now that the pieces are being cast in the final game, I must be there for her."

Kaska placed a small hand on his shoulder. "You need to know that my spies tell me Cimmis has ordered your death."

He gave her a gap-toothed grin. "Then I had better hope I'm not caught before I'm done."

She clapped her hands. "Sand Wasp, provide Red Dog with a bag full of rations. Then have one of our warriors escort him to the trail."

Sand Wasp nodded. "This way."

Red Dog took one last look at the shields—he swore their eyes followed him—before he ducked beneath the hanging.

Once outside, Sand Wasp called, "Banded Eagle?"

The guard instantly ducked under the hanging and ran across the lodge. "Yes, War Chief?"

"Please see that this man is provisioned and escorted back out the side gate."

Banded Eagle bowed. "Yes, War Chief."

Sand Wasp watched Red Dog disappear beneath the far door hanging, then softly said, "He is gone, Matron."

"Come and speak with me."

Sand Wasp entered her lodge and stood stiffly, waiting for orders. Her perfect triangular face had gone tight with worry.

She searched Sand Wasp's face, as if the answers lay there. "What are we going to do? Cimmis has ordered me to have our warriors march near the front of the procession. What excuse can I give for marching in the rear?"

"We leave before dawn tomorrow. He will not wish to alter his plans. Not this close to our departure."

"No," she said softly, and her brows slanted down over her dark eyes.

He could see her thoughts whirling, trying to decide. "This plan of Rain Bear's, is it a good one?"

She nodded, staring down at the squiggles Red Dog had drawn in the dirt. "Well, we are committed, then. May Gutginsa bless us with luck."

Sand Wasp said, "Matron, perhaps it is time—"

"No, not yet," she said again softly, and bowed her head. "I'll tell our most trusted warriors when the time is right. But not yet, Sand Wasp. The longer they know, the longer they have for second thoughts. Cimmis and the Council would pay a matron's ransom to anyone who would betray us."

"Yes," Sand Wasp agreed absently, "at least that much."

"I will assign warriors to spread the word just before we reach Whispering Waters Spring."

"Yes, Matron." He stood stiffly, jaw clamped.

"Is that fear I see in your eyes?"

"Yes, Matron. Betrayal is a frightening thing."

Red Dog yawned, barely aware of his breath frosting on the cold air. The night was like charred sap: thick and black. He carefully skirted the trail that led from Salmon Village up the mountain to Fire Village. If guards were out, he had to hope the inky blackness would hide him.

Gods, he was bone weary, his thoughts thicker than matted buffalo wool. He plodded on, one weary step after another. His hips, knees, and ankles ached. Tomorrow would be the beginning of the end.

He had taken this last trip without the permission of either Cimmis or Ecan. Kaska's warning that Cimmis had ordered him killed hadn't come as a surprise. It was a miracle that he'd gone undiscovered for this long. But how was he going to get past the gates, overcome the guards, and sneak Dzoo and Pitch out?

If only he could clear his head for a moment, shake the terrible need to sleep from his body for one more day.

"There you are, old friend," a familiar voice called from the trees at the side of the trail.

Red Dog stopped, peering into the shadows cast by a lonely stand of firs. "What are you doing out here?"

"Caught me one of Rain Bear's spies. Want to see?"

One of Rain Bear's spies? Which one? And, more to

the point, what was he going to do about it? This close to the beginning of the attack, it could mean disaster.

Red Dog stepped into the shadows, blinking in the inky darkness. "I can't see a thing. Let's drag him out onto the trail where—"

The whistling war club came out of nowhere, catching Red Dog full on the side of the head. The blow flashed yellow lightning behind his eyes. He heard as well as felt the bones snapping as his head recoiled from the force.

As his swimming vision cleared, he realized he was on the ground, unable to move.

The last thing he saw was the faint outline of a giant coyote's head against the sky.

"Dzoo is mine, you silly fool. All mine."

The words barely penetrated the ringing in Red Dog's head as his vision faded to gray.

Dusk

"**S**oul Keeper?" I whisper.

"Yes, I'm here."

I breathe, "I...I'm afraid. I don't want...to die."

I no longer have the strength to open my eyes, but I know night is falling. The light that filters through my eyelids is dark gray. I'm almost used up. For the past hand of time, I've felt myself going cold inside, like an ember slowly fading to ash.

Wind Woman sweeps across the beach and flaps the Soul Keeper's cape. I listen as he resettles himself.

"There is a very old story," he begins, "about Wolf and Coyote in the Beginning Time."

I take a deep breath and let the words flow around me. There are tens of such stories. Which one does he want me to hear?

"In the Beginning Time, no one died. They ate a plant called the Everlasting Flower that kept them alive. Coyote's brother, Wolf, said, 'I think people should die,

246

but rise after two days' Coyote disagreed. He said, 'There are too many people in the world. I don't want people to rise. They should die forever."

"Coyote...won," I say.

"Yes, he did. But when Coyote's only son grew ill, he panicked. Coyote ran like lightning across the world searching for one single blossom from the Everlasting Flower."

My soul must be climbing out of my body, because I do not recall this version of the story. I say, "Did he... find it?"

"Oh, yes. Yes, he did." The Soul Keeper's voice is grave. "Magpie told him about a cave where the last flowers grew. Coyote ran hard and fast. The cave sat at the foot of a mountain. When Coyote entered the cave, he heard a buffalo's startled grunt; then the animal moved, and the fetid odor of rot filled the cave. Coyote trotted deeper, and he saw the flowers growing at the edge of a still pool. Bright and silver, like Sister Moon's flesh, they glowed in the darkness.

"As Coyote rushed forward to pluck one of the blossoms, a hideously diseased buffalo stepped out of the shadows. It was all but a skeleton. It could barely stand. Hair hung like filthy rags from its rotting hide.

"'What happened to you?' Coyote asked.

"Buffalo said, 'Do not pick that blossom.'

"'But I must. My son will die forever if I don't.'

"Buffalo wobbled toward Coyote on rotten legs. I ate those blossoms when I was a calf.

"'But how can that be?' Coyote asked. 'You look like you might die at any moment.'

"'Yes,' said Buffalo in a deep, rumbling voice, 'but I

won't. I should have died tens of seasons ago and gone to the House of Air to graze green meadows with my Ancestors. But I am condemned to live in this world. All of my family and friends are long dead. No living buffalo will talk to me. I am a rotting carcass to them. I rot a little more every day, without the hope of death.'

"Coyote backed up a step, his yellow eyes wide. 'Are you saying that the Everlasting Flower grants eternal life, but does not rejuvenate the body?'

"The moldering buffalo nodded. 'It just prevents death.' He hung his massive head and heaved a sigh. 'I pray every day to Buffalo Above to grant me the peace of death, but it never comes. So, I stand here to warn others of the cost of the Everlasting Flower.'"

A smile tugs at the corners of my mouth. If I'd been Coyote, I know very well what I would have done.

I say, "I would have...grabbed it...and run."

"Yes, I suspect most parents would. But what a supreme act of selfishness—condemning a son to live forever because you cannot bear to lose him. How do you think your son would feel when you died? Do you think he would praise your name? Or curse you?" I understand the lesson.

Does the old fool think I'm no smarter than a common rock? He's telling me I should stop struggling and look upon Death as salvation. It is so difficult.

My soul keeps wandering through memories of things I've done...bad things.

How can I believe that salvation awaits me?

I manage to get enough air to ask, "Will you...keep... my soul?"

He does not answer for a time, and I know he must

be thinking of what people will say. They will condemn him. Maybe even kill him.

He hesitates before he says, "I have not decided."

A swelling emptiness sucks at me.

Chapter Twenty-Seven

Cimmis stumbled in the night. He bit off a curse as he looked up at the cloudless sky. The stars reminded him of foam on the sea.

Odd, he hadn't had a poetic thought for cycles.

He sniffed the cold air, but only smelled his musty cloak, heavy now with the clinging smoke from the Council Lodge. He had spent the last hand of time in the stifling interior going over the final details with White Stone. Time after time they had sketched the organization plan into the dirt.

He had worked it down to a fine system, the warriors going from lodge to lodge, waking the occupants, sending them down the trail in just the right sequence so that everyone moved in an orderly fashion.

Oh, to be sure, there would be grumbles in the predawn darkness, and people would stumble and fall, but by first light, they would be well on the way to Salmon Village. With any luck at all, by the time Rain Bear beat, flogged, and cajoled his Raven rabble into position, it would be to find nothing left but their tracks.

And Rain Bear could attack all the tracks he wanted.

Unless, of course, he tried to keep his unwieldy force together and surrounded Wasp Village. With starvation on the land, that had as little chance for success as rain falling upward.

Cimmis made a face as a stitch of pain shot through his hip. Gods, and he had to walk for the full day tomorrow. Or at least try to. If his warriors had to carry him, it would shame him.

As he approached the lodge, he stopped, staring thoughtfully at the high domed shape. Tomorrow night, it would be vacant, dark and cold within.

He laid a gentle hand on the bark wall, feeling the moss and lichen that had grown there. Here, he had lived most of his life with Astcat, risen with her to the pinnacle of authority. Inside these walls his daughters had been born. Here, too, their young son had choked on a plum pit and died.

"It is so hard to leave it all behind," he said softly.

"Father?" Kstawl called, worry in her voice.

He bent, wondering what terrible thing had befallen Astcat, and ducked inside.

In the fire's red glow, he could see his daughter waiting by a steaming stew hanging from its tripod. Automatically, he glanced at Astcat's bed, only to find it empty.

"Where's Mother?" Kstawl asked. "You know better than to keep her so long at the Council meetings." Her eyes had fixed expectantly on the door behind him, as though awaiting her appearance.

Cold, like a curling breaker, washed through him. "She's not here?"

"I thought she was with you!"

Cimmis blinked, stepping across the lodge to stare dully at her bed. Her favorite robes were missing. He turned, expecting to see her small bag of ornaments resting in its place, only to find the dirt bare.

"Merciful gods," he whispered. "We have to find your mother! She may have wandered off, gotten lost."

She pointed to a basket, its contents covered by a wicker lid. "A man brought that not more than several fingers ago. He said it was for you."

Cimmis, an incipient panic rising, lifted the lid. In the dim interior, he could just make out Red Dog's blood-streaked face, the matted hair gluey with gore, the eyes half opened.

"I do not tolerate betrayal," he murmured. "Gods, we've got to find your mother. Quick. Go wake White Stone. I want this village turned upside down!"

As Rain Bear walked through the darkness, his bones had a rickety feel, and he kept stumbling over little irregularities in the rocky surface. The tension in his muscles reminded him he wasn't a young man anymore.

Overhead, the stars were gleaming in a frosty wash across the sky. They cast just enough light that Rain Bear could see the outlines of their camp. His warriors were bundled in their blankets, most snoring fitfully. For some, exhaustion vied with anxiety about the coming battle. For the rest, fatigue momentarily had the upper hand.

In my next life, I'm going to be a simple hunter. Hunters, he figured, got more sleep than chiefs did.

He rubbed his gritty eyes and pinched the bridge of his nose, as if doing so would squeeze the weariness from his head. It didn't.

He turned faltering steps toward his flickering fire where it glowed near the middle of their camp, and was surprised to see Evening Star sitting on his robes. She had a long stick that she used to play with the flames, lighting the end, then lifting it until the yellow tongues died before poking it back into the coals.

"I'm surprised that you're still awake."

She glanced up, shot him a radiant smile, and shrugged. "I knew you had to make one last inspection. I thought I'd see if you wanted company tonight?"

He glanced out at the slumbering warriors.

Her lips turned up wryly. "It's not as if they didn't already guess. Besides, we'll stay dressed. If I'm half as tired as you look, neither one us will have the energy for anything but sleep."

He nodded, loosened his cape, pulled off his moccasins, and climbed under the thick buffalo robe beside her.

For long moments, they held each other, the combined warmth of their bodies leaching the misery out of his bones and muscles.

"We made better time than I thought we would," she said.

"We got a break in the weather. If it had been snowing, we'd have covered half the ground."

She tightened her hold on him. "Will we make Whispering Waters Spring in time?"

"I think." He filled his lungs and tried to exhale the tension inside him. "So many things could go wrong."

"For Cimmis as well," she reminded. "It's up to the gods."

He reached up, running his fingers along the curve of her soft cheek. "If we live, will you be my wife?"

She hesitated. "You're a Dreamer."

"As long as I can Dream you."

She smiled, and he felt the foggy warm sensation of sleep creeping through his soul.

Yes, enjoy this. If you know nothing else, it's that you have this one moment of bliss. After tomorrow, you may have nothing but eternity.

Chapter Twenty-Eight

itch jerked awake and stared around the lodge, his heart hammering. In the faint glow of the fire, he could see Dzoo where she sat upright, a seagrass blanket over her shoulders. From the blank expression on her face and wide glassy eyes she might have been seeing something far distant across time and space.

He was starting back to sleep when he heard the voice: a hollow whisper. He could barely make it out, the words unintelligible. Sitting up, he frowned.

"Dzoo?"

At his call, the voice stopped short.

Dzoo raised a warning hand; her face remained slack, emotionless.

The faintest rustling came from behind the wall, as if hide clothing had scuffed the bark.

"Who was that?" Pitch demanded.

"Coyote."

Pitch blinked and felt his heart skip. "He's here? Just outside the lodge?"

"Oh, yes," she said simply. "He comes and goes. Mostly, he just listens at the wall. Tonight he came to warn me."

"Warn you of what?"

Her eyes moved; then her face began to melt into a ghastly smile. "That our joining approaches."

"Dzoo, we have to get out of here. Given the choice of Cimmis or Coyote, I'd rather take my chances dying while trying to escape."

"There is no escape," she said simply. "Ever since Antler Spoon's village, I've been working to lure him ever closer."

Before Pitch could ask, shouts came from outside. "Now what?" he muttered.

He reached for his shirt. As he slipped it over his head, the voices grew louder. He was already on his feet when a warrior threw back the door flap.

"Grab your things!" He was young, skinny, with a melon-shaped skull.

"Why? What's happening?"

"We're leaving Fire Village."

"Now? In the middle of the night?" Pitch stood and tied his pouch to his belt. "I thought we were leaving at dawn."

"Hurry. The chief wants us out of Fire Village within one finger of time."

Dzoo was still smiling her eerie smile. Gods, was she actually looking forward to this? Pitch swung his cape around his shoulders and ducked beneath the door flap. Another warrior, older, with hard eyes, stood outside.

"Follow me," the man said, and turned to walk up the trail.

Some of the warriors carried torches, which illuminated a knot of people who stood near the palisade gate.

Pitch leaned toward Dzoo, whispering, "I still think we should make a break for it."

The young guard prodded Pitch's back with a spear. "Quiet. Walk."

Pitch walked.

Star People glittered across the midnight sky with an icy crystalline brightness. In the plaza, people hugged each other, and he heard weeping as they said goodbye to this place that had been their home.

A coil of gray smoke rose from the dying plaza fire and trailed across Fire Village like a sleepy serpent. The air smelled pungently of burning sagebrush.

"Stop at the gate. The great chief is coming."

Pitch stopped and glanced at Dzoo. In the faint light, he could still see that enigmatic smile. It brought a shiver up his back. Through the gate Salmon Village was visible farther down the mountain slope. Distant warriors bore torches—but pinpricks of light—while people trotted around the palisade, carrying litters and bundles.

It took Pitch a moment to recognize Cimmis when he hobbled out of the darkness. Could this be the same Cimmis who had scared the soul half out of him earlier? His face was a mask of worry, the eyes glittering as if lost. The man walked with a slight limp, his withered left arm hanging from his shoulder. He wore a blue shirt beneath a hide cape. He looked like an ordinary warrior. Nothing more. He'd even coiled his gray hair into a bun at the base of his skull—like every other warrior standing close by.

At that moment, War Chief White Stone came trotting at the head of a small party of warriors.

"Great Chief," he called. "We have discovered what happened to the matron."

Cimmis spun on his feet, crying, "What? Where is she? Take me to her!"

White Stone stopped short, his head cocked, puzzlement on his face. "Well, it seems that she has already left."

"What? Left how?"

"Deer Killer was on guard at this same gate earlier today. He said that the great matron—carried on her litter by four warriors—passed through the gate."

"I don't understand!" Cimmis bellowed. "Was she a prisoner? Was she...was her soul loose?"

A frightened young man stepped forward, visibly shaken. "Great Chief"—his voice quavered—"I swear, she was fine. She sat atop her litter and gave orders to the warriors carrying her. She seemed completely in control of her senses. She—"

Cimmis stepped forward and slapped the man across the face. "Why? Why did she leave me?"

The blow wasn't that powerful, but the warrior collapsed to the ground. His voice was almost a wail when he shrieked, "I heard her say she'd see you at Wasp Village!"

Cimmis bent down over the huddled figure. *"Why didn't you stop her?"*

"She's *the Matron*]"

Cimmis blinked, stepping back. "Yes. She's the matron." He shook his head in confusion. "Did she say anything else?"

"Yes! I heard her bid Fire Village farewell. But that's all. I swear it on my life, Great Chief."

Cimmis straightened, turning to White Stone. "Then let's get this column moving. Someone inform my daughter."

Where she stood beside Pitch, Dzoo leaned her head back. The sound of her laughter rising on the cold night air was unnerving.

"Separate them," Cimmis ordered, flicking his finger between Pitch and Dzoo. Then he turned and stalked down the slope toward the muscular warriors who stood with the Four Old Women's litters on their shoulders, awaiting orders to move. The old women resembled dark mounds of flapping hides. More litters lined the trail, loaded heavily with packs and roped with grass cords.

"I'll see you later," Pitch cried hopefully as Dzoo followed the shaken Deer Killer off into the night.

People stood alongside the Four Old Women's litters, calling last words. Several wept openly and tore at their clothes.

The warrior called Thunder Boy hissed, "I swear it's the end of our world."

His companion, Ground Hog, a young man with wide blue eyes and copper-colored hair, shook his head. "Not yet. The reckoning is yet to come...when we meet Rain Bear."

Wind Woman's cold breath fanned Pitch's hair around his shoulders. He took a deep breath and gave Fire Village one last look.

Chapter Twenty-Nine

Hunter tried to look confident as he strode toward the gate. He could feel Dzoo's presence, like a malignant wind, blowing a chill onto his back. His hair was prickling, as if someone rubbed a phantom fox hide over his skin. Of all the luck, why did Wind Scorpion constantly order him and Deer Killer to guard the witch?

The Raven People slaves milling around the fires hushed as they passed. They resembled lean hungry wolves. The few Raven People who'd decided to remain had already piled their belongings in front of the lodges they would be claiming and had posted family members to protect them, but he suspected there would still be fights. He could feel the tension in the air. When the elite were finally gone, there would be a great tumult of greed.

Dzoo's soft steps padded behind Hunter as he walked through the gate. He glanced back to see Deer Killer, shaken and wobbly after his experience with the great chief. He was the last man who should have been assigned to this duty.

Soon, the three of them would be marching out in front of the procession like the triangular head of a snake. All night long, he'd been praying to every Ancestor Spirit he could think of that Deer Killer wouldn't bolt or fall first in the battle.

Blessed gods, what will I do if I suddenly find myself alone with her?

The thought must have stopped him in his tracks, because Dzoo walked up beside him. She stared him in the eyes for a long time, as though reading the path of his soul, before she walked ahead.

Hunter fought to steady his nerves.

Deer Killer gave him a weak grin. "Try not to throw up. Everyone is watching."

Hunter grabbed him by the cape ties. "From now on, *you're* leading the way." Then he shoved Deer Killer ahead.

Deer Killer glanced over his shoulder and said, "I was just joking!"

Tsauz lay in the cold windswept darkness, listening. All around him, fragrant branches whispered in the moving air, the sound mixing oddly with the snores of tens of warriors.

They had traveled for two days through the forest and up into the alder thickets west of Eelgrass Village. Rides-the-Wind slept beneath the hides to his left, his back to Tsauz. The rest of the camp was behind them, scattered across the slope.

Tsauz reached out and put a hand on the old Soul Keeper's shoulder. He just needed to touch someone.

Each step he took, he was getting closer to home, but he had to keep reminding himself that he wasn't going home. Fire Village would never be his home again.

Rides-the-Wind patted his hand and whispered, "Are you all right, Tsauz?"

"I'm not sleepy."

"What's wrong?"

Tsauz blinked at the darkness. "Chief Cimmis could still win the battle, couldn't he?"

"Yes."

"What will happen if he does?"

Rides-the-Wind yawned. "The North Wind People will probably continue their march to Wasp Village, where they will live until the Raven People finally overwhelm them."

"Are you sure?"

"Some things are inevitable." Rides-the-Wind put a warm hand on Tsauz's arm. "You've done everything you can, Tsauz."

He sucked in a deep breath and held it. He'd flown on Thunderbird's rain-scented back, diving and soaring through the glistening Cloud People. He had glimpsed the future, but Thunderbird had told him they were just things that *might* be.

He looked up and searched the blackness.

Father once told him that Mother had become a tiny point of light in the belly of Old Woman's enormous sky. He tried to imagine where she would be shining. Every day since she'd died, he'd longed for her.

Tsauz closed his eyes and lifted his hand, holding it out to her.

If I die, Mother, will you please come for me?

"Tsauz, you mustn't dwell on these thoughts. They siphon your strength. Bad thoughts are like tiny holes in a water bucket. Pretty soon they'll make you dry and empty."

Tsauz closed his eyes. He tried to calm himself by imagining the countryside. "I know."

He smelled water.

They hadn't traveled long enough to be near Whispering Waters Spring. They must be on Water Storage Plateau. He and Father had camped here on the way north. The flat expanse of lava was covered by wind-carved potholes. When it rained or snowed, the holes filled and served as cisterns.

Rides-the-Wind flipped onto his side. His hair smelled of wood smoke and sweat. It had been a long hard march, and Rides-the-Wind had held his hand the entire way, guiding him around brush and away from holes where he might fall and break his leg.

"Where are we? Would you tell me what you see?"

Rides-the-Wind sighed and lifted his head. "Tens of black humps."

"Sleeping warriors?"

"Yes. And more stand on the high points, keeping guard over Water Storage Plateau. Every so often the obsidian points of their spears glint in the night."

"Elder, do you think..." He paused, hating to ask, unable to help himself. "Do you think Thunderbirds can lie?"

"Why do you ask?"

Tsauz smoothed his cheek over the soft buffalo hide. "I've just been wondering, that's all."

"Well, I've never heard of a Spirit Helper lying, though they often play tricks on people."

"No, I mean, would a Spirit Helper try to turn a battle in favor of one side?"

"Of course he would."

Wind Woman breathed across the plateau, and the foot of their buffalo hides flapped. Cold air ate at Tsauz's bare feet. He didn't say anything for a while, just breathed in and out as he remembered what Thunderbird had said about his father.

Apprehensively, the old Soul Keeper asked, "Which side do you think Thunderbird might be favoring?"

Tsauz swallowed hard. "The North Wind People."

"Why would you say that?"

"I—I don't know. It's just a feeling." He rubbed a hand over his aching heart. "Right here. It hurts. Like I can already feel a spear point lodged in my lungs."

Rides-the-Wind put his hand over Tsauz's heart. "I wouldn't worry. That's probably the dried fish you had for supper. I swear Rain Bear has had that fish for cycles. It looked a little green to me."

"Did it?" Tsauz asked hopefully. Anything would be better than thinking his Spirit Helper was Trickster in disguise.

"You wouldn't sound so happy if you'd seen it. I would have rather chewed on a moldering dog leg. I was just too tired to go out and hunt one down."

"Elder, do you fear death?"

"Not as much as I fear Rain Bear's cooking."

Chapter Thirty

Gispaxloats glanced uneasily at Kitselas. Their small fire had burned down to ashes, and as the first faint light of dawn sent rose colors through the thin high clouds, it was apparent that the great matron's soul had fled. What was even worse, they were lost. He had no idea where the trail was that they were supposed to take, and without Astcat to tell them, all he could do was stumble on ahead and hope he was doing it right.

Blue Hand and Spotted Arm both sat across the fire, blankets around their waists as they yawned and rubbed their eyes. That didn't hide the worry as they shot quick glances at the matron.

She lay in her litter just west of the fire, where the evening breezes would drift the fire's warmth over her. This morning, however, her face was slack, her mouth hanging agape. Drool slipped silver down the side of her chin.

Gispaxloats shook his head, muttering, "What now?"

They had stopped for the night and set up camp in a shallow cove just up from a stream crossing. The location was bounded on three sides by basalt outcrops and partially screened by brush. Thick grass had made for good bedding, and enough snags had been snapped from the nearby conifers to keep the fire going all night.

"We follow our orders," Kitselas said with resignation as he watched the old woman's shallow breathing. "She is the great matron. That's all there is to it."

"But it doesn't make any sense!" Spotted Arm muttered as he stood, watched his frosty breath in the cold air, and then walked into the brush to relieve himself.

"Who cares if it makes sense?" Blue Hand, his younger brother, kicked his blankets off, rose, and followed. From behind the screening of brush, he added, "Kitselas is right. She's the great matron of the North Wind People. We keep going."

"Cimmis is going to pull our hearts out of our chests and boil them while they're still beating."

Gispaxloats pulled his war bag over, lifted the flap, and stared inside. "There's enough food here for one breakfast. I say we cook it, eat it, and do as the matron told us."

"Yes. Let's," Kitselas agreed. "We might as well eat it all. I've always wanted to die with a full stomach."

Blue Hand stepped out of the brush and ran his fingers through his hair as he stared at the listless Astcat. "Why did she choose us for this?"

"Because we're the best." Gispaxloats tossed more firewood onto the coals. "Kitselas, take that bladder over there and walk down to the stream. Bring me some water. I heard that the great chief always trickles water into her mouth when her soul comes loose."

Kitselas took the water bladder and stood. "What if the great chief catches us before we can complete the task we've been given?"

"Then he'd better find the matron receiving the best of care." Gispaxloats stared hopefully at Astcat. "I just hope she brings her soul back in time to explain for us."

Reluctantly Blue Hand said, "Well, let's get about it. We have the matron's orders. I'll build up the fire. You go cut green branches. If she wants a big smoke, we'll make it so that the whole country can see."

"Yeah," Spotted Arm muttered as he stepped out of the bushes. "It's a toss-up as to who is going to find us and kill us first."

"Do you see the smoke, my Chief?" Young Thunder Boy called.

"What smoke?" Cimmis asked.

Over ten tens of people twisted at once to look back at Cimmis. He felt like he was gazing into a writhing sea of disembodied faces. The North Wind procession resembled a snake with a chipmunk in its belly as it wound down the ridgetop trail. The triangular head of the snake was composed of three people. Immediately behind them, a group of around five tens of warriors marched. A bulbous circle of spear throwers encircled the Four Old Women's litters. Another group of warriors brought up the rear, and the tail of the snake slithered out behind.

Just ahead of him, the Four Old Women shifted on their litters to see what the commotion was.

Thunder Boy said, "Someone is sending a signal down along the base of the mountain." He swung around and pointed to the southwest. "You can still see the column of white smoke where the wind has blown it back into the trees."

Cimmis stepped away from his guards to get a good look at the location. He knew this terrain; every groove and bump was familiar. If Rain Bear was sending the message, he couldn't be too far from the spire. Probably...there. Less than two hand's run from Water Storage Plateau.

"Are you sure that was a message and not just some hunter drowning a campfire?"

Thunder Boy swallowed hard. "It was a white plume of smoke, Great Chief. We thought you should know."

Cimmis turned, beckoning to Wind Scorpion, who walked several paces back. The grizzled old warrior trotted forward.

"Yes, Great Chief?" When Cimmis pointed, the cunning old eyes turned to where the faint white plume of smoke rose over the distant trees.

"Do you know what that might be?"

Wind Scorpion's eyes narrowed. "A signal of some sort, I suppose. The first thing that comes to mind is that Rain Bear has split his forces. One group is signaling to another. He surely wouldn't attack here. This ground is too open."

He gestured down the slope. A fire five summers ago had denuded the slope where the trail followed the ridge down toward patches of trees.

As they walked, Cimmis couldn't help but glance periodically at the plume of white. It seemed to strengthen, and then diminish, only to be replenished again. It looked to him more like a beacon than a signal smoke. Beacon? For what? For whom?

As if he had overheard Cimmis's thoughts, Wind Scorpion said, "The threads of Power are being drawn tight."

As the sun rose ever higher in the sky, Hunter kept shooting wary glances at the witch, as did Deer Killer; but Dzoo had her unblinking eyes focused on Ecan. She seemed possessed of an absolute stillness. With her dark hood flapping around her beautiful face, she looked almost godlike.

"Witch!" Hunter called. "Are you sleepwalking?"

She didn't appear to hear him.

"I asked you a—"

"Red Dog's soul is stalking yours." She said it so calmly.

Deer Killer cried, "Red Dog? No one's even seen him for days. Word is he ran off to Rain Bear."

Hunter glanced warily around; the very notion of something stalking his soul chilled his blood. "What makes you think he's dead?"

"A witch whispered it to me last night."

"We were guarding you all night. No one came close." Deer Killer thumped his chest in emphasis.

"I shall miss the two of you," she said simply. "Give my regards to Red Dog's spirit when you see it. Tell him I will always honor his memory."

"That makes no sense," Hunter muttered, but he kept glancing over his shoulder to see if a ghost was there.

As Dzoo walked, a heaviness lay in her heart. She had liked Red Dog. When Coyote had whispered that he'd killed him outside of Salmon Village, her heart had deadened. She had known that Red Dog cared for her, had seen it grow in his eyes while he healed under her care.

Scoundrel that he was, she would miss his wit, the dogged persistence of his character. He would never have filled the hole left by her Pearl Oyster: She had had one husband, one love of her life.

She could feel Ecan's presence long before she was aware of him marching up to her.

"Hunter, Deer Killer, leave us." The Starwatcher made a gesture with his hand.

The guards faded off to each side, leaving a bubble of space around them. Dzoo sniffed, catching the subtle odor of damp moss. "You are tainted, Starwatcher." She glanced at his pinched expression. "What was his reaction when he laid hands on his fetishes again?"

Ecan missed a step. And recovered, one hand to his breast. "What...what are you talking about?"

She let the faintest of smiles bend her lips. "I'm talking about the bargain you struck with Coyote. Was Red Dog part of it, or was killing him Cimmis's idea?"

"Cimmis deals with Coyote?" Ecan seemed genuinely surprised.

"Of course. But for a thread of Power, Coyote would have already killed Tsauz and removed him from the complex web we find ourselves in. Curious, isn't it, that he didn't kill Matron Evening Star that night in her lodge?"

Ecan was watching her as if she could spin miracles. "Coyote was sent to kill both Evening Star *and Tsauz?*"

"You owe your son's life to the Soul Keeper, Rides-the-Wind. Why do you think the old man went to Rain Bear in the first place? It was to save the boy."

"For which I shall reward him when the time comes." Ecan seemed suddenly reserved, as if putting new pieces into an old puzzle. "As to Evening Star, I would prefer to deal with her on my own."

"If *he* will let you."

"I control—"

"Is that what you think?" She laughed at the man's temerity. "What makes you think he would *serve* you?" She lowered her voice to a hiss. "You're no doubt congratulating yourself on having drawn him away from Cimmis. Do you really think Coyote would choose to ally himself with a dead man?"

He barked a sharp if unsettled laugh. "You keep calling me that, and my heart keeps beating."

She shrugged. "Even without your prompting, he would have killed Cimmis and Astcat sooner or later."

Ecan's face went ashen. "I would *never—*"

"You still don't understand, do you?" She searched his eyes, seeing all the vainglorious arrogance welling behind them.

"Understand what?"

"The reason he took your payment, the reason he'll kill Astcat and Cimmis in the end. You see the reason he left Evening Star alive is because he needs her to be his matron. When this is all over, *he will be great chief.*"

Chapter Thirty-One

From his place in the line of march, White Stone watched as Ecan staggered away from Dzoo. The Starwatcher stopped in the middle of the trail, his eyes focused on something in the distance. White Stone gazed curiously that way, but could only see Raven Bay, Gull Inlet, and the distant islands.

Dzoo, meanwhile, was looking down the slope ahead of them, where patches of firs grew. He followed her gaze first to the low rise to his left—at which she smiled for a time—then down to the grove of firs. Dzoo's face turned stoic enough to have been carved from some pale hardwood.

White Stone lifted his war axe and called, "Hunter! Close up on the prisoner." She wouldn't think of trying to escape into those trees, would she?

As the procession continued plodding down the winding trail toward the trees, the ocean breeze mixed with scents of mud and damp firs to form a heady fragrance. The Four Old Women on their litters hissed questions to each other. Everything was going as planned, and they were ahead of schedule.

He watched his two lead scouts trot into the trees. He had almost forgotten Dzoo's interest in the trees when two warriors in mangy hide capes charged out from the timber. A half heartbeat later, a screaming horde broke from cover. Keen obsidian points glinted on the tips of their spears.

White Stone shouted, "Get into position!"

Just as Cimmis had planned, three tens of spear throwers separated from the circle around the Four Old Women, and the men behind moved forward to take their places. The first group ran downhill to form a solid wall against the attackers.

The litter bearers quickly set their burdens down and huddled around the Council and the matrons accompanying the party.

All except Kaska, who stepped off her litter, shoved through the ring of guards, and looked down the slope at the Raven People. White Stone smiled at the thought of her confusion. By now, according to her plan, Sand Wasp should have been looking to her for orders.

Instead, the Salmon Village war chief stood tall, his jaw set, not two paces from White Stone. White Stone said, "Sand Wasp, have your warriors form a second line behind the first!"

"Yes, War Chief."

For a moment, when he turned around, Sand Wasp's gaze touched Kaska's. The man seemed to freeze; then he motioned to his warriors. "You heard White Stone, form a second line!"

Three tens of Kaska's warriors ran down the slope and knelt behind the first row of defenders.

"Ready!" White Stone called as the Raven People dashed up the slope, their spears over their heads. Casting uphill was risky at best, but on the run?

As they neared casting range, the Raven People split in half in a clumsy pincer movement.

Blessed gods, they're fools! White Stone watched the ineffective tactic develop. The attacking warriors were panting from their long run up the hill. Worse, their formation was disintegrating as they scrambled over the rough hillside.

White Stone filled his lungs. "First line, cast!"

Sunlight flashed down the polished shafts as the spears arced into the sky, seemed to hover like birds for a few eternal instants, then plunged down.

The lethal missiles met flesh; the screams began—ragged, breathless. At least half of the Raven People fell. Most writhed on the ground, trying to jerk the shafts of wood and stone from their bodies. Some stood dumbfounded, staring at the carnage. Others threw down their weapons and ran, but a few kept coming.

The few enemy spears gleamed as though afire as they lanced through the sky. Three of the throwers in the first line went down. Then two more.

"Second line, cast!" White Stone ordered.

Kaska's warriors took aim and threw.

White Stone turned to look at Dzoo. She stood tall, utterly unafraid, watching the battle. Cimmis had hoped that by leaving Dzoo out front, it might stem the ardor of the enemy spear throwers. The great chief had apparently miscalculated.

"Ready!" White Stone's remaining warriors nocked spears in their atlatl hooks.

"Let them get closer, closer..." When the Raven

People were less than two tens of paces away, he shouted, "Cast!"

Several went down instantly, but the others charged forward, screaming like gutted birds.

"Use your clubs!" he shouted, and as his men rushed to obey, tens of spears clattered onto the ground.

The war chief who led the enemy warriors headed straight for White Stone. He was stocky, with a scarred face and granite-headed war club.

White Stone lifted his axe, braced his feet, and waited for the man to come to him.

"Meet your death!" The Raven warrior swung his club at White Stone's head.

White Stone sidestepped, pivoted, and drove his axe into the panting man's back as momentum carried him around. The Raven warrior let out a surprised yip as the blow severed his spine. He tumbled to the ground, screaming, his upper body flopping helplessly. Several others went down around White Stone as Sand Wasp waded into the onslaught.

Then, abruptly, the few remaining Raven warriors broke and ran.

"Hold!" White Stone bellowed to keep his warriors from dashing in pursuit. Nevertheless, a handful did, carried away by the moment. He ground his teeth. Better if they were killed by the fleeing Raven warriors than if they had to face his wrath for disobeying orders. At the calls of their fellows a couple turned back, glancing sheepishly in his direction.

Cimmis came striding down the line. His gray bun had come unpinned and hung around his wrinkled face. White Stone watched as Matron Kaska lifted the hem of her cape and fell into step behind Cimmis.

As Cimmis passed the Four Old Women, he ordered, "Lift these litters! Be ready to move at my command!"

In less than five heartbeats they'd hoisted the litters and stood stiffly waiting.

"Where is Rain Bear?" Cimmis demanded when he arrived. His sharp old gaze darted over the dead and wounded that scattered the slope.

"I didn't see him, my Chief."

"Where could he be? Still in the trees?"

White Stone shook his head. "It isn't like Rain Bear to hide in the trees while his men go out to meet the enemy. He usually leads the charge."

"Hunter?" Cimmis sharply called. "Go and search the bodies for Rain Bear."

"Yes, my Chief!"

White Stone turned to watch Hunter kick over the first body and barely heard the soft grunt behind him.

He turned back in time to see Sand Wasp stagger as Kaska repeatedly drove a stiletto into his back. The war chief didn't even try to fight back, but wavered as his knees buckled and he collapsed at her feet.

Sand Wasp gasped, "Forgive me, Matron. I did not wish to...to do it, but..." His gaze flickered to Cimmis, as if caressing his face.

White Stone clutched his axe a little more tightly and noticed the two new shiny copper nuggets that gleamed on the dying war chief's throat.

Kaska shouted at her warriors, "You obey my orders now, and mine alone! Return to your positions. We must make it to Wasp Village as soon as possible!"

White Stone glanced at Cimmis and raised a questioning eyebrow. *Kill her now?*

The great chief shook his head.

White Stone wasn't sure he agreed, but perhaps this really wasn't the time.

Cimmis whispered, "I'll have my special agent attend to it tonight. When everyone else is asleep."

White Stone nodded.

Kaska's warriors muttered, stared forlornly at Sand Wasp, then started back to regroup in front of the litters.

Kaska had turned her hard glare on Cimmis, knowing full well he was going to kill her, and calmly went back to climb onto her litter.

"That's a brave woman," White Stone said softly.

Cimmis ground his teeth. "Yes, much too brave. I want her separated from her warriors."

"But my chief, we need every—"

"It would demoralize our men to have to kill their own people, War Chief. Do as I say."

He bowed stiffly. "Of course."

Occasional screams still rose from the firs down the slope, but White Stone had no way of knowing if they were torn from his men, or from Raven warriors.

Hunter trotted back up the slope and said, "My chief, I have looked into the eyes of everyone lying on this slope, alive or dead. Rain Bear is not here."

Cimmis wiped his mouth with the back of his hand. "Then who are these people? They are Raven warriors, aren't they?"

"They are Raven warriors," White Stone said. "It took me a few moments, but I recognized the man who attacked me. He was the war chief of Shell Maiden Village."

Cimmis seemed to be considering that. "I may have underestimated Rain Bear."

"I hope not. He is the one man in the world I would not wish to underestimate. Especially not now when we are tired from marching all night. Our quivers are half empty, my chief. If this was some kind of diversion, it did work to weaken us."

Cimmis rubbed his chin. "Tell our warriors to pick up every spear that can be thrown, even if the point's broken. Then we'll go. We won't be safe until we're in Wasp Village."

White Stone lifted his axe and shouted, "Move through the meadow. Collect every spear!"

People ran through the grass, picking up spears, pulling stilettos from the bodies of dead warriors.

He turned, looking down the mountain's flank to where a green thumb of land protruded into Raven Bay. A faint blue haze of smoke could be seen.

Their haven still lay a hard march away.

And somewhere out there, Rain Bear and his warriors were waiting.

Chapter Thirty-Two

R ain Bear sat quietly in the shadowed patch of timber that overlooked Whispering Waters Spring. Below him, he could see the grassy meadow where he fully expected Cimmis to stop for a midday rest.

To his right, Evening Star crouched over the body of Cimmis's scout. He had already been stripped, Falcon Boy donning his clothes so that he could wave the all-clear when the North Wind procession arrived at the spring. If all went according to plan, they would begin to relax, and then, as they let down their guard, Rain Bear's warriors would charge down the hill.

The advantage of surprise would be his. Cimmis's people would be tired, off their guard. The terrain here favored an attack, allowing momentum to carry his people through their lines. Better, the defenders would be casting uphill at rapidly moving and bobbing targets.

As soon as his people had broken the lines, Kaska's warriors would rally to their aid. If it worked as planned, within moments, Dogrib would have taken the

Four Old Women. That was the key. Hold them, and all North Wind opposition would crumble.

He glanced back at the low knob above Raspberry Creek where the curious white plume of smoke had appeared. They had seen it a hand of time ago as they moved into position. It looked like someone was burning green branches to make so much smoke. Like a beacon.

But for whom? He had dispatched Sleeper and a handful of scouts to find out, fearing a flanking move by Cimmis.

"He's dead," Evening Star said as she stood. The scout's body looked pathetic and forlorn in the meadow grass. "Look at him there. Just one more young man who has lost his future. All of his Dreams are gone, Rain Bear. Within days, his flesh, too, will be stripped away. By this time next year, the grass will have grown through a few white bones. Porcupines will gnaw at his remaining ribs, and mice will build a house inside his skull."

"It's how Song Maker made the world." Rain Bear gave a shrug. "It's such a waste, but what can we do? Name a single people who don't make war, who don't raid."

She nodded. "I know, but I don't have to like it."

He glanced at the warriors who had lain down in the shade behind him. He wanted them as completely rested as they could be.

A day this warm was unusual for the middle of the winter. Just days ago snow had coated these same trees. Now the needles looked green in the bright midday sun. It felt like spring.

Evening Star cocked her head. "Did you hear that?"

"What?"

"It sounded like someone shouted in the distance."

He listened, hearing the soft sigh of the breeze through the fir branches, the melodic trill of a chickadee.

"Definitely shouting," she said, her blue eyes narrowing.

Rain Bear shrugged, wondering if age had robbed him of hearing as well as flexibility in his joints and muscles. "If there's anything to report, Talon will let us know. He and his scouts are keeping—"

"Great Chief!" Sleeper called from below. The war chief was waving for all he was worth.

Rain Bear frowned. "Curious. Stay here. I'll go down to get his report."

He started down the ridge, nodding to his warriors as they dozed, checked their weapons, and waited.

As he stepped into the sunshine, it was to see Sleeper's small party of scouts weaving through the trees, followed by what seemed to be a litter. The dress of the bearers couldn't be mistaken for anything but North Wind.

Sleeper's expression immediately set Rain Bear on edge.

"Did you find that fire?" Rain Bear asked.

"Did we ever." Sleeper's eyes were wide. "You were right. It was a signal for us. We crept up the Raspberry Creek bottom and look what we found." He extended his arm toward the litter bearers.

Rain Bear read the awed expressions of Sleeper's warriors. These were the men who had shadowed Ecan, definitely not callow novices.

He stepped forward to meet the litter. The four young men carrying it were muscular, fit-looking. Beautifully dyed blue war shirts hung to midthigh, and each was decorated by a wealth of stone, shell, bone, and copper beads. They carried themselves well, each as alert as a hawk sailing into an eagle's territory.

Rain Bear raised a hand. "What is your purpose?"

As one, they slowed to a stop, the right-hand man asking, "Can you take us to the great chief, Rain Bear? We come in response to his promise of safe passage."

That caught him by surprise. "I am Rain Bear. If your purpose is peace, your safe passage will be honored."

The speaker smiled uneasily, and at a gesture, lowered the litter. "I am Gispaxloat. I am here on the orders of our great matron. We place ourselves under your protection, Great Chief, and invoke the honor of your oath."

"What is this?" Rain Bear stepped forward, hands raised. "I grant you my protection, but why are you here? Who's in the litter?"

Gispaxloat carefully reached over, pulling back the corner of a stunningly decorated and painted robe to reveal an old woman, eyes sunken, her mouth agape. He'd have thought her dead but for the faint rising and falling of her chest.

Gispaxloat stood stiffly at attention. "Great Chief, I present the matron of the North Wind People, Astcat. She has asked us to tell you that when her soul returns, she wishes to speak with Matron Evening Star, Soul Keeper Rides-the-Wind, and the boy Tsauz."

Wind Woman blew Evening Star's long red hair over her face. She brushed it away and stared out at the vista. From the top of the timbered ridge, she could see down the coastline and along the rugged terrain. On the distant point below them, Wasp Village could be seen. It seemed so peaceful on such an unseasonably warm day.

Movement caught her eye, and she turned to watch a man trotting down the hillside. His white hair shone like polished seashells. Glancing down the backside of the ridge, she wondered what was keeping Rain Bear. He'd been gone nearly three fingers of time.

"Is that Dogrib?" Rides-the-Wind asked and pointed with his walking stick. He sat on a rock not far from the dead scout's body.

"With blazing white hair like that? It's got to be. He's back sooner than I'd have thought."

"Perhaps they're closer than we think and he didn't need to run farther."

Dogrib trotted up and stopped. He bent, his chest rising and falling as he caught his breath. His gaze searched the people nearby before he whispered, "Where is Rain Bear?"

Evening Star said, "Sleeper returned from a scouting trip. Rain Bear went to take his report. What did you find?"

"I met our scout, Salt Boy." He gave Evening Star a suspicious look, as though not certain he should trust her with the information. "He was running down the trail as fast as he could. There was a battle up on the old burned ridge."

"I don't understand? Who was fighting?"

"The renegade chiefs who refused to support Rain Bear mounted their own attack at the spring."

Evening Star took a deep breath, expecting the worst. "And?"

Dogrib shook his head. "Salt Boy said Cimmis's warriors cut through them like an obsidian knife through hot fat. Apparently Bluegrass's faction managed to gather about six tens of warriors. They were badly outnumbered to start with and bungled the attack."

"The fools!" Rides-the-Wind spat the words and clutched Tsauz's hand more tightly.

Evening Star absently stared at the old alder leaves blowing up the trail. "Cimmis isn't anyone's fool. He'll think it was a trick, a way to make him lower his guard for the real attack."

Dogrib nodded, a new respect in his eyes. "I agree, Matron."

"What of Kaska's forces? Did Salt Boy see them?"

"He watched the battle from that point, Matron." Dogrib pointed to a hilltop north of the spring, where a thick stand of firs grew. "Salt Boy said he couldn't tell one group of warriors from another, but they all worked as one, obeying Cimmis's orders. However, when the battle was over, he's sure he saw Matron Kaska plunge her stiletto into Sand Wasp's back. Many times."

Rain Bear's familiar steps sounded behind her, but she didn't turn. "What happened then? Did Cimmis kill Kaska?"

Dogrib shook his head. "Salt Boy says no."

She tucked windblown hair behind her ears. "If he's smart he'll wait. He won't want to alienate her warriors when he might need to use them against us."

She waited while Dogrib made his report to Rain Bear.

Rain Bear stared at the ground, kicking pensively at the old leaves and duff. "Do you think there's any chance our decoy scout can just wave them in?"

"Not anymore. We must choose another place," Dogrib said. "A place far enough ahead that we will have time to get into position. If we attack at dusk, close to Wasp Village, when they're utterly exhausted from running and fighting, we'll have an advantage."

"They've been hit once today; they'll be waiting for us around every bend."

Evening Star touched his arm. "Think about attacking at Gull Inlet. It's close to Wasp Village. They will be rushing to get there, thinking they are almost safe."

Rain Bear nodded; then his black brows drew together. "Red Dog said they expected our attack there."

She saw his mind wasn't on war and asked, "What is it?"

"Something unexpected has happened. I'm not sure what to do about it."

"What?"

"Matron Astcat has taken me up on my offer."

Evening Star blinked. "What offer?"

Rain Bear turned and used his chin to gesture. Evening Star frowned down the hill at the litter being carefully placed in the shade. Four blue-shirted warriors were watching carefully as Sleeper and his men kept curious warriors at bay.

"I don't..." she started, then stopped. Yes, she did understand. "She didn't. She wouldn't!"

"She would and did." Rain Bear lifted his brows, silently asking her what he was supposed to do now.

Evening Star looked at the litter again. "Is she all right?"

"She's alive. But her soul is gone."

Dogrib said, "What are you speaking about?"

"See that new litter?" Rain Bear asked.

"Yes."

"That's Matron Astcat."

Dogrib looked like he'd been bludgeoned. *"What?"*

Rides-the-Wind stepped forward, and his gray beard flapped in the wind. "Great Chief, Astcat has placed a strand of Power in your hand. How will you pull it?"

Rain Bear made a calming gesture with his hands. "I just need some time to think."

Evening Star's gaze drifted down the coastline, noting every unusual rock formation and the way the surf curled against the cliffs. "Well, you had better think fast. With each step, the North Wind People are closing the distance to Wasp Village. Once they are behind that palisade, you won't be able to strike at them."

"And you are now responsible for the great matron's welfare," Rides-the-Wind reminded. "If anything should happen to her all of your hopes will be dashed like a clamshell on the rocks."

Rain Bear stepped out of the trees to stare down at the distant Wasp Village. "I am very aware of that, Elder."

Evening Star watched him stroke his chin, a reservation behind his dark eyes. He stood so deeply lost in thought that he might have been stone.

He stiffened as if struck, a light behind his eyes. He glanced at Evening Star, then at the Soul Keeper. "Having the matron complicates things, but I think I know how to do this. If we are to succeed, I need your help. And you, Dogrib, can you carry out a particularly dangerous task?"

Chapter Thirty-Three

Rides-the-Wind squeezed Tsauz's hand and looked over the side of the trail to the surf below. Mother Ocean raged beside them, throwing water at the passing people as though to wash humans from the face of the world. In the distance, Thunderbirds hunted a dark wall of Cloud People, flashing and soaring. If he concentrated he could hear the deep boom of thunder on Wind Woman's breath.

Immediately to the south, Gull Inlet cut a wide notch in the cliffs. The trail split just before the inlet. One branch ran up over the cliffs, then followed the ridge where it jutted out into Raven Bay. The other branch, which Rain Bear's warriors currently followed, ran parallel to the ridge.

If Rain Bear's audacious plan worked, Rides-the-Wind could see a way out of their current dilemma. So much depended on timing and Rain Bear's control of his warriors in battle. Even more depended on Evening Star's courage, and Matron Astcat's condition. May the gods help them if her soul returned too soon. If the

North Wind lines held and Rain Bear's warriors fled the wrong way, they'd end up cut off from retreat and would be driven into Gull Inlet. He could imagine tens of people fleeing into the surf, trying to swim through the rough swells. Many would drown.

Astcat's four litter-bearers seemed tireless as they bore the great matron onward. In fact, their pace only seemed slowed by Rides-the-Wind and Tsauz. His old bones were hobbling along as fast as they could go, but already he was tired, fearful of his heart where it hammered so hard against his ancient ribs.

They had one hand of time, maybe.

"Soul Keeper?" Evening Star called just above a whisper.

He turned. "Yes?"

"I have a little dried fish left in my pack, and Tsauz has some dried seaweed. It's not much, but anything will help keep your strength up."

"Your kindness is appreciated." Rides-the-Wind was freezing and hungry. "Pull the yellow bag from my pack and we can chew the last of the pemmican as we go."

"Yes, Elder."

As Evening Star reached to fish around in Rides-the-Wind's pack, she almost pulled him off balance. She handed sections to him, Tsauz, and the litter bearers. They all ate as they walked.

"Is she all right, Elder?" Evening Star indicated the litter.

"I think she's alive, though I can't prove it."

Tsauz bent around to peer blindly at Rides-the-Wind. Worry tightened his young face. "But she's breathing, isn't she?"

"Not that I can tell, but that may mean nothing. Several times in the past six tens of summers I have sat beside people who did not seem to be alive. They did not breathe. They had no heartbeat. Yet, two or three days later, they awakened and smiled at me." He stared at Astcat, catching glimpses of her face. Damp locks of hair spread across her blankets like a dark gray halo.

"She'll get well, Elder. I know it." Tsauz seemed so sure of himself.

"I pray you're right."

Tsauz was genuinely concerned. He could see it in the boy's eyes and the worried set of his mouth. "Was the matron kind to you?"

"Oh, yes. After Mother's death she used to speak to me when no one else would. I think people were frightened by my blindness, but Matron Astcat treated me just the same as she had before Mother's death."

"She has guided her people well."

"She tried to, but when her soul started to fly away, things changed."

Evening Star's delicate brows lowered. "How so?"

"Father said the Council of Elders had become like a boat without a paddler. There was no one to tell it which way it should go. It just seemed to flounder without her. Then Old Woman North decided to make the decisions."

"And we all know what that led us to," Evening Star said darkly.

Tsauz nodded. "We only started attacking the Raven People after Matron Astcat's soul left her body."

It surprised Rides-the-Wind that the boy knew what a bad decision that had been. He hadn't gotten that from his father, since Ecan seemed to thrive on murdering Raven People.

In a barely audible voice, Tsauz said, "I want to marry her, Elder. I *have* to."

Evening Star turned. "What will you do if you become chief, Tsauz?"

He wiped his nose on his sleeve. "Stop the war. Then I—I'll free all the Raven People slaves. I have to. I've seen it."

"Seen it?" Rides-the-Wind frowned. "You mean in a Dream? Thunderbird showed it to you?"

Tsauz's blind eyes seemed to be drifting over the white-crested waves that tormented Mother Ocean just below their trail. "No, this is a Dream I had the night I went blind. Mother was...was dead, and Red Dog left me sitting alone on a hillside with the people who'd been hurt in the fire. They all died, of course; and I was scared. I tried to climb off the rock and fell and hit my arm." He wet his lips. "Father later said that once I got used to being safe again, I'd stop having the Dream, but it's never gone away."

"What happens in the Dream, Tsauz?"

Tsauz looked nervous, his feet feeling for the trail as he held Rides-the-Wind's arm. "After I have made peace with the Raven People I'm swimming in a lake of blood trying to save a baby boy who's drowning, and there are strange feathered Spirits—"

"Ah," Rides-the-Wind said in a soft voice. "I know that Dream."

Tsauz jerked his head around, almost falling. "You do?"

"Oh, yes. As a matter of fact, I've never known a

Dreamer who hasn't had that Dream at least once in his life. The greatest Dreamers have it many times."

"But why, Elder? What does it mean?"

Rides-the-Wind gestured uncertainly. "I think it's a warning. Something far in the future, I fear."

As though trying to memorize it, Tsauz whispered, "A bloody boy far in the future."

As they wound down the mountain trail through the leafless alder groves, Ecan gradually dropped to the rear of the procession to walk beside Pitch. No one seemed to notice. Almost everyone had shifted positions after the battle. Cimmis now walked in front, beside Dzoo. Kaska's warriors followed them; then came the three concentric circles of warriors around the Four Old Women. Kaska's litter was the last in line as they descended the steep trail, and she had new litter bearers—Cimmis's warriors. Cimmis had effectively separated her from her people.

She had to know that upon arrival at Wasp Village, they would separate her permanently.

With Sand Wasp dead, her warriors were like a headless serpent, writhing about aimlessly. Ecan had heard two disheartened men whisper that they should just go back to Salmon Village and live out their lives without a matron.

Pitch walked two paces to Ecan's left, the Singer's narrow face a stoic mask, his gaze trying to keep track of Dzoo way up at the front.

Ecan shifted to watch her through the weave of people. Ahead, the gray cliffs of Gull Inlet scooped out the coastline. Her eyes seemed to be on the wind-twisted firs that crowded the rim.

Is that where Rain Bear has set up his ambush?

The trail made a wide curve around a thicket of head-high alder saplings. Ecan saw Cimmis gesture, and two warriors sprinted to the thicket and began thrashing it with their spears, trying to flush any enemy warriors who might be hiding there.

Cimmis was saying something to Dzoo.

When her soft laughter echoed in return, the entire procession backed away.

Ecan narrowed his eyes. *Coyote will kill him after we arrive at Wasp Village. And if Dzoo is right, I have to kill Coyote as soon after as possible.*

He shot a glance back at Kaska where she rode the litter. He was going to need a great matron. His first attempt to whip Evening Star into submission hadn't gone so well. Would he have better luck with Kaska? Would she be willing to divorce her husband and marry him, say, if he were to save her life and the life of her daughter?

Coyote. How do I kill Coyote?

Gods, he didn't even know who the man was!

Chapter Thirty-Four

At the call from the guards at the main gate, War Chief Tsak left his son in charge of the final inspection of the lodges. In all of his years in Wasp Village, this was the most upsetting of times. He kept glancing up at the sun as he walked across the plaza toward the main gate. They couldn't already be arriving, could they?

No, he needn't look at the sun; all he had to do was see his lengthening shadow to know that by the time the sun set, he would no longer be the war chief of Wasp Village. He might indeed serve his matron, but his authority would be subject to White Stone's approval.

Dwelling on the notion wasn't something that made Tsak overly fond of the coming commotion. He would be courteous and respectful, of course, and greet the Council and Cimmis with the homage due them, but inside, part of him would be dying.

As he walked, he took in the new lodges with a side-long glance. Where Wasp Village had once been airy and spacious, it now resembled an overstuffed hive. In every open spot, the slaves had built new lodges, most of them larger and more imposing than those of the original inhabitants.

"Maybe it won't be so bad," he muttered under his breath. He was lying to himself, of course. He had known White Stone for years. They had a mutual respect for each other's abilities, and a formal relationship that had never been strained by long and intimate association.

"No," he corrected, "this is going to be a disaster."

Down in the depths of his soul, he wondered if Rain Bear needed any volunteers. The thought tickled the rude and obnoxious part of him that he had spent most of his life trying to keep under firm control. He just couldn't help it—that little voice inside was always making fun or mouthing off in the most disrespectful way. People often saw a wry smile on his lips and wondered why.

He approached the eastern gate, where the two guards stood looking up-country, their spears resting butt down on the ground.

"What is it?" Tsak asked as he stepped between them and stared up the main trail past the slave village. The ridge was open for two spear casts before a stand of fir and spruce masked the trail. There, in full view, he could see a litter being borne by four blue-shirted warriors. Behind them came a small knot of people: a woman, an old man and child, and a ratty looking—but heavily armed—party of perhaps five tens of warriors walking five abreast.

As word of their arrival spread through the slave village, Raven People trooped out in the muted afternoon sunlight to watch.

With a sinking sensation, Tsak looked down to see his shadow gone. A quick glance over his shoulder showed that a dark cloud had obscured the sun. Gods, the weather had been too good to be true. By nightfall, it would be raining again.

Turning his attention back to the approaching party, he steeled himself and walked out the gate, motioning his guards to accompany him. His heart beat like a sodden drum. Who were these people? The four leading warriors were certainly Cimmis's: They wore blue, the fabric dyed from a combination of octopus blood and larkspur petals.

He threw his head back, calling, "Who comes?"

"The great matron, Astcat, and her party," came the reply from one of the blue-clad warriors.

Tsak waited with the finality of a man doomed. As they came close, he could recognize Astcat's bearers: Gispaxloat, Kitselas, and the Raven warriors. And behind them, yes, that was Matron Evening Star, whom he had thought a fugitive; and there was the Soul Keeper, Rides-the-Wind, also supposedly with the Raven People at Sandy Point Village. The first tingling of unease grew within him. Especially as he got a good look at the hard-jawed ranks of warriors coming behind.

"Please lower the litter," he called, reaching for his war club. "I want to see Matron Astcat for myself."

Gispaxloat nodded to his companions, and they carefully eased the litter to the ground. Kitselas pulled a corner of the ornate blanket back to expose the matron's lax face.

"Her soul has fled," Rides-the-Wind said as he stepped forward.

"We would like to take Astcat to her new lodge as quickly as possible."

Tsak hesitated. "Matron Evening Star? I thought you were Outcast?"

"Enslaved," she said bitterly. "It's not quite the same thing." She tilted her head toward the litter. "The great matron has seen fit to reinstate me."

Tsak glanced at Gispaxloat, but the stern warrior betrayed nothing. "And you, Soul Keeper? Is it true that you were staying among the Raven People?"

Rides-the-Wind thrust his face uncomfortably close. "Is it true, Tsak, that you're going to keep us waiting out here answering stupid questions while the Great Astcat is in need of shelter, food, and water?"

"But these warriors?" He indicated the hard-eyed warriors who had formed a knot on the trail behind them. They looked nervous as they fingered their weapons and appraised him with wolfish eyes.

"Are the protective escort for the great matron," Evening Star said hotly. "If you're not going to allow us entry, let us know so we can tell Chief Cimmis to turn the entire procession around and send it back to Fire Village."

"He's close?"

"A hand or two behind us. Cimmis deemed it *important* to bring the great matron ahead." She crossed her arms, those imperious blue eyes narrowing.

He hesitated for a moment, some voice of warning crying out inside him. But it made sense. If Astcat was incapacitated Cimmis would want her stowed away somewhere out of sight.

"Yes, yes," he muttered. "Go on. Inside, all of you."

He turned his attention to the warriors. "Who is in charge here?"

A wiry young man in a torn cloak, mud-spattered moccasins, and grimy war shirt stepped forward. "I am war chief."

"Camp your men just inside the gate. I'll figure out what to do with you later."

Gispaxloat had already raised Astcat's litter. And so it was that she, her party, and Sleeper's five tens of warriors were ushered past Wasp Village's gate, War Chief Tsak trotting at their heels.

On the ridge above Gull Inlet, Dogrib experienced fear like he had never known it. His mouth was dry, his hands damp. His skin crawled as alternately fear-sweat beaded on it or shivers traced patterns across it. He hated the runny feeling in his bowels. His jaw was clamped so hard his cheeks were spasming.

He had hidden himself and four other men in a patch of raspberries just off the Wasp Village trail. They had burrowed down into the old musty leaves, thorns scratching and burning any exposed skin. He and his warriors now waited, each locked in his thoughts as the long moments passed.

He heard them coming, talking among themselves. Then came the moment of greatest terror. The North Wind scouts jabbed halfheartedly at the brush while, huddled in the center, Dogrib and his warriors shivered.

And then they passed.

Dogrib exhaled the terrible tension from his body

and grinned at his companions through a hole in the thorns.

White Stone had commanded superb discipline at the burned ridge. When he broke Bluegrass's attack, most of his warriors had stood firm, refusing to break formation. Now, everything depended on Dogrib, on his ability to break that control.

Dogrib lifted his head, wary of exposing his white hair. Through the tangle, he could see Great Chief Cimmis walking beside Dzoo and White Stone. In that moment, he saw what fate had granted him. *Cimmis...*

His heart hammering like thunder, he wet his lips. *Let them come closer.*

Wait. Just wait. That's it.

Then, as they were almost even, he rose, shouting, *"Now!"*

He cast, putting all of his body behind the atlatl as it catapulted his finest spear. The missile flew true, as if drawn toward Cimmis's heart...

White Stone was caught completely by surprise. With one arm he shoved Cimmis, and slapped out with his other, touching the shaft, deflecting it at the last instant. It was enough. The spear meant for Cimmis's heart drove deeply into the bone of the old man's hip.

At the same time, Dogrib's other warriors had cast. He had no time to see the results. He shouted, *"Run!"*

They thrashed their way out of the raspberry patch, ripping their skin, tearing their war shirts. Feet beat the ground behind him as they raced toward escape. He heard screams, curses, and then the most glorious sound: White Stone bellowing, *"After them!"*

It was working! A quick glance over his shoulder showed warriors pounding in pursuit. A spear thudded into the ground ahead of him, the shaft vibrating with the force.

He leaped a fallen log and hurtled down the steep hillside almost out of control. He couldn't have stopped if he'd wanted to. His only hope was to guide his head-long flight around obstacles—like boulders—that might kill him. Another spear hissed past him to shatter on an angular basalt boulder.

"It's Dogrib! Get him! Run faster!" an enemy warrior called.

Over his shoulder, Dogrib shouted, "Eat maggots and die, you worms!"

Two more spears came close enough that he could feel the wind of their passing. He shot through a small hollow surrounded by trees and headed straight for an opening in the far side.

"Oh, my Ancestors, please help me!"

Just when Dogrib was certain he was dead, he heard Rain Bear shout:

"Hold...hold! *Cast!*"

Spears glittered as they shot from the trees ten paces ahead and to either side. Dogrib dove for the ground, hit, and rolled, the wind knocked out of him. In a retching agony, he covered his head. The sound of the spears cutting through the air above him was like tens of falcon wings hissing by. When they'd flown over, he jerked around to look.

The spears arced into the midst of the enemy warriors. Every man in the front row shrieked, tumbled as if broken, and fell writhing to the ground. Some jerked futilely at the spears embedded in their flesh. Others stared in disbelief, mouths open in horror. Others whimpered with pain and fear.

The remaining warriors rushed onward, coming ever closer. Dogrib figured that if he stood, he'd look like a mouse who'd roused a porcupine.

"Hallowed Ancestors," he whispered, "let me live through this and I promise I'll never—"

"*Cast!*" Rain Bear shouted.

Another volley hissed angrily through the air barely ten hands over Dogrib's head. He tried to curl into an invisible ball in the grass.

The screaming grew louder. A man fell on top of him. Dogrib stared into the fellow's wide, panicked eyes. The spear had taken him through the heart, but his body didn't know it yet. The man struggled to rise, a horrible sucking sound coming from his impaled chest.

Dogrib looked past him to see another two tens of warriors racing down the hill, straight into Rain Bear's trap.

When the few surviving North Wind warriors turned and ran, a great roar went up.

Dogrib held his breath, waiting.

Then he heard it. On the hill above him, White Stone ordered more warriors down the hill. Their distinctive North Wind war whoops ululated as they ran.

"*Come on!*" Rain Bear cried and burst from cover. "Keep them running!" He pointed to the fleeing North Wind warriors.

Dogrib watched his fellows rush from the trees, screaming their war yell—a sound like the hoarse throaty caws of a flock of ravens.

Within moments, the ululations and caws mixed with the whistling of spears to form a terrifying sound that resembled an avalanche tumbling downhill.

Dogrib froze until the last of the Raven warriors dashed by him; then he rose. His four warriors poked their heads up, wide-eyed as they gasped desperately for breath. He could see the amazement in their expressions. Like him, they were stunned to be alive.

Dogrib began to laugh. Starved for breath, surrounded by maimed and dying men, peal after mad peal of laughter shook him.

His men took it up. Together they laughed with the intensity of the insane.

Chapter Thirty-Five

Rain was an old companion. Cimmis ground out a cry as Deer Killer tried to pull the slim spear from his hip.

"The stone tip is lodged in the bone, Great Chief." Deer Killer looked as if he was going to throw up.

Cimmis blinked, his vision sliding in and out. He couldn't seem to catch his breath. "Just pull it out! You, Hunter, grab on to that shaft and yank!"

They both grasped the polished wood, looked at each other, and pulled. The scream tore out of his throat, deafening even to him.

He felt his body jerked, and then both Deer Killer and Hunter tumbled backward, the slim shaft clutched in their hands.

"Quick, you fools! Take my cloak. Wad it up. Use my belt to bind it over the wound to stop the bleeding."

By Gutginsa's balls, where was a Healer? He considered calling Dzoo for a moment and decided against it. She might take the opportunity to finish the job that three-times-accursed Dogrib had started.

"Great Chief?" Deer Killer asked, his voice tight with fear.

"What?"

The warrior held up the spear as Hunter attended to his wounded hip. "The point, Great Chief. I think it's still inside. The binding gave way."

Cimmis blinked, staring at the end of the spear. Although blood soaked, he could see the broken sinew that had once held a keen stone point. "Men have lived with points in them before."

He almost bit his tongue as Hunter pulled the makeshift bandage tight. Gasping and sweating, he asked, "How is the fighting going?"

Deer Killer turned his attention from the spear to the fighting below. "Our warriors are after them. I think it was just a small party."

"Yes, well, there will be a larger one waiting. Call up Kaska's warriors and be ready for a counterattack. If I know Rain Bear, this won't be as easy as it was at the burned ridge."

Rain Bear led his forces to meet the howling North Wind warriors, leaping brush and deadfall, bursting through the tall grass. The spears of the enemy glinted like tens of membranous wings.

When they were within thirty paces, the voices of his men rose to a roar. Spears whistled by as his warriors cried out with the thrill of battle or shrieked in pain. He saw gaps in his line after the North Wind warriors cast their first volley—but he kept going, leading his men headlong into the North Wind warriors. They met with a clattering of spears, wild shouts, screams, and howls.

A tall North Wind warrior headed straight for Rain Bear, his mouth wide open in a scream of rage.

Rain Bear drove a spear through his chest. All around him, men clashed in a snarling, grunting chaos.

He waded into a tangle of North Wind warriors and brought his club down hard on a man's head. The warrior fell like a limp strand of seagrass.

"Rain Bear!" Wet Fern shouted. "Behind you!"

He leaped sideways as a club smashed into his left shoulder. Pain staggered him, and the North Wind warrior whooped in victory as he lifted his club to finish the job. Rain Bear ducked the blow meant for his head and broke his attacker's ribs. The man's breath shot from his lungs in a loud *whoosh*.

Rain Bear's next blow took him squarely in the chest. Amid the screaming and shouting, he barely heard the man's breastbone crack.

The familiar odor of battle permeated the air: a powerful mixture of sweat and the coppery tangs of blood and torn intestines.

Rain Bear pushed himself up the hill. He could see White Stone.

The war chief stood like a sun-bronzed statue, his face stern as he shouted orders. Dzoo was poised slightly behind him, her long red hair blowing around the dark frame of her hood. Where was Pitch? Ecan?

And in that instant, the North Wind line broke, went tumbling back. Warriors dropped their weapons to flee up the hill. Rain Bear shouted in triumph, knowing that this single greatest victory would have to be surrendered.

"We can take them!" Talon bellowed as he smacked his war club into the back of a fleeing man's spine. The warrior staggered. Before he could fall, Talon split his skull.

"No!" Rain Bear cried. "Follow the plan! You *must* follow the plan!"

He might have been a whisper in a gale. His warriors went charging past him, heading up the hill.

"No! Do not do this! You are making the same mistake Bluegrass did!"

"Bluegrass led cowards!" Three Shells bellowed in reply as he charged headlong up the hill. Rain Bear watched as Three Shells ran down a straggler, beating the man's head in with a stroke of his club. "For War Gods Village!"

"For War Gods Village!" The cry was picked up by the charging warriors.

On the ridgetop War Chief White Stone separated from the group of warriors that surrounded the Four Old Women and strode forward, shouting orders.

"Back!" Rain Bear shouted after his warriors. "Come back! Follow the plan!"

A few of the Sandy Point warriors glanced at White Stone, longing in their eyes, but instinctively moved closer to Rain Bear.

The others rushed past, their excitement a living thing. He could feel it creeping through his own blood like tiny worms. Every fiber in his being cried to follow, to take the fight to Cimmis.

"Hold!" he ordered his remaining warriors. "We've got to prepare. They've got their blood up now, but they'll be headed back soon."

"But great chief!" one of the warriors cried. "If we don't support them, they'll be killed."

He stomped toward the men, anger building. "Yes! They will, unless we devise a plan to save them!" He thrust out his club. "You and you, into that patch of brush. Robin, I want you and others to take cover in that patch of fir trees." He searched their frantic eyes, knowing he was about to lose them to the fever of combat. Imploring, he asked, *"Do you remember the plan?"*

It was Bark Hare who said, "Yes, Great Chief. I do." He looked at the others. "Gods, yes. It's up to us. We've got to lay the ambush."

"That's it." Rain Bear slapped his shoulder. "Hurry. We don't have that much time. Gather as many spears as you can. We're going to need them."

He quickly placed his warriors, judging which route his absent warriors would take when they fled the fight. Looking down the hill, he could see where Dogrib should be, the war chief still assuming that the plan was working.

"When we go, you run there!" Rain Bear pointed to the gap in the rocks. "After we pass, we set up another ambush. Remember how it works?"

The craziness of battle had been replaced with a rabid excitement. He'd held them.

Even as he laid his trap, the first of the Raven warriors, a man streaming blood from a head wound, came pelting past. He was but the first of a flood.

Up on the ridge, Rain Bear knew that White Stone had called in his reinforcements. Kaska's warriors would have joined the fight.

Now warriors fled in absolute panic past Rain

Bear's position. As the first of the North Wind warriors came whooping down in pursuit, Rain Bear stood, signaling his warriors. Each picked a target and cast.

Rain Bear turned and ran for all he was worth.

A flood of warriors rolled down the hill with him. "The gap!" he called, pointing. "Make for the gap!"

He shot a quick glance over his shoulder. The North Wind warriors were close, but some slowed as they stopped to kill a straggler.

"My warriors!" he screamed against his tearing lungs. "Stay with me! Stay close and don't lose your weapons!"

He led the way through the gap, followed by wheezing and gasping men. As he passed the rocks, he could see Dogrib, a spear balanced in his hand. Yes, blessed gods, Dogrib was where he should be.

Past the rocks, Rain Bear pointed to the stony outcrop below. "There! We'll set the next ambush there!"

Lungs laboring, he scrambled up into the rocks in time to look back. Screams erupted from the gap as Dogrib and his men stood, bodies twisting as they speared the first pursuing North Wind warriors.

Then Dogrib and his three remaining companions turned and ran for all they were worth, headed straight past Rain Bear's outcrop.

The race would be long, fraught with danger, and if he failed to cross the finish line ahead of Cimmis, a great many people were going to die.

Chapter Thirty-Six

Tsauz sat beside Matron Astcat and listened to her labored breathing. She hadn't moved at all since they'd arrived in the spacious new lodge in Wasp Village. The place smelled of sappy wood, green bark, and freshly cut vines. Packs had been placed along the walls, and a row of magnificent shields stood across from him. He had run his fingers over them, learning their size and shape. On one, the figure of Killer Whale had been created out of round beads.

Longing tingled in his chest. He needed to speak with her, to ask her advice.

"Just fill Matron Astcat's bowl with broth," Evening Star had said. "No meat." Then she had gone back outside to ensure that the prisoners were safely locked away and guarded. War Chief Tsak's shouts of rage and disbelief as he was marched off at spear point still echoed in Tsauz's ears.

Tsauz lifted his pointed chin, and the cold ocean breeze tousled his shoulder-length black hair. The rich scent of fish soup made his empty stomach growl, but he was saving it for Astcat.

A flash.

Tsauz tilted his head and stared toward what he assumed to be Mother Ocean. The roar of her voice grew louder, and tiny fleeting spots of brightness lit up the dark curtain behind his eyes.

"What's the matter, Tsauz?" Rides-the-Wind asked as he entered the lodge.

"Are—are the Thunderbirds coming?" Fear stung his veins.

"Yes. Why?"

He swallowed hard. "I see them."

"See who?"

"Their flashes are bouncing around behind my eyes."

Rides-the-Wind tucked a bowl into Tsauz's hands and grunted as he sat down. "Eat, Tsauz. If Thunderbird is coming for you, you'll need to have a full stomach."

Tsauz felt for his horn spoon and tasted the soup. The flavors of the fish and venison pemmican created a mouth-watering combination.

Rides-the-Wind slid across the sand, and the matron's blankets rustled.

Around a mouthful of pemmican, Tsauz asked, "What are you doing, Elder? May I help?"

"No, you just eat. I'm arranging the matron's head on my lap so that I can try to feed her."

After a few instants Rides-the-Wind said, "Matron Astcat, I'm going to put a few drops of broth in your mouth."

Tsauz heard Rides-the-Wind stir the broth—the

spoon raked the sides of the wooden bowl—then Rides-the-Wind said, "That's good. See if you can swallow a little more."

"Is she eating?" Tsauz asked hopefully and touched her soft cheek.

"She's taken two swallows so far. I'm slowly trickling another spoonful into her open mouth."

Tsauz heard her swallow this time; it sounded difficult, as though she might be on the verge of choking.

"I'll just pat her hair, Elder," he said, and drew his hand away from her wrinkled cheek. When he started stroking her hair, she gasped suddenly and coughed with such violence he jumped back.

"What's happening?" he cried. "Is she choking?"

She drew in a sharp breath.

Rides-the-Wind's voice went so gentle Tsauz almost didn't recognize it. "Matron? Can you hear me?"

"I...I hear you...Holy Hermit."

Tsauz's eyes jerked wide at the hoarse sound of her voice.

"Please, lie still. Don't move too quickly. Your soul just came home. We want it to stay."

"How...long?"

"Have you been gone? I don't know, Matron. Your warriors brought you to us for safekeeping. But I think you've been away for at least a day."

She took several deep breaths, as though enjoying the feel of air moving in her lungs. "R-Rides-the-Wind," she asked in a pitifully small voice, "do you have any...willow bark tea? It seems to help fasten my soul down."

"I do, Matron. Let me get it from my pack."

Rides-the-Wind rose, and his pack rustled.

"Matron, are you all right?" Tsauz asked, and edged as close to her as he could.

She took several breaths before she said, "I always feel confused, empty, for a time after I return. But I think I'm all right."

He could feel her staring at him as she asked, "Did you fly very high on Thunderbird's back?"

"All the way to the Star People, Matron."

"I do not understand this."

Tears welled in his eyes. "I don't understand it either, Matron. I just know that you need me."

She let out a breath, and her hand crept out and found his. "I saw you in a Dream, boy. You were standing, tall and bloody. You had stones for eyes."

"Will you marry me?"

"Your mother was one of the Raven People."

Tsauz blinked. Bolts of lightning shot around behind his eyes again, flashing so brightly they hurt. "Thunderbird...Thunderbird said that Father murdered her because she was Raven." He winced. "I asked Rides-the-Wind if Spirit Helpers ever lied."

"In that case, no." She seemed sad. "Red Dog told me about it."

"Why would Father do that? He loved her."

She said nothing, but he could feel a sad anger brewing within her. When he looked her way, he could see a glow behind his eyes.

Frightened, he said, "Does that mean you don't want to marry me? Because of my Raven blood?"

She squeezed his hand with no more strength than a sparrow. "Quite the contrary. Power is all around us. And in the end, you can't fight Power."

"No," Rides-the-Wind whispered from the side.

"Poor Cimmis. Oh, gods, this is going to hurt him."

"There is no way out of this that isn't painful, Matron," Rides-the-Wind said. "Not for you, or for Cimmis. Each of you must make choices. Power will be the judge."

"Very well." The matron's fingers felt icy in Tsauz's grip. She swallowed and said, "Do you give me your oath...that you will be a good and faithful chief? That you will always put the good of both peoples before your own happiness?"

Tsauz's throat constricted. "Yes, Matron. I will try very hard to be a good chief."

"Then I think perhaps I will take you as my husband." Tsauz wet his lips nervously. He'd heard her say those words before, when he'd been riding Thunderbird's back, but they sounded different, kinder, coming from her own lips. "Thank you, Matron."

Dzoo crouched over a dying warrior, placing a finger on his neck to feel the pulse weakening. As she did so, she slipped an obsidian knife from his belt and tucked it into her legging. When she straightened, it was to see the Four Old Women staring bug-eyed at Cimmis where he was being placed on a litter by Deer Killer and Hunter. Blood smeared the bindings on his hip, scarlet in the slanting light.

Dzoo looked just in time to see the last of Rain Bear's warriors break. Even as they turned and fled, they were being run down. As with the dying warrior, she could do nothing for them. Idly she turned her attention to the brown stand of cattails that filled a hollow to the south of the trail. The dry stalks were head-high, winter-brittle, and rattling.

Cimmis had ordered Kaska's warriors forward, but for the moment White Stone was keeping them out of the battle. They didn't look happy about it. Many grumbled and stamped their feet, eager to be in the fight.

She could see Ecan leading Pitch down the slope to stand at the head of the party. Presumably so the Raven warriors would see him. Hunter and Deer Killer had taken positions on either side of Cimmis's litter. Her own guard, Wind Scorpion, had disappeared. She looked again at the cattails. Threads of dark Power filtered through the stalks like a malignant mist.

"Of course we're winning!" Old Woman North shouted gleefully from her litter. "It will only be a matter of moments before we push the Raven People into the sea!"

Old Woman South lifted her wrinkled chin and said, "Good riddance. The Raven People have always been thieves and maggots."

Chuckles burst from the others, and Dzoo's heart went cold.

Old Woman North called, "Warriors! Prepare to move. We are going closer to get a better view."

"But, Elder!" one of the guards objected. "The battle could shift! You should remain here where it's safe."

"I said we're moving lower on the mountain! Accompany us!"

Dzoo's attention fixed on Cimmis. She had seen the warriors pull the spear from his hip, but how badly was he wounded? He was propped in his litter, calling orders, using his shriveled arm to point this way and that.

She glanced at the cattails. *Yes, it is time, my stalker. The final Dance has begun.*

She glanced out at the storm brewing over Raven Bay. Sunlight outlined the tall bank of clouds in a halo of gold. She waited for another crack of lightning. In the rolling growl that followed, she stepped into the cattails.

A cheer went up when Cimmis's forces charged after Rain Bear's fleeing warriors. With that as cover, she made another step. And then another.

She sniffed: The dank odor of cattails barely masked the mossy scent she had come to associate with him.

Step by step she made her way through the stalks and leaves. With a careful hand she parted the dry plants, looked around, and was in the process of taking another step when a shape rose from one side. She started to turn as the whistling club slashed through the cattails and blasted lightning behind her eyes.

As she fell, she heard the Thunderbirds booming in defiance. *Yes, Coyote. How clever you are. Ever the patient one...*

Chapter Thirty-Seven

Despite the pain Cimmis smiled to himself as his litter swayed. A runner had arrived with word that the great matron was waiting in Wasp Village. A weight, like a huge stone, had lifted from Cimmis's chest. He still didn't know why she had gone on ahead, but by Old Woman Above, she was safe.

From his perch atop his swaying litter, he watched as the remains of his party wound through the last stand of firs and into the clearing. In the growing dusk, he could see the welcoming palisade of Wasp Village just ahead. The gates were open, warriors standing at them, spears in hand.

It was over. They had made it. Though White Stone had only made a quick count, it seemed that some seven tens of warriors were missing after their final fight with Rain Bear. But given the extent of the rout, most of them would come trickling in through the night, jesting and waving trophies taken from the dead.

As he studied the meadow before Wasp Village an idea came to him. "White Stone?"

His war chief dropped back to walk beside the litter. "Yes, Great Chief?"

"I'm thinking about setting a row of poles on either side of the trail here. Tomorrow, I want you to send a party of warriors out to cut the heads off the dead Raven warriors. We'll stick a head atop each of the poles. It should create quite the stir among the Raven villages, don't you think?"

White Stone gave him a sober look, and asked, "Are you all right, my Chief?"

"A little dizzy."

White Stone shot a speculative look at the slave village just to the north of the village gates. "It might not be such a bad idea after all."

Cimmis smiled as White Stone trotted back to his advance guard.

Behind him, the Four Old Women chattered like ruffed grouse in spring. The young Singer, Pitch, marched with his head down, a dazed look in his eyes. Yes, well, his head could join the others.

Dzoo, perhaps to no one's surprise, was missing. Slipped away like smoke.

Let her enjoy it. In the end, I'll send Coyote to bring her back.

Ecan walked like a man in a trance, his eyes slightly out of focus. The expression on his face was that of a man who had unexpectedly rounded a forest turn and found himself eye to eye with a spring-starved grizzly.

Cimmis blinked, dizzy again. He took a deep breath, feeling oddly light-headed. Touching a hand to his wadded cloak, he found it saturated with blood.

"Set me down. Starwatcher! Bring me your cloak."

As great chief, he wasn't going to make his grand entry dripping blood like a beheaded rabbit. Besides, the time had come to put Ecan in his place.

The warriors lowered him gently to the ground. Ecan stepped over, eyes dull. He hardly seemed aware as he slipped off his snowy cloak and handed it to Deer Killer.

Cimmis winced as Hunter and Deer Killer untied his belt. Swiftly, efficiently, they wadded Ecan's white cloak and bound it tightly to keep pressure on the wound.

When they were finished, Cimmis beckoned. "Ecan, a word please." He placed a hand on the Starwatcher's shoulder when the man bent over him. "Well, we are here. The Raven People have taken not one but two defeats, and we have flushed all of our adversaries."

"We have indeed," Ecan agreed, despite the distance in his eyes. "I assume that I can bargain for the return of my son now."

"Bargain?" Cimmis smiled in a fatherly way. "I don't think you have the talent for it. You're not good at making deals with people. You don't seem capable of reading their true souls." He shrugged. "The way I heard it, you'd bargain away your future for a sack of stone trinkets."

The color drained from Ecan's face.

If he placed Ecan's head on the first pole outside the gate, he wouldn't have to walk so far to see it. Better, he could place a wager with White Stone as to how long it would take for the flesh to melt away from the bones.

But who should I appoint as the new Starwatcher?

When Ecan stumbled back, the strength seemed

gone from his legs. Cimmis chuckled and shot a glance behind him. The silly old women were preening in their litters, arranging their jewelry.

Four paces in front, White Stone was staring pensively at the distant Wasp Village gate, as if worried. Cimmis squinted at the clouds blowing in from the west. What did White Stone have to worry about? It wasn't like the storm was going to catch them out in the open.

"Yes, War Chief?" Cimmis gestured toward the gate.

"Nothing, Great Chief, just a feeling. As if something terrible is about to happen." He smiled. "Are you comfortable?"

"Oh, quite. Everything is finally in place."

"You are a dead man." Dzoo's words echoed inside Ecan's hollow soul. So, too, was his son. He'd seen that in Cimmis's eyes. No matter what happened, the boy was going to die.

Without his cloak, Ecan felt the chill as he stepped away from Cimmis's litter. The great chief was talking light-headedly with White Stone while the Four Old Women attended to their appearances. The rest of the remaining warriors lounged and chatted about the battles, their talk filled with animation. The threat was vanquished, and the time for bragging had arrived.

"You'd bargain away your future for a sack of stone trinkets." Coyote had betrayed him.

Ecan threw his head back and looked up at the dark

clouds rolling down upon them from the sea. Lightning flashed. Distant thunder rolled.

It would come in the night, silently, without warning. The next morning someone would go to wake the tardy Starwatcher—only to find Ecan's mutilated body lying in his blood-soaked bedding.

How did it come to this?

He felt at his belt but had no weapon. He turned, seeing Kaska, surrounded by her guards.

Is that how I want to go? But perhaps there was still a way to save his son and perhaps save himself.

No weapon.

He crouched, cupped his hands around an angular piece of basalt, and lifted. The stone loosened in the damp soil, then peeled free.

Ecan lifted, savoring the head-sized stone's weight. He turned, took two steps, and raised the heavy rock high.

"For my boy," he said softly.

Cimmis had just looked up, his eyes going wide. Ecan slammed the stone squarely onto the great chief's chest.

He heard the thump, the cracking of ribs, the gush of air blown from the old man's throat. The expression of shock and surprise gave way to a rasping gasp as Cimmis struggled for a breath.

It took a moment of stunned disbelief before Ecan realized what he'd done. He was still staring into Cimmis's eyes when a voice whispered, *"Run"*

Ecan leaped Cimmis's litter, pelting full tilt through the following warriors, shoving slaves out of his way as he raced for the screen of fir trees. It was a blind flight, spurred by panic. He had no idea where he was going, how he was going to escape.

He had just reached the trees when White Stone's spear impaled him from behind. The force of it staggered him, and an odd tingling chill like spearmint mixed with the sharp pain.

Chapter Thirty-Eight

Coyote carried Dzoo into the winter-bare alders and gently laid her on a pile of old leaves. Her long red hair, matted with sticky blood, spread across the leaves in glistening waves. She looked serenely beautiful. He touched his fingers to the side of her head, feeling to make sure the skull wasn't broken. Then he raised his fingers to his nostrils and savored the coppery scent of her blood.

He'd deliberately pulled his blow, hitting her only hard enough to temporarily cause her soul to fly. She would wake soon. She had to, because he wanted to look into her eyes when he took her.

He ran his finger down her jaw and could barely contain himself. The need within him was alive, a palpable presence that churned in his guts and bones.

He bent down and nuzzled his cheek against hers, then whispered in her ear, "Are you ready? We are together at last."

He'd waited so long for this that he feared he might rush and ruin it. But it was getting dark, and a storm was breaking. He didn't wish to do this in the dark while rain pelted their naked bodies, so he had to hurry.

He held out his shaking hands and flexed his fingers several times; then he reached down and untied the laces of her cape. When he threw it back, he saw the beautiful crimson dress she wore. The shell beads that covered the bodice winked and glimmered in the flashes of distant lightning.

She was limp as he lifted her and slid the dress from her smooth pale skin. Carefully, deliberately, and with great tenderness, he arranged her on his cloak. Rolling her dress, he made a pillow for her head, and then like an artist painting a shield, he stretched her matted hair out so that the red tresses lay like rays of sunlight on the dry leaves.

Fighting to still his trembling, he massaged her full breasts. At the touch of her smooth warm skin, an electric sensation flushed his veins. He ran his palms over the curve of her ribs, down the dip of her waist, across the bone in her hips to the flat above her pubis. His fingers traced the downy softness of her curly pubic hair. He bent down and filled his lungs with the scent of her womanhood.

He ripped off his war shirt and stared down at his stiff penis where it jutted out from below his muscular belly. Need, like a fire, burned inside him. His erection had become a tingling ache as he positioned himself between her muscular legs.

He whimpered as he lowered himself onto her. His fevered penis slipped along the inside of her thigh, and he gasped at the point of ejaculation.

You're going too fast! You've Dreamed this ten tens

of times! You are supposed to savor her! Use your tongue to taste her before you—

Dzoo opened her eyes.

His face was less than a hand from hers. He was panting as he thrust his fingers into her and opened her to his manhood.

She didn't struggle but rolled her hips back, ready to receive him. Her dark luminous eyes began to drink his soul. She must have wanted him as badly as he'd wanted her.

"Are you ready?" he whispered huskily.

She was dry when he forced himself inside; her eyes widened slightly.

Gripping a handful of her red hair, he took it into his mouth. He could taste her blood; it stoked his desire even more. He sucked at her hair and thrust as hard as he could. Her legs were rising, tightening around him. He should have removed her leggings! Then it would only be her skin against his sides, across his back.

By the gods! Yes! Yes! He felt the tingling sensation building at the root of his penis. She was watching him, a gleam in her eyes, a faint parting of her lips as she anticipated the explosion of his loins.

His whole body convulsed with each jetting of his seed inside her.

From the corner of his eye, he saw her reach for her legging. Then her pale hand lifted...

Chapter Thirty-Nine

From the platform within Wasp Village's walls, Evening Star stared in amazement as Ecan plucked a head-sized stone from the ground and crushed Cimmis's chest. She watched White Stone start at the sight, barely hesitate, and then race in pursuit of the fleeing Starwatcher. She saw the war chief's arm whip back as he sent a spear flying after Ecan. Gods! Had she just witnessed what she thought she had?

In confirmation, the North Wind party broke into shouts and began running back and forth in confusion. White Stone turned back, bellowing orders, and the litter bearers bent over Cimmis. From her vantage inside Wasp Village, Evening Star could see Cimmis's legs as he writhed and kicked in pain.

She glanced at Sleeper, himself gaping in disbelief. He asked, "Should we attack them? Even with our five tens, there could be no better time. They're disorganized, stunned."

"No." She shot a quick glance at the lodge closest to the gate. "Stick to the plan. Be patient."

He nodded, looking unsure.

She glanced back across Wasp Village. At the far end she could see ten of her warriors surrounding the two lodges where they had confined Tsak and his warriors. Here and there she could see her people prowling, swinging their axes or cradling spears as they ensured the rest of the villagers stayed put in their lodges.

She remembered the stunned look on Tsak's face as she stepped up and pressed a bone stiletto against his throat. Even as the Wasp Village warriors had begun to understand, Sleeper's warriors had surrounded them, sealing their fate. Rather than die, all but a handful had surrendered. The bodies of those who had not lay hidden under a cover of seagrass matting.

Turning her attention back to Cimmis, she could have predicted what happened next. His warriors packed him up on the litter and charged for the gate. As they neared, they cried, "Make way! Make way for the great chief! He's wounded. We need help!"

Sleeper climbed nimbly down the palisade, dropping to the ground. "Let him in! And then let the Four Old Women in. After that, try to close the gate with the warriors outside."

Evening Star leaped to the ground as Cimmis's litter was borne through the gate and carried to the Council Lodge. As the four bearers lowered it to the ground, she gestured, sending several of her warriors to surround them.

The four bearers looked up in astonishment as

Evening Star stopped before them. "We have no wish to kill you. If you wish to save his life, you will surrender your weapons and walk peacefully to that lodge." She pointed to the large storage lodge where Tsak and his warriors waited under the vigilant noses of Dogrib's warriors.

"I say we do it," the first muttered as he took measure of the hard-eyed warriors surrounding him. The others nodded, tossing stilettos and war clubs to the ground.

As they were being led off, the Four Old Women were being ceremoniously borne through the palisade. Evening Star shot a glance over her shoulder in time to see Sleeper's men roll the gate closed in White Stone's face.

Angry shouts broke out as the North Wind war chief howled in protest.

Then Rain Bear emerged from the lodge where he'd been hiding. He shot her a smile, but looked haggard, still breathing hard from his long run. His body remained sweat-streaked and filthy. An ugly bruise had swollen and discolored his left shoulder. She watched him climb painfully up the rickety palisade. He cupped his hands and shouted, "We have Cimmis and the Council! You will disband, surrender your weapons, and leave this place!"

"Rain Bear?" White Stone cried in dismay.

"It's over. We have won."

The shout caught everyone by surprise. Not only that he could do it, but that a man with a crushed chest could muster the volume. Cimmis shouted, *"Attack! Kill them all!"*

White Stone waved his men back, Cimmis's order ringing in his ears. Attack! His chief commanded.

"Assemble here!" He pointed to the grassy flat just out of casting range from the palisade. "I want someone to run to the forest for a log! Not a rotten one that will splinter on impact, but one that will take that gate down!"

Ten of his warriors turned on their heels and left at a run for the distant stand of firs.

White Stone paced back and forth. Everything was out of control. He shot a glance at the masking trees behind them. Ecan was hit; he was sure of it. Some part of his soul insisted that he send warriors to hunt the Starwatcher down. Sense told him he needed all of his strength here.

He studied the Wasp Village palisade again. No way around it—this was going to be a bloody affair. His people would die on the way to the gate. With Kaska's forces, he had enough warriors to storm it, but once inside? Who knew how many capable fighters Rain Bear had behind him.

Rain Bear? He was supposed to be fleeing southward around Raven Bay. How in Gutginsa's name had he gotten into Wasp Village in the first place?

Kaska stood as her guards set her litter down and went trotting up to join White Stone's assembling warriors.

She blinked in amazement. No doubt about it—that was Rain Bear's silhouette above the palisade. No one could mistake his voice as he warned White Stone not to attack.

She pushed her way forward and stormed up to the war chief. "You're not seriously thinking of attacking, are you?"

White Stone gave her a cold glare. "My chief has given me an order."

"It will be a bloodbath!"

"Then it will be a bloodbath, but those are my orders! *I have sworn to obey my chief!*"

She could see he didn't like it, but a lifetime of obedience ruled him where sense should have.

"Is this what we've made ourselves into?"

She turned, taking stock. Her warriors stood to one side, shooting uneasy glances at her, White Stone, and the Wasp Village palisade. Unlike White Stone, they certainly didn't have any illusions.

She hurried forward, fully aware that she had little time before White Stone had her either killed or silenced. She lifted her hands to the storm-filled twilight and shouted, "My warriors, listen to me! It is time for you to choose!"

Her men knew something had gone terribly wrong. They must be confused, frightened. Would they obey her?

Kaska stabbed a finger at Banded Eagle. "You are now my war chief. Prepare to lead our warriors against the people who murdered Matron Gispaw!"

Banded Eagle's eyes glowed. He whirled around and shouted, "Follow me! For the matron! Let's teach these fools a lesson they'll never forget!"

"Prepare!" Kaska shouted as she took a position beside Banded Eagle. She would live or die with her warriors.

"Kaska!" someone shouted.

"Kaska! Kaska! *Kaska!*" her warriors began to shout. She raised her arms in time to rhythm. *"Kaska! Kaska! Kaska!"*

White Stone was staring, astonishment writ large on his face. One by one his warriors began to shift behind him, some almost dancing away as they realized the seriousness of their situation.

"Come on," Kaska growled under her breath. "Give up. Can't you see? It's over."

White Stone stood rigid, his back arched. Then he sagged and made a weak gesture to his warriors, calling, "It's over. They have won."

Kaska stood tall and straight, trembling, praying, wondering if she had just saved her people, or condemned them.

Chapter Forty

From his position in the Council Lodge, Rain Bear studied Great Chief Cimmis. The North Wind chief lay under a blanket, breath wheezing in and out of his crushed chest. A double strand of rope had been tied around his hips to keep the compress over the spear wound. Firelight flickered like burnished copper on his sagging cheeks. The old man's eyes were fevered, pain-bright, but he was alert, knowing full well what was happening.

Behind him, the Four Old Women sat silent, owl-eyed, still stunned as the realization of their captivity sank in.

"What's to talk about?" Talon thrust out his arm and looked one by one at the occupants of the Council Lodge. The place was huge, but when the old women had ordered it built, they'd had no idea what its first use would be.

"Kill them," Sleeper agreed. "For the pain they have caused our people, I say that we boil them alive and leave their corpses on the beach for the gulls and crabs to pick at."

"Yes!" Goldenrod agreed.

"Death." Black Mountain slapped a hand to his thigh in agreement.

Rain Bear glanced at Evening Star and Kaska, who watched with uneasy eyes.

Rides-the-Wind eased back from where he'd been inspecting Cimmis's wound. "You may kill them most gruesomely if you wish, but I would ask you, is that the message you want to send to the rest of the North Wind People?"

"The time of the North Wind People is over," Black Mountain growled. He looked at the two matrons. "Besides, Evening Star and Kaska have served us well."

Kaska flared, "I do not serve the Raven People, Chief. My goals are not yours."

"We'll remember that," Black Mountain said darkly, "later."

Rain Bear interjected wearily, "This isn't about peoples."

"Then what is it about?" Goldenrod asked bitterly. "For years we have served the—"

"And they have served *us*\" Rain Bear thundered. "Like I said, this isn't about peoples; it's about them!" He pointed at Cimmis and the Council. "It's about the decisions they made that led to the murder of tens of tens of people, Raven and North Wind alike!" He rose painfully to his feet, glaring. "What we do here will affect everyone. Don't you understand? It's our families that we're talking about. If we choose the wrong path here today our sons and daughters will continue to kill each other until we are all so weak the Cougar People or the Buffalo People will move into our lands, and we will be *their* slaves."

"He is right," Evening Star said. "We must confine our punishment to the Council and the great chief alone." Images of her dying family flickered in the back of her mind. "Death."

"Death," the others assented.

"*Life!*" a sharp voice barked.

All eyes turned to see Matron Astcat standing in the doorway. She held Tsauz's hand. Carefully, she walked into the Council Lodge and braced herself. She shot a fond look at Cimmis. "Hello, my husband."

He couldn't seem to find words, but nodded a faint greeting as he labored for air.

Astcat turned, taking in the chiefs. Rain Bear felt the Power in her as their eyes met. She gave him the briefest of nods.

"Oh, yes," Astcat said wearily, "something must be done to atone for the Wolf Tails, and the raids, and the fear." She narrowed her eyes, staring at the Four Old Women. "You have ruined the Council. You have brought us to the teetering edge of destruction. Because of you, our time is done."

"You don't—" Old Woman North began.

"*Quiet!*" Astcat cried.

"Why shouldn't we kill them, Great Matron?" Rain Bear asked reasonably.

Astcat gave him a wary smile. "I will bargain with you, Great Chief. If you will allow me to declare them Outcast, I am prepared to divide up the North Wind clan grounds among the Raven People. We will surrender our villages to you, live among you, and teach you everything that we know. We will work beside you, gathering clams, digging roots, and fishing."

"Great Matron!" Kaska cried in dismay.

Astcat fixed her with keen eyes. "My soul has been away for a long time, Kaska. I was lost in a vision of the future, and this is how it shall be. We are losing ourselves as it is. Let us make the process as painless as possible, shall we?"

"But our traditions," Evening Star cried. "Who will keep them alive?"

"We all will." Astcat pointed to Rain Bear. "Look at the great chief. His daughter is my granddaughter. She is married to a Raven Singer." She pointed to Pitch, who watched soberly from the side. "Tsauz here is half Raven, and he will be my husband."

Talon made a hacking sound as he cleared his throat. "We can have all of your territory anyway, Matron. What if we just take it and turn the tables, enslave the North Wind People as they have enslaved us? Why should we do it your way when we can do it ours?"

Astcat's keen gaze bored into him. "That's a fair question, but the Wolf Tails are still out there, and I am the great matron. At my order, they can either disband, or you may awaken some morning to find your children headless—assuming they survive the wars. I assure you the North Wind People will fight for their lives. I offer you an opportunity to let your children grow up, War Chief. How do you want it? Easy, or hard?"

Talon had visibly paled. "You would do that? Disband the Wolf Tails?"

She nodded. "I never liked the idea anyway."

"And who would follow you?" Sleeper asked.

"What if we ended up with someone like Old Woman North as great matron? Or an Ecan as great chief?"

"Evening Star will succeed me as great matron. If she hasn't earned your trust, no one can."

Rain Bear took a deep breath. "Chiefs, I think there is a great deal of wisdom in the great matron's words."

Astcat turned, her face like carved wood as she met her husband's eyes. "Cimmis, you and the Four Old Women are hereby declared Outcast! I order Matron Kaska to assign a party of her warriors to bear you across the mountains to the lands of the Striped Dart People. There, she will leave you with any who wish to accompany you. You, and your followers, and any such descendants as they may have, may never return to our lands under pain of death."

"Why," Cimmis whispered, "my wife?"

Her voice, tight with love and pain, almost broke as she said, "It is the price of my people's survival, husband."

She turned, eyes like wounds, and hobbled slowly from the Council Lodge. Tsauz clutched tightly to her withered hand.

Ecan curled on his side. He lay screened from view by a skirt of low-hanging fir branches. Brittle fir needles prickled against his sweat-hot cheek and stuck to his skin. His breath came in fast gasps. With each inhalation, with each heartbeat, the spear sticking through his body moved.

Ecan opened his mouth, blinking against the pain and fear. His belly was on fire, burning as gut juices leaked from his torn intestines and gurgled inside him. The stink of it clogged his nostrils where intestinal fluids and blood continued to leak out of the wound.

He heard them, the rapid pounding of feet as two warriors hurried past. Twisting his head, he could see them through the screening branches. Cimmis's men, they ran with a purpose.

Hunting me?

But they didn't even look his way, trotting past, casting anxious looks over their shoulders. Fleeing. But from what?

Ecan lowered his head back to the duff, his hands gripping the spear point that stuck out from just to the right of his navel.

Gods, he was dying. The spear had caught him from behind, lancing through his right kidney, angling down through his stomach and intestines. He'd cut enough people open, listened to their screams as he'd pawed through their living guts, to know how he was hit.

I'm dying! The thought sent a shiver of fear through him.

"I am to be great chief," he whispered to the shadows where he lay. "Do you hear me? Great chief!"

It was all so unfair! He'd been betrayed at every turn. Betrayed by Evening Star, White Stone, Coyote, Cimmis—all of them!

He blinked, aware of the hot blood that dribbled from the spear shaft onto his hands. He tightened his fingers around the spear, feeling the keen edge of the point. Did he dare pull it out?

Could he? The very thought of feeling that long shaft sliding through his guts sickened him.

Fear coupled with shock and sent a feverish heat through him. Sweat prickled on his skin just before his body jerked, and he threw up great gouts of clotted blood.

Whimpering, he lay back, the stench of his wound rising to tease his nostrils. Tears leaked from his eyes and turned the world silver.

Movement! Something creeping through the branches. He blinked to clear the glassy sheen from his eyes. Then blinked again.

Yes, it was a puppy! A little black dog with a white face.

"Runner?" he gasped. The puppy was watching him intently, studying him.

But if Runner was here, was Tsauz close by? His heart leaped. Tsauz! Yes, his son had come for him!

"Tsauz?" he tried to cry, having a hard time finding the breath.

The world seemed to shimmer and float in a way that was watery and liquid. A warm haze began to gray Ecan's vision. Only Runner remained in focus as he stepped ever closer, his black shiny nose sniffing warily.

"Take me to Tsauz," Ecan gasped, fighting to keep the world in focus. All he could see was the puppy. It was smiling now, wagging its tail in anticipation.

Then he remembered War Gods Village, recalled driving the spear into the little puppy's side, hearing the shriek of pain and fear. Gods, was that why Runner was here? To claim him?

As if in answer, the little dog threw its head back and yipped in delight.

As his soul loosened from his body, Ecan knew the true taste of fear.

Chapter Forty-One

"What are you feeling?" Rides-the-Wind asked as he crouched next to Cimmis. The great chief lay on his litter, a blanket covering all but his head and arms. Around them, people passed. They shot uneasy looks in Cimmis's direction, whispering behind their hands. Two guards ensured the old man's safety.

Cimmis managed a bare whisper. "Rage." Blood caked his lips. When blood from his punctured lungs built up, racking coughs expelled clotted phlegm. The pain had to be excruciating.

Rides-the-Wind looked down into the old man's pain-glazed eyes and felt, what? Sympathy? No, more curiosity than anything else. "I have often wondered if for every good there is an evil. A balance in the way the world was first Sung."

"There is only suffering," Cimmis whispered dryly. "If I could stand, only for a moment…"

"You would do what?"

"I would choke the life from her body!" He winced with the vehemence of his words.

"Do you have so little love for her?"

"No," the old man whispered. "It's because I still love her that I want so badly to make her pay." He turned his head away, tears leaking from the corners of his eyes.

"Do you wish to tell me anything, Cimmis?" Rides-the-Wind considered the old man. "You will be standing before Gutginsa's spear soon. I am curious as to how you will be judged."

"I'll live," he swore. "Just wait and see! From exile, I'll come back, and when I do…"

"Yes?"

"I will see them scream in agony."

"Have you no room in your heart for anything but anger?"

He reached up, gasping from the pain in his crushed chest, and wiped his eyes. "I loved…her…"

"Then," the old Soul Keeper mused, "perhaps there is hope."

"Hope…is a myth."

Rain Bear stepped around the edges of the Joining ceremony, heading to where Rides-the-Wind knelt beside Cimmis. He'd been there all day, right at the edge of the palisade, talking with the captive chief. A hard-eyed guard of Kaska's warriors ensured his safety.

Pitch's voice carried in the clear morning air. "And will you, Astcat, matron of the North Wind People, accept this man Tsauz as your husband, to become great chief of the North Wind People?"

Astcat took Tsauz's hand and called in a loud voice, "I accept Tsauz."

Over ten tens of people had come, including many from the once slave village. They watched with wary but curious eyes. Tsauz stood to Astcat's right, a tall boy with his chin up, wearing Pitch's red ritual cape.

"So, it is done," Evening Star said as she walked up and took Rain Bear's hand. "And now, I have a question for you."

"Yes?"

"Will you, Rain Bear, great chief of the Raven People, join with me, Evening Star, of the North Wind People, to be my husband, and to eventually become the great chief of the North Wind People?"

He studied her for a moment. "Are you sure you want to do this?"

Her steady blue eyes seemed to bore into his soul. "If I have to build a new world for my people, I want to do it with the man I love. My people will trust you."

He hesitated for a moment, just staring into her eyes. "Yes, Matron, I will join with you."

"Great chief?" Dogrib said. "You had better come see this."

Rain Bear left the Council Lodge where he, Evening Star, Talon, and Kaska had been talking.

"What is it?"

"Dzoo." Dogrib shot him a grim glance. "She just appeared headed this way down the trail."

"Is she all right?"

"She looks fine. She's leading a party bearing someone on a stretcher."

"Thank Gutginsa she's safe." They'd been worried. Dzoo's blessing would be critical if they were going to maintain the fragile peace. "Do you think she found Ecan?"

"I can't say, my chief. No one has found him yet."

As Rain Bear followed Dogrib through the gate he could see her. In the clear morning light, Dzoo walked at the head of a small party of former slaves. They carried a litter, upon which a person lay.

The way Dzoo moved was magical, almost as if she floated above the ground. Her body dipped and swayed as she sang a melody that was at once haunting and joyous.

Above her, a column of crows wheeled and cawed, as if drawn by the bizarre sight.

Rain Bear and Dogrib stepped out to meet her, and both men shivered as Dzoo's voice rose to a high pitch and ended in laughter.

"Dzoo?" Rain Bear asked. "Are you all right? We've had warriors searching for you."

When her large eyes fixed on his, he felt the world sway, and reached out to brace himself on Dogrib's shoulder.

"I thank you for your concern, Great Chief. I have been Dancing with Coyote. It has taken a while to teach him to fly."

"Coyote? Fly?" He glanced at the litter, noticing for the first time that the bearers looked scared half out of their wits.

At a gesture from Dzoo, the litter clattered to the ground—and no sooner were the bearers free of the poles than they broke and ran like quail from a weasel.

Rain Bear stepped forward, frowning, trying to

make sense of what he saw. The gruesome thing indeed looked like a huge bloody bird.

"Wings," Dzoo whispered as Rain Bear puzzled over the flaps of skin that hung down from the spread arms. "Skinned wings."

The organs had been removed from inside the torso, leaving a blood-caked hollow, the spine visible where the ribs curled up. The eyes were gone; the face had been carefully sliced away from the underlying bone. But the thing that drew the eye was the erect penis that stuck up from the crimson-caked pubis. A stick had been inserted to extend it far beyond human dimensions.

A dizzying sense of Power whirled through the air, and Rain Bear stepped back, wincing. Dzoo caught him and kept him from falling. Dogrib was making a sucking sound, as if he couldn't quite fill his lungs with air.

"It's all right, Chief Rain Bear. He can't hurt you." She smiled as she held up a blood-streaked obsidian fetish. It had been carefully chipped into the shape of a coyote's head. "I've placed Coyote's soul in here. It's obsidian, so sharp and brittle. All I have to do is snap it in two, or crush it under a rock, and his soul is gone forever." Her smile was predatory. "And he knows it."

Dogrib had turned away, a green color rising in his face.

She pulled the familiar coyote-tracked bag from the belt at her waist and dropped the fetish inside.

Rain Bear would have sworn he heard a faint, high-pitched scream.

Night

"After everything we'd done together, everything we'd been through, she cast me aside like a cracked cup. I can't believe it. I loved her with all my soul." I force a difficult breath into my lungs.

They have been waiting for me to die. But I continue to fool them. For three moons I've been devouring myself from the inside out, until now I feel like a drum; all beating heart, but no insides.

"She had to make a choice: you or the survival of two peoples. You know that. Just as you know that she made the right choice."

"Perhaps, but I have been betrayed. I feel completely empty."

The old Soul Keeper's voice is gruff: "It is emptiness that makes a vessel useful. What would a bowl or cup be without its hollow interior?"

"Well, then, my wife has turned me into something very useful—I have become a yawning black abyss." Anger tinges the words. My love has turned into a huge burning ache. More than anything, I wish I could have *betrayed her in kind. A great many women would have flocked to me, worshipped me.*

"Very soon now you must decide whether that abyss will be eternally filled with anger and resentment or love and peace. Which will it be?"

As he rises, the Soul Keeper's cape flutters then flaps in a gust of wind. He smells spicy, like the leaves of the Spirit plants he's been using to Heal me.

He doesn't know it, but I already understand his words—only too well.

It is the empty chamber that makes a drum beautiful, or a flute melodious. Without emptiness, there would be no music.

Emptiness is also what makes love possible. If a human being felt full and contented, he would have no need for love.

But at this late date, what does such knowledge bring me? I understand that I am now the perfect vessel. Waiting to be filled...but with what? Perhaps I just need a purpose. Any purpose, beyond simply dying and ridding the world of my presence, would be welcome.

"Do I have a purpose?"

Through hazy eyes, I see him watching me. "If I could Heal you, what is the first thing you would do?"

I wheeze the words, "I would seek her out, and strangle that boy before her eyes."

He nods cryptically. "Despite what you would have me believe. You are not empty, Chief. Unfortunately you are still full."

Full? Of what? I wonder as the darkness closes in around me. At first it is soft and gray. The world is fading as I fall toward...what?

Epilogue

The small camp was located in the floodplain beside the north bank of the great river. A cool stand of cottonwood trees gave respite from the oppressive heat that came rolling out of the arid uplands. Summer here, in the dry plateau, was brutally hot compared to the cool damp coast where the people had lived. Deer Killer had chosen this spot out of necessity. Not only had Cimmis needed the shade, but Rides-the-Wind suffered under the direct sunlight.

Cimmis's dead body lay beneath the hides, his eyes staring wide into the distance of death. His shriveled face bore the faint sheen of sweat. Beads of it dotted his lashes.

Since the day Kaska's small band of warriors had left them and turned back to the mountains, Cimmis and his group had wandered the sagebrush barrens. Making a living had depended on the few strong young warriors who had accompanied them.

But for the gift of the camas roots, they'd have starved in the first few weeks. Deer Killer, despite his

Raven People blood, had become their chief. No one had said anything when Kstawl moved her robes to his lodge and began sharing his bed.

Rides-the-Wind thoughtfully studied the dead man before he reached over and pulled Cimmis's eyelids closed.

"Soul Keeper?" Kstawl called. "How is he?"

Rides-the-Wind replied, "His soul is hovering inside his nostrils."

She took a breath, head bowing. "Then, my father is finally dead?" She pinched the bridge of her nose. "I'm sorry, but it's a relief."

Rides-the-Wind picked up a stick that he'd placed to one side and held the end in the smoke. He kept it over the heat until it began to smolder, then held it under Cimmis's nose.

Kstawl kneeled beside him and saw that it was a lock of gray hair tied to the stick. The smoke came from a smoldering bundle of sweet grass and cedar bark that lay in the ashes.

"You're smoking Father's hair?" Kstawl asked in disbelief. Then she realized what he was doing. "You're *sealing* his soul in his body? For the sake of the gods, let it go!"

A perfectly cut square of buffalo-hide rested beside Rides-the-Wind's knee. He tucked the smoked lock into the hide, then folded it up and tied it with a seagrass cord. When he tossed it into the ashes, it landed with a thump and began to blacken. The first tongues of flame caressed its edges.

Kstawl gasped in horror, backing away. Her disbelieving eyes went from the fire, to Cimmis, to Rides-the-Wind.

"It isn't time for his soul to be set free," the Soul Keeper said. "It must stay here, with his bones."

"Why, Elder?"

Rides-the-Wind stood, and his gray hair and beard whipped around his face. One by one he looked into the sober eyes of Deer Killer's small band. "Everyone deserves the chance to stand before Gutginsa and explain his actions. Even Cimmis. Though it may be a long time before Cimmis understands what he did and Gutginsa allows him to go free."

"How long?" Kstawl demanded.

"Who knows? That is up to Cimmis's soul. It may be for a people long removed from us to finally send him to judgment."

As he walked across the grassy silt, he looked out at the wide river, at the bluffs wavering in the midsummer sun beyond. Terrible sadness had settled upon his aged shoulders. "I will leave tonight. I have no more business here."

In the haze, far to the west, Thunderbirds played over the distant mountain peaks; lightning leaped through the clouds.

"Do you think that's true?" Kstawl asked Deer Killer as she studied her dead father. "That everyone deserves the chance to explain?"

Deer Killer shrugged. "Who are we to judge, my wife? For the moment, I am more concerned with making a grave for your father. As to his soul, well, that's up to Gutginsa's spear."

Afterword

So, who were the first people to arrive in North America?

The question has tantalized archaeologists for over a century, but we are only now just beginning to piece together the answer.

When we wrote *People of the Wolf* in 1988, it was generally accepted that the earliest peoples, called "Clovis Culture," arrived in North America down an ice-free corridor between the massive Cordilleran Ice Sheet and the Lauren-tide Glacier around 13,000 years ago. In the past thirty-five years, new information derived from archaeological excavations and technological advances has altered that view.

For example, in 2017 an archaeological team at White Sands National Park in New Mexico was called in to help preserve fossilized mammoth trackways. When the team arrived, they discovered that along with mammoth tracks, there were human footprints. They archaeologists dated the layers of sediment and discovered the human footprints were around 23,000 years old, providing evidence of a much earlier human expansion into North America. Who were these people? At this point in time, no one can answer that question.

We are also fairly certain now that the first peoples did not strictly come by land down the ice-free corridor along the face of the Canadian Rocky Mountains. We suspect they also had boats and paddled down the coastlines, fishing, hunting, and gathering as they traveled, and some may well have travelled across open ocean to get to the Americas—which would explain the Australoid DNA in 10,000 year old Brazilian sites.

It is likely that the earliest inhabitants of North America lived along the Pacific coast of Canada and the northwestern United States. We say that for two reasons. First, the greatest diversity of Native American languages is found along the Pacific coast. It takes time for languages to diverge. They are most different in areas where people have lived longest. Second, though much of the northern Pacific coast was covered by the Cordilleran Ice Sheet 16,000 years ago, parts of the Queen Charlotte Islands in British Columbia and Prince of Wales Island in southeast Alaska appear to have been ice-free. As well, recent geological evidence indicates that the continental shelf, which was exposed by lowered sea levels 13,000 to 14,000 years ago, was also free of ice. The ice had, in fact, retreated from British Columbia's coastal mountains by about 13,000 years ago. By 10,600 years ago, lowered sea levels had exposed large areas of the Hecate Plain east of the Queen Charlotte Islands, the bottom of Queen Charlotte Sound, and the areas adjacent to the north and west coasts of Vancouver Island.

But what were the food resources?

Paleobotany, the study of pollens, seeds, and phytoliths—the silicate skeletons of plant cells—tells us that those ice-free areas were vegetated. By 14,000 years ago, southern British Columbia supported heath, a variety of grasses, sedges, and herbs. There were also conifers present. By about 12,000 years ago, lodgepole pine and poplar grew on the Queen Charlotte Islands and had spread to southeast Alaska. Close behind were sitka spruce and hemlock.

In addition, from 8,000 to 12,000 years ago, Prince of Wales Island supported brown bear, black bear, red fox, otter and ermine, and other small mammals, as well as fish resources.

This was a period of extreme stress. Sea levels were rising rapidly, the land itself was "springing back." This is called "isostatic rebound." Imagine putting a block of ice on a piece of foam. As the ice melts, the foam "springs back." Continents do the same thing. As the massive weight of the glaciers vanished, the land rose. But it seems to have happened at different rates in different places. For example, the sea level on Prince of Wales Island between 9,000 and 9,500 years ago was about twenty feet higher than today. Farther south, 9,300 years ago, the sea level on the Queen Charlotte Islands was approximately 475 feet higher than modern sea level Qosenhans et al., 1995, 1997).

Sediment cores taken off the Oregon coast show that wind patterns also reversed at this time, weakening the coastal upwelling and reducing marine productivity (Sanchetta et al., 1992).

Adding to this problem, as the Cordilleran Ice Sheet continued to melt it flooded the rivers, streams, and finally the ocean with silt-laden fresh water. This decimated shellfish beds and lowered salmon runs, affecting the food chain and reducing the numbers of sea mammals, birds, and human beings who could survive.

Of the thirty-nine individuals found in North America who date to more than 9,000 years ago, only two are fairly complete: Spirit Cave Mummy from Nevada and Kennewick Man from Washington. Even with this limited data, we can glean critical details about who they were and what happened to them.

Keep in mind this is a period of rapid transition from the Pleistocene Ice Age to the warmer Holocene period that we now enjoy. Most of North America's earliest inhabitants endured periods of starvation. Malnutrition temporarily interrupts bone growth and leaves mineral deposits that we call "Harris lines" in the limb bones; it also appears as ripples in the teeth called dental hypoplasia. We see changes in the skull as well. The girl from the Spirit Cave site in Nevada showed multiple growth interruptions in her teeth, indicating a life of repeated nutritional privation. The Spirit Cave Mummy (10,700 years old) had a number of Harris lines in his limb bones, as did the Buhl Woman from Idaho (12,800 years old). The lines on the Buhl Woman's femur, or thigh bone, were so regularly spaced that hunger seems to have been a yearly occurrence. The bones of the man from Horn Shelter Number Two in Texas (11,200 years ago) also show he suffered extreme hunger in his life.

Though afterlife traditions can only be guessed at, the treatment of the dead gives us clues to what they might have believed, and given the diversity of burial styles, their religious traditions appear to have been many. Ten of the thirty-nine were cremated. Thirteen were buried. Two were "bundle" burials, that is bundles of cleaned bones wrapped in beautiful blankets and deposited in caves or rock shelters. We call these "secondary" burials. We occasionally find grave goods. The Buhl Woman in Idaho and the woman from Colorado's Gordon Creek site were buried with stone knives. The Horn Shelter Girl, Marmes I, and Buhl Woman all had needles as grave offerings. Buhl Woman also had a badger's baculum—penis bone—with her. A beautiful group of spear points accompanied the man from Browns Valley. The man at Horn Shelter Number Two in Texas had more than one hundred grave offerings, including a large chert knife, two antler wrenches for straightening spear shafts, sandstone slabs for working bone or shell, and a necklace of four canid teeth surrounded by more than eighty snail-shell beads from the Gulf of Mexico. Red ocher is the most common offering; it was used to coat the bodies of the people found at the Gordon Creek site; the Anzick site in Montana; Browns Valley; the woman from Arch Lake, New Mexico; and probably Stick Man from Washington. We also find raw lumps of the pigment included with the dead—as though they would need it in the afterworld, just as they would need knives, needles, and spear points.

Eight of the earliest skeletons are children. The Anzick-1 child (12,900 years old) was about eighteen months old. The Horn Shelter girl lived to be around twelve.

Interestingly, only the men show dramatic injuries, which tells us a great deal about how they lived and died.

Spirit Cave Mummy had fractures to his skull, spine, and hand. Stick Man and the Marmes III Man also had skull fractures, as did Kennewick Man. The Grimes Burial Shelter teenager tells a similar story. One cut on his rib contains obsidian fragments—residue left from the weapon used to inflict the wound—and there are two cuts present, indicating that the youth's assailant stabbed him at least twice. Since no healing is apparent, it's probable that the teenager died from this assault.

Kennewick Man shows, by far, the most traumatic injuries—all of which he survived. Several months, or even a few years, before his death, his chest was crushed, breaking several ribs. He also had an infected wound in his skull, on his left temple. He was relatively tall for the time period, five feet nine inches, and was around fifty years old when he died. In addition, Kennewick Man had a "Cascade" spear point embedded in his hip.

In our current collection, 67 percent of the males from this time period demonstrate serious injuries. This is a very high rate, especially when compared to European burials. Mary Brennan, who was working on her doctorate at New York University, studied 209 skeletons from southern France dating to between 10,000 and 100,000 years ago, and found only five fractures, or a little over 2 percent. As another example, Thomas Berger and Eric Trinkaus studied over 1,200 skeletons from modern humans and Neandertals and found less than one hundred injuries, or around 8 percent.

The high rate we see among Paleo-American males could be sampling error—we don't have many examples to learn from—but it likely represents interpersonal violence. We only find skull fractures on males, and most of those occur on the left side of the head, toward the front, as if caused by a blow delivered by a right-handed opponent.

Women, on the other hand, show few such injuries. Only the Minnesota girl had a fractured rib. But women also had a much shorter life span than men. While men often lived into their forties or fifties, or even older, Paleo-American women generally died between the ages of eighteen and twenty-three. We don't know why this disparity exists, though the physical and nutritional stresses associated with child-bearing almost certainly played a role.

In their extensive study, *Kennewick Man: The Scientific Investigation of an Ancient American Skeleton,"* Dr. Richard Jantz and Dr. Douglas Owsley showed that the most ancient skeletons in North America fall into two distinct "craniometric" groups: one group that has features similar to the Ainu or Polynesians and a second group that appears very Indian-like. These groups are so different from each other that Owsley and Jantz proposed they were from two distinct populations of people who migrated separately into North America.

Today, we know that that basic assumption seems to be correct. Kennewick Man (8,900 years old) and the Anzick-1 child (12,900 years old) are different. Nuclear genomic analyses conducted in 2018 suggested that there was a split of Native America ancestors between 18,000-14,000 years ago, creating two separate branches. Also, fifteen ancient genomes analyzed from the across the Americas revealed two distinct migrations from North to South America—from Alaska to Patagonia—between 8,700 to 21,000 years ago. To complicate the matter, Dr. Jose Victor Moreno-Mayar and colleagues sequenced DNA from a little girl who lived in Alaska around 11,500 years ago and discovered that she'd been part of an isolated group of ancient Beringians that separated from modern Native Americas about 20,000 years ago (https://www.the-scientist.com/new-evidence-complicates-the-story-of-the-peopling-of-the-americas-69928).

From another interesting study of gut bacteria, published in 2021, an international team of scientists took samples of *Heliobactr pylori* from the stomachs of 500 humans living in different regions of Siberia and Mongolia and compared the genetic sequences of these bacteria to other strains from around the world, which revealed that the genetic strains of bacteria split around 20,000 years ago. One strain of bacteria apparently remained in northeast Asia, while the other showed new mutations that were introduced when people left Siberia, then returned thousands of years later. Moodley says, "the bacteria that these people had in their stomachs 24,000 years ago, it's still alive and well in Siberia." While that distinct ancient group of people may be gone, the bacteria that originally inhabited the stomachs of these ancestral Eurasians is alive and well.

What's surprising about this is that it surprises

anyone. Genetic diversity is the key to the survival of species.

The remarkable thing is that it has taken us this long to find the evidence, but that's archaeology. The research is never finished. We do not know enough to reconstruct the past completely. We never will. All we can do is take the best information we have...and try.

A look At Book Six:
People of the Moon

The Chaco Anasazi ruled a vast empire spanning New Mexico, Colorado, Utah, and Arizona. For over two centuries, they built monumental great houses, engineered expansive road networks, and stored immense food reserves. Guided by the stars and ruled by powerful Matrons, their priests promised rain and prosperity—but could not stop the disasters to come.

A volcanic eruption coupled with relentless drought sparked famine and rebellion. As Sister Moon returned to her sacred birthplace, signaling the end of a great cycle, an empire teetered on the brink of collapse. Bloodshed and betrayal would seal its fate.

Spurred by Cold Bringing Woman's prophecy, four young men from the conquered Moon People—Bad Cast, Spots, Wrapped Wrist, and Ripple—find themselves at the heart of the rebellion. Ordinary men thrust into extraordinary circumstances, their fates entwine with gods, exiles, a rogue woman warrior, and the mystical witch known as Nightshade in a desperate fight for survival.

Hunted by the ruthless Deputy Leather Hand, their quest is fraught with betrayal, sacrifice, and devastating loss. Will they succeed in toppling an empire, or will they pay the ultimate price for their defiance?

Based on cutting-edge Southwestern archaeology, *People of the Moon* is a sweeping tale of power, survival, and the enduring fight for freedom.

AVAILABLE APRIL 2025

About W. Michael Gear

W. Michael Gear is a *New York Times*, *USA Today*, and international bestselling author of sixty novels. With close to eighteen million copies of his books in print worldwide, his work has been translated into twenty-nine languages.

Gear has been inducted into the Western Writers Hall of Fame and the Colorado Authors' Hall of Fame —as well as won the Owen Wister Award, the Golden Spur Award, and the International Book Award for both Science Fiction and Action Suspense Fiction. He is also the recipient of the Frank Waters Award for lifetime contributions to Western writing.

Gear's work, inspired by anthropology and archaeology, is multilayered and has been called compelling, insidiously realistic, and masterful. Currently, he lives in northwestern Wyoming with his award-winning wife and co-author, Kathleen O'Neal Gear, and a charming sheltie named, Jake.

About Kathleen O'Neal Gear

Kathleen O'Neal Gear is a *New York Times* bestselling author of fifty-seven books and a national award-winning archaeologist. The U.S. Department of the Interior has awarded her two Special Achievement awards for outstanding management of America's cultural resources.

In 2015 the United States Congress honored her with a Certificate of Special Congressional Recognition, and the California State Legislature passed Joint Member Resolution #117 saying, "The contributions of Kathleen O'Neal Gear to the fields of history, archaeology, and writing have been invaluable..."

In 2021 she received the Owen Wister Award for lifetime contributions to western literature, and in 2023 received the Frank Waters Award for "a body of work representing excellence in writing and storytelling that embodies the spirit of the American West."

Selected Bibliography

Bancroft-Hunt, Norman, and Werner Forman. *People of the Totem.* Norman, Okla.: University of Oklahoma, 1988.

Beck, Mary. *Heroes and Heroines in Tlingit-Haida Legend.* Anchorage: Alaska Northwest Books, 1989.

Benedict, Jeff. *No Bone Unturned.* New York: Harper Collins, 2003.

Bonnichsen, Robson, and Karen L. Turnmire. *Clovis: Origins and Adaptations.* Corvallis, Oregon: Center for the Study of the First North Americans: 1991.

Bringhurst, Robert. *A Story as Sharp as a Knife. The Classical Haida Mythtellers and Their World.* Lincoln: University of Nebraska Press, 1999.

Bryant, Vaughn M., and Richard G. Holloway. *Pollen Records of Late-Quaternary North American Sediments.* Dallas: The American Association of Stratigraphic Palynologists Foundation, 1985.

Capes, Katherine H. *Contributions to the Prehistory of Vancouver Island.* Pocatello, Idaho: Occasional Papers of the Idaho State University Museum, Number 15, 1964.

Chatters, James C. *Ancient Encounters: Kennewick Man and the First Americans.* New York: Simon and Schuster, 2001.

Cove, John J. et al., editors. *Tricksters, Shamans and Heroes: Tsimshian Narratives I and II.* Ottawa: Directorate, Paper No. 3, Canadian Museum of Civilization, 1987.

Crawford, Michael H. *The Origins of Native Americans. Evidence from Anthropological Genetics.* Cambridge: Cambridge University Press, 1998.

Dauenhauer, Nora, and Richard Dauenhauer. *Haa Tuwunaagu Yis, for Healing Our Spirit: Tlingit Oratory.* Seattle: University of Washington Press, 1990.

Dixon, James E. *Bones, Boats and Bison.* Albuquerque: University of New Mexico Press, 1999.

Emmons, George Thornton. *The Tlingit Indians.* Seattle: University of Washington Press, 1991.

Enrico, John, and Wendy Bross Stuart. *Northern Haida Songs.* Lincoln: University of Nebraska Press, 1996.

Selected Bibliography

Fagan, Brian M. *Ancient North America: The Archaeology of a Continent.* Third edition. London: Thames and Hudson, 2000.

Fienup-Riordan, Ann, ed. *Our Way of Making Prayer. Yup'ik Masks and the Stories They Tell Us.* Seattle: University of Washington Press, 1996.

Gunther, Erna. *Ethnobotany of Western Washington. The Knowledge and Use of Indigenous Plants by Native Americans.* Seattle: University of Washington, 1999.

Harkin, Michael E. *The Heiltsuks. Dialogues of Culture and History on the Northwest Coast.* Lincoln: University of Nebraska Press, 1997.

Harris, Arthur. *Late Pleistocene Vertebrate Paleoecology of the West.* Austin: University of Texas Press, 1985.

Jaffe, A. J. *The First Immigrants from Asia.* New York: Plenum Press, 1992.

Jantz, Richard and Douglas Owlsley, eds. *Kennewick Man: A Scientific Investigation of an Ancient American Skeleton,* College Station, Texas A & M University Press, , 2014.

Josenhans, H. W. et al., 1995. "Post Glacial Sea-Levels on the Western Canadian Continental Shelf: Evidence for Rapid Change, Extensive Subaerial Exposure, and Early Habitation." *Marine Geology* 125: 73-94.

--. 1997, "Early Humans and Rapidly Changing Holocene Sea Levels in the Queen Charlotte Islands-Hecate Strait, British Columbia, Canada." *Science* 277: 71-74.

Judson, Katharine Berry, ed. *Myths and Legends of the Pacific Northwest.* Lincoln: University of Nebraska Press, 1997.

Kan, Sergei. *Symbolic Immortality; the Thlingit Potlatch of the Nineteenth Century.* Washington: Smithsonian Institution Press, 1989.

Krober, Paul D. *The Salish Language Family; Reconstructing Syntax.* Lincoln: University of Nebraska Press, 1999.

LaBlanc, Steven. *Constant Battles.* New York: St. Martin's Press, 2003.

Linderman, Frank B. *Kootenai Why Stories.* Lincoln: University of Nebraska Press, 1926.

Martin, Paul. *Quaternary Extinctions: A Prehistoric Revolution.* Tucson: University of Arizona Press, 1989.

Matson, R. G., and Gary Coupland. *The Prehistory of the Northwest Coast.* San Diego: Academic Press, 1995.

McFeat,Tom, ed. *Indians of the Pacific Northwest*. Seattle: University of Washington Press, 1989.

McIlwraith, T. F. *The Bella Coola Indians*. Toronto: University of Toronto Press, 1948.

Miller, Jay. *Tsimshian Culture, a Light Through the Ages*. Lincoln: University of Nebraska Press, 1997.

Millspaugh, Charles F. *American Medicinal Plants*. New York: Dover Publications, 1974.

Owsley, Douglas W., and Richard J. Jantz. "Archeological Politics and Public Interest in PaleoAmerican Studies: Lessons from Gordon Creek Woman and Kennewick Man." *American Antiquity,* September 2001.

Pielou, E. C. *After the Ice Age: The Return of Life to Glaciated North America*. Chicago: University of Chicago Press, 1991.

Reid, Bill, and Robert Bringhurst. *The Raven Steals the Light*. Seattle: University of Washington, 1988.

Ruby, Robert H., and John A. Brown. *Indians of the Pacific Northwest*. Norman: University of Oklahoma, 1981.

--. *Dreamer-Prophets of the Columbia Plateau: Smohalla and Skolaskin*. Norman: University of Oklahoma Press, 1989.

Samuel, Cheryl. *The Raven's Tail*. Vancouver: University of British Columbia, 1987.

Sanchetta, C. et al., 1992, "Late-Glacial to Holocene Changes in Winds, Upwelling, and Seasonal Production of the Northern California Current System, *Quaternary Research* 38:359-370.

Savinelli, Alfred. *Plants of Power: Native American Ceremony and the Use of Sacred Plants*. Tennessee: Native Voices Publishing, 2002.

Smith, Harlan I. *Ethnobotany of the Gitksan Indians of British Columbia*. Hull, Quebec: Canadian Museum of Civilization, Paper 132,1997.

Steward, Hilary. *Totem Poles*. Seattle: University of Washington Press, 1990.

Straus, Lawrence Guy et al., eds. *Humans at the End of the Ice Age: The Archaeology of the Pleistocene-Holocene Transition*. New York, Plenum Press, 1996.

Suttles, Wayne, ed. *Handbook of North American Indians: Northwest Coast*. Washington: Vol. 7. Washington, Smithsonian Institution Press, 1990.

Thomas, David Hurst. *Skull Wars. Kennewick Man, Archaeology and the Battle for Native American Identity.* New York: Basic Books, 2000.

Turner, Nancy J. *Plant Technology of First Peoples in British Columbia.* Vancouver: University of British Columbia, Royal British Columbia Museum Handbook, 1998.

--. *Food Plants of Coastal First Peoples.* Vancouver: University of British Columbia, Royal British Columbia Museum Handbook, 1995.